Mur

Park

Phillip Strang

BOOKS BY PHILLIP STRANG

DCI Isaac Cook Series

DI Keith Tremayne Series

Steve Case Series

Standalone Books

Copyright Page

Dedication

For Elli and Tais who both had the perseverance to make me sit down and write.

Chapter 1

A Sunday, the first warmth of the coming summer and a clear sky. The sort of day when Detective Chief Inspector Isaac Cook should have been with Jenny, his girlfriend, either out and about or enjoying an early-morning spell of lovemaking. But yet again, a phone call. This time it was his second-in-command, Detective Inspector Larry Hill, a man who appreciated time at home with his wife and children at the weekend.

'Hyde Park,' Larry Hill said. 'A body.'

Isaac raised himself from his bed; the lovemaking had seemed preferable to a walk or a run around the block. 'Whereabouts?'

'Hyde Park, the Serpentine, the Kensington Gardens side. You'll have to park back from the murder site, Lancaster Gate on Bayswater Road, and walk down, two minutes if you walk briskly, four if you don't.'

'Local?' Isaac asked.

'A Chinese tourist out with a group found the body, as they were heading up to Kensington Palace, hoping to look over the fence, catch a glimpse of a royal.'

'Who's at the scene?'

'A couple of uniforms, a gaggle of tourists who keep wanting to take selfies of the body with those sticks they carry.'

'Ghoulish.'

'It's what tourists do. No doubt it'll be all over Facebook, or whatever they have back in China.'

'Doesn't help,' Isaac said. Even before the alarm had been sounded, he wondered how many had trampled over the evidence, disturbed the body, made a straightforward murder enquiry more difficult.

He had hoped that the Homicide Department at Challis Street Police Station could have had a break for a few weeks at least, the chance for him to take Jenny to Jamaica to visit where his parents had come from. He knew she would be disappointed; he knew she'd understand. That's what he liked about her, loved even, although he wasn't sure why that word scared him. Maybe it was fraught with memories of lost loves, missed opportunities, or was it a fear of commitment? Was he the perpetual bachelor? he wondered. Always saying that he wanted to settle down, but when the opportunity was there, he felt a gentle doubt that became more intense, and then came the tension in his voice, the irritation at something minor that his latest love had done, and the sorrowful breakup. It had happened more than once, and he knew that for him policing was a vocation, not a job, and that his preference was for maintaining law and order, not for staying that extra time at home and working on the relationship.

'I've made you a cup of tea,' Jenny said as she gave Isaac a kiss on the cheek. 'Toast?'

'I'll grab something on the way. I'll drink the tea, though,' Isaac said, realising that it was the wrong response. 'Something on the way' was going to take longer than for Jenny to make his breakfast, but there had been a murder. And once free of the flat that the two of them shared, he would be focussed, making phone calls, rallying the team, checking with the crime scene investigators. He could see by her expression that she wasn't pleased. He hoped it wasn't the beginning of the end.

A quick shower, dressing in a suit, even though the weather was more suitable for an open-necked shirt, even a pair of shorts.

'Jamaica off?' Jenny asked.

'Not sure yet. Let me see what we have,' Isaac said, fully aware that the trip probably was off, but unwilling to say so. He knew that he and Jenny never argued, that they were compatible, and she had never once mentioned his long hours away from home, the unwillingness to discuss important things when he came home, preferring either to sleep or to sit quietly, not talking. But there were things to talk about, Jenny knew that. A trip to Jamaica to visit Isaac's parents who had retired back to the island, was an acknowledgement that marriage was the next step.

Isaac knew that Jenny was hoping for a proposal, and he was considering it. He realised that marriage led to children and then on to old age and retirement, and then the inevitable. He didn't want to contemplate the fact that he was getting older, not wanting to avoid it, but not just yet. For him, Jamaica was going to be a make or break with Jenny, although he knew that he was wrong to feel that way with a woman who deserved better. She had hinted on more than one occasion that her biological clock was ticking, a none too subtle nudge for him to make up his mind.

'See you later,' Isaac said as he walked out of the door of the two-bedroom flat. 'I'll call you if it's an open and shut case.'

'It won't be,' Jenny said.

Outside on the street he looked up at the flat, saw her looking out of the window. She appeared to have a wistful look about her as if she wasn't sure what to do. Turning away, Isaac got into his car and drove to the murder scene.

***

A Sunday morning, the tourist season in full swing, not that the city was ever devoid of visitors, but then that was London. A cosmopolitan melting pot of peoples from all around the world, most making their way on foot or by bus or taxi around the prime sights to visit. To the west of the murder scene, Kensington Palace. To the east, Hyde Park, albeit that officially Hyde Park had been divided into two, the area west of the West Carriage Drive renamed as Kensington Gardens.

As expected, another tourist sight had sprung up, even more popular than the Princess Diana Memorial Fountain, even more than Speaker's Corner where anyone was free to get up on a box and make a speech, regardless of whether it was nonsense or intelligent debate, religious or not. The only rule was that whatever was said, it had to be lawful and not likely to incite violence. Not that it worried some, and most of those who spoke were open to ridicule. A great sport in his younger days, Isaac knew, to come down to Hyde Park, listen to the orators, to heckle some, to silently agree with others. Karl Marx had stood there, so had Vladimir Lenin, George Orwell.

But today was not the time to listen to the speakers or to walk through the park and on to Buckingham Palace. Today was the time to investigate a murder.

At the entrance to the park, Isaac parked his car, pulling off onto the pavement, a uniform standing there to show him where. Bayswater Road was busy and getting busier by the minute. Not far away, Kensington Church Street, the turnoff down to the Churchill Arms, full of Churchillian memorabilia and good beer, a decent restaurant. Larry visited it on a regular basis, Isaac infrequently; no royals in there, though.

'You'll have trouble controlling the people in the park,' Isaac said on his arrival. Larry was already there, although he wasn't dressed as well as Isaac and it was clear he had had a heavy night. Isaac could see that his inspector was struggling again and that he was starting to put on weight; his complexion was ruddy, and his general physical health was not as good as it should be.

Last time the man had had a drinking problem it had been Isaac who had officially warned him about the issue, Larry's wife reinforcing the ban on the excessive consumption of alcohol, if he wanted to avoid sleeping downstairs on the sofa.

But Inspector Larry Hill wasn't the biggest problem that day; it was the body that had been found floating in the reeds at the side of the Serpentine, the recreational lake in Hyde Park, its name due to its snakelike, curving shape.

'What do we have?' Isaac said.

Isaac would have said it was scenic there, the statue to Peter Pan at his rear, the water in front of him. A couple of moorhens in the water, a pigeon nearby, hopeful of the crumbs from the sandwich that he had

5

purchased on the way. He thought back to Jenny and her offer of breakfast. He had made the wrong choice, as the sandwich, cheese and ham, was neither fresh nor agreeable, purely filling a place in his stomach. And it was not as if he could do much at the present moment. The area had been secured by the uniforms, and no one could come along the pathway; no doubt a few tourists would be complaining. So far, the crime scene investigators, led by Gordon Windsor, wasn't on site, and they would be another ten minutes. Then the barriers preventing entry by vehicular traffic onto the pathways had to be dealt with. Isaac remembered when the barriers had been installed: three weeks after a car had mounted the pavement in a shopping mall and mowed down six people, three dying at the scene, another in hospital. It had proved not to be terrorist related, but an elderly man suffering a heart attack, but it had been enough to raise the fear that it could happen again, and the next time, it could be a terrorist. Hyde Park could have been a target, so could Kensington Palace, even an infiltration into the building with heavy weapons, and then…

And now there was a body in the Serpentine, a tranquil lake, boats for hire, swimming down at Lansbury's Lido, the Peter Pan Christmas Day Race where hardy individuals would swim a one-hundred-yard course in the lake. Isaac had swum it once, and received a medal for competing, though not gold or silver or bronze. He had been a runner in his day, good enough to have been considered championship material, but then an injury, and his running days had come to an end. He had been born in London, although the bitter cold winter days still troubled him, and as he looked at the water, he remembered the intense cold when he had dived in before.

'We've not disturbed the scene any more than we had to,' one of the uniforms said. 'We just brought the body ashore. There was a possibility that he was still alive.'

'Was he?'

'No. There was a doctor in the park. We asked him to look. An ambulance, standard procedure, had already been called. The doctor checked the body, nothing more.'

'Any evidence destroyed?'

'Not by us.'

'The person who found the body?'

'A Chinese tourist, no English, although there's a translator with the party. Talk to her if you want any more, but you'll not get much. They saw the body, took photos, phoned their friends and family back home, and called us.'

'In that order?' Isaac asked.

'Probably.'

'Larry, you were here before me. Anything to add?'

'Male, in his thirties, Caucasian, dressed in a tee-shirt and shorts, an iPhone strapped to his upper arm, running shoes.'

'Early-morning jogger?'

'I'd say so. No identification though.'

'You've checked the phone?'

'Water ingression. Forensics might be able to dry it out, get access to the memory. Apart from that, there doesn't seem to be any other way to identify him.'

'No credit cards, driving licence?'

'Not that we can see. I've not checked him that closely, nor did the medical men, only what was necessary to administer first aid and to see if he could be resuscitated.'

'How long in the water?'

'You should ask Gordon Windsor when he arrives.'

'He's the senior crime scene investigator, but you should be able to come up with a rough idea.'

'One to two hours. It was raining heavily last night, and it's unlikely a jogger would have been in the park. I can't be certain about that, as some of them can be fanatical about their daily adrenaline hit.'

'A crazy bunch,' Isaac agreed, remembering back a few years when he ran each day.

'The body's not showing any signs of exposure to the elements, although the water's cold. It'll take more of an expert than me to be more exact.'

'Why murder?'

'A heavy object to the head, some bleeding.'

'Drinking more than you should?'

'It helps,' Larry said.

'Helps with what?'

'It helps with coming down to Hyde Park on a Sunday morning to see a dead body.'

Chapter 2

Midday, the scene of crime officers (SOCOs) were in full force at the murder scene. Celebrities in their own right, as the hordes of tourists stood close to the crime scene barriers watching the proceedings.

'Inspector Hill's right on this one,' Gordon Windsor said. A smallish man with thinning hair, he barely came up to Isaac's shoulder.

'I thought he was,' Isaac said. Not that it quelled his anxiety about his inspector. The conversation earlier about Larry's level of alcohol consumption, his reply that seeing dead bodies was the cause, didn't ring true. The man had never shown aversion or disgust at a murder scene before, so why now and why this body?

Isaac had welded together a good team, he knew that; almost like a family in that each helped the other, played off each other's strengths. Back in the office, Bridget Halloran, a wiz with a computer; she dealt with the department's paperwork – prepared the prosecution files, followed up those responsible for collating the evidence, filing the reports, made sure the myriad of other sundry bureaucratic requirements was dealt with. She also had the added responsibility of helping Detective Sergeant Wendy Gladstone, her best friend, with her reports. Bridget was fifty words a minute on the keyboard, Wendy was lucky to manage five, and then there would be grammatical mistakes. Not that Bridget complained. She and Wendy had pooled their resources and were sharing Wendy's house, strictly platonic. Wendy was glad of the company after her husband had died. Her cat – inherited from an old woman in a previous case who had grieved and subsequently died after viewing her dead son's body – had helped, but it slept a lot and only came near when it was feeding time. Bridget, financially secure, thanks to a wealthy aunt who had left her some money, had grown tired of her layabout lover and had kicked him out.

Larry was attempting to find out if anyone else had seen anything at the crime scene. The Chinese tourist who had found the body had not been able to give any more information. The body lay on the ground, ready for moving to Pathology after consultation with the pathologist. Gordon Windsor was wrapping up and removing his coveralls.

'No identification?' he said.

'Not on this one. You've not found anything?' Isaac said.

'Nothing that helps. The man's in his thirties, good physical condition; before obviously.'

'Jogger?'

'You've already asked, but yes. The clothing doesn't offer much help. Made in China, no doubt you can buy it here as in any other country. The running shoes, Nike, are expensive, good quality. New, only been worn a couple of times. Forensics will give you a better idea on that.'

'A local?'

'Probably, but it's not conclusive.'

'The time of death?'

'Early this morning, probably still dark when he was attacked.'

'Attacked, are you sure?'

'A severe blow to the head. No other reason for him to be in the water.'

'In the water unconscious doesn't mean that he would have drowned.'

'He may have been able to run, but that doesn't make him a good swimmer. If his fat content was low enough through excessive running, then he might not have been a natural floater.'

Isaac could understand that. When he had been running competitively in his youth, short distance, not marathons, he was all muscle, very little excess fat. He had never been a great swimmer, the reason, apart from the cold, that he had not received more than a neutral coloured medal for competing in the Christmas race on the lake that was in front of them. There had been a group of them from Challis Street, young, keen, all proud of their physical prowess: Ben Tidworth, an up and coming sergeant at the time, Sally Jenkins, an educated woman who was very ambitious, very aggressive at the station when she thought she was being sidelined because of her sex, and Archie Corker, a Scot from Glasgow. A hard drinker, a hard man, who was popular in the station on account of his optimistic outlook on life, and his willingness to join every club he could and to enjoy life to the full. The only bane in his life was when someone called him Scotch. 'That's a damn drink,' he would say. 'I'm Scottish.'

Of the four of them, Ben, Sally, Archie, and Isaac, Ben was now an inspector at a station in the north of the country, Sally was teaching law at a university, Isaac was standing by the side of the Serpentine, and Archie had died one night, a hit and run driver.

At the Christmas Day race, it had been Archie, the most unlikely of the four, who had taken the bronze medal, the other three just finishing.

11

A wave of nostalgia swept over Isaac, good times past. One of the police divers surfaced and came over to where he was standing.

'Not much to see down there,' the diver said, once he had removed his mouthpiece. 'No visibility, not that it's deep, but it's the mud. As soon as we probe around, up it comes.'

'No sign of a wallet?'

'An old bike, even a shopping trolley, a few sad looking fish, but no wallet. We'll try for a couple more hours, and then we'll have to call it quits.'

'Thanks for trying,' Isaac said as he moved away. He hadn't expected them to find anything; a serious jogger always travels light, although not finding a debit card inside the mobile phone cover was unusual. Even he carried little cash nowadays, preferring to flash the card across the machine when he was buying fuel or even a lifeless ham and cheese sandwich, as he had that day.

And now the trip to Jamaica was off, and he had to phone the travel agent, and then phone Jenny, and then...

After the look on her face when he had left, he wasn't sure what to say to her. She deserved better, but he had a murder enquiry, although many would say that a personal relationship took precedence over work, and his leave had been approved, and that he should go. But that wasn't how he was wired, he knew that. To him, a murder enquiry was personal, and whoever was responsible, they were answerable to him. It was he as the senior investigating officer and his team who would solve the crime and bring the perpetrator to account.

***

It was late on the first day, and the team were in the office in Challis Street. The clothes and the shoes were good quality,' Bridget said. 'I've seen an initial report from Forensics.'

'I've not,' Isaac said. He was leaning back on his chair, not unusual for him when the heat was on. He had just finished speaking to Jenny back at their flat. She had sounded fine, but he was sure she was not. He knew that when he finally arrived home, much later, she would want to talk, whereas he would not. It wasn't directed at her, but after a hard and long day, with a surfeit of facts to digest, an attempt to separate the murder from his personal life was necessary, even if he rarely succeeded.

He knew that Larry would use alcohol as the means of separation, but he had never been a drinker, not even in his youth. Larry wasn't the first police officer who had used alcohol as a crutch. But Larry was on his team, and he didn't intend to lose the man due to alcoholism, an easy way to be drummed out of the police force.

'You will soon,' Bridget said. 'I've got a contact down there, let's me see it before it's been signed off by the Forensics officer.'

'What does it say?'

'The clothing and shoes could have been purchased in England, as well as overseas. I'll work on it tomorrow, contact the importer, find out where the stock had been dispatched.'

'Any more, seeing that you have friends in high places?' Isaac said, a smile on his face, not that he felt jovial.

'The SIM card in the phone. Vodafone, purchased in a supermarket probably, prepaid.'

'A tourist?'

13

'We can't be certain. Plenty of people don't want to tie themselves to contracts, others have more than one phone.'

'And some toss the phone and the SIM card out after a week.'

'Criminals would, but the man had the latest iPhone,' Larry said. 'If he were a criminal, then he would have purchased something cheap.'

'The media?' Isaac asked.

'A death in Hyde Park, Chinese tourists, no more than a five-minute walk to Kensington Palace. It's touched the public's imagination, the fear that the man's death was not random, and there's a madman on the loose,' Larry said.

'Just what we need, public hysteria.'

'Not yet, but it could become that if there are more.'

'It would have needed something for him to have stayed in the water,' Larry said.

'Have you swum in there?'

'Not likely. Too much dirt and duck poo for me.'

'The dirt's on the bottom, but it's cold, freezing cold.'

'You've been in?' Wendy asked.

'Not recently. The water comes from three bores in the park; it used to be fed from the River Westbourne, but that's been diverted underneath and around the lake. If he wasn't a good swimmer, the cold would have sapped his strength on contact with the water, and then panic sets in, and if it was dark, the man, uncertain of his bearings, strikes out for shore. Confusion, fear, possibly jet-lagged if he's a tourist, and then death.'

'Sad way to die,' Wendy said.

'Who was he? We need to know and within twenty-four hours,' Isaac said.

'Six in the morning meeting?' Bridget said.

'Until we solve the murder.'

'Jamaica?'

'It's off for the time being.'

'Someone will be disappointed,' Wendy said.

Isaac chose to ignore Wendy's comment, true as it was. He stood up, put on his jacket and left the office. Tomorrow was another day; he knew that tonight at home was another problem.

***

Torrential rain greeted Isaac as he left his flat at five o'clock the next morning, but it was a welcome relief from the frosty atmosphere inside.

He knew that he'd have to make it up to Jenny, and as soon as the current murder investigation was over, he'd rebook the flight to Jamaica, even pay extra if necessary.

One advantage of the rain was that Hyde Park would have fewer tourists, although one or two joggers would be winding their way through, determined that without their early-morning hit they'd never get through the day. However, any remaining evidence at the murder scene would no longer be available. He pitied the two uniforms still at the site.

In the office, the team were there. Even though they had all been in the office five hours previously, the early-morning meeting was a rule that Isaac rarely broke during an investigation.

In the small kitchenette, Bridget had prepared tea for everyone, even bringing a homemade cake with her.

In his office, Isaac, after the customary 'thanks for coming', led off. He had a mug of tea in his hand, no sugar, although Larry had two spoons, and Bridget and Wendy had sweeteners, the two of them attempting to lose weight for their upcoming week in the South of France, the hope of finding love or lust, joking mainly about the unlikeliness of either.

'We need to know who this person is,' Isaac said as he took a sip of tea.

'I'll focus on the clothing, Inspector Hill can focus on the SIM card,' Wendy said.

'Also, the iPhone. Bridget's running it through the system for me, although without it switched on, we've not much to go on,' Larry Hill said.

'Needle in a haystack if it was purchased overseas or on eBay.'

'Worth a shot,' Isaac said, glancing over at Larry who wasn't looking the best. He would have to have that talk soon with him.

'The SIM's a better chance. Although the serial number may not help much. Detective Chief Superintendent Goddard, we can expect his dulcet tones in here soon?'

'Sometime today. The media attention will ensure his becoming involved,' Isaac said.

A short meeting, it was still too early to start making phone calls, knocking on doors. Bridget went back to her computer. Larry researched how easy it was to get hold of a SIM card for a mobile; remarkably easy, as it turned out that few checks were conducted.

Wendy busied herself with checking the suppliers of the clothes and the shoes the dead man had been wearing. She soon realised that there were more than she could ever door knock or phone, and if they were counterfeit, brought from a shady seller down a dark lane and off the back of a truck, then they would be impossible to trace. According to Forensics, the fabric in the shorts the man had been wearing indicated that they were genuine, although they couldn't be sure with the shirt. The shoes seemed genuine as well.

The dead man was either a saint or a rogue, or possibly somewhere in between, but no one had reported him missing. Not a concern in itself, as it was only twenty-four hours since he had died. Missing Persons would contact Homicide if anything came in. Bridget had scanned their website, sad to see so many people there with no names, other than John or Jane Doe: washed up on the shore, three months floating around in the sea, dead under a bridge, some in their teens, others old and unwanted. People who had loved or been loved, now forgotten.

And now one more to add to the list, a man in the Serpentine, but Wendy was sure the day would reveal his identity. After all, he had been carrying a late-model phone, he had been dressed appropriately for jogging, he was not a tramp or a refugee. He must have money and loved ones somewhere. Wendy realised that that was the soft-hearted side of her, the side that looked for the best in people and circumstances. The man could have been a savage killer, an abuser of children, a villain, but until that was known, she would only think the best of the man who was lying on a metal table waiting for the pathologist to conclude his autopsy and to update the team.

Wendy scrolled down the list of clothing that had been provided by the crime scene investigators.

Shoes. Nike Air Zoom Pegasus 35 Shield – Black – Size 10.

Shorts. Nike Challenger – Black – Medium.
Nike Dri-FIT Medallist – Short-sleeve – Black –
Medium.

All of it one brand, which indicated that a Nike
shop or a section in a department store might be able to
supply the details, assuming a credit card was used. Cash
was unlikely. Who carried cash these days, Wendy
thought, although she still preferred money in her wallet,
not fully trusting the card to work when she wanted it to,
not always sure if there were sufficient funds in the bank
account to cover whatever she purchased.

Larry sat at his desk, realising that the iPhone
would not be of much use unless it was powered up. The
phone was with Forensics, drying out. No attempt would
be made to switch it on until the process had completed.

'You'll fry what little's left of it if you try,' the
smart and eager young man in the white lab coat had said
when Larry had stuck his nose around the door the night
before. Forensics wasn't too keen on working on a
Sunday, the same as everyone else, but for a murder the
person on standby duties had been brought in.

Larry looked at his watch. 7.20 a.m. He'd give it
another ten minutes, and he'd be over to Forensics, no
doubt making a nuisance of himself, hopeful of a result.

Chapter 3

'It'll cost you a pint,' Jerry Blaxland said. He had arrived at the Forensics lab at eight in the morning, expecting to have a chance to grab a cup of coffee and check his emails. It wasn't to be as Larry had arrived ten minutes earlier.

Blaxland, a man in his forties, with jet-black hair, had a perpetual frown as though the world was about to end. His initial comment, 'it'll cost you a pint', said before the usual courtesies, did not concern Larry. Apart from Blaxland being a good forensics laboratory officer, he was also a drinker, and he and Larry had often shared a few glasses of beer.

'I'll buy you two if you can get the phone to work,' Larry said.

'Five minutes while I log in, check a couple of emails and grab a coffee. One for you?' Blaxland said, not willing to forego the early morning ritual.

'One sugar.'

'Cutting down?'

'I'm trying to, but you know how it is.'

Blaxland was another man who struggled with his weight, not helped by five pints of beer every night at his local pub, a predilection for McDonald's hamburgers, the biggest they had, every lunchtime.

'The wife?' Blaxland said.

'She's complaining, and I'm waiting for my DCI to have another go at me.'

'Tough.'

'Sometimes we see things that no man should see.'

'Not in here,' Blaxland said. Larry looked around the laboratory, could see what the man meant. The area was sterile, with hardly anything to show for what passed through the doors: blood-stained clothing, guns and knives, some still bloodied, some that had killed, and sometimes body parts, heavily decayed and writhing with maggots. Yet, each day, the fear of contamination and disputed evidence ensured that the place was left spotless. A faint smell of chemicals pervaded the air.

'We've had the phone on low heat for twenty-three hours,' Blaxland said. 'If it's going to work, it'll be now or never.'

'The memory, any chance of finding out contacts from it, images?'

'Do you remember back in 2016 when the FBI tried to unlock an iPhone belonging to a suspected terrorist and Apple wouldn't help?'

'Vaguely,' Larry replied, not sure of the relevance.

'The FBI managed to unlock it in the end. We may have a password on this phone as well.'

'Is that likely?'

'Fifty-fifty. It's a prepaid card, so if someone stole it and made a long-distance call to a relative in Australia, the money would have run out soon enough. Depends though.'

'On what?'

'Whether whoever this phone belonged to was neurotic, or he used it to phone a girlfriend while his wife sat at home with the kids.'

'Assume the best. Just switch it on.'

Blaxland set the phone on one of the benches in the lab. He then connected the charging cable – nothing.

'It's dead,' Larry said.

'You've got a phone. What happens when the battery goes flat?'

'It switches off.'

'And when you connect it to the charger, it thinks about it for a short while before anything happens. I'm only applying a trickle charge, the lowest setting that I can. It'll take a few minutes. Time enough for another coffee.'

'I'd rather stay with the phone.'

'A watched kettle never boils. You must have heard that saying?'

'My mother, all the time.'

'Your mother had more sense than you. A coffee and then it'll be ready to try.'

The two men retreated to the coffee machine, Larry not keen to go, but complying with Blaxland. The man was good, Larry knew that, and if anyone was going to have success, it would be him.

Five minutes later, the two men were back at the phone. The screen was illuminated, a charge of eight per cent indicated.

'It's a bit low, but it's promising,' Blaxland said.

Larry wanted to pick up the phone and scroll through it, find out the phone's number, instigate a search on the calls made. 'Can't you try it now?' he said.

'It cost the FBI a fortune to break the password on that phone in America,' Blaxland said.

'The most I can manage is a couple of pints of beer if that's what you're hinting at.'

'That'll do. There's no password.'

'What's the phone's number?'

Blaxland scrolled through to the settings to show the number. Larry messaged Bridget; she'd know what to do.'

'A list of phone numbers called, received?'

'You've got the phone's number. It's easy from here on.'

'Humour me. Give me the last ten with times, also any messages. Are there images?'

'No images, two messages. "See you soon, can't wait", "Ready and waiting, lover".'

'Phone numbers for the messages?'

Blaxland typed the information on his laptop. Not long after, Larry left Forensics with a printed sheet of paper containing the details of the two messages complete with their phone numbers and eight phone numbers dialled, but no emails, as the phone had not been fully set up.

***

Wendy had to admit relief in that the focus had turned from the clothing the dead jogger was wearing to the phone calls, especially the two messages. Of the eight phone numbers dialled, four of them were the same as the messages.

'A wife?' Isaac said in the office.

'You've a trusting nature, DCI,' Wendy said. 'The man had a fancy woman, a bit on the side. That's why the prepaid phone, the coy messages, the short phone calls.'

Isaac knew that Wendy was probably right.

He had had a troublesome night, with Jenny wanting to talk for hours on end, and just as he was dropping off to sleep, she'd nudge him in the ribs and start on again about the need for commitment, the time to prioritise what was important in his life.

She was right, he knew that, but what could he say? There was a murder enquiry. He had had no words, and it had been the first time that she had complained. He hoped it would blow over, but he wasn't confident that it would.

She was only exercising her right as the person who shared his life. In the end, she had left the bed and had gone to sleep in the other room. When he had left early in the morning, he had tiptoed past her, not sure if she was asleep or whether she was pretending. He felt sorry, but he couldn't say that they'd leave for Jamaica as promised, nor could he say that he loved her and all would be well. He had been down this road before, and it was invariably rough before it got to the end. He wished it could be different.

'*A mistress,*' Wendy said, this time louder than the first. She had seen the distant look in her DCI's face, realised what the problem was. Of all those in the department, she had known him longer than anyone else, even longer than Detective Chief Superintendent Goddard. Isaac had been in uniform when she had first met him, a lowly constable attempting to make his mark. Back then, he had been irresistible to the women in the station: over six feet tall, black complexion, always immaculately dressed, even in his police uniform. And now, many years later, the looks had not changed, only aged a little and become more distinguished, and now he wore a suit.

Isaac, embarrassed that he had drifted away for a few seconds, refocussed on the meeting. 'Yes, of course. Do we know who?'

'It's another prepaid,' Bridget said. 'I've found out where it was bought, although not a name.'

'Local?'

'Paddington.'

'Wendy, Larry, focus on finding the owner of this phone. Any more you can give us, Bridget?'

'Not so difficult now with the number. I can tell you where the phone calls to and from the jogger were made.'

'And?'

'The dates go back six days. The jogger phoned the number four times, the other end phoned him twice, plus a couple of messages.'

'We'll check where the other phone number's SIM was purchased, and then it's legwork,' Larry said. 'Any more you can give us, Bridget?'

'The other mobile's relatively static. I've got the SIM provider checking further, but we're assuming Paddington, and we should be able to narrow it down to two to three streets, maybe a bit more.'

'That's still a lot of territory to cover. We'll be looking forever. Any other phone calls made from the other number?'

'Only to the jogger, which indicates that Wendy is right. Clandestine lovers indulging in subterfuge.'

'It got the man killed,' Isaac said.

'It's a good enough motive.'

***

'Do you know how many SIMS we sell in a day?' Brent Anderson said. He was standing behind a shop counter at Paddington Station. In front of him, a glass-fronted kiosk had an array of cheap mobile phones. Behind him, hanging on hooks, SIM cards for all of the major mobile phone networks.

'The phones you're selling? Fakes or stolen?' Larry said.

'I've got receipts for all of them. This is a respectable business.'

'Respectable, I don't think so,' Wendy said. She didn't like the look of the man. He had a great location in the railway station, a lot of passing traffic, yet he stood there with unkempt hair, a one-week beard growth.

'If I have to close you down, get your stock checked out, I will,' Larry said.

Anderson looked away, took a puff of a cigarette.

'No smoking in here,' Wendy said. 'Can't you see the signs.'

'Is this your store, or are you just an employee?' Larry asked.

'What's it to you?'

'We came here in a civil manner, showed you our warrant cards. If you don't want to help, then we'll call in some people from the station to close you down, check your records.'

Wendy had got to know the previous station master well during another murder enquiry. She knew what he would have thought of the man selling phones. The station master had been a stickler for rules and regulations and for keeping the trains on time, the station modern and efficient. Although in his office it was like stepping back in time, the leather chair where Wendy had sat recovered from a carriage on the last steam train to leave Paddington. Now the trains were slick and fast and clean, Wendy was not nostalgic for their smelly and slow predecessors. She imagined that Anderson would have liked them. Back then everyone smoked, and there were no restrictions.

'Tell us what we want, and we'll leave you to it,' Wendy said. She didn't want to indulge in a slanging match; she was there with Larry for information. Later on, she would make a phone call to the new station master, mention her friendship with the previous incumbent who had since retired. She'd make sure that a smart-arse like Anderson got his comeuppance.

'How long ago?' Anderson said with a resigned look on his face.

'Eight to nine days ago.'

Larry handed over the phone number.

'It depends whether the person paid cash or not. Male or female?'

'We can't be sure.'

Anderson ran through the records on his computer where he had activated the SIM, entering the information into Vodafone's database. 'Found it. Christine Hislop, 24 Talbot Square, Paddington. A two-minute walk from here.'

'It's also the Fitzroy Hotel,' Larry said.

'That's the address the woman gave.'

'Do you remember her?'

'If she was a looker, I might have, but no.'

'Bogus address?' Wendy said, not appreciating Anderson's derisory comment, not that she had expected more of the man.

'That's not my concern, is it?' Anderson replied. 'I gave you what you wanted. The woman paid cash. Now if you don't mind.'

'We do,' Larry said. 'If there's anything more we'll be back. You've got a driving licence, proof of address?'

'I've done nothing wrong.'

'We're not saying you have, but if we find the woman, we may ask you to have a look at her photo, let us know if it rings any other bells.'

'Have it your way,' Anderson said as he handed over a driving licence, still valid, just, as well as a utility bill, overdue, good address.

'Your parents' place?' Larry asked.

'Mine and paid for. I got lucky with a lottery ticket. Bought myself this hole in the wall, paid for the house.'

'Then why work here?' Wendy asked.

'Schizophrenic, if you must know. If I sit at home, I'd be smoking more than twenty Marlboro Gold a day. This keeps me sane.'

Wendy could see that the unpleasant man had some redeeming features, not many though, although he had reasoned that sanity was preferable to the alternatives. 'Thanks for the help,' she said, even managing a weak smile.

***

'I'm sorry, I can't help you,' the neatly-turned-out man said at the Fitzroy Hotel's reception said. 'The woman could have been a guest.'

'She may still be. The first phone call in this area was six days ago, the last thirty-six hours,' Larry said.

'As I said, we don't have a Christine Hislop here.'

'Do any of the staff live on the premises?'

'A few, but I don't recognise the name.'

'Can you check?' Wendy asked. She had looked around the hotel as she had entered, seen that it cost over five hundred pounds a night for a small double, more than she spent in a month on her half share of the house she shared with Bridget.

'Sure, no trouble.'

Wendy compared the man behind the hotel reception to Brent Anderson. The latter would have had more money but didn't deserve it. The receptionist was probably paid a pittance, worked long hours, yet remained civil and friendly. Life wasn't fair, Wendy knew, but sometimes the injustices of the world got to her – the reason that the television at home was switched off when the news was on, which appeared to be most of the time. She no longer wanted to hear about corrupt right-wing politicians and their agendas, the starving in Africa, those fleeing war zones. Not that she couldn't sympathise with the downtrodden and the neglected; it was just that there was too much closer to home, too much in the area to deal with. A man, not missed by anyone yet, lay dead; that was enough for her to deal with for the present.

'We've got a Christine Mason on the books.'

'Where is she?' Wendy asked.

'She handles the accounts. I'll give her a call.'

'Don't bother. Just point us in the right direction,' Larry said.

'Behind me, second door on the left down the corridor. Is she in trouble?'

'Routine enquiry, that's all.'

'But you're from Homicide.'

'We've not come here to arrest anyone, just to ask a few questions. How long are you on duty for?'

'Another three hours. Why?'

'We may have some more questions for you.'

'She's a good person, is Christine.'

No doubt the dead man was, Wendy thought, but he's still dead.

Larry and Wendy walked through the door at the back of reception. The impressive décor out front soon degenerated into drab white-painted walls. The first office

28

along the corridor had a sign on the door stating it belonged to the assistant manager. Across from there, on the other side, two printers occupied an alcove. The corridor did not stretch far, only six offices from what they could see. On the second door on the left, the sign said accounts manager. It wasn't an impressive brass plaque; this was plastic and cheap, held on by a couple of screws.

Wendy knocked; a voice came from the other side. 'Come in.'

Wendy showed her warrant card first, Larry second.

'You've come about the body upstairs? I'm not the person to see. You'll need housekeeping. They deal with the occasional guest that dies on the premises, two in the last three months.'

'We're from Homicide,' Larry said. He took a seat, as did Wendy. 'Are you Christine Hislop?'

'I was a Hislop once,' the woman said, no longer sitting comfortably, no longer working on her accounts.

'You purchased a SIM card from a vendor at Paddington Station nine days ago. A scruffy-looking individual.'

'I may have. Sometimes for the guests, a special favour.'

'Why would you do that?'

'Some of them struggle with English. It's easy enough for me to do, gets me out of the office for a while.'

'We need to be blunt, Miss Mason,' Wendy said. 'Mrs.'

'Very well, Mrs Mason. The phone that was activated with the SIM you purchased had sent some messages, as well as a number of phone calls, to one

29

phone number in particular. The English on the messages was perfect.'

Larry held his phone out of sight of Christine Mason. He dialled one number, the number they were now discussing. A delay of five seconds, and then the ringing of a mobile.

'Mrs Mason, who were you phoning? Who did you call "lover"? Please think carefully before answering.'

'We were friends, nothing more.'

'We're not here to discuss whether you were friends or lovers. We're from Homicide, investigating a murder,' Larry said. 'We need a name.'

'My husband, the children. I can't.'

'It's more serious than that,' Wendy said. 'We need his name.'

'He was a guest here once or twice. We got to talking, and then, well, it wasn't too good at home. My husband's a good man, but he leaves me cold.'

'I'm sorry, but we must insist on a name. Afterwards, we can discuss the right and wrong of it, how you met, and so on.'

'Is he…?'

'Did you suspect that something had happened?'

'Not really. I phoned him one day ago, maybe two. We had arranged to meet, but when he didn't turn up, I didn't think too much about it. Sometimes we don't see each other for months, and then three times in a week. My husband travels, so did Colin, overseas a lot of the time.'

'Colin who?'

'Colin Young.'

'An address?'

'We decided when we became involved not to talk about our home life or where we lived. I didn't love him,

30

not that much, but he was kind. Two lonely souls, to use a cliché.'

'We need to find his next of kin.'

'Colin? I thought you were referring to someone else.'

'You seemed to understand before.'

'It's just that I can't…'

'Believe it, is that it?' Wendy said.

'He was so fit, so full of himself.'

'A jogger?'

'Serious, every day, wherever he was. We snuck in a couple of nights away once, and five in the morning, he's out there running around. And I'm there waiting for him, and now he's dead, and I'll never see him again. How will I survive? He kept me going, and now he's gone. How?'

Wendy could see the woman resolutely holding back the tears.

'Hyde Park, near the Serpentine.'

'But why? He wasn't staying here. Where was he? He doesn't live in London, I know that, and he always comes to see me.'

Larry could recognise the truth. Colin Young was a player, a man that had more than one woman, the married and susceptible his speciality. Not that it explained why Christine Mason, also known as Christine Hislop, would have been attracted to him. She was in her forties, blonde hair, articulate and educated.

Chapter 4

The team in Homicide had a name and an address that the man had used when he had signed in at the Fitzroy Hotel on four separate occasions, even at the small and discreet hotel in the countryside where Colin Young and Christine Mason had enjoyed a romantic two-day tryst. But that was it.

Isaac was frustrated. The case had been split wide open with the naming of the dead jogger. Pathology had confirmed that he had been semi-conscious in the water and he had swallowed sufficient water to drown. The blow to the back of the head with something heavy was clear enough, and the force had thrust him backwards into the Serpentine, and that it was still murder.

The team met early in Isaac's office. The weather outside was miserable, interminable rain, the clouds heavy and dark.

'Colin Young, what do we know?' Isaac asked.

Wendy sat quietly; a late night the previous day and back at six in the morning didn't sit well with her. Larry, without the customary few too many pints of beer at the end of the day, was more alert.

'Christine Mason, I suppose we should call her that, rather than the name she used when she purchased the SIM card, is forty-seven years of age. She must be fifteen years older than Colin Young,' Larry said.

'You're still trying to make out that Christine Mason is a floozy, desperate for a man,' Wendy said accusingly.

'I agree that the woman didn't seem to be that sort, but what do we know about her? Profiling would indicate that she's not the type for a young lover, but the facts are the facts. You've checked out her story, confirmed that her husband, a salesman for an engineering firm, travels a lot, and that there are two children, old enough to look after themselves.'

'What kind of engineering?' Isaac asked. He was in a better mood than the previous day. He and Jenny were talking again, though not yet loving, and the relationship was going to survive; he was sure of that.

'Military,' Larry said. 'Something to do with weapon guidance systems.'

'No more than that?'

'Not that I could understand. Tony Mason is a high-powered salesman, trips into the Middle East, Saudi often. And then, he travels to other countries in the region, some that the British Government doesn't approve of.'

'Illegal?'

'Even with sanctions imposed, it still continues.'

'So the man's secretive?'

'We've not spoken to him yet. We don't know what his reaction will be when he finds out about his wife and her lover.'

'Not pleasant, we'd assume,' Isaac said. 'He'll need to be interviewed at some time. In the country?'

'According to Christine Mason, he's due to leave again in a couple of days,' Wendy said.

''Very well. Focus on Colin Young. What do we have?'

'An address in Bristol, bogus,' Bridget said. 'No point going there unless you want to enter a convent.'

'Sense of humour, our Mr Young.'

'Sense of something,' Wendy said. 'It's hardly humour if he has been stringing along other women.'

'Apart from that, we know that the address is bogus. Payment at the Fitzroy?'

'Credit card, valid. It was in the name of Colin Young. The bank that issued it has an address, this time in Bath.'

'Which indicates that he comes from around there?'

'The address in Bath is a secretarial service. We've been on to them, although all they do is receive the man's correspondence, put it into a post office box.'

'Which he picks up from.'

'It's a busy location, a lot of pedestrian traffic. We can start by asking people on the street if they've seen anyone open the box, but it's a needle in a haystack. The man wouldn't have stood out from the crowd.'

'Coming back to London,' Isaac said. 'The man's in jogging gear near to the Serpentine. It's early morning, so that tells us he spent the previous night in London, and somewhere close. If it's not the Fitzroy, then where?'

'We've had people out door knocking the hotels, although we got nowhere. We'll continue, widen our search if we have to,' Wendy said.

'He had no money on him,' Larry said. 'He must have been staying nearby, within walking or jogging distance.'

'Which could mean for a man so obviously fit, anywhere up to five miles, even more.'

'Needle in a haystack, as you say,' Isaac said, aware Jenny would be disappointed that the murderer was not going to be found soon.

'We've asked other people to check on the clothing,' Wendy said.

'Focus on finding out what you can about this man. It's no use chasing red herrings, interviewing Christine Mason's husband unless we have reason to suspect him.'

'He must be a suspect,' Bridget said.

'He is, but of what? He may not have known about his wife. What do we know about her? Is this behaviour of hers out of the ordinary? Is Colin Young her first lover?'

'Since being married, you mean?' Wendy said.

'I'm not trying to insult the woman or imply anything. But if she's got a habit of hooking up with guests at the Fitzroy or elsewhere, we need to know about her. There could be another lover, disturbed that he's not the only one. From what you said, she didn't love the jogger, only used him as a plaything, someone to get her rocks off with, to use the vernacular.'

'I'm meeting with her later today,' Wendy said. 'Outside of the hotel, neutral territory. She seems upset and she wants to talk.'

'She doesn't want her husband to find out. Good provider, is he?' Larry, who could not see the woman in the way that Wendy did, remained sceptical. To him, Christine Mason, a woman his age, wouldn't take a young lover unless there were other forces at play.

'I'll find out, let you know.'

'Christine Mason's husband is involved with selling weapons,' Bridget said.

'And your point?' Isaac said.

'If what he's doing is secretive, could Colin Young have been keeping a watch on him, using the man's wife to delve deep, industrial or military espionage, possibly a foreign power?'

'We deal with the facts for now.'

'Just a thought.'

'A good thought, I would agree. And personally, I don't want to go down that road. What we have, until we know differently, is a young and fit man seducing a woman who may have had a difficult home life, feeling in need of attention.'

'Sad,' Wendy said.

'Sad or otherwise, find out who Colin Young is. Once we know that, then the pieces of the puzzle will fit together.'

'You hope,' Larry said.

'It'd be good to have an easy win, for once.'

'And a trip to Jamaica,' Wendy said.

'Don't go there, Wendy,' Isaac said. 'Deal with the murder enquiry, not my personal life.'

'But we care.'

'That may be, and I thank you for your concern, but it's going to be alright this time. And now, after our heart to heart, please get out of my office and give me results,' Isaac said, embarrassed that he had opened up more than he should have.

***

Larry and Wendy accepted the mantle to find out who Colin Young was and what his movements had been in the hours leading up to his death.

Wendy took a couple of uniforms with her, both juniors at Challis Street: Constable Katrina Taylor, a tall, slim Scottish woman with dark, shoulder-length hair. Personable, attractive, and a woman with a future in the police force, Wendy thought. The second constable, Elvis Mortimer, was in his early twenties. A stocky individual with a chip on his shoulder, and parents who must have

loved the American singer. It was a good job, Wendy
thought, that she hadn't named her eldest son Cat, after a
famous English singer that had been popular, and then
had found religion and became Yusuf Islam. She couldn't
see Cat Gladstone or Yusuf Gladstone working, any more
than the pairing of Elvis and Mortimer. For one thing,
the man couldn't sing, and he wasn't the sort of man for
girls to swoon over, although there had been complaints
that he had rubbed up against a couple of the women in
the station, including Katrina Taylor. The man was on a
short leash. One more incident and he would be out on
his ear.

'We'll keep to the south of Hyde Park, focus on
Knightsbridge and Kensington. That's a lot of hotels, and
if we need help, we'll bring more people in,' Wendy said
to the two constables who sat some distance from each
other.

'There would be hundreds,' Mortimer said.

'So?'

'It will take forever.'

'And you've got something better to do? Meeting
up with the chief superintendent later on for a drink?'
Wendy realised that she was allowing her prejudice against
the constable to show. The man had been warned
officially; it wasn't for her to aggravate the situation.

'Constable Mortimer's right,' Katrina Taylor said.

'It's a tough one. Bridget Halloran is preparing a
list of the hotels, discounting some that we've already
canvassed. First off, we'll start making phone calls, send
an email back up with a photo and name, as well as the
addresses.'

'Isn't there a central reservations database for the
hotels in London?' Mortimer said. Wendy didn't warm to
the man, but he was no dummy. He was asking the right

questions, had been able to see the path to take to maximise the possibility of a result, minimise the legwork. Wendy would grant that the latter was not something she looked forward to, having done enough in her time.

'We'll work with Bridget on that. Most bookings are made over the internet, and they would require a credit card. He's used Colin Young on the card he used to pay the bill at the Fitzroy. If he stayed in one five-star hotel, we'd assume that he stayed in another of similar quality. A bit hit and miss on that one, but we need to eliminate those further.'

'He could have walked in off the street, paid cash, or he could have rented an Airbnb. They're good. I've used them myself once or twice,' Katrina Taylor said.

'Our man stayed somewhere, and we need to find it.'

'I read the reports about him,' Mortimer said.

'What do you reckon?' Wendy said.

'If he was a keen jogger, then maybe he belonged to a club, competed in marathons.'

Wendy knew that she had picked well. Constable Taylor had the enthusiasm; Mortimer, apart from his leering eyes that stripped naked every young female in the station, had the makings of an excellent investigative officer, if he lasted that long.

***

Larry knew that Colin Young was an enthusiastic jogger, which meant he had probably run to where he had died, but from where?

Sergeant Dean Cousins, Challis Street Police Station's premier athlete, who competed in the London Marathon each year, was a whippet-thin man. Every lunchtime, if he was in the station, he would put in five miles while the others were taking a rest or eating their lunch, or even grabbing the opportunity for sleep. And then once a week, he'd jog the eleven miles from his home to the station, a backpack with his essentials, a spare uniform hanging on a hook in the changing rooms.

'What's your best time?' Larry asked. The two of them were standing by the side of the Serpentine.

'I ran sub three hours a couple of years ago, two fifty-three.'

'Impressive.'

'The winner ran it in two hours and five minutes. But he was a professional. I can't hope to run that fast, not if I keep my day job, not even if I quit. Most of the winners these days come from Africa.'

'And you come from Barnsley. A major disadvantage there,' Larry said.

'Some, but that's not why we're here, is it?'

'You've read the case file, what do you think?'

'Judging by the time in the morning that the man would have been running, his physical condition, I'd say he was a man I'd identify with.'

'Crazy?'

'Of course. Who else would find pleasure pounding around London, inhaling the petrol fumes, dealing with angry drivers and breaking the ice underfoot in winter?'

'What do you reckon? The man's running along on the path here; we can't tell which direction. I need a rough idea as to where he entered the park, where he would have exited, and more importantly, where he may have come from.'

'You don't want much.'

'I thought you could help. Sergeant Gladstone's conducting a blanket investigation south of the park. Now, I don't want to go heading off in the wrong direction. If you, a man who thinks like the murdered man, may be able to assist, it'd be appreciated.'

'Not all joggers think the same, and we tend to vary the route, prevent boredom.'

'I thought you people were fanatical.'

'We are, and when the adrenaline rush kicks in, then it's great. But you can't guarantee that every time, especially when the weather's not so good. The muscles don't warm up enough and the times are down.'

'Crazy, as I said.'

'Mad as a hatter, but that's what jogging is about. Overcome the adversity, enjoy the outdoors, push through the pain barrier, reap the rewards.'

Larry looked at the water, the tourists walking behind them. 'Tranquil, it's kind of beautiful standing here. Not the place for murder, that's for sure.'

'Where is? You want my thoughts on where the man would have run?'

'If you can.'

'I run around it sometimes. The park is closed from midnight to five in the morning. If he came after five, then he could have entered anywhere. Before that, he would have had to jump the fence, and the parks are patrolled at night.'

'From 5 a.m. is fine.'

'It would help if CCTV cameras had picked him up outside.'

'It was dark and an early-morning fog.'

'You said he stayed in a hotel in Paddington on a couple of occasions.'

'Four to be precise, but not this time.'

'If it were Paddington, then he would have probably jogged down Westbourne Street. If he had chosen Lancaster Terrace, that would have been one more road to cross. Nothing a serious jogger likes less is to be held up by traffic lights and pedestrian crossings.'

'Let's assume he stayed somewhere close to the Fitzroy.'

'He would have crossed Bayswater Road and entered by the gate near to Buckhill Lodge. You can rent it out sometimes, expensive though, and beyond my salary.'

'Assume Buckhill Lodge as his entry point.'

'Have you checked with the people staying there?'

'We have; no luck.'

'If he had gone down Lancaster Terrace, he would have entered through Lancaster Gate. It's not far from Buckhill Lodge, and it makes little difference as to the route he took. He's in the park now, which way to go?'

'What would you choose?'

'It's just over two miles to run around the Serpentine. Scenically, it would be attractive, but a serious jogger's looking for more than that.'

'How many miles do you run a day?'

'If I've got a marathon coming up, I'll aim for ten.'

'And you achieve it?'

'It's hard, but yes. Most weeks, I'll run five a day.'

'You're in the park, what then?'

'Head left down towards Marble Arch, then run down alongside Park Lane, keeping in the park. Before I reach the end, I would swing right and run alongside the lake, keeping to the Kensington side, up past the swimming pool, take the tunnel under West Carriage Drive and up to where we're standing.'

'And the alternative?'

'In reverse. If the man was a keen jogger, it's the route he would have taken.'

'But the person who struck him, ensuring that he fell back into the water wouldn't have been jogging, just waiting.'

'Then the murderer must have known the man's movements. And if he was predictable, then others must have seen him.'

'Who?'

'Other joggers, people walking through the park, the staff at the Lido Café.'

'Too early for the café, and it would need people who were here on a regular basis.'

'Sorry, can't help you anymore. I can put you in touch with some friends who run through here more often than I do, although I reckon that's the route he would have taken.'

Chapter 5

'No idea on this one?' Chief Superintendent Goddard asked. He was sitting behind his desk, the panoramic view of London behind him.

'Until we know the man's real name, we're hitting a brick wall,' Isaac said from his side of the desk. 'The man's suspicious, but there's no record. We've checked the usual: DNA, dental, photo.'

'Yet he uses a false name and address.'

'He's been stringing along a married woman. We don't know if it was love, or whether it was just a dalliance. Not that he ever took money from her, not that we know of. The woman's husband is involved with military technology. It's an avenue that may be pursued at some stage.'

'Espionage, attempting to find out details of the technology?'

'Something like that. We've not spoken to the husband, and his company is subject to the Official Secrets Act. We could go barging in, blow the woman's alibi, or whatever she's been using to hide the truth from her husband.'

'You think that the dead man could have been involved with a foreign power?' Goddard asked.

'I hope not. We became involved with the secret service on a previous case. Ended up getting messy, almost destroyed our careers.'

'It could have got you killed.'

'That's why I don't want to go there,' Isaac said. 'Pandora's box. If we open the lid, who knows what or who will come out.'

'Don't pursue that angle yet. You reckon that the dead man was involved with other women?'

'Assumptions, and not very good at that. He used a bogus address and name, credit cards delivered to a post office box.'

'Unusual in itself, not strictly illegal.'

'The account where the credit card draws its money is offshore, but it's paid off in full each month.'

'He may be an overseas contractor, paid offshore.'

'Then why the false name?'

'I can't help you there. How's Jenny?'

'She's fine. We were going to Jamaica, but with this murder, I've put it on hold.'

'Once it's over, come over to the house, the two of you. You can call me Richard there, not sir.'

'You know I can't, never have, never will.'

Goddard laughed, knowing full well that in all the years they had known each other, the times they had met socially, his DCI had never once referred to him as anything other than 'sir' or 'chief superintendent'.

Isaac left and returned downstairs to his office. A report had to be dealt with; he was not excited at the prospect. Too much time spent in the office, too much time dealing with reporting and budgetary constraints, trying to justify the need for extra staff, receiving the customary rejection.

Restless, Isaac left his office and went and sat with the two constables that were working with Wendy. 'Any luck?' he asked.

Katrina Taylor, he knew; Mortimer, he did not, other than by reputation. It was not for him to form an opinion of the man, and he could only be civil to him.

'No luck, DCI. Sergeant Gladstone's meeting with Christine Mason. We're ploughing through the hotels, phoning some, emailing others. It could take some time,' Katrina Taylor said.

'We could do with some help, sir,' Mortimer said.

'We all could,' Isaac replied. 'Unfortunately, I can't get you any yet. Find where Colin Young has been, and then maybe.'

As Isaac left the two constables, he leant over and whispered in Katrina Taylor's ear. 'Any trouble?'

'Not yet. Best behaviour. You've heard?'

'I have. If it happens, or you think it's about to, give me a call. Wendy says he's competent, just that his eyes are too big for his head,' Isaac said.

***

Wendy could see that Christine Mason was an insecure woman. Even when meeting at a café close to Paddington Station, she was nervous.

'Sorry I'm late,' the Fitzroy's account manager said. 'Trouble with balancing the books.'

'What sort of trouble?' Wendy said. She had arrived earlier and had ordered a latte and a slice of cheesecake.

'Can I see him?'

'After here. You're the only one, proof positive, that can confirm that it's the man you knew.'

'It's him.'

'We're certain it is, but you seeing him may jog something in your memory. Something you've failed to tell us.'

'I've told you all I know. I loved him, you know.'

'That's not what you said before. The truth, please. Did you love him, or are you now upset that he may have been playing the field, spending time with you for the benefits?'

'What benefits?'

'Financial.'

'Well, I did lend him some money once, but he paid it back.'

'All of it?'

'Not all. That's the problem at the hotel.'

'You've been borrowing money from the hotel, IOUs, and you've not paid it back? That's a criminal offence.'

'I know, and now I don't know what to do.'

'Your husband has money, so do you.'

'Joint accounts and he's fastidious. He'd know if I did that.'

'It's going to come out at some time. Did you kill him?'

'Who? My husband or Colin?'

'Colin Young. Had you contemplated leaving your husband and moving in with him?'

'Silly dreams, the same as a pubescent girl, her first crush on a boy. Imagining the two of you living the "happy ever after".'

'We grow out of it, most of us do,' Wendy said, remembering back to Bradley Lawson. The two of them, just fifteen, and there behind the barn on his father's farm. She had lost her virginity to him, him plighting his troth, telling her it would be forever. And then two weeks

later, she had caught him with her best friend, Theresa.
The same barn, the same corny lines, another gullible
teenager. She smiled as she thought back to that day, not
that she had smiled at the time. She had been so angry,
and stronger than most of the boys at that age, that she
had pulled him off her now ex-friend, his trousers around
his ankles, Theresa's skirt up high. With one shove, she
had pushed him onto a cowpat, his naked backside
sinking in deep. As he struggled to stand, she had hit him
square in the face with a clenched fist, breaking two teeth
and his nose.

Bradley, the young lover, had required dentistry to
fix the teeth, although the nose always remained off to
one side. Not a good look for someone who had become
a lawyer, not that anyone would have ever asked. Those
who would have seen it as they sat in his plush office in
Sheffield would have thought it was from rugby at school,
not from a helpless woman he had seduced and then
rejected.

Theresa, the friend, had not fared any better that
day. After punishing Bradley, Wendy had grabbed her by
the hair and thrust her face down into the cowpat. No
one would have known but Theresa, humiliated and
upset, had told her mother – leaving out some of the
sordid details – who had then complained to Wendy's
father and the headmaster at school. Not that either of
them had been under any illusion. Her father was a man
of the soil, a farmer. He knew the truth, so did the
headmaster.

In the end, lacking resolution and an apology,
Theresa had blabbed to her other best friend in the
strictest confidence. But it was a school playground
confidence, and one hour later the whole school knew.
Wendy was the heroine, Theresa, the tart, and Bradley

Lawson was a weakling to some due to a woman besting him, a source of admiration to others in that he had made love to the two of them; not that love was the word used, not in a school, not amongst young men.

'That's the problem,' Christine said. 'I knew it was wrong, but every time Colin phoned, I couldn't say no.'

'How much money?'

'Two thousand pounds. Not a lot in itself, but my husband, he's the jealous type.'

'And he would know? Couldn't you tell him that you had to buy some clothes, some furniture for the house, a surprise for him?'

'You don't know him, or you wouldn't even think it, let alone suggest it.'

'Violent?'

'Never, not with me.'

'Capable of murder?'

'You think he might have found out?'

'It's a possibility. It's normally the nearest and dearest who commit the murders.'

'He's the nearest, I'm not so sure about the dearest.'

Wendy ordered another latte and a slice of cheesecake. Christine ordered the same. Wendy liked the woman, although she couldn't understand why she had been so foolish. It was increasingly looking as though the woman had been the target of a skilled seduction, and if Colin Young could seduce one, then he could seduce two, possibly more.

Regardless of who the dead man really was, Wendy's conversation with Christine Mason revealed one thing: the woman's husband was a possessive man, a man who probably regarded his wife as one of his possessions. The sort of man that profiling would consider to be a prime candidate to commit murder if he knew. And that was the question that needed to be answered. Wendy looked across at the woman who was starting to drift away, a glazed look in her eyes.

'What is it?' Wendy asked.

'It's a mess, isn't it?'

'Your problems seem more serious than mine.'

'Tony will find out eventually, won't he?'

'He will. Have you told me the whole truth?'

'I think so. Can I see Colin?'

Christine Mason excused herself for a couple of minutes. Wendy could see that she wanted to cry.

'Stay with her,' Isaac said when Wendy phoned him.

'She might remember something else, or she might be holding back. Ask DI Hill to check out her husband. He could be dangerous, and when he finds out, he could attack his wife.'

'Are you suggesting she gets away from him?'

'It's not for me to suggest. We need to document what she's told me, what I've said to her, just in case.'

'Make sure it's in your report when you type it up, or should I say when Bridget does. Just get the facts straight, that's all.'

'We're going to look at the body.'

'Have they been told?'

'I phoned Pathology. They'll attempt to make him look presentable.'

***

Neither Roy Eardley nor Adrian Clark was as whippet-thin as Dean Cousins, the jogging police officer. Larry thought Cousins looked anorexic, but he knew that wasn't

49

the case, having seen him on a couple of occasions eating with gusto.

'Burns the calories, jogging,' Cousins had said that day in Hyde Park. Which to Larry sounded great in principle, not so much in reality.

'Dean's a legend,' Eardley said. A thick-set man, he looked to be of average build to Larry, not the archetypal jogger, but then he wasn't sure what the archetypal jogger was. Around where Larry lived, there they were every day running up and down the street: some with dogs on leashes, even a woman pushing a pram, the baby inside gaining the benefit of bouncing up and down, whether it liked it or not. There was one hardy individual who'd been out there, rain or sun, snow even. The man had lived two doors down from Larry, a friendly enough person in his sixties, always ready for a chat when he wasn't jogging or using the side of his house for stretching exercises. In the end, he had suffered a heart attack; too much exertion was the reason given.

'Legend's not an accolade I would have ascribed to Dean Cousins,' Larry said.

'London Marathon, two fifty-three. That's a great time.'

'What have you run it in?'

'Three times, I've started, not finished one yet. I got close, real close the last time. This is my year, I'm determined to get to the end.'

'And you, Adrian?'

'Three twenty-six, not as good as Dean, but he's determined, never misses a day, and that run once a week from his home. Not sure I could do it.'

Larry thought back to the man two doors down from him, six feet under, imagined the epitaph: *Herein lies a fool. Thought he was fit, but found out the truth – the hard way.*

Cynical, Larry realised, but he had had enough of the get fit brigade, knowing that his wife would be enamoured of them and that she'd be out buying him the shirt and the shorts, the running shoes. He had tried cycling once, didn't mind it, but it was dangerous on the road, an idiot in a red car had caused him to swerve and had put him in a ditch. Jogging was the last thing he needed now.

'Both of you run around Hyde Park?'

'During the week. We both work in an office not far from here. There's a group of us, four most days, sometimes five.'

'The others?'

'Dean thought we'd be the most likely to be able to help you. We've seen a few strangers running around the park, not sure if one of them is your man.'

'Would you recognise him?'

'Difficult,' Roy said. 'We're focussing on the run, and if he's wearing glasses, or has a cap on his head, then it's not likely.'

'You'd recognise a serious athlete, someone super-fit?'

'We see them from time to time, not that we'd ever talk to them. Maybe a nod of the head.'

'Are you two up to having a look at a dead body?'

'If it's important,' Adrian said. 'When?'

'Now. Thirty, thirty-five minutes, no more.'

'Don't hold out too much hope, but we're willing to help if we can,' Eardley said.

Chapter 6

Graham Picket, the pathologist, was a tall, thin man who regarded humour as a wasted commodity, civility as a marginal necessity. He did not appreciate the two women coming through the door and into his inner sanctum.

'Don't worry about the pathologist,' Wendy said as the man came towards her and Christine Mason.

'You're DCI was on the phone. Told me I've got to let you see the body,' Picket said.

'I'm sure that DCI Cook would have followed procedure.'

'We're busy here.'

'Mr Picket, may I introduce Mrs Mason. We believe that she knew the deceased.' Wendy said.

'Very well,' Picket said, ignoring Christine Mason. 'And now I've got DI Hill coming here with two more. I hope you won't be long. I'll get someone to take you in. Sign the book on the way in, on the way out.'

'We will.'

'Unpleasant man,' Christine said when Picket was out of hearing range.

'Too much time in here. It gets to them all in the end. Too depressing seeing dead bodies, then cutting them up.'

'Do they?'

'How do you think they conduct an autopsy?'

'I've never thought about it. A check of the body, take DNA, check the teeth, a sample of blood.'

'Check out YouTube if you've got the stomach for it. They do what you've said plus more. The organs are removed, so is the brain. Then they stitch the body up, make it presentable for the family.'

'Colin?'

'Sorry. A bit too close to home for you, I suppose.'

'Let's get this over with.'

'If it becomes too much, exit the area as soon as you can. They don't like the place dirty.'

'Do many? I mean…'

'I know what you mean and yes. Some people look stunned as if they were a dead fish, some will break down in tears, others will bring up their lunch. You're the teary type.'

'You can tell?'

'Yes. If you're holding back on me, I'll know after this. Everyone feels guilt, wants to talk. The easiest way to loosen tongues, not the most pleasant.'

'I'm not holding back the truth. We had something special. You'd not understand.'

Wendy said no more, realising that the woman had it bad. The first flush of ageing when she was no longer the young woman with her choice of men, no longer as firm in the body as she had once been, no longer able to turn a man's head with a swish of her hair, a wiggle of her hips.

Wendy had passed that stage in her twenties, by then married with two sons, a career in the police force. She had been content, even when the sons had gone through the rebellious stage, coming home drunk, attempting to sneak in a random female, their first tattoos. And her husband had always been there for her, attentive, decent, never looked at another woman, apart from the Christmas party at the council offices where he had worked. She had seen him there, the mistletoe, one too many glasses of wine. The next day, sober, he remembered nothing, never fully understanding why Wendy hadn't spoken to him for a week, hadn't shared his bed for two.

And now, she was standing beside a woman, more attractive than she had been, although Christine Mason was only eight years younger than her. Yet Christine Mason, the accounts manager at the Fitzroy Hotel, was not a happy woman. Further checks on her husband, the erstwhile Tony, had revealed that the man was taciturn, well respected for his negotiating skills, his ability to successfully bring back a contract for his company's products from countries that did not fare well for their human rights records. A contact, name not given, had updated Richard Goddard about the man. Isaac was sure that it was Lord Shaw, the previous commissioner of the London Metropolitan Police, who had passed on the information after consulting with senior people in the Foreign and Commonwealth Office.

Lord Shaw had mentored Richard Goddard from the first year of his career, and now Isaac was being mentored by Goddard.

Christine Mason said nothing, only looked around her at the clinical and cold surroundings. Wendy could tell she was regretting her request to see the body, but she had come so far, she was going to continue. Wendy was determined on that. The woman still needed to open up to her, to lay bare her innermost thoughts, her fragility, her need for a younger man, the reason why she thought that Colin Young was interested in her for herself, and not using her for his perverted pleasure.

A young woman came through the swing door at the end of a long corridor and walked up to the two women. She was wearing a surgical gown. 'You're here to see Colin Young?' she said.

'Sergeant Wendy Gladstone, Christine Mason,' Wendy said.

'We've prepared him for viewing. Are you up to this, Mrs Mason?'

A pause before replying. 'Yes, I think so.'

The badge pinned to the young woman's gown said Siobhan O'Riley, although her accent was not Irish, but London cockney.

Inside, the viewing room was bare apart from the table where the body lay, a sheet covering it.

'I'll uncover the face,' Siobhan O'Riley said. Slowly she drew the sheet back, revealing the face of the dead man.

'Oh my God,' Christine said, her legs going weak. Wendy put her arm around the woman to steady her.

'Do you want a chair?' the young pathologist asked.

'No. It came as a shock,' Christine said. 'He was always so tanned, so fit, so alive.'

'But now he's pale, is that it?'

'Yes.'

'Yours is a normal reaction. You've handled it well.'

'Can I see more?'

'Only the face, I'm afraid. Standard procedure.'

Wendy knew that if the sheet had been pulled further back, it would have revealed the mutilated body where it had been sliced open. Even so, the man lying there seemed peaceful, inert, and Christine Mason had not vomited or shed a tear. The woman was transfixed, focussing on the face, not wanting to go, not wanting to stay.

In the end, Wendy took hold of her arm and led her out of the room. 'A good cup of tea is what you need,' she said.

The English answer to everything, Wendy thought. A cup of tea. Her mother had sworn by the remedy.

***

Thankfully, Larry Hill didn't have to deal with the acerbic Picket on arrival at the viewing room. As Wendy was leaving, Larry was coming in – a cursory acknowledgement of each other.

Larry could see that Wendy had the bit between her teeth and that the woman she was with – it could only be Christine Mason – was in tears. And besides, he had his own problems. Roy Eardley was holding up, although Adrian Clark was looking green around the gills. Larry could see him throwing up.

'Busy today,' Siobhan O'Riley said when she introduced herself to the three of them.

'Mr Eardley and Mr Clark may be able to help to put the pieces together,' Larry said. 'Anything else you can tell us about the body?'

'You'd need Mr Picket for that.'

'Good or bad mood?'

'The usual,' Siobhan said with a grimace.

'Bad, then.'

'Your friend, is he going to be alright?' Siobhan asked, looking over in the direction of Adrian Clark.

'I'll be fine,' Clark said. 'It's like a hospital in here, and I've never liked them.'

'You'll not be the first,' the young woman said as she gave him a bag to hold. 'It'll be me cleaning up afterwards.'

A mouthed 'thank you' from Adrian Clark.

'A hot drink may steady him,' Larry said to Siobhan.

'Unfortunately, it won't. Get him out as soon as you can, then a walk around the block.'

She handed Clark a mint. 'Suck on this, it'll help.'

The four moved through to the viewing room, the sheet pulled back. Clark moved back, managing to get his bag in place in time.

'It would have been a hot drink as well,' the young woman said.

'I've made a fool of myself,' Clark said after he rejoined the group. The bag was left on the floor behind them. A faint odour from it pervaded the air. Nobody in the room looked well, not even Siobhan.

'You never get used to it totally,' she said.

'It's causing me some problems,' Larry said. 'Too much misery, too many unpleasant sights.'

'We get counselling if it becomes too much of an issue. Have you considered it?'

'Not yet. We're meant to be strong, to rise above it, to be professional.'

'We're still human. Even Mr Picket gets upset sometimes, especially if it's a child killed by the parent.'

'Give me the name of the person you use. I'll consider following your advice.'

'Don't consider, do.'

Larry could see that the woman could hold her own with Graham Picket, though he couldn't. He was pleased that the man had not shown his face.

Roy Eardley looked at the face of Colin Young, studied it for a while. 'I can't recognise him. As we said, glasses and a cap, and the man's unrecognisable.'

Adrian Clark swallowed, taking down the taste of his vomit. He approached the body and looked at the face. He said nothing for twenty seconds, before taking two steps back. He then rushed to the toilet, grabbing the bag from the floor.

'Thanks,' Larry said. 'I believe that we've taken enough of your time.'

'My pleasure, do come again,' Siobhan said. 'And remember, talk to the counsellor. No point allowing it to get to you.'

'I'll take your advice, but for now, I'd better look after Mr Clark.'

Outside the building, a cold nip in the air. The three men walked along for ten to fifteen minutes, the colour in Clark's face returning. 'I could do with a drink and something to eat now,' he eventually said.

'We need to talk,' Larry said. 'Are you sure you didn't recognise him?'

'Not him, but her.'

'Whom?'

'One of the two women coming out as we were going in. The blonde-haired one.'

'The other one was Sergeant Wendy Gladstone.'

'I've never seen her, but I've seen the other one.'

'When, where?' Larry said excitedly.

'Some food first, and I'll tell you.'

'You didn't mention it at the time.'

'At the time, I wasn't speaking. I was trying to keep my breakfast down, waste of time that was.'

McDonald's was not a favourite of the serious jogger, but it was what Adrian Clark wanted and needed. He ordered a Big Mac, as did Roy Eardley.

'I was feeling queasy in there, as well,' Eardley said.

Larry assumed that even the athletic needed a break from routine once in a while. Protein bars and fruit juices had to become boring in time, as he, Larry Hill, knew only too well. His wife, always thinking of his well-being, had fed him enough strange diets, most of them faddish, over the last few years. He was a man who worked hard. A man who needed chips with his steak, a pint of beer with his pub lunch.

'Make that three Big Macs,' Larry shouted to the person behind the counter. Tomorrow, he'd worry about his weight.

Adrian Clark gulped the Big Mac down, almost stuffing the chips into his mouth. He then took hold of his milkshake, chocolate-flavoured, and sucked on the straw. He looked over at Larry.

'Four days ago, in Hyde Park.'

'Where?'

'Where you fished the man out. She was standing around the back of the Peter Pan statue.'

'Are you sure it was her?'

'I was on my own, and it was raining. Not heavy but enough to be annoying.'

'Describe the scene, take your time. I'll record you on my iPhone.'

'It was just after five in the morning. I came into the city early, attempting to catch up on some work that was overdue, have a run around the park. I'm coming up past the statue, minding my own business. I was making good time, the best for the last few weeks, and there she is.'

'The blonde?'

'Yes, her. There's rain coming at me from the rear, and it's cold, but I've been running for some time, so I didn't notice it. And then, out from behind the statue, the woman. She's agitated, ducking behind the statue, coming out again, looking up and down. She's nervous, I can tell that, and it's raining, and she's wet. All she's wearing is a white blouse and a skirt, knee-length.'

'Shoes?'

'High heels, so she's not a walker.'

'You saw a lot for someone who was running past, making good time.'

'The lace came loose on one of my shoes. I wouldn't have stopped, not for her. I'm about twenty yards up the path, heading towards Lancaster Gate.'

'Okay, you've seen her, and you've stopped. Then what?'

'My time was shot, so I stood there catching my breath. I'd overdone it, I knew that, but I had been determined, and then my shoe. I watched her for a few minutes, and then I carried on. Nothing more after that.'

'Any idea as to why she was there?'

'No. I didn't think much about it after that. There was a meeting in the office at ten, and I wasn't prepared, not as well as I had to be. I hurried back to the office, a quick shower, and then I focussed on a report. The oxygen in the brain helped, and I completed the report earlier than expected.'

'Did you see the woman again, or before that day?'

'Never.'

'How about you, Roy?'

'Not me. To me, she was a stranger.'

'Does it help?' Adrian Clark asked.

'It brings in another element to the investigation,' Larry said. 'But why didn't you tell us before?'

'We only met this morning, and I'd pushed it to one side in my mind. Running early or even late, especially in summer, you see some sights. Couples copulating, people arguing, dogs defecating, the owners looking the other way, not bothering to pick up the mess. I even saw a couple strip off their clothes and jump in the Serpentine for a swim, and it wasn't summer. Probably high on drugs, but I said nothing.'

'Thanks for your help. Adrian, I'll need you down at the station to make a formal statement. You as well, Roy. Midday suit you both?'

'We'll be there,' Roy said. Adrian Clark nodded his head.

The two men walked out of McDonald's. Larry ordered another Big Mac. He phoned Wendy.

Chapter 7

A gushing of emotions, the need to talk: that was what Wendy had expected from Christine Mason after seeing and confirming that the dead man was indeed her former lover.

Wendy was not disappointed in the woman as they sat in a café not far from the pathologist's. Outside, on the street, people hurried by, some going to work, others just out for a stroll or for window shopping, the chance to spend their money.

'Seeing him there, it wasn't what I expected,' Christine said. She had removed her jacket; the café was warm.

The tea had arrived in a teapot, along with two cups, a jug of milk, a bowl of sugar cubes. Wendy called the waitress back, complained about the tea being tepid. The woman had pulled a face but had taken the teapot, returning in a couple of minutes with another.

'In your own time,' Wendy said.

'So pale, so cold, so…'

'Dead is the word. The man was murdered, we're sure of that, but why? You're holding back. Is it a fear of your husband? A fear of something else?'

'I never really knew who he was. It was just… I know it sounds silly, but he made me feel special.'

'And you still think he cared?'

'I wanted to believe him, but he was so attractive. The sort of man that could have had any woman, but he chose me.'

'Christine, you're not a stupid woman, not uneducated. Why do you continue to talk as if you're a teenager? This is not reality television. This is real life where attractive men take advantage of vulnerable women, people overdose on drugs, murder people in Hyde Park. Colin Young, whoever he was, was up to something, or he had upset someone.'

'I wouldn't know.'

Christine Mason didn't look to be naive and silly, yet she was. She had fallen for the dead man, even though he was younger than her, probably only a few years older than her own children, yet somehow she saw it as all possible, that the man was sincere, that he cared, that he came to London every few weeks to see her first, to conduct business second.

'And when he wasn't in the hotel?'

'We kept in contact.'

'How?'

'By phone. He would phone me every few days.'

'No mobile number?'

'He changed it every two weeks.'

'Why? You've not told us this before. What reason did he give?'

'He said that he preferred secrecy, and if you kept a phone for long enough, you'd be plagued with nuisance calls.'

'And you believed him? You're an accounts manager for a five-star hotel. They don't employ dummies, or do they? Are you pretending to be competent, making a damn good show of it, fiddling the books? How much more than the two thousand pounds that you've mentioned?'

'Please, it's too much.'

'It's here or down at Challis Street. We know that Young was not on the straight and narrow. People do not change their phones every few weeks, nor do they keep it a secret where they live, not from those they care for, not unless there's a wife, or a business partner, or a criminal organisation after them. You know something, and you're not telling. What is it? Your husband will have to be told if we hold you for twenty-four hours, forty-eight possibly, pending enquiries. You're the most likely culprit at this time, and we're desperate for an arrest. You'll do for now.'

Wendy looked over at the waitress, could see that she was talking to another employee. All in all, the café had been a disappointment. The tea had not been that hot the second time around, and the sandwiches, cut into triangles, that the women had eaten but not enjoyed had been neither delicious nor fresh; too few in quantity, as well.

'Next time, I'll call the inspectors in to check your kitchen,' Wendy said as she paid the bill.

'Who do you think you are?' the waitress said, leaning down to whisper in Wendy's ear, ensuring the other patrons didn't hear.'

Wendy flipped open her warrant card. 'Police, you want to make something out of it?'

'No tip, then?'

'Not a chance.'

***

Christine Mason sat on a chair at Challis Street. She hadn't been charged with a crime, and Wendy still wanted to believe her story. If it hadn't been for Larry's phone call as she had driven the woman back to the Fitzroy Hotel, their accounts manager would have been back in

64

her office balancing the books, checking the money that had come in that day, the money going out, the staff salaries, the expenses.

'I'm sorry about this,' Isaac said, as he sat down beside the woman. Wendy could have sworn that Christine Mason, nervous and confused as she was, visibly relaxed as Isaac spoke to her.

'DCI, Mrs Mason has some explaining to do. I don't think that we should regard her as an innocent bystander at this time,' Wendy said.

'Sergeant Gladstone's right. We've received further information. We should be in the interview room. Do you have legal representation?'

'I don't want my husband to find out,' Christine Mason said.

'It's gone beyond that but we have no intention of contacting him, not just yet. It depends on what you tell us.'

Wendy took hold of the woman's arm and led her to the interview room. She sat her on one side of the table, and she and Isaac sat on the other. Isaac informed Christine Mason of her rights, the procedure that would be followed.

Larry listened from another room. He should have been in the interview room, as it had been him who had received the revelation from Adrian Clark. He had passed up the opportunity, as both Eardley and Clark were in the station. They were writing their statements, and once finished, Larry would speak to them once more, see if there was any other snippet of information that Clark could remember. If there was, it would be passed onto his two colleagues.

'Mrs Mason, you made a statement to Sergeant Gladstone,' Isaac said.

'Call me Christine.'

'Very well. Christine, you made a statement, admitted to a relationship with Colin Young.'

'Yes, that's correct.'

'There are anomalies in your statement. Facts you've not revealed, inconsistencies you've not explained.'

'I've been honest, believe me. I had an adulterous relationship with a younger man. Isn't that enough? I should be ashamed, and maybe I am sometimes, but it was good, he was good, and now he's lying dead on a metal table. What did he do to deserve that, you tell me?'

'That is why we are here,' Isaac said. 'With a full statement from you, we will find out who he was, where he was from, who killed him. Was it you?'

'Never. I loved him.'

'As you have said before.'

'He told me he only cared for me.'

'But did you trust him?'

'Yes.'

'Was he married, single?'

'He told me he had never met the right woman.'

'Do you have a lot of money?'

'My husband has.'

'Could you get access to it?'

'I don't understand why you are asking these questions. I've done nothing wrong, I only fell in love with a good man.'

'DCI Cook's trying to help you, Christine. It pains me to see you subjected to this,' Wendy said. 'You were seen in Hyde Park.'

Christine Mason's face turned ashen, the blood draining away. 'It's a lie. I've never been there.' Her voice weakened.

'We have a witness. Four days ago. Not the day Colin Young died, but you were there. You were at the exact spot where he was murdered. Now, what do you have to say? The truth this time, not some half-baked story that it was eternal love, and it transcended the age difference,' Isaac said. 'You, Christine Mason, are either a naive woman or a predator, fixated on younger men, men who can satisfy you whereas your husband can't.'

'You can't talk to me like that.'

'We can and we will. You had the motive, and you had the place, even the strength, to kill him. Now, once again, did you kill him? Are you going to tell us the truth?'

'I need a lawyer.'

'We'll halt the interview. Do you have someone we can call?' Isaac said.

'My sister. She'll come for me.'

'Please phone her. Sergeant Gladstone will arrange transport for her, allow her time to talk to you. For your sake, I hope she's competent.'

'I'd trust her with my life. She can't be here until tomorrow.'

'Why?'

'She's busy.'

'If that's the case, you'll be spending the night here. Is that what you want?'

'No.'

***

Wendy would have said that Isaac had been badgering Christine Mason. Not strictly by the book, but she had seen him use the tactic before. A woman in love was a formidable force to break and broken she had to be. Her being in Hyde Park at the place where the man had died

67

was damning. In the hands of a skilled prosecution lawyer, and if it was found that the dead man had been playing the field and Christine Mason had known, the circumstantial evidence could be enough to sway a jury. If the woman didn't clear up the doubts at Challis Street, it would go against her. And what if she had confronted the man that day that Adrian Clark had seen her? If she had, then why was he still running that same path?

'Sorry about that,' Isaac said. 'I had to do it, you know that.'

'Not that she'd agree, but yes, it had to be done. I've been trying to get her to be honest. I don't believe she did it, though.'

'A woman's intuition or police evidence?'

'Both, I suppose.'

'Her husband, where is he?'

'He's still in the country. Is it time to call him?'

'Not yet.'

Larry sat with Roy Eardley and Adrian Clark. Clark was looking better, and he gladly accepted a coffee from the machine that dispensed something with a taste resembling treacle. At least, that was how Bridget described it. She had an espresso machine in Homicide, but the three men were sitting in a room on the ground floor.

'Anything else before you sign your statement, Roy?'

'Nothing from me.'

'Adrian? Did you see her more than the once?'

'Not that I can remember. Strange, her being there.'

'She's in the station, upstairs. We need her to open up.'

'A woman scorned, and all that?'

'What makes you say that?'

'It stands to reason. A man's murdered, the woman had been looking for him. She did it, I'm sure.'

'Speculation,' Larry said. 'No proof, no evidence, that's the problem.'

'If she saw me, she might remember me.'

'Why? Any reason?'

'None that I can think of. I looked over at her as I ran past, nodded my head. I certainly had no intention of stopping for her, not with the time I was making.'

'Would you have at another time?'

'Damsel in distress. I like to think I would, but no. Just talking out loud. You seem to want more from us, but we can't help.'

'It would help if we could be sure that she saw Young in the park.'

'Did she kill him?' Eardley asked.

'We're not even sure that's his correct name. We call him Colin Young because that's what the woman called him, and what he signed in at the Fitzroy as.'

Eardley and Clark left the station soon after. Larry had exhausted what he was going to get from them. He took the lift to the third floor and sat down at his desk.

'Long face,' Isaac said as he sat down beside him.

'Who is this man?'

'The credit card? Any leads?'

'He used it at the Fitzroy each time he stayed there, nowhere else. It's the same with the phone calls he made. The man was either an inveterate womaniser or a villain of the first order.'

'It's too contrived, too much skulduggery. The hotels, how's the checking going?'

'That's Wendy's responsibility. You'd better ask her. I went with the jogger angle, trying to find out where the man could have run from. He entered from Bayswater Road, I'm certain of that.'

'Why?'

'If he entered on the south side of the park, he would have chosen another route around the park, and Christine Mason was there and waiting for him near the statue. Has she opened up?'

'We're getting her legal representation. She's going to need it.'

***

The two-hour delay before the interview extended to four. Christine Mason's lawyer, her sister, had been in court – a messy divorce. The team at Challis Street knew that they would have to agree to the delay.

On the dot, four hours as stated, the sister walked into the station. 'Homicide, DCI Cook,' she said at the desk on the ground floor. Wendy went down to meet her, escorting her up to where her client sat.

Gwen Hislop was an efficient woman, Wendy could tell. She had entered the station dressed in a blue suit with a white open-necked blouse. She was older than her sister, and no ring on her finger. If Wendy didn't know otherwise, she would have said she was not the sort of woman who wanted a man, not like her sister. Not that it reflected badly on the lawyer, and her manner and the way she carried herself, proud and haughty, indicated somebody who'd be a formidable adversary in a court of law. Or maybe she was a woman in a man's world, pushing that little bit extra, to not let the men's club ride over her, male chauvinism still in existence. Regardless, she was Christine Mason's lawyer, and she was entitled to however long she needed with her client.

70

Inside the room where the two women sat, a hush, neither wanting to speak. Eventually, Christine broke the silence. 'How are you?'

'And now you ask? How long has it been? Four, five years?'

'Longer. You look well.'

'I can't say the same for you. What is it this time? I thought you would have learnt your lesson. Is Tony involved in this mess? They gave me a case file on the way in.'

'Tony's beastly to me, won't let me out. I'm no more than a drudge to him, a slave to his every whim.'

'Can you blame him after the last time? Do the police here know about your last escapade?'

'It wasn't in this country, you know that. It's best if they don't find out.'

'And what happened to the man? Dead in the desert, died of thirst. And you in jail for three months before they could get you out.'

'We were in Dubai, you know that. They're strict about those sorts of things.'

'They're not too keen on adultery here, either.'

'I didn't kill him in Dubai, you know that.'

'And now, what are we going to do? Defend the indefensible?'

'You're my sister. I need you to get me out of here.'

A pregnant pause while the two warring sisters considered their respective positions.

'Very well, the full story,' Gwen Hislop said. 'And don't give me any of that poor little me, no drooping eyes, no crocodile tears.'

'I loved him.'

'Stop it! The facts, not the platitudes. Don't throw your guilt trip on me. It was you who walked out of the family house at sixteen, pregnant.'

'I lost the baby.'

'Screwing anyone you could get your hands on, including my boyfriend. What did you expect?'

'But you married him.'

'At nineteen, in a church, white dress. Naive back then, and I believed him when he told me he hadn't been with you. I kicked him out after three years. Did you see him again?'

'Never, but he seduced me. I couldn't help myself.'

'Rubbish. Nobody ever seduced you. No doubt the police think of you as Little Miss Perfect.'

'I was seen in Hyde Park the day before Colin died. I can't deny it forever, but what can I say?'

'If I'm to help, you'd better start giving me the facts. The police will find out eventually, even about your past history.'

'It was hushed up.'

'Nothing's hushed up, you know that. Tony's up to God knows what, his wife's having an adulterous relationship with a man young enough to be her son, another relationship overseas that ended up in the man's death, you in jail. I'll get you out of this mess for now, but I can't guarantee that I can clear you of everything. Now, give me the answer straight. Did you kill Colin Young?'

'No, I swear it.'

'Don't put your hand on a Bible for me. If you do that, then I know you're lying.'

Gwen Hislop pushed her chair back and walked to the door. She knocked on it, a uniform opening it.

'We'll need something to drink, and any chance of some food?'

'Pizza, sandwiches?' the uniform replied.

'A pizza and two cappuccinos, not the type that comes out of a vending machine.'

'We have a standing order with a place next door. Cappuccinos, large or small?'

'Large, and a pizza, Hawaiian will do. Thank you.'

Gwen sat down again, taking her laptop out from her bag. 'Now, the facts, and don't give me the sanitised version. You're a tart, always were.'

Chapter 8

Wendy checked on Constables Taylor and Mortimer. Isaac and Larry would conduct the interview with Christine Mason and her sister when they were ready. The day was coming to a close, and the sky was darkening outside. Not that it concerned the Homicide team, as they were used to very long hours, with a minimum of sleep in between. But Christine Mason had a husband who was known to be difficult, and the woman wasn't leaving until she had answered all the questions.

Mortimer had a reputation at Challis Street for leering, sidling up to the young women in the station; the printer room was ideal, just room enough for two to squeeze past each other. But there they were, Katrina Taylor and Mortimer, working alongside each other, laughing.

'Sorry, Sergeant,' Katrina said as Wendy walked in. 'He told me why his parents named him after Elvis Presley.'

'I've no problem with humour,' Wendy said. 'Any luck?'

'We've reduced the search area. We've excluded south of the park. Knightsbridge and Kensington are no longer part of the search,' Mortimer said.

'Are you sure?'

'As sure as we can be. We went out to a few hotels ourselves that looked promising, pulled in favours from some of the other uniforms.'

'Favours? You've not been here that long in the station.'

'Everyone likes a drink of a night. We've offered to pay.'

'Good initiative, but not finding the man after so long is a worry. Are you sure you've been approaching this the right way?'

'I'm sure we have,' Katrina said. 'Constable Mortimer set up a grid pattern for us, and we've been charting and then checking off the hotels one by one. We thought we had a promising lead in Kensington, but it wasn't our man. Apart from that, nothing.'

'Inspector Hill reckons that the man was in the area of Bayswater, Notting Hill, possibly Paddington. I'm not so sure, too close to the Fitzroy Hotel, the possibility that Christine Mason might have seen him.'

'If you can narrow the search area, it will help,' Mortimer said. 'Katrina's doing a great job.'

'So's Elvis,' Katrina said.

Wendy wasn't sure what to say. The two of them appeared to be very cosy. Maybe she was misreading the signals, but whatever it was, they were working as a capable team, although coming up with nothing.

'We need to find out who this man is. If I have any more, the two of you will be the first to know.'

***

Finally, Christine Mason was ready. Isaac and Larry had taken the opportunity while waiting to pop out for a meal at a Chinese restaurant nearby. Wendy was in the office with Bridget, Larry taking her place, a fresh face to throw Christine Mason off balance.

The two women entered the interview room. Neither looked pleased to be there.

'I hope this won't take long,' Gwen Hislop said.

75

'We've a lot of unanswered questions,' Isaac said.

The four sat down at the table. Isaac dealt with the formalities, noting the time and the names of those present.

'Christine, you said before that you were not in Hyde Park. Do you still hold to that?' Isaac asked.

The woman shifted uneasily in her seat, placing her hand on her sister's arm. She did not speak.

'I'll answer for my client,' Gwen Hislop said. 'She wishes to change her previous statement.'

Larry sat forward on his chair, anxious to hear what was said. The woman's sister, the lawyer, was easier to read: studious, sensibly dressed, obviously intelligent. Christine had the looks, not Gwen, although he wouldn't have described her as unattractive, more a person who did not care whether a hair was out of place, or her lipstick was not applied to perfection.

'Do you wish to make a statement on your client's behalf?' Isaac said.

'Yes. My client is also my sister, as you know.'

'The statement?'

'Very well,' Gwen said through gritted teeth. The chemistry between the two women was not good, both Isaac and Larry could see that. Maybe there was bad blood, a past history.

'In your own time,' Isaac said, the delay in the statement noticeable.

'I don't need instructions on how to conduct my business. Any coercion or attempt at railroading these proceedings will be noted. If you decide to use false evidence, circumstantial or otherwise, against my client, then how you and your inspector conduct this interview will be noted. A judge will take exception to anything other than the correct procedure being followed.'

Sister or no sister, Isaac thought, the woman was skilled, a worthy person to have on her sister's side.

'I need to make a phone call.'

'Your prerogative.'

Isaac paused the interview; Gwen Hislop took out her mobile and dialled. 'Tony, Christine's staying with me for the night. Nothing to worry about. It's just that I've got the flu, and she's acting as a nursemaid.'

'Will he believe that?' Isaac asked. 'How many years since you and Christine have seen each other?'

'What he believes or does not is not your concern, is it?'

'It is if it has a bearing on this investigation. We are led to believe that the relationship between Mrs Mason and her husband is strained, and you two don't seem to be close.'

'It's not relevant.'

A hard woman, Isaac thought, whereas according to Wendy, Christine Mason was a mellow, friendly, easily-led woman. What secrets lurked behind locked doors? Was Gwen Hislop involved? And if so, then how?

The interview resumed, Isaac once again asking Gwen Hislop to read the statement. Once again, a delay.

'I was there. I was in Hyde Park, it's all true,' Christine said. Her sister looked at her in disgust.

'Leave it to me,' Gwen said.

'I loved him, and he was cheating on me. I know he was.'

'How?' Larry asked.

'My sister is emotional. I will answer for her,' Gwen said. 'Please, Christine, let me tell them,' she said, looking at her sister.

'I'm sorry,' Christine replied. Her eyes were moist, and she was shaking.

'As you can see, my sister is a fragile person.'

'The statement,' Isaac reiterated.

'I, Christine Mason, am innocent of the murder of Colin Young. I was in Hyde Park on the day mentioned, and I was there hoping to see him. But he never came. I knew that he ran around the park whenever he was in London, and I knew the route, having walked around it once with him. I was sure that he loved me, and he treated me well. And then I saw him in London, not far from the Fitzroy Hotel. I knew then that if he wasn't with me, he was with someone else. I was frantic, unable to contain myself, and Tony was at home, and I had a job at the hotel. Somehow, I managed to continue, to pretend that nothing troubled me when it did. I did not kill him in Hyde Park, although I was angry and hurt that day that I was seen. I couldn't have killed him, it wasn't possible. He was my sanity, and now he's gone.'

'We'll enter it into the record,' Isaac said. 'Now, Christine, we need to know two things. What was his real name, and where was he staying in London? You must know both of these.'

'My sister does not. She is innocent, and unless you have further evidence, we will wish you goodnight.'

'It's not that easy, Miss Hislop. Your client has consistently lied, altering her story as it suits her. Firstly, she denied any knowledge of the man, and then we find out that he was her adulterous lover. And now, another revelation. What next? That she was in the park, determined to confront him and kill him? We'll accept that when she was seen in the park, she did not see Young and that he was somewhere else. Where he was is critical, but first, we have to understand what we have here. Colin Young would not have been in the park on the day of his murder if he had been confronted by Christine on a previous occasion. A logical assumption, not cast iron, of course.'

'Why not?' Gwen asked.

'Christine had an unhealthy relationship with this man. Maybe, to her, it was sweet and innocent, but she's not a stupid woman. She must have realised there was something untoward about the man she was sleeping with, the credit card that was only used at the hotel, the phone number that kept changing. And how did you know that, Mrs Mason?'

'I didn't. I only knew the number of the last phone that he had. Before his number had been secret, and he only phoned me,' Christine said.

'Then why did he allow you to phone him on the last phone?'

'He said he wanted us to be closer. To form a bond of trust between us.'

'And you believed this?'

'Yes.'

'My sister has a Mills & Boon romantic notion of love,' Gwen said.

'Sugar and candy, innocent love, sweet words under the apple blossom tree? That sort of thing?' Isaac said.

'Exactly. Not the reality of love and lust and heaving bodies, words of love spoken in the heat of passion, rejected afterwards. If Christine says that she believed this man loved her, then she is not lying.'

'A history of such relationships?'

'Not necessarily adulterous, but yes.'

'My sister does not like me,' Christine said.

'It does not affect the situation,' Gwen said. 'You're family. I'll support you whatever.'

'Even if she committed murder?' Larry asked.

'Even then. He's not the first man to break her heart. He won't be the last.'

'You're not the sort to be susceptible.'

'I'm not here being interviewed, my sister is.'

'Christine, let us come back to when you saw him,' Isaac said. 'Where was this?'

'I was walking to Paddington Station.'

'Another SIM card to purchase for a guest?'

'Not this time. I just needed to get out of the hotel, and it's as good a walk as any other. I'm waiting to cross the road, and he drives by in the back of a taxi. He's got a woman with him.'

'Nothing you can do at the time?'

'No.'

'What did you do afterwards?'

'I was confused, not sure what to do. I thought the worst.'

'Any reason to?'

'He was a lovely man. He could have had anyone. Why me?'

Gwen Hislop let out an audible sigh, rolled her eyes.

'Don't look at me like that, Gwen,' Christine said.

Isaac ignored the friction between the two sisters, surprised that Gwen, a lawyer, was allowing personal issues to affect a police interview. Most unprofessional, he thought, realising that the hatred between the two ran deep.

'The taxi? What did it look like? Did you get the number?'

'Black, the same as all the others.'

'Not a minicab?'

'It was black.'

'And the registration number?'

'LD08 CYP.'

'How do you know that?'

'I remember numbers, work with them all day.'

'Photographic memory,' Gwen said. 'We had an aunt who thought she was a freak, scared her so much that she wouldn't visit us. Not that we cared, she was a dragon.'

'Why didn't you tell us this before?'

'I didn't want to remember,' Christine said.

'Time and place?'

'The corner of Praed and Spring Streets. 11.46 a.m. Five days ago.'

'Photographic memory again?'

'I looked on my phone, tried to take a photo.'

'Did you?'

'No, the lights changed, and the taxi took off.'

'No more questions for now,' Isaac said.

Four minutes later, the two sisters left the station. Eight minutes later, the team assembled in Homicide, this time joined by Katrina Taylor and Mortimer. It was close to midnight. No one was going to get much sleep that night.

***

Wendy was seriously annoyed with Christine Mason. 'I gave her enough opportunities to come clean. It wasn't as if we were moralising about her behaviour. As far as I was concerned, she could have been screwing every last member of the Household Cavalry.'

'Ease up,' Isaac said. He could understand her frustration, but anger wasn't going to resolve anything, facts would.

'Easy one, the registration number,' Bridget said. 'I've accessed the Automatic Number Plate Recognition database. Every registration is in there.'

'A win,' Larry said. 'Any luck with the taxi's movements.'

'I can't give you that. The taxi company will keep records, also the driver. It's part of their conditions for the licence.'

'Where are they? Who do we talk to?'

'This time of the night may not be so easy. It's not the same as it used to be, the twenty-four-hour phone number, the dispatcher radioing the location of the pick-up, the name, the destination. Nowadays, it's online, on your phone.'

'Who's going to knock on a door?' Isaac said.

'I'll go with Larry,' Wendy said.

'Constable Taylor, Constable Mortimer, any more to add?'

'The taxis would have GPS tracking, and the taxi company will have fleet management software,' Mortimer said.

'Okay, everyone. Do what you can, and we'll meet back here at six in the morning,' Isaac said. 'Try to get a few hours' sleep if you can. If you can't, then sorry.'

With the two constables out of the room, Isaac looked over at Bridget. 'A handy man to have around,' he said.

'I thought he was on the way out,' Wendy said, 'and now he's friendly with Katrina.'

'You think that something's going on?'

'Takes all sorts. She's pretty, and he's no oil painting. Still, Christine Mason fell for a young man; he for her, supposedly.'

Chapter 9

Isaac arrived home at twenty past two in the morning. It had been some time since Jenny had spoken to him in anything other than a manner that could be described as terse, although she had otherwise been agreeable, had ensured that he had an early breakfast, a meal in the microwave or the oven on his return. She had even discussed the trip to Jamaica, made it clear that she understood, and how important his work was, and that people could walk the streets at night due to his efforts.

Isaac had thought the 'people could walk the streets at night' was the warm up to 'we can't continue like this' speech – he had heard it before. For the last few days he had expected her to make the final decision, but each night she was there, a meal waiting for him, not that he always wanted it, but keeping the peace was more important than the alternative.

'I thought we could have a glass of wine,' Jenny said as Isaac closed the door to the flat. She was wearing a dress; her face was made up. 'It's the only time we can talk, with you being so busy.'

There was no suitcase in the hall, no sad face.

'I can't change you, not that I want to,' Jenny said. She came over and kissed him, flung her arms around his neck. 'I've missed you, you know.'

'The same for me,' Isaac said.

The meal remained untouched, the wine as well. It was the first time since that night when she had given him the cold shoulder that they made love.

***

No one was looking their best for the 6 a.m. meeting. Isaac arrived twenty minutes late, a smile on his face. Wendy wanted to comment but did not. Isaac had been able to get some rest, she and Larry had not, apart from an hour on a chair in the office. Bridget had brought in fresh clothes for her.

Larry was still wearing his clothes from the day before; he was not looking so good. Constables Taylor and Mortimer were still in the office, both alert and cheerful.

The stamina of youth, Wendy thought. She remembered when she had stayed up all night partying as a teen, and then gone out as a constable on the beat, but now she needed eight hours sleep a night to feel her best, and she had only received a fraction of that over the last few days.

'Bright and breezy,' Isaac said as the team came to order. On the table in the conference room, a selection of food from a local bakery, as well as six coffees.

'Everyone's hungry, I suppose,' Bridget said.

Isaac said he was, as did the others, but for him, it wasn't true. In the short time at home, he had made love to Jenny, slept for two hours, and even had breakfast.

So much for my weight, he thought, as he helped himself to some of the food.

'We'll go around the room for your updates,' Isaac said.

'We've got an 8 a.m. appointment with the taxi company,' Wendy said. 'We phoned the manager, woke him up. He wasn't pleased and sounded drunk. His language wasn't the best, full of invective.'

'Not our problem.'

'He sharpened up once I told him who we were and why we were phoning.'

'Good job he did.'

'If he hadn't, we would have knocked on his door, woken him and the neighbours up.'

'You had to threaten him?'

'He was courteous afterwards. Apparently, one of the men in the office is getting married.'

'Stag night, a few too many drinks, a stripper,' Larry said.

'He told you?' Isaac asked.

'Not in so many words. I just added the stripper in for effect.'

'We don't want to hear about your stag night,' Wendy said. 'No doubt you had a stripper.'

'Two, if you must know. Don't tell my wife, will you?'

'I won't if you don't go into any more details.'

'Larry, Wendy, focus,' Isaac said. 'We've got two young and impressionable constables sitting in with us. We don't want them to get the wrong idea.'

'Don't worry about us,' Katrina Taylor said.

'Did you get the data we wanted?'

'According to the manager, their expert was worse than him,' Larry said. 'He promised he'd be in the office when we arrive.'

'Bridget, CCTV cameras in the area?' Isaac asked.

'There's a lot of traffic. I started last night, and although I can see a taxi, almost certainly the one in question, the tracking back to where it came from, where it was going, is not so easy. We agreed that it was best to wait till this morning.'

'We need the driver and the taxi. Where is it, by the way?'

'It's out of service, engine trouble. We'll ask the CSIs to check it out, but it doesn't seem that much will be gained,' Larry said.

'Nothing,' Isaac agreed. 'We'll meet at midday, either here, or phone in. We need to know everything about this taxi trip. See if you can find out who the mysterious woman is.'

'Christine Mason?' Wendy said.

'No more to say to her at present. Did she stay with her sister?'

'We believe so. I'll phone her at the Fitzroy Hotel later today.'

***

Wendy remembered the last time she had visited the principal office of a taxi firm, more years ago than she cared to remember. It had been a smoke-filled environment – everyone smoked back then – the smell of tobacco, a fan attempting to keep the place cool, two dispatchers in radio communication with the taxis, pieces of paper clipped to a board, a line drawn through them as the job was allocated. On the other side of the cramped room, a dozen people operating the phones, taking a customer's details, and then clipping the job to the board, a runner, a young lad no more than seventeen tasked with the job. It had been bedlam, but it had been alive.

'Times have changed since then,' Patrick Gleeson, the owner of the company said. He was a ruddy-faced man, barely up to Wendy's shoulder, although he wore a smile that stretched from ear to ear – it seemed to be a permanent fixture. He had arrived at the premises not long after Larry and Wendy. No black cab for him, but a Mercedes.

'Business good?' Larry asked.

'The minicabs eat into the pie, and then we had those damn Ubers cutting corners, not paying taxes, and the drivers wouldn't even know where Buck Palace was, even if they were standing on the balcony with Her Majesty.'

Wendy and Bridget had been in Spain for a short break earlier in the year, and the Uber from the airport to their hotel had got lost twice, or maybe he was padding the bill. They were never sure which was correct, but regardless, Wendy had complained vigorously to the man who had pretended not to understand English, not even Spanish when the local police had arrived. Wendy had produced her warrant card – she wasn't giving up without a fight. The stern faces of the local police, ready to deal with another belligerent English tourist, changed in an instance. The driver hadn't had a chance, and the police had checked his permit to be in the country, found it to be invalid. In the end, the driver had been hauled off to the police station, and the local police had helped Wendy and Bridget into the hotel with their bags.

'They've been given a temporary licence,' Larry said.

'The Ubers? I know, but it won't last long. They don't have the discipline nor the drivers. With our company, you can be sure of arriving at your destination. You'll want a copy of the data, is that it? Young Douglas over there is the guru, not me. I can barely manage an email, and as for typing, I'm woeful.'

A man she could identify with, Wendy thought. Another one-fingered typist.

The three walked across the scrupulously clean room to where young Douglas sat. 'Young' was subjective as he was in his forties. He was a thin man with red hair down to his shoulders, he stood up and warmly shook the two police officers' hands.

Over in another part of the room, two women sat behind computer screens.

'The blonde is Maisie, the lady with the tattoos, that's Hannah. They run the place,' Gleeson said. 'I wouldn't know how we'd manage without them.'

'Their jobs?' Larry asked. Maisie, he could see, was a woman of advancing years; she wore horn-rimmed glasses, her hair neat and tidy. A pleasant woman, he decided, although they did not go over and talk to her. Hannah was a fright to look at, with tattoos covering both arms, a spiralling design of some description on one side of her neck. She had a ring in her nose and pendulous earrings that drooped down.

'I'll introduce you later. Don't let appearances deceive you. Maisie checks the records, follows up on any payment discrepancies, not that we get many these days, everyone flashes the plastic for payment, very little cash. Hannah, an ace with the payroll, ensures the drivers are paid on time, their insurances are up to date.'

'You were saying?' young Douglas reminded Larry and Wendy.

'We have a time, a date, and a place.'

'Registration number?'

'LD08 CYP.'

'That makes it easy. Time, date, where?'

'The corner of Praed and Spring Streets, Paddington. 11.46 a.m. on the twenty-third of this month.'

'The Pride of Paddington on the corner. They serve a decent beer, a good pub lunch.'

'You know your London,' Wendy said.

'I did "the Knowledge". I drove for a couple of years. After that I found an affinity with technology, and I've been in the office ever since. It suits me fine, although Patrick is still nostalgic for the old days,' Douglas said. 'We get the occasional person trying to check up on a loved one, or they've left a handbag in the taxi.'

'You help?'

'The police if they've got the right accreditation, the general public with lost articles. We're not getting involved in domestics, more than our licence is worth.'

Larry and Wendy along with Douglas looked at the computer screen; the manager had moved over to talk to Maisie and Hannah.

'Here you are,' Douglas said. 'The cab was hailed off the street, the corner of Pembridge Villas and Chepstow Crescent, four blocks from Portobello Road. There are some expensive properties around there, out of my price range.'

'Out of ours,' Larry said.

'How many passengers?' Wendy asked.

'Two.'

'Would the driver know who they were, recognise them?'

'Not unless they were regulars, or they were getting friendly on the back seat.'

'Is that likely?'

'Not at midday. Late night after a few drinks, maybe. Not that the drivers complain as long as it doesn't get out of hand.'

'Let's assume no hanky-panky,' Larry said. 'What else do you have?'

'He dropped them off outside Harrods in Brompton Road, Knightsbridge. That won't help you, will it?'

'Unless they were shopping, used a credit card.'

'The taxi was paid with a card. I've got the details.'

'Can you email it to this address,' Wendy said as she handed over Bridget's details.

'The name on the credit card?' Larry asked.

'Matilda Montgomery.'

'Our man likes to live dangerously. The chances of being seen were too easy. You'd think if he were playing the field, he'd keep his women separated by more than a few miles,' Wendy said.

'It could be innocent,' Larry said.

'Not with Colin Young.'

'Did you get what you wanted?' the manager asked as Larry and Wendy said goodbye.

'Young Douglas is worth more money,' Wendy said.

'He tells me often enough to become irritating. I let him marry my youngest daughter. I reckon that's got to be worth something,' the man said with a smile, looking over at Douglas and the two women in the far corner, all three enjoying the joke.

Chapter 10

Bridget was excited as Larry and Wendy walked back into Homicide. 'I've got it,' she said. Isaac was not in the office; he was upstairs with Chief Superintendent Goddard.

'Got what?' Wendy asked. She knew that her friend was excitable, especially when she had hitherto unknown information, the result of her computer skills.

'An address.'

'Matilda Montgomery's?'

'Yes. The woman exists, and the credit card's valid. I pulled in a few favours, and the bank helped out.'

'Near where the taxi picked them up?'

'55 Pembridge Mews. Parking's difficult there, so you'd better park nearby and walk down.'

'DCI Cook?' Larry asked.

'I've messaged him. He'll be down here soon enough.'

'Have you phoned the woman?'

'I've not got a mobile number for her, and there's no phone registered at the house.'

'Not many are these days,' Larry said.

Wendy grabbed a biscuit out of a packet in the small kitchen area on the way out, Larry did not.

Larry was driving, and there were roadworks on Challis Street which took ten minutes to clear. He turned into Bayswater Road, tempted to push through the traffic, but he did not. It was not an emergency, just a visit to a potential witness, a person who could help them with their enquiries. At Marble Arch, the nineteenth-century white marble-faced triumphal arch, he followed the one-way system around it. Which triumph the structure celebrated, he didn't know, but it wasn't important, not now – getting to Pembridge Mews was.

They travelled down Bayswater Road, passing Buckhill Lodge, the first of the two entrances into Hyde Park that Colin Young could have used, the second being Lancaster Gate. That was passed quickly enough, then Kensington Church Street, the next intersection of interest, the road down to the Churchill Arms.

Two intersections later, Larry turned right into Pembridge Road, taking the right turn after four hundred yards into Pembridge Villas. Two more intersections and Pembridge Mews was on the left. Larry parked close to the entrance, this time placing a sign on the car dashboard that it was parked on police business and exempted from the thirty-minute time restriction.

The mews houses, formerly stables, usually with carriage houses below and living quarters above, had served the large city houses in front of them. But now, two hundred years later, there were no horses, no servants, only very exclusive residential dwellings. Visually, they looked the same as they had in the past; inside, most had been gutted and rebuilt to the highest standards. Wendy thought that Matilda Montgomery's house was the prettiest in the street.

Larry knocked on the door, Wendy standing back to see if there was any movement inside. She then peered through a window, to see that no lights were on. Larry knocked on the door again, this time louder than before.

A woman came out of a door on the other side of the mews. The street was narrow and not suitable for cars, although a motorbike was outside one house, a couple of cycles propped up against another, a strong lock around them. 'Matilda's not been there for a few days,' the woman said. She was neither friendly nor dismissive.

'Sergeant Wendy Gladstone,' Wendy said as she opened her warrant card.

'Matilda? What would the police want with her?'

'Routine enquiries.'

'She lives alone. I hope she's not been in an accident.'

'You know her well?'

'For the last two years. She comes over to my house, I go over to hers.'

'We need to find her,' Larry said, having decided that the door had been knocked on enough.

'She never said anything the last time I saw her. Sometimes, she goes away, but most times she lets me know. Although I've been away myself.'

The woman was elegantly dressed, she was also tall and slender, statuesque, a model perhaps.

'Your name?' Wendy said.

'Amelia Bentham, the Honourable.'

'Your father?'

'Lord Bentham. He doesn't use his title, nor do I mention it normally.'

'You told us.'

'You're the police. Mind you, it comes in handy when I'm booking a good table at a restaurant. A title still opens doors in this city.'

Wendy did not comment that she thought very little of the class structure and those who hung onto it. The whole system should have been abolished a long time ago, around the time that Pembridge Mews had stopped being a place for the horses and the downtrodden servants of those in the big houses.

'We need to check her house,' Wendy said.

'I've got a key.'

'If you walk around with us, otherwise we'll need a court order.'

Larry phoned Isaac, now back in Homicide and keen to find out about Matilda Montgomery, Bridget having detailed what had been messaged to him in a précised form on his mobile.

'Make sure Amelia Bentham is with you at all times. I don't want any comeback on this.'

'There won't be. I'll stay outside, just let the two women go in. Supposedly, Matilda Montgomery and Amelia Bentham have an agreement to look after each other's properties, feed the cat, the fish, whatever.'

'Is there a cat?'

'I'm speaking figuratively. So far, we don't know much about Miss Montgomery.'

'Miss?'

'According to Amelia Bentham. Her brother comes to stay occasionally.'

'Is it him?'

'It's probable. We've not shown a photo to the young woman yet.'

'Her age?'

'Amelia Bentham's in her twenties. She speaks posh, which should upset Wendy, but the two women are getting on like a house on fire.'

'Matilda Montgomery's age?'

'Miss Bentham, how old is Miss Montgomery?' Larry shouted over to the two women. Up the street, a couple of curtains moved, and an old man, bent over and with a walking stick, listened, adjusting the volume on his hearing aid. A dog barked from inside a house further down.

'Damn nuisance,' Amelia said. 'A neurotic Chihuahua, but then, aren't they all?'

'Matilda Montgomery's age?' Larry repeated the question.

'Twenty-nine last week. We went to the local Starbucks, shared a cake to celebrate.'

'Not to the pub?'

'Neither of us drink, not much anyway. Her brother likes to occasionally, but he's not been around for a while.'

'How long since he's been here?'

'I'm not sure. I saw him three weeks ago, and I've been away for ten days. I returned three days ago.'

'Photo shoot?' Wendy said, hazarding a guess.

'Yes, a photo shoot. I'm a model. You've not been buying any magazines lately?'

'That's why you're familiar.'

'Six weeks ago, although it's only just been published. This time it was next winter's fashion range for one of the top labels. Norway, and it was cold. I can show you the proofs if you're interested.'

'You got all that?' Larry said to Isaac.

'Check the house, and then show a photo to Matilda's friend. It looks as though we're on to something,' Isaac said.

***

Larry walked back to his vehicle. A parking enforcement officer – the term traffic warden no longer favoured – was looking at it suspiciously. The man's attitude changed after Larry showed his warrant card.

'You can never be too sure,' the officer, a man in his forties, said. Judging by his accent, he was from

Africa. Probably only in the country for a year or two, he had drawn the short straw in the job market. There wasn't any profession that people disliked more than a traffic warden.

'It's a police vehicle, the sign in the car's clear enough.'

'Sometimes they forge the signs. I picked up an obvious forgery with a disabled driver. I was giving the vehicle a ticket. The driver, fifty yards away, stood up from where he had been slouching and made a dash for me, Olympic pace.'

'Tough job.'

'So's yours. Can you make sure that you move the vehicle before 3 p.m.? We'd have to move it then, police or no police.'

'I'll remember. If not, I'm in the mews.'

'I knock off in a couple of hours, so it won't be me. I've made enough for the council.'

'Not to deter the wrongdoers?'

'What do you think? It's for generating revenue, not that they pay me much. Back in Nigeria, I was a schoolteacher, a lot of respect.'

'Why did you leave?'

'Less money back there. I'm better off doing this, copping the abuse, and taking night classes to upgrade my qualifications for England.'

'Best of luck,' Larry said as he took three pairs of overshoes and gloves from the boot of the car.

'Here, put these on,' he said to Wendy and Amelia on his return.

Amelia turned the key in the lock of the front door of Matilda Montgomery's mews house. Inside, Larry could see that the place was neat and modern. Whoever the woman was, she wasn't poor. Larry stayed outside. The old man from further up the mews came over.

'A good-looking woman,' he said.

'You know her?'

'We speak from time to time. Very polite. If I'd been younger, she would have been my sort.'

'You're not that old.'

'Eighty-three next month. My days of chasing pretty girls are over.'

'For me, too,' Larry said.

***

Inside the two-storey house, Wendy led the way, giving explicit instructions to Amelia to keep her hands in her pockets as much as possible, and not to deviate from the route she took through the house. It was clear that the house had been extensively renovated.

'Was Matilda here when the renovations were done?' Wendy said.

'Some of the time. These buildings are old, they need constant work. She has good taste.'

The ground floor was open plan, and the kitchen, a skylight above it to let in natural light, could be seen from the front door. Where the garage door was at the front on the left, there was no room for a car, but there was a bedroom with an en suite instead. There was nothing out of place, and the cleanliness did the woman credit.

Upstairs, two more bedrooms and a roof terrace. Wendy checked the first bedroom, neat and tidy, everything in its place, a picture of a sea view on the wall, a flat-screen television secured by brackets. In the wardrobe, the woman's clothes, some with plastic covers over them, the rest neatly pressed.

A scream came from the other room. Wendy, looking around, realised that Amelia Bentham, though under strict instructions not to wander off, had done so.

'Oh my God,' Amelia said as she staggered back, Wendy grabbing hold of her. She moved the woman to one side, a chair conveniently to hand for her to sit on.

Wendy rang Larry. 'It's a crime scene. Let DCI Cook know.'

'I heard the scream. Is it...?'

'She's hanging from a beam.'

Wendy turned around, found Amelia blankly staring into space. She was muttering to herself.

'Amelia saw the body. I'm leaving here and going over to her house.'

'I'll be up to have a look,' Larry said.

'No point, not unless you're fully kitted up. I'll backtrack with Amelia, try to keep the traces of our presence minimal.'

'Suicide?'

'There's no sign of a struggle.'

Chapter 11

'It's not going to become a habit, is it? Two bodies in a week?' Gordon Windsor, the senior crime scene investigator, said. It wasn't the first murder investigation that he and Isaac had worked together, and the flippancy reflected the two men's respect for each other.

Isaac looked up at the dead woman, considered what had driven her to such despair. She'd been dead for twelve to fourteen hours, Windsor had said, even though it wasn't his responsibility to offer an opinion, knowing full well that the DCI would be anxious to follow up on the woman's death.

The two men were both kitted in the standard wear for a crime scene: coveralls, overshoes, nitrile gloves. Larry was out in the street with the uniforms, and Wendy was across the road with the Amelia Bentham. Pembridge Mews, a cul-de-sac, was closed off at the junction of Pembridge Villas; the only traffic allowed through, the crime scene investigators and the local residents. The traffic on the busy thoroughfare on Pembridge Road was heavily delayed as a result of Matilda Montgomery's death. The parking enforcement officer's statement that after 3 p.m. any vehicle, police or otherwise, would be removed no longer held true, at least for the police. Camera crews from two of the television stations had attempted to take advantage, one of them receiving a ticket for their nerve, and then a tow truck, while the other, sensing the situation, had driven down another street, finding a spare parking spot.

'Are you confirming suicide?' Isaac asked as he stood back from the body. No one in the house showed any emotion, although one of the CSIs had said that he liked the house, and how much it would be to buy a place like it, and there was no way he could do it on the measly pittance he received.

Isaac knew the man wasn't insensitive. It was how some dealt with the situation, others succumbing to a few too many drinks of a night, and one or two were known to vomit in the gutter at the end of their shift. Isaac wasn't any of those, inured as he was to death. And hanging there, the body of Matilda Montgomery. He could see, in spite of the pained expression on her face and the cord around her neck, that she had been an attractive woman in life. Yet she had committed suicide. Colin Young was now known to be Barry Montgomery, her brother, proven by a photo of the two in the kitchen, Amelia in the background with a beaming smile.

'You couldn't be wrong about the suicide on this one?' Isaac asked.

'Pathology will check if she had been taking drugs, but I doubt they'll find anything. The woman committed suicide, open and shut case,' Windsor replied.

Isaac didn't like open and shut cases, they invariably had a flaw somewhere, but he trusted Gordon Windsor. The woman, if she had not been seen out and about for several days, must have stayed in the house, and then decided to kill herself. Downstairs, the CSIs were working their way through the rooms, relaying to Windsor and Isaac that nothing was out of order. No one else had been in the house, at least for a week, and food had been taken from the refrigerator, cooked and eaten, the dishes washed up afterwards and neatly put away, handles at the front, labels on the jars of food pointing forward. A clear sign of a possible obsessive-compulsive disorder.

'Did she kill her brother?' Windsor asked. The two men were now downstairs and on the street.

'It's a possibility,' Isaac said. 'Inconsolable grief at what she had done, followed by days on her own, commiserating with herself, and then what we saw upstairs. How long before you remove the body?'

'Later today. A messy hanging, the way the rope was around her neck. She would have suffered for a while.'

'And regretted it?'

'Who knows the state of her mind. Most suicides are either drugged or drunk, sometimes both. Not with her from what we can see. The beam's only eleven feet off the ground, so she climbed up the step ladder, threw the rope around the beam, and the noose around her neck, and then stepped off. It's almost as if she wasn't sure whether to go through with it.'

'The ladder was tipped over,' Isaac said.

'She could have panicked, thrust her foot out in despair, hoping to find the ladder, kicking it over.'

'Not a nice way to go.'

'At least that's solved the murder of Colin Young. Confirmed as the brother?'

'Their parents will be in Challis Street within a couple of hours.'

'Fratricide. You don't see it often.'

'The act of killing a brother. Not a lot; in fact, I can't remember another case. According to Matilda's friend, the dead woman was close to her brother. But he's still an unknown. We may have a name, but his movements are still unclear, and why was he with Christine Mason?'

'He could have been serious about the woman, ashamed to admit that he felt love for her. An Oedipus complex, the Mason woman being the mother substitute. Mind you, they always get it wrong. If you read your Greek mythology, Oedipus didn't lust after his mother. He never knew who she was, and when he found out, he gouged out his own eyes, not wanting to see the wickedness of the world and what he had done.'

***

Isaac knocked on the door of Amelia Bentham's house and went in. In the living room, Wendy sat with Amelia. The situation appeared calm, and there were no tears.

'This is Detective Chief Inspector Cook,' Wendy said.

'Pleased to meet you,' Amelia said, standing up to shake his hand. She was a fine-looking woman, he had to admit, reminded him in some ways of Jess. *Why do I keep thinking of her, when I'm with Jenny?* Isaac thought to himself.

'A coffee?' Amelia asked.

'A juice, if you've got one.'

'Fresh orange. I squeezed it myself this morning.' Amelia got up from the sofa where she had been sitting and went into the kitchen. A minute later she returned with a jug and three glasses. Isaac poured the juice for them all, taking a gulp before speaking.

'Matilda?' Amelia asked.

'I'm sorry to say it, but she committed suicide.'

'How long ago?'

'Not long, twelve to fourteen hours.'

'Gordon Windsor?' Wendy asked, preferring something stronger than orange juice, but not mentioning it to the woman who had a well-stocked drinks cabinet on one side of the room.

'He doesn't believe that alcohol or drugs are involved.'

'Not Matilda. She could be a bit on the puritanical side sometimes. No drugs, weakens the resolve she would say. And alcohol made her come out in hives. At least that was what she said, although I'm not sure she believed it, just used it to avoid accepting drinks from drunken fools at the pub.'

'She visited them?'

'And clubbing. She liked to have a dance, a good laugh, and then be back at a reasonable hour.'

'And you, Miss Bentham?'

'I like to kick on sometimes.'

'Men?'

'There was one man that Matilda went out with a while, but he never stayed the night.'

'Waiting for the right man,' Isaac said.

'She'd have you convinced that she was, but I doubt it. She had a notion of eternal love, no such thing nowadays.'

'These days they want the honeymoon before the wedding.'

'They always did,' Wendy said. 'It was up to the woman to control the situation.'

'Guilty, I'm afraid,' Amelia said. 'I've been known to have the occasional one-night stand. I doubt if Matilda had.'

'Let's come back to the current situation,' Isaac said. He enjoyed talking to the woman, refreshingly open, no doubt a lot of fun. 'Barry, her brother, you knew him?'

'Very well.'

'How well?'

'If you want to know whether I slept with him, then you'd better ask.'

'Miss Bentham, did Barry Montgomery and you have an intimate relationship?'

'Infrequently, but yes. Matilda disapproved, not that she ever mentioned it, and it didn't affect my friendship with her. Matilda was not always at home, and if Barry was there, and I was free, then we'd hook up. A few drinks, an early night. Nothing serious, and not love. He was a philanderer, a man who liked to put it about.'

'A jogger?'

'At 5 a.m. sharp, every day, rain or shine, whether I was in his bed or he was in mine. I'd joke with him that he was wasting his energy on running while I was around.'

'His reaction?'

'He'd just smile, and it never stopped him running.'

'Matilda, any signs of obsessive-compulsive behaviour?'

'The jars in the cupboard, nothing in the fridge past its use-by date?'

'Yes.'

'She was always cleaning, even when I was over there. It wasn't irritating, but she had the symptoms.'

'And Barry Montgomery?'

'The 5 a.m. jogging, rain or shine, when there was meat on the plate?' Amelia gave a smile. 'What do you think?'

'Barry died not long ago. Did you know about that?'

'Not until your sergeant told me. And you think that Matilda did it?'

'Logically that would be the conclusion. The sister, grief-stricken, dwells on the enormity of what she's done, sits in her house, her mind churning over, impossible thoughts, disturbing thoughts, and then in a fit of remorse kills herself.'

'I always thought she was stable, more stable than me. But she was young and without a man, who knows? Maybe she was frustrated, maybe she had an unhealthy relationship with her brother.'

'Incestuous?'

'I've never considered it, but who knows what goes on behind closed doors.'

'Miss Bentham, have you someone to be with you?'

'It's not needed, not now. Wendy's been a dear. My mother is arriving in thirty minutes. I'll go home for a few days.'

'I'll take you to where you can meet her,' Wendy said. 'The uniforms will be restricting access to the street for some time.'

'I'll pack a bag. Just drop me off at Starbucks, up the road.'

'Your address, mobile number, email?' Isaac said.

'I've already got it,' Wendy said. 'Miss Bentham's been an ideal witness.'

***

Matilda Montgomery's body was finally taken down and transported to the mortuary at ten in the evening. The floodlights which had illuminated the house were extinguished at eleven.

The old man who had spoken to Larry earlier in the day, before the woman had been found, had complained that the police were disturbing his sleep with their constant noise. Larry had dealt with the public

relations and ensured him that he was an invaluable help
to the investigation, and the woman that he had expressed
a fondness for, too young for him, he had admitted, had
died a sad and lonely death. It was a time for forbearance
and forgiveness. In the end, the old man had wandered
back to his house. Others in the mews had been
interviewed, their details taken. No one had a bad word to
say about Matilda Montgomery, all saying that she was
quiet, no loud parties, no strange men.

The owners of two houses had made mention
that Amelia Bentham, well-connected with a titled father,
was not as quiet and that she had the occasional man
over. Not that the latter observation came as a surprise, as
the woman had admitted to Isaac and Wendy that she
wasn't a shrinking violet.

In a comfortable room at Challis Street, the
parents of Matilda and Barry Montgomery sat. 'Our
daughter, we'd like to see her,' the father said. He was in
his sixties, his hair greying, signs of baldness on top. An
upright posture and he was tall, even taller than Isaac.

'You've been made aware of the situation?' Isaac
asked.

'We have,' Mr Montgomery said. Wendy looked
for signs of emotion from the man but couldn't see any.

'After we've spoken, gathered a few facts, we'll go
to where your daughter is.'

'Now look here, Inspector Cook. I'm not used to
waiting, and she's our daughter. I demand to see her.'

'Your daughter has died under tragic
circumstances. Surely you don't want us to hurry our
investigation?'

'No, of course not,' the father blustered. 'But I
don't want lamebrained excuses, either.'

'May I ask your profession?' Isaac said.

106

'Senior civil servant, Home Office.'

Short and sweet, Isaac noted. The man had said all he intended to, and he had no intention of revealing more about his life.

The mother of the dead siblings sat demurely. Compared to her husband, she was a small woman.

'Mrs Montgomery, I'm sorry for your loss,' Wendy said.

'I'll speak for us,' her husband said. 'There's a chain of command here, and I'll communicate with DCI Cook, he will communicate with me.'

Wendy was not sure if it was male chauvinism, misogyny, or just pig-ignorance, but decided that it was the latter, as the man, tall as he was, had a roundish face, eyes that were too close to one another, and a flattened nose, almost pig-like. It was a character assassination, she knew it, and if she had said it out loud to the man, she would have been on a disciplinary. Even though he was a grieving father, he was still a pig.

'I believe that a formal interview will be necessary,' Isaac said.

'Not today, it isn't.'

'As you say. Is there anything you can tell us that will help us to understand what drove your daughter to such an act?'

'She's a Montgomery. A Montgomery doesn't indulge in such weakness. Re-examine your evidence. Matilda did not die by her own hand.'

'Our investigation leads us to the conclusion.'

Matilda Montgomery could possibly have been traumatised by an overbearing and bombastic father, Isaac realised – the reason for her need to line up the jars and the food containers one next to the other, as if they were on the parade ground, her father inspecting that all was spick and span, a charge if they weren't, a thrashing, bare backside, for a misdemeanour.

'I believe that we need a comment from Mrs Montgomery,' Isaac said.

'Very well. Janice, say something,' her husband said, giving her a nudge with his hand.

'I'm sorry that Matilda's died, but Stanley's correct. You must have got it wrong. A Montgomery would not do such a thing.'

'What was their childhood like?' Wendy asked.

Montgomery looked over at her as if she was not worthy to lick his boots. 'Boarding school for both of them.'

'At what age?'

'What's this got to do with it?'

'It's important,' Isaac said. 'Sergeant Gladstone is attempting to get a profile of their childhood, find out who may have known them, wished them harm.'

'Matilda was sent to boarding school at the age of seven. She came back for the holidays, and she wanted for nothing.'

Except for a mother's love, a father's guidance, Wendy thought.

'And your son?'

'I don't have a son.'

'But we know that Barry Montgomery was your son.'

'I disowned him years ago.'

'We need to know the reason.'

'Not here, not now. My wife wants to see her daughter, not to indulge in idle speculation.'

'We'll need to know eventually.'

'That's as may be. Are you going to sit here wasting our time, or are you going to show us our daughter?'

'Sergeant Gladstone will drive you over,' Isaac said.

Chapter 12

Christine Mason realised that she had made an error of judgement. 'I knew it was innocent, and that he loved me,' she said.

Wendy had decided that she needed to know the truth about the other woman in the taxi, not out of compassion, but to measure her reaction.

The two women sat in the café at the hotel. 'Free to us,' Christine said. 'Choose what you want.' Wendy did.

'She was his sister, and now she's dead.'

'You didn't tell me that,' the handkerchief coming out again. 'How? Why?'

'That's the question, isn't it?' Wendy picked up one of the sandwiches placed in front of her. Momentarily silenced, she looked over at Christine Mason. The woman was dressed conservatively, more so than on their previous meetings. Wendy wondered if it was the influence of Gwen Hislop.

'When you tried to confront him in Hyde Park, was violence on your mind?' Wendy said.

'I don't think so. I might have slapped him across the face, but that's all. I don't think I could kill anyone. Colin's sister, are you sure?'

'She committed suicide yesterday.'

'And you think she killed her own brother?'

'We don't know what to think. Our investigation is continuing, but here's the conundrum. You saw him with a woman, thought the worst. His sister commits suicide after he is murdered in Hyde Park. And he was using his correct name with his sister, but not with you.'

'Am I still a potential murderer?' Christine said. She looked up, saw the hotel manager staring at her with steely eyes. 'It's my break, and it's not as if I'm a junior, but he gives me the creeps.'

'Why?'

'I don't know. Undresses me with his eyes, not that he's got a chance, not him.'

Wendy stole a glance, could see a man in his forties, well-dressed and very presentable. She liked the look of him, Christine didn't. Wendy made a mental note to check into the manager's background.

'If Colin Young felt affection for you, then why the false name? And why this hotel, when his sister had a house not far from here?'

'As long as he cared for me, that's all that matters. Until you tell me otherwise, I'll continue to believe that he loved me, and the rest of it is unimportant. Maybe he was something to do with the government?'

'A James Bond, is that what you're saying?'

'I'm not sure what I'm saying. He was good-looking, and he certainly knew how to seduce women.'

Wendy saw no point in telling the lovestruck Christine that he had seduced more than one woman, Amelia Bentham being another – better to let the woman have her delusions for the time being.

'Your husband?'

'He's overseas again. I'm certain that he's happiest when he's not with me, not that he'd ever say it.'

'A woman overseas?'

'I don't know, don't care. I had Colin, but he's gone.'

'You intend to find another?'

'None are as attractive as he was.'

'Tell me, Christine, are you levelling with me? If you're not, it will go against you.'

'I've been honest. Why wouldn't I be?'

'Why, indeed? You've been hoodwinking your husband, consistently lying to us as to what you know. I can't trust you, not totally, and if DCI Cook thinks you're holding back, he'll have you charged.'

'Gwen will get me out.'

'What is it with you two?'

'We didn't communicate for many years, not until she came to the police station the other day.'

'Why? And why were you so sure she would come? You placed a lot of faith in her. Illogical if there was any tension between the two of you,' Wendy said.

'I walked out of the family home when I was sixteen; she stayed.'

'Walked or kicked out.'

'It was either me going earlier or my father forcing me to do something I didn't want to.'

'Which was?'

'I was pregnant, a silly girlish belief that the man cared for me and that it was eternal.'

'The sugar and candy view of the world that your sister mentioned. Life's not a Barbara Cartland novel, you do know this?' Wendy said. There was still something about the woman, hidden depths that needed to be plumbed. Christine Mason, enamoured of childish notions of love, was not foolish, and her need to continually look for it indicated psychological issues. The sort of issues that could easily be transposed into extreme violence, the need to lash out, to kill and maim, the need to hit a man over the head and to push him into the cold water of a lake in Hyde Park.

'My life's been difficult,' Christine said. Wendy had little sympathy. She had grown up in Yorkshire, the daughter of a farmer who had barely made enough money, a period of promiscuity in her early teens – a few of the local males had learnt of love and sex courtesy of her.

The records indicated that Gwen's and Christine's upbringing had been middle class, the father, an accountant, the mother, a teacher. Bridget had done some checking and had found out the mother was still alive. The father had died on his fifty-ninth birthday, a massive heart attack, the result of stress. Officers at the local police station close to where the mother still lived knew the family well, and could only offer praise for them.

'Life's what you make of it. The truth, why leave home?' Wendy said.

Christine shifted uneasily on her seat, looked up at the ceiling and around the area. 'It was Gwen's boyfriend. He was the father.'

'Does Gwen know?'

'She knew later on that I had slept with him, not that there was a bed involved.'

'Then where?'

'It was the three of us one night after the pub. We were all underage, but we could make ourselves look older, and no one asked for proof of age, not where we lived. And besides, the publican didn't care as long as we paid cash. Gwen was a drinker back then, teetotal now. Her boyfriend, athletic and full of himself, was a prefect at school, played football for the school as well. Anyway, there's the three of us. We stopped on the way home. Gwen had been drinking beer and vodka, mixing her drinks. She was seriously out of it. I'd kept to the beer.

113

'Gwen passed out in the local park, and it's me with her boyfriend. He looks at me, I look at him, and there we are, going hell for leather.'

'Sexual intercourse?'

'Not the word he used, but yes. Four weeks later, I'm convinced something's amiss. My period's late and I've no one to talk to. I can't tell Gwen because she'll start asking questions, and I could never keep a straight face, never could lie. Don't have me for a poker partner. I'm frantic, don't know what to do. My parents, Roman Catholic and devout, would have had a fit, and no doubt shuffled me off out of sight.'

'They would have been angry, but they wouldn't have kicked you out.'

'I know that, but it was my child, no one else's.'

'They would have arranged an abortion, had the child adopted.'

'I didn't want either. To me, the child belonged to no one else. No one was going to tell me what to do or how to care for my child. I packed a bag and walked out. I left a note for my sister telling her what I was doing and telling her why. I didn't say that the child was her boyfriend's. She married him two years later, not knowing the truth.'

'Did she find out?'

'Three years later, I met her, confessed to her. Even when I was away from home, I used to phone my parents once a week. They were upset at my leaving, and they constantly pleaded for me to come home, but I never did. My father started to send me money, not a lot, but enough to rent a room in a shared house.'

'The child?'

'I miscarried at four months. I wanted to go home, but I couldn't. There would have been lectures, and then I'd be confined to my room, and endless questions. I couldn't face it.'

'And then after three years, you met your sister?'

'Sort of. I hadn't moved far away, and there was always the risk of bumping into one or other of my family. I had seen my mother once from a distance. I had wanted to run over to her and to give her a hug, beg her forgiveness.'

'Why didn't you?'

'I wasn't dressed properly.'

Wendy knew what was coming next. She had heard it before: the fallen female, the drugs, the degradation, the disgrace.

'After I lost the baby, I was at a low. I had no support mechanism, and I had bills to pay, the same as everyone else. My father's money paid for me to subsist. I tried to get a job, but it was only stacking shelves in a supermarket, cleaning offices. I was intelligent, even though I was young and had no qualifications. One of the girls I shared the house with, she had a friend who had a friend who could help me to make some easy money. Naively, I thought it was door-to-door, selling cutlery or some other nonsense. I went to the meeting that had been recommended and found it was for modelling.'

'A euphemism for something else.'

The hotel manager kept watch on the two women. He approached their table. 'Has the payroll been dealt with?' he said to Christine.

Wendy looked up at the man, not an attractive face she decided on reflection. 'Mrs Mason is assisting with our enquiries,' she said, flashing her warrant card.

'I saw…' Christine hesitated, trying to come up with a convincing story.

'What Mrs Mason is trying to say is that she witnessed a traffic accident two weeks ago. A pedestrian was knocked over and subsequently died. She may be asked to give evidence if the driver is charged with manslaughter. Now your payroll, when's it required?'

'Not for another day,' the manager, his nose out of joint, replied.

'Then I suggest that you leave us alone.'

'Christine, when you're finished, could we meet to discuss outstanding work,' the man said to Christine, looking past Wendy.

'Any recriminations, any attempt to badger Mrs Mason, and I'll be back here to discuss that rat dropping under the next table. And while I'm here, the woman sitting near the entrance. Who is she?'

'I've never seen her before.'

'But you know what she is. She's a local whore waiting for one of your guests to take her to his room.'

'That's not illegal.'

'I would agree, but it will reflect badly on you now that I've told you, won't it?'

'Please take your time,' the manager said as he walked away.

'There'll be trouble later on,' Christine said.

'You need to stand up to bullies. The man's a bore. Good at his job?'

'Not really. The place has gone down since he took over, and the staff turnover is above the average.'

'Coming back to where we were. The friend of a friend of a friend, prostitution?'

'Standing in various poses, naked or dressed provocatively, yes.'

'Men with cameras; if you go a little further, there'll be some extra money.'

116

'I didn't want to do it. Not that I had any problem with the money, or even selling myself, but some of the men were fat and ugly, one or two even smelt.'

'When you saw your mother?'

'As I said, I looked the other way.'

'Your sister married the man who made you pregnant. Is that correct?'

'That's what I told you. Why are you repeating what I've already said? And I must go. I do have a lot to do, and my husband's coming back tonight. No idea why I bother. He's not overseas doing business all the time. The people he deals with play the game by different rules.'

'Bribery, corruption, women laid on to sweeten the deal?'

'You know about this sort of thing?'

'Christine, when you've been a police officer as long as I have, you learn a lot. The minor villains arrested for stealing a car, a dodgy respray, the hoodlum mugging someone for a credit card, a handbag, some cash to feed their drug habit, have nothing on the people your husband comes across. He either plays by their rules, or he gets no business. Coming back to your sister's husband. You've become pregnant by him before they were married, and then you lost the child. Does your sister have children?'

'No.'

'Did her husband know about the unborn baby.'

'Not at the time, but when my sister divorced him, the truth came out. Gwen, before she knew about him and me, had a fertility check, a sperm count for him.'

'And?'

'Gwen was fine, but he had a medical condition, low-quality sperm, supposedly. Apparently a genetic or a health problem. I don't know which, but in his teens, seventeen and at his maximum virility, he had managed the one time to impregnate a woman, and she had miscarried.'

'Where is he now, the seducer of sisters?'

'He's around. Two more wives, two more failed attempts at fatherhood.'

'He could be bitter towards you. Sees you as the hussy who cheated him out of a son and heir.'

'It was a daughter, I know that.'

'Regardless, the man's bitter, and over the years it festers in him, eventually bursting out in violence, against you, against anyone that you get close to.'

'I wouldn't know,' Christine said. She was looking at the clock, fretting over work not done, a husband flying in. Wendy wrapped up the interview, thanked the woman and left the hotel.

Chapter 13

Barry and Matilda Montgomery's father identified his daughter, declined to do the same for his son. Not that there was much that anyone could do about it, though the mother had wanted to see her son, according to Siobhan O'Riley, the junior pathologist who had shown Wendy and Christine Mason the man's body before.

But with DNA and dental records, Barry had been identified conclusively.

Next day, in the office at Challis Street, the mood was more upbeat, although Wendy, more emotional than the others, was upset by the attitude of parents who should have cared, but didn't. Amelia Bentham had phoned to let her know that she was with her parents and that she'd stay for a few more days. Christine Mason was busy pandering to her husband, a man she did not love, and the unpleasant manager at the Fitzroy Hotel had not heeded Wendy's warning, and was becoming a nuisance. Wendy knew she'd have to deal with him in due course.

'Larry, what do you have?' Isaac asked. He noticed that his detective inspector had smartened himself up and that he was wearing a new suit. He made no comment, although Wendy and Bridget had. The conversation in his office, Isaac knew, had done the trick. He never felt comfortable giving warnings, preferring the conciliatory approach, the word in the ear, the gentle nudge, but with Larry, he had had to get serious.

'Matilda Montgomery, late of 55 Pembridge Mews. I've checked her out,' Larry said. 'There's a boyfriend from last year, although he said it wasn't serious, and that he had liked her, but she was emotionally barren.'

'What does that mean?' Wendy asked.

'You've been with her parents. I'd say it had something to do with them.'

'Did he explain it better than that?' Bridget asked. 'I've done some checking on her parents. The mother says little, the father is a tiresome and argumentative bore, constantly intruding in the local community where they live, complaining about a barking dog, a noisy car. The sort of person that if the local kids kick a ball over the fence, he'll stick a knife in it before throwing it back.'

'Where did you find that out?'

'One of the neighbours is a police officer. He told me about it. Said he had complained to Montgomery, a heated exchange according to my contact.'

'What did he do about it?'

'He went and bought his son another ball. Montgomery hadn't done anything wrong, not legally.'

'Okay, we know the man's a tyrant, treats his wife abysmally, and he treated his children with the same contempt. Does that explain Matilda committing suicide; her killing her brother?' Isaac asked.

The investigation was moving forward, the pieces were coming together, the key players were all in play, and there was a flight to Jamaica still available, the chance to arrive before his parents' wedding anniversary. It would make a great surprise if he and Jenny could arrive as the cake was being cut.

'It doesn't,' Larry said. 'According to the ex-boyfriend, he had dated Matilda for a couple of months, secretive meetings at an out-of-the-way cinema, a distant pub. He said she could be affectionate but never spoke about her childhood. He was surprised when I told him about her brother.'

'Had he been to her house?'

'Never. She never told him where it was; he'd never bothered to find out. He'd initially accepted her for what she was but in the end he had despaired of her, and he had stopped phoning her; she never rang again. He thought she had found someone else, and he moved on; just too much hard work.'

'He sounds cold,' Wendy said.

'From his point of view, she was not easy to understand, and there was a barrier that neither he nor anyone else could break through,' Larry said.

'Amelia Bentham implied the same. It was only with her brother that Matilda was truly happy. The dancing, the singing, the visits to the pub, were always affectations, a façade.'

'Is there any reason to believe that her relationship with her brother was anything more than that of siblings?' Isaac asked.

'That's a terrible thought,' Bridget said. 'According to Pathology, she hadn't had sexual intercourse for some time.'

'That's possible, but they are looking for penetrative intercourse in the last few days. We know the woman had been on her own for six days before committing suicide, and we're not assuming that she had had sex any time before that. The question remains, did she harbour feelings for her brother that went beyond sibling affection?'

'Did she and her brother have an incestuous relationship, is that what you're asking?' Wendy said.

'It needs to be known. Try Amelia Bentham again. See what she can tell you. Also, Larry, the neighbours, the old man with a walking stick. He likes to talk, no doubt he keeps a watch for what's going on.'

'He fancied her, I know that. An old man's folly, looking at Matilda Montgomery, imagining that he was the young stud again.'

'This is abhorrent,' Bridget said, 'what we're talking about.'

'It's the human condition,' Isaac reminded her. 'We're here to solve a murder investigation. The world's a messy place, full of depravity and iniquity. We need the truth.'

Isaac could see that the meeting was digressing. He suggested a five-minute break. Afterwards, the team reassembled. Isaac had taken the opportunity to get himself a coffee, the two women, tea, and Larry, resorting to type, a cigarette outside the building in the car park. Not that he brought the smell of it back, but the strong mint he was sucking was the giveaway.

'Are we sure about Matilda Montgomery's guilt?' Isaac asked. He sipped his coffee, realised that it wasn't as good as when Jenny made it at their flat.

'No,' Larry said. 'She committed suicide, and the timing for her seclusion aligns with her brother's death, but it's not conclusive.'

'She must have known.'

'That appears likely, but how? Assuming we give her the benefit of the doubt on this, what do we have?'

'Nothing. An older woman who loved him thought he was cheating on her. Hell hath no fury like a woman scorned, to paraphrase William Congreve,' Isaac said.

'Reading the classics again?' Bridget said.

'It's just something I remembered from school,' Isaac said, slightly embarrassed that he had shown his education.

'What do we have?' Wendy said. 'A vengeful woman, a loving sister, a father emotionless at his son's death, only mildly more concerned about his daughter. And then Barry Montgomery is pretending to be Colin Young and staying at the Fitzroy Hotel.'

'Don't forget Amelia Bentham,' Bridget said.

'It's not her,' Wendy said.

'Why?'

'She had been sleeping with him, but she's an easy lay.'

'Have you checked on the skeletons in her cupboard? What if she knew of a relationship between the brother and sister? What if she had experienced abuse as a child – her father, an uncle? Who knows what torments lurk in the mind of the innocent, the promiscuous, the devious?'

'Fanciful,' Isaac said. 'We've had Wendy with conspiracy theory. Now we have intrigue and sexual deviancy. What next?'

'Christine Mason's husband,' Larry said. 'Where does he fit into all this? What do we know about him? Barry Montgomery could have been using the man's wife as a way to find out what her husband was involved in, who he was meeting, that sort of thing.'

'The woman doesn't know. All she knows is that he travels a lot, no doubt he's bribed with money and women, returning the favour as needed.'

'A woman knows more,' Isaac said. He thought back to when he had been with Jess. Jess was a potential murderer, and they had been discreet, not once sleeping together, wanting to, keeping to a restaurant or a pub, a kiss at the end. And then a meeting with another woman, her sharing his bed that night. Jess had known instinctively the next time they had met. There was no exclusivity, only an unspoken agreement between her and Isaac, and he had violated it. Even with forgiveness from her, and apologies from him, it had doomed their relationship, so much so that one day her case was packed, and she had left.

'Very well,' Isaac continued. 'We need to move on. Larry, focus on Matilda and Barry Montgomery, much as it upsets the ladies. Wendy, ask Amelia Bentham to confirm one way or the other, and Christine Mason. Are you convinced she's telling you the whole truth?'

'She could have still killed him.'

'That's what I thought. Push her if you have to. We'll need to bring her husband in at some time if we don't get a breakthrough.'

'If we make an arrest, there'll be a trial, Christine Mason will be called as a witness. He'll know then.'

'Better sooner than later, if that's the case. If he knew of his wife's affair… And the woman's admitted that she used to put it about. She's probably had other affairs, find out about them. And this lost child? Proven or was it born, adopted? How old would it be if it was still alive?'

'Late twenties,' Wendy said.

'Find out from the woman when and where and how? Backstreet abortion or natural causes?'

'She'll clam up if I dig too deep.'

'We've got no time for the niceties, push her.'

'Bridget, Christine's teenage love, Gwen's husband. Find out who he is, where he is.'

***

After a few days, Pembridge Mews returned to normal. It hadn't been the first murder in the cul-de-sac, although the death of a scullery maid one hundred and fourteen years previously did not concern the team, especially Larry who was back at the scene. The old man with the walking stick, identified as Eugene Smith, had been an impresario in middle age, having worked in the theatre district near Shaftesbury Avenue.

'Good times, met them all. Even royalty,' Eugene said. He was sitting in his favourite chair in his house. Larry sat opposite, holding a glass of brandy. The house wasn't renovated, not in the style of Matilda Montgomery's and Amelia Bentham's. It was well-worn, the dividing walls were still in place, the small and dark kitchen at the rear. The main room of the house was warm and homely and smelt of old leather. On two walls, bookshelves, an upright piano hard up against another wall.

'Great taste,' Larry said. His wife was all for modern, but somehow the old-fashioned look appealed to him more. Not that he would ever tell his wife.

'You're asking about Matilda and Amelia, aren't you?' Eugene said.

'We're not sure what to make of Matilda's death.'

'You're convinced it's suicide?'

'We've no reason to doubt that verdict. If someone had been in there, strung her up, there would be evidence, there always is.'

'Always? No such word.'

'It's possible to leave no obvious signs, but you'd need to know what you're doing. And besides, the woman would hardly have voluntarily stood up there on instructions from someone else.'

Larry gladly accepted a top-up to his glass of brandy, Smith leaning forward with the decanter.

'She always seemed so well-balanced, and so did he, not that I saw him often.'

'Amelia Bentham, what about her?'

'Likeable, attractive.'

'She's admitted to a healthy sexual appetite. Did you know about her and Barry Montgomery?'

'Very vocal, Amelia. I could hear her from here.'

'Orgasmic raptures?'

'Not that anyone cared. We're a disparate bunch, mostly theatricals, entertainers, in one way or the other.'

'Any parties at her place?'

'Sometimes. I'd hobble down and have a drink with them. Fifty years ago, I would have been throwing the parties, indulging in the fun.'

'Was there fun?'

'Couples pairing off, that sort of thing? I'm sure there was, not that I saw it. I stayed downstairs, had a couple of drinks, then hobbled back.'

'Any issues with the neighbours?'

'Not that I know of.'

'Matilda, did she go?'

'Never. Not her scene. I don't know much about what she got up to. I assumed she had the occasional man, but if she did, I never saw him. Only Barry Montgomery.'

'He went to Amelia's parties?'

'Not often, but yes. He and Amelia were friendly, I've already said that, but it wasn't serious, just a roll in the hay. Can't blame the young man, an attractive woman.'

'More attractive than Matilda?'

'No way. Matilda had an innocence about her. Quite unique in her way.'

'Yet she had had a troubled childhood. Did you ever see her parents here?'

'Once, her mother. Not that I was introduced.'

'How long ago?'

'Three weeks, more or less. I don't think she was there long. I asked Matilda afterwards about it.'

'What did she say?'

'She shrugged it off, said it hadn't been anything important.'

'Which you interpreted as…?'

'I didn't think any more about it. Not everyone gets on with their parents, and Matilda was an adult. The house was in her name, I know that.'

'A lot of money for a woman her age.'

'Maybe, maybe not. It depends on how she earned it, who she had inherited from.'

Eugene Smith had drunk two large brandies. He was asleep. Larry topped up his glass, gulped it down in one go, and left the house.

***

A wrought-iron gate, firmly closed, prevented Wendy from progressing. To her right, an intercom. She pressed the button, a voice with a Yorkshire accent answering.

'I've come to see Amelia Bentham,' Wendy said.

'Is she expecting you?' the voice said.

'Yes. I'm Sergeant Wendy Gladstone, Homicide, Challis Street, London.'

'Drive to the front of the house and ring the bell. I'll open it for you, show you the way.'

The remotely-controlled gates swung open. Wendy put her car into gear and drove the hundred yards up to the front of a Georgian mansion.

Amelia had said that her parents were titled, but she had never said they were exceptionally wealthy.

The door to the house opened, a man in his fifties, dressed in a blue suit, stood there. 'His Lordship will greet you in the drawing room,' he said.

Wendy had never heard a Yorkshire accent spoken with the haughtiness that the butler imparted. To her, it was odd.

In the drawing room, larger than Wendy's house, she looked around. The room had an aura of old-world wealth, the peasants toiling in the fields, the squire cavalierly dispensing his orders with no concern as to who was inconvenienced or who it hurt. On the wall, a Rembrandt, a Van Gogh, even a Picasso, but it looked out of place.

'The most valuable in the room,' said a voice from behind her. Wendy looked around to see a man well over sixty, closing in on seventy. He was dressed casually.

'I'm Lord Bentham,' the man said, extending his hand to shake Wendy's, a bear-like grip.

'Sergeant Wendy Gladstone.'

'Yes, I know. Amelia said that you looked after her after she had discovered the body. Why was she in the house in the first place?'

'She had a key. If I'd entered without her, I would have needed a search warrant.'

'Surely you would have required one anyway.'

'Debatable. The woman's brother was dead, and we'd just found out about his sister. She had not been seen for a few days. Amelia helped us out.'

'Explanation accepted. Please take a seat, Sergeant.'

'Yes, my lord.'

'Geoffrey's the name. The title comes in handy, and so do the privileges, but apart from that we're simple folk.'

'I doubt that, Geoffrey,' Wendy said. 'Not with all this,' she said, as she looked around the room.

'You don't approve?'

'It's not the way I was brought up.'

'Honesty's the best policy. Amelia has some issues, as well. Picked them up from the school we sent her to. Education for the nobility on the promotional blurb.'

'It wasn't?'

'I could have had them for false advertising. A hotbed of revolution, rich children sponging off their parents, idealising about the inequalities in society.'

'Not that they were willing to divide their share.'

'That's the problem, Sergeant. You and I understand, both worked hard over the years, made a contribution.'

'Have you?'

'I inherited this pile from my father, a waster of the first order: gambler, philanderer, risk taker. Left me with nothing, other than a mansion I couldn't afford to renovate, and his debts. I set up an engineering company with my brother, a garage at the back of a trading estate. Ten years later, a few close shaves, sailing too close to the wind too often, and then we broke through, manufacturing mining equipment. This place was renovated at my expense, and that place in Pembridge Mews, we bought it for Amelia.'

'My father was a farmer, no money, but he worked hard, looked after the family. I started as a constable in Sheffield, saw the inequality between those with plenty, those with nothing.'

'Then, Wendy, if I may be so bold as to use your first name, we understand each other. Now, what is it that you want with my daughter?'

'My time was limited with her on the day, and she was upset. If I could spend a couple of hours with her, then she may be able to help us with our enquiries.'

'A tragedy, Matilda dying like that.'

'You knew her?'

'Every few weeks, my wife and I would make the sixty-mile trip to London, business mainly, some pleasure, take in a show, visit one of the tourist attractions. Amelia and her mother would go to Oxford Street more often than I liked, but I couldn't refuse. Matilda would come out with us sometimes.'

'You seem to be a devoted family man.'

'I am.'

'Matilda's was not.'

'Amelia seemed to know something about it. The woman was a friend to Amelia, and we mourn her passing.'

'Her brother?'

'I met him briefly once. He seemed to be a pleasant man. Amelia liked him.'

'And…?' Wendy waited for an answer. So far, Amelia had not shown her face.

'We are an open family. Amelia has a good heart, and we did not interfere with her life in London. If, as it seems you might be implying, she had a relationship with Barry Montgomery, then I would suggest you ask her.'

'You're not what I expected,' Wendy said.

'You expected me to be clothed in ermine, shouting down at the peasants, is that it?'

'Well, not quite, but I didn't expect such a liberal attitude.'

130

'We trust our daughter and her sound judgement. If she liked the brother, spent time with him, then that's her business. Is it relevant to your murder enquiry?'

'Amelia is the closest person we have to the two of them. Her insights are invaluable.'

Geoffrey Bentham poured two glasses of wine and gave one to Wendy. 'We will wait for her. She's out riding. In the meantime, you and I will sample my wine collection. You do appreciate a drink?'

'Of course. What's with the butler?'

'He's been with us for over thirty years. He's more family than a servant, but he likes the airs and graces.'

'He certainly does,' Wendy said as she sampled the wine, a Shiraz. She was sure there would be a few more before her return to Challis Street.

Chapter 14

Isaac relished the opportunity to get out in the field and away from the office. He and Larry made the trip to the Montgomery family home. It wasn't far, located just north of the city in Hampstead, on the edge of Hampstead Heath.

On their arrival, the door was opened by Stanley Montgomery, the head of the household.

'I've said all I intend to say,' Montgomery said. The door had a security chain on the inside, and the man peered through the small gap that it allowed as the door was opened.

'Mr Montgomery, this is a murder investigation. Either you cooperate, or we'll haul you down to Challis Street, in handcuffs if necessary. Is that what you want? Flashing light, siren, the works. Let the neighbours get a good view,' Isaac said.

'What concern are they of mine, a bunch of low-achieving nonentities?'

'Your attitude is noted. You're either a complete moron, or you're hiding something. It was your son that was murdered, your daughter that committed suicide. Doesn't that mean something to you? Are you a sociopath, devoid of any feeling towards others? How about your wife? What does she have to say? Surely she must be upset?'

'My wife is not of concern. She agrees with me.'

Isaac turned to Larry. 'Phone for a patrol car. We're taking this man in. I'll go with him, you can stay with his wife.'

'You can't do that. I have my rights,' Montgomery said. He released the chain on the door and opened it wide. 'Come in, we can talk here.'

'No, we can't,' Isaac said. 'You are obviously mentally incapacitated and a possible suspect in your son's murder. Challis Street is the only place for you. If you need a lawyer, you'll be given the opportunity to make a phone call.'

'My wife can't stay here on her own. She's too upset.'

'And *now* you care about your wife? I don't remember you showing her any consideration before,' Larry said. 'In fact, the opposite. She wanted to talk before, but you stopped her. What are you hiding? Your daughter, disturbed, struggling with her emotions? And yes, we've spoken to an ex-boyfriend, found out from him about her emotional detachment. Years of abuse in this house, your wife forced to turn a blind eye.'

'How dare you accuse me of such a thing. I loved my daughter.'

'Your son?'

'Once, before…'

'Before what?'

'I've no more to say.'

'How long before the car is here?' Isaac asked Larry. Before Larry had a chance to reply, a siren could be heard. The curtains next door moved, a face appeared in a window across the street.

'Bastards,' Montgomery said as he slammed the door in Isaac's and Larry's faces.

Isaac knocked on the door again. It opened. 'The choice is yours. You either come voluntarily, or I'll have to arrest you as a hostile witness.'

'You'll need a court order.'

'An expert in the law, are you? We'll discuss it at the station.'

'My wife...?'

'She'll be fine. Inspector Hill will stay with her. We'll ask a uniformed officer from the local station to be present.'

'Not him next door?'

'A female officer skilled in counselling, not the man with the child's football that you slashed.'

'But...'

'No buts, just step out here and get into the back of the police car, the one with the siren and the flashing lights.'

'You can't do this.'

'We can, and we are. You, Mr Montgomery, who should be shown care and consideration for your loss, will receive none. Not this time or in the future. Where is your wife?'

'She's in her bedroom.'

'Larry, we could have done with Wendy.'

'She's with the Benthams,' Larry said.

'That shameless hussy with her men and her wicked ways,' Montgomery said.

The man was sociopathic, the two police officers could see that clearly. Not that it made him a murderer. Isaac and Larry could only imagine the torment that his wife and children had suffered over the years.

'Constable Elaine Sands,' said a woman, no more than mid-twenties, as she came through the gate at the front of the house. She shook hands with Isaac and Larry. Montgomery looked away.

'Follow me, Constable,' Larry said.

'You can't, not without a warrant.' Montgomery, clutching at straws, continued to protest.

134

'Your wife is in the house. We've not seen her, and her condition is our primary consideration. You, Mr Montgomery, are due at Challis Street. We are going to have a long chat as to why you disowned your son, how your daughter came to own a house in Pembridge Mews, and what it was that drove her to suicide.'

'She killed Barry,' Montgomery blurted out.

'Proof?'

'It had to be her. She was a sensitive soul. He was not.'

'That's hardly a reason for murder. Your proof?'

'There is none, but I knew her, knew him.'

'Challis Street, please,' Isaac said. One of the police officers in the car came over and placed a hand on Montgomery. The man meekly complied and got in the back of the vehicle. The vehicle pulled away, its flashing light still going, its siren still wailing. A crowd had formed on the street outside the house.

'I'll wait for you at the station,' Isaac said to Larry. 'We'll interview him together. Check on the man's wife first. If she's traumatised, phone for an ambulance. God knows what this man has put his family through.'

'It doesn't explain Pembridge Mews, does it? The place must be worth two million pounds, and we know it was in Matilda's name and there was no mortgage. Could he have killed Barry?'

'It still doesn't explain what happened to Matilda,' Isaac said. 'Do what you must here, and ensure that Constable Sands stays with Mrs Montgomery.'

***

There was something about the Benthams' house that made Wendy relax. She shouldn't have liked Lord

135

Bentham, but she did, and now, with Amelia still not back, she and Geoffrey, as he preferred to be called, were onto their fourth glass of wine. This time a Cabernet Merlot.

'Cullen Diana Madeline Cabernet Merlot, 2001,' Geoffrey said.

'South African or Australian?' Wendy's slurred reply.

'Margaret River, Western Australia. Seventeen months in French barriques, a great wine.'

'Father's found a willing partner,' Amelia said as she came into the room. Her mother was with her.

'We've been out riding,' Lady Bentham said.

'Father likes to show off his wines. Mother doesn't drink often, and I can't tell a Merlot from a Shiraz.'

'Philistine,' Geoffrey Bentham jokingly said to his daughter.

'I'll be back in five minutes,' Amelia said. 'We can talk then.'

'We've another bottle to test,' her father said.

'Sergeant Gladstone can stay for dinner. And besides, she's not in a fit condition to drive back to London tonight. I knew them both better than anyone else. Strange, I should be more upset, but it wasn't as if I ever knew Matilda really.'

'What's the reason that got Matilda's brother evicted from the family home?' Wendy asked.

'I can't remember it being mentioned. You'll be asking me how Matilda could afford such a lovely house, won't you?'

'I will.'

'Then have your drink with father, praise his wines, and after dinner, you and I will talk.'

'As I was saying, seventeen months in French barriques,' Geoffrey Bentham said.

Wendy nodded in acknowledgement, spoke about the wine – the intensity, the colour, the nose – taking the lead from her teacher. She did not have any idea what a French barrique was.

After her introduction to wine tasting, Wendy was shown her room by the haughty butler.

'I've laid out clothes for you, and there are clean towels in the bathroom,' he said.

'Casual for dinner?'

'Always,' the man said as though he regretted it.

'What time?'

'Eight o'clock. Don't be late. It's fish tonight. His lordship's chosen a Cabernet Blanc from his cellar for you.'

'I don't think I could drink any more.'

'Not so from where I was standing,' the butler said. 'You looked as though you were just settling in for the long haul. They're good people.'

'Yes, they are.'

'I hope they're not in trouble.'

'So do I,' Wendy said.

***

Upstairs in the Montgomery house, Larry and Constable Sands found Janice Montgomery's room, the woman answering from the other side of the door.

Elaine Sands turned the door handle. 'It's locked,' she shouted out.

'Stanley locked it. He has the key. He doesn't want me to see you,' Mrs Montgomery replied.

'Is there a spare?'

137

'Downstairs, hanging from a rack in the kitchen.'

Larry ran down the stairs, found the key quickly enough and returned. He put the key in the lock. It turned, and the door opened. Inside, Janice Montgomery was sitting up in bed.

'Are you alright?' Larry asked.

'Yes. Why shouldn't I be?'

'Your husband…'

'That's Stanley. He cares in his own way, wants to protect me from the nastiness outside.'

'Don't you leave the house?' Elaine asked.

'Sometimes, but I prefer it here.'

The room was well decorated and bright. In one corner, a budgerigar in a cage. It was chirping. In the centre of the room, a queen size bed with a wooden headboard. Mrs Montgomery seemed to be consumed by the voluminous pillows that supported her.

'Stanley has made it very nice for me, don't you think?'

Larry could only agree, but it was still a gilded cage, and the woman looked as if she had become institutionalised, a captive to her husband's paranoia, his need to control. Getting answers from her would be difficult, but he had to persevere.

'Mrs Montgomery, your husband is helping us with our enquiries into the deaths of your children.'

The woman sat still in her bed. She clutched a doll. 'Matilda loved this doll,' she said, a tear rolling down her cheek. 'Why did she have to die?'

'We need to know,' Larry said. Elaine Sands dabbed a handkerchief on the tearful woman's cheek. Janice Montgomery clutched her arm, as in an act of affection.

Larry, not a psychologist, just a detective inspector, thought that the woman had been deprived of affection for a long time. The young police constable had supplied what she had wanted.

'Thank you,' Mrs Montgomery said. Elaine Sands went downstairs, returning after a few minutes with a cup of tea and toast for her.

'We need to talk,' Larry said. The circumstances of the woman in her room did not indicate neglect or maltreatment, though she was childlike, a mere shadow, perilously thin.

'You want to know about Matilda?'

'And Barry. We don't understand why Matilda needed to die.'

'My husband is a good man, you must understand that. It is just that he is…'

'Controlling?'

'He wants everything and everyone his way. Barry could never accept it, although Matilda was more forgiving, and she loved her father, I know she did.'

Loving the father seemed more than Larry could accept. Nobody could love a tyrant, other than from fear of causing displeasure, hanging on to the only thing they had ever known. But Matilda hadn't been a child. No one calmly throws a rope over a beam, not unless their life has taken a turn for the worse, a broken heart, a financial crisis, guilt.

The last reason, the most viable of all the possibilities, was hard to contemplate.

And now there was Stanley Montgomery, a man who had no friends, a family that he ruled with an iron rod, just his wife remaining.

'How did Matilda leave this house?' Larry asked.

'She was a good girl, did well at school, and then there was university. Always the best for her, but she would spend more time away, not always coming home every night.'

'What did your husband do?'

'He confronted her at a house she was sharing, accused her of cheapening herself, cheapening the good name of Montgomery. Not that she could cheapen it any more than it already had been.'

'What do you mean?'

'Check on the Montgomery family history. You'll find out what I mean.'

'We will, but first, can you tell me?'

'Stanley's great-grandfather fought in the Boer War in South Africa.'

'A long time ago.'

'Not to Stanley, it wasn't. Cecil Montgomery, a captain in the Cheshire Regiment. He deserted, couldn't take the bloodshed, the wanton loss of life, the treatment of the captured Boer families. They charged him with desertion and cowardice. They executed him by firing squad and buried him in an unmarked grave.'

'Why should that concern your husband? That's over a hundred years ago. No doubt we've all got relatives that have committed crimes, shown weakness in a time of adversity.'

'The family history of military service. There had been a Montgomery at every major battle for three hundred years before that, an earldom, an estate in the country, wealth and influence.'

'After the execution?'

'All gone within five years, ostracised from polite society, reduced to servitude and living in the slums.'

'Your husband did not grow up under such conditions.'

'No, but the memory ran deep, the need to hide that shameful past. Stanley is a driven man, not a man to show emotion, but Barry hurt him deeply, and then Matilda not coming home. He became worse, but with me he remained calm, even loving on occasions.'

Larry realised that the woman could not face the reality of her life. He'd leave her with her delusions if it helped to deal with the current situation.

'The house in Pembridge Mews?'

'Stanley purchased it for her.'

'Did you ever visit?'

'I met Matilda every few months, Stanley never did. In fact, he never saw her again after the problem with Barry.'

'What about Barry?'

'Stanley wanted someone to restore the family name. To regain the prestige that it once had. Stanley couldn't do it, he knew that. He did not have the charisma or the likeability to influence people, but Barry did. Barry was a lovely young man, a true gentleman. He knew the right people, and he would have made a great success of his life.'

'What happened between your son and his father?'

'It was the last time with Matilda. Barry was there at the house that she shared. Stanley was insisting that she come home, Matilda resisting. Barry stood up to his father and said no. There was a fight, and Stanley lost. For once Barry had bested him, and my husband could never forgive him, never to allow his name to sully this house.'

'It was an argument, his son. Surely, with time?'

141

'Not to Stanley. To him, Barry was Cecil, the coward, the man who had turned his back on tradition and history, the pariah who had to be expunged at all cost.'

'Even murder?'

'I can't believe that of Stanley.'

'Why not?'

'He never raised a hand to the children. He controlled by his voice, his strength of character. He loved Barry, even more than Matilda, and he had been let down.'

'Had you seen him since?'

'No. We occasionally spoke on the phone, and Matilda would pass on the news about him. I never saw my son again.'

'Is there anyone that can stay with you?' Larry asked.

'No. Please, I'm fine. I've got the television and Stanley will be home later. He'll be hungry when he comes in. You'll not keep him for long, will you?'

It was Elaine Sands, the young constable, who spoke first outside the house. 'The woman's mentally stunted if she puts up with that,' she said.

'Are you convinced that her husband is the saint that she portrays him as?'

'He's either Saint Stanley of the Divine Benevolence or the devil incarnate. Personally, I'd go for the latter.'

'So would I,' Larry said as he shook hands with the constable. 'Best of luck, see you around,' he said. The constable walked back to her police station; Larry got into his car for the drive back to Challis Street.

Chapter 15

Wendy knew she wasn't going to drive back to London that night. At the head of the table, Geoffrey Bentham was dressed casually, as the butler had said. His wife sat at the other end. Wendy thought that she was the more aristocratic of the two: her high cheekbones, her flawless skin, her elegant figure. In spite of the more than twenty-year difference between mother and daughter, she could have passed as Amelia's sister.

The butler hovered, ever attentive, ensuring that everyone's glass was topped up. On the plate in front of Wendy, salmon with all the trimmings. Nothing like the fish and chips she'd sometimes buy on the way home from Challis Street.

'Best china for you,' Amelia said.

'I'm not sure what to say,' Wendy said. She looked at the array of cutlery, polished to perfection, the tablecloth freshly pressed, the flowers in the middle of the table.

'Bruce, we can't stop him,' Denise Bentham said. 'We've tried enough times to make him sit down with us, but he won't. Someone's got to maintain the tradition, I suppose.'

'I suppose,' Wendy said, not sure if they did, not caring particularly at the present time.

'Tell us, Wendy,' Geoffrey Bentham said. 'You don't' altogether approve of how we live, do you?'

'It's not that. I grew up in the north of England. We weren't poor, not rich either, but it was a loving family. Every day my father would go out into the fields,

143

rain or shine, snow or sleet. And in Yorkshire, up in the dales, most days were not ideal. He never complained, not as long as he could have a pint at the end of the day, a chance to talk about what was wrong with the world, not that he ever saw any of it.'

'So why the disapproval? If some people have money, either through hard work or being born with a silver spoon in the mouth, would your father have cared, should you?'

'If a person carves out a good life for themselves through honest hard work, then I've no issue. I sometimes wished that my husband had been more ambitious, and I had had the discipline to have educated myself better, but that's behind us now.'

'Your husband?' Amelia asked.

'He died young, dementia at the end.'

'I'm so sorry.'

'No need to be. He was difficult during the last few months, and now I'm sharing the house with Bridget, one of the ladies in Homicide. There's enough money between the two of us to go on holidays twice a year.'

'The silver spoon?' Geoffrey reiterated.

'In the countryside, I didn't see it much, but when I got to Sheffield, there they were, the late teens, the twenty-somethings, with their pockets flush with cash, partying, getting drunk, drugged, not caring who got in their way. It just seemed unjust, and then there was Margaret Thatcher attempting to bring to heel anyone who opposed her. Good people suffered. Don't get me wrong, I'm not a storm the Bastille socialist. It's just that I feel that people should be treated better, a fairer division of wealth. The rich helping the poor.'

'I'm a socialist,' Geoffrey said. 'Small "s", though. When Denise and I were first married, and before I inherited the title, before Amelia was born, we were doing it tough. We've experienced the other side, not that we ever want to go back.'

'You've all been very hospitable,' Wendy said. 'I could get used to this.'

'Then enjoy your time here. There's another wine I'd like your opinion on.'

'I still need to talk to Amelia,' Wendy said.

'There's all night. Enjoy your meal and your wine,' Amelia said. 'We will go into the other room later. There's a log fire in there.'

***

It was two in the morning before Wendy and Amelia finally had a chance to sit down and talk. The retreat to the log fire, the heat it gave off, the subdued music playing in the background, and Wendy, the worse for wear after a good meal and more wine than she had drunk in a long time, slept for three hours, her feet on a stool in front of the chair where she was sitting.

'I left you to sleep it off,' Amelia said when Wendy finally stirred. 'I've brought you a pot of black coffee. I hope that's alright.'

Wendy got up, slightly embarrassed because she had visited the Benthams on official business, not to indulge herself.

'Mum and Dad don't socialise much,' Amelia said. 'They're not into foxhunting and hanging out with the local gentry.'

'Foxhunting's banned, isn't it?'

'They still have their hunts, make out they're tracking an animal-based scent. Fox urine, usually, and they've still got the hounds. It's proof, that's the problem.

145

Even now, there are attempts to overturn the ban in Parliament.'

'Matilda?' Wendy said as she drank her coffee.

'What can I tell you that I haven't already?'

'We know from her mother that her father bought the house for her.'

'She never spoke about her father. Not even her mother from what I can remember.'

'According to the mother, a nervous, timid woman, very much brow-beaten and controlled, she used to meet with Matilda on an occasional basis.'

'As I said, Matilda never spoke about her parents, always changed the subject. Sorry, I can't help you there.'

'We know that Matilda's father was, still is, a controlling individual. Off the record, the man's a horror. He must have subjected his daughter to untold mental anguish.'

'Physical abuse?'

'It's not been proven one way or the other. We'll continue to check, but we don't believe that he did. He gave the house in Pembridge Mews to Matilda with no conditions, and the family home is attractive and well maintained. His wife has also been cared for, although not a life that you and I would enjoy.'

'Man, the provider; woman, the child bearer and homemaker? Her father's view of how the world should be?'

'It's more than that. According to Inspector Hill, the woman was locked in her room. Not neglected or maltreated, far from it. The room was luxurious, and the woman wanted for nothing.'

'Except her freedom.'

'The one thing that she had been conditioned not to want. It was subtle brainwashing, that's for sure. But Matilda must have been affected by it, though.'

Amelia put another log on the fire before continuing.

'We've spoken about this before. Matilda never opened up about her life, and whereas she'd go out and enjoy herself, she'd never get drunk or take a man home with her.'

'And then she commits suicide. If she had murdered her brother, the most likely scenario, what's the reason? We know she was close to him, but did it transcend sibling love into something else?'

'It could have, but why? Barry was interested in other women, including me. I can't see why he'd want to be sleeping with his sister.'

'Amelia, take your head out of the sand for a minute,' Wendy said, sounding awfully close to a preaching mother, she thought. 'You have kind and loving parents, a good life, not only here, but an interesting career. Matilda had a strict upbringing as a child, no horses to ride, no freedom to make mistakes, to sleep with the wrong boy or man, to get drunk. Nothing that you and I take for granted, apart from the horse.'

'You grew up on a farm,' Amelia said.

'Okay, a horse that worked on the farm, pulling a cart, my father riding it to check around the place. I saw your horse; it wasn't a nag.'

'Do you ride?'

'When I was younger. We're digressing. Let's talk about Barry. You slept with him on a few occasions.'

'Three, from what I can remember.'

'Remember or know?'

147

'It was more than three. Once after a night at the pub, and another time when Matilda was asleep, and he crept over, used my key under the flowerpot and climbed in with me. The other times when the opportunity presented itself.'

'You didn't suspect it was someone else coming into the house?'

'I don't make it a habit of letting strange men into my house and into my bed. Mind you, five in the morning, and he'd be out there and running around.'

'And you were just getting in the mood for a return bout.'

'I'm a healthy young female with needs, the same as everyone else.'

'I'm not criticising,' Wendy said. 'I've been there, done that, got the badge.'

'I bet you have,' Amelia said, a smirk on her face. 'The fire still burns hot?'

'Not as hot as it once did. Now, getting back to Barry. He had another woman; did you know that?'

'Not that it was any of my business, but no. We were friends, nothing more.'

'This other woman was older than him by a few years, married.'

'Attractive?'

'Yes, but not as attractive as you.'

'Thanks, but that's how I need to be. A life of starving myself and doing the right exercises. Not much fun sometimes. Mother does nothing and look at her.'

'This woman is nearly twenty years older than him, old enough to be his mother. Barry had spent time with her, professed love.'

'Love? Barry?'

'Incapable?'

148

'I'm not saying he is, but the man was beautiful. An unusual term to use about a man, but he was. Physical perfection, a woman's ideal.'

'But you didn't fall for him?'

'You've met my parents, sensible people. I take after them. Perfection is fleeting, a façade that fades with time. It's the inner person that ensures contentment; the outer layer is for the momentary pleasure.'

'A good lover?'

'The best. I've tried a couple since, but they don't measure up. I don't know where he learnt his technique, but he was a master at his trade.'

'A gigolo?'

'Not with me. I wasn't about to give him money, he knew that. This other woman, what about her? Rich, starved of love?'

'Starved of love appears likely. She's not noticeably rich, although she had access to some; not enough for a serious gigolo.'

'What's enough? Not everyone's driven by greed. What if he only wanted enough to live well, sleep with whoever?'

'He had that, and then when he wanted, the young and nubile.'

'There was me. Go on, say it.'

'We thought he might have been fixated on older women, but if he slept with you, that tends to destroy that argument.'

'Not in itself. What man would get up before the crack of dawn when there's a woman ready and willing? That never made sense to me.'

'The man could have had commitment issues; not willing to allow himself to be emotionally or sexually controlled.'

'If Matilda was screwed up, he could have been as well.'

***

Stanley Montgomery sat in the interview room. After what Larry had seen at the man's house, he couldn't care less that he did not have a cup of tea, a comfortable chair.

Larry Hill did not like the man, although that didn't make him a murderer. Regardless of what other crimes he may have committed, whatever antisocial and sociopathic actions he may have done, it was still homicide that interested the team.

Larry remembered Constable Elaine Sand's parting comment: 'He's either Saint Stanley of the Divine Benevolence or the devil incarnate.' He had thought it an accurate observation of a man who appeared to care, but was it care? Or control? A need to maintain his assets in good condition, the car regularly serviced and washed, the house neat and tidy. Could it be that he approached his wife and children in the same way, treating them with reverence, showing them the way, mollycoddling them, not allowing them to cross the road?

And then, Barry, the son, moves on and out. Disinherited, forgotten, his name never to be mentioned. But then, Matilda had moved out, and Stanley Montgomery had stood by her, had given her a house, money probably. Yet he had never seen her again.

Larry felt that the man needed a psychiatric evaluation, but that could wait. For now, the truth; later the defence's arguments that the man had had a difficult childhood, never knowing a moment's peace, beaten by an uncaring father until his skin was raw. Even if the man had killed his son, the chance of a conviction, a custodial sentence in prison, was unlikely. More probable was that he would spend time in a high-security psychiatric hospital, drugged into complacency, never feeling guilt, never being cured.

Isaac was the first to enter the interview room. He proffered a hand as a courtesy. Montgomery glowered back, his hands folded.

'Let's get this over with,' Montgomery said. 'My wife?'

'You've already been told. I've spoken with her,' Larry said.

'You've no right.'

'Mr Montgomery, do you want a drink before we start?' Isaac asked.

'Not in this place.'

'Very well.' Isaac went through the procedure, informed Mr Montgomery that he was helping them in their enquiries into the murder of Barry Montgomery.

Montgomery sat still, said nothing. His head did not move. He did not see the light up above, the heater in the corner, the sun streaming in through a window set high up, the bars on it. All he saw were the eyes of the two police inspectors: Detective Chief Inspector Isaac Cook and Detective Inspector Larry Hill.

Isaac saw it as an attempt at intimidation, and it was not going to work. He had stared down a few villains in his time, and Montgomery was not up to their calibre.

'We found your wife locked in her room,' Larry said.

'If you had bothered to check, you will find that my wife is absent-minded. It was for her own protection.'

'A medical condition?'

'I believe so.'

'Has she been to a doctor's?'

'Is this relevant?' Montgomery said. 'She is a person with a nervous disposition. I have ensured her well-being after the death of our daughter. We are both grieving, and you still have the temerity to drag me down here, to embarrass me in front of our neighbours.'

'Mr Montgomery,' Isaac said, 'why don't we stop this charade? You are an insensitive man, a man that it is easy to dislike. You do not care what your neighbours think or do, as long as they keep away from you. A police car to bring you here can only enhance your reputation, or lack of it. You should be pleased with what we did for you.'

'Is this it? A slanging match while you insult me. I've a wife to care for, a daughter to bury.'

'A son that needs justice.'

'I will not hear that man's name mentioned.'

'You're not in your house; you're in a police station. Barry Montgomery was your son. He's been murdered. Now, we have some possibilities. One, it was a married woman he was having an affair with, or it was her husband. We're not convinced about the woman, although the husband remains a possibility. Then we come to you and Matilda. You hated your son, and we are told he struck you, told you to let Matilda live her life the way she wanted.'

'My wife was not there. She doesn't know the truth, only what Matilda told her.'

'Not Barry?'

'He would not have said anything...'

'Assuming it's not you, then it's Matilda, burdened with guilt over her relationship with her brother.'

'Are you implying that my children were sleeping together? My dear Matilda with that brute?'

'We're implying nothing. It is you that is expressing the possibilities. Did you drive them together, their defence against you and their upbringing?'

'They always had the best.'

'You keep saying that, but they left as soon as they could. Your house is a prison. Tastefully decorated, and comfortable, but children, as they are growing up, need the chance to develop, to make mistakes, to fall in love, to fall out again.'

'That may be your family, not mine. I protected them, and then they deserted me, left me with their mother.'

'You don't love your wife?' Isaac asked.

'She is getting old, and Matilda, she was so beautiful and innocent. I wanted her to stay that way.'

'You transferred your physical affection from the mother to the daughter, is that the truth?' Larry said.

Montgomery jumped up from his seat and grabbed Larry by the throat. The man's grip was firm, and Isaac couldn't release it. Two uniforms, on hearing the commotion, came into the room, separating Montgomery from Larry.

Larry took a seat, attempting to catch his breath. Isaac stood, not sure how to make sense of what had just occurred. Montgomery sat stunned, taking deep breaths, his face red.

'Fifteen-minute break,' Isaac said, pausing the interview. 'Mr Montgomery, tea, coffee, something to eat.'

'My apologies. You touched a raw nerve.'

Twenty-five minutes later, the interview resumed. By that time, Larry had had the chance to recover, and Stanley Montgomery had been looked at by a doctor. The man was declared to be in good health, but suffering from stress.

'The man's got a pulse, we know that,' Larry said sarcastically when the doctor updated him and Isaac.

Isaac again went through the procedure before recommencing the interview. As far as he was concerned, Larry had baited the man, not that he could blame him. It should be kid gloves with the father of a murdered man, a daughter who had committed suicide. The man's impenetrable barrier was unnerving Larry, and Isaac knew that he would have liked to grab the man and throw him about until he started telling the truth. Each time they met the man, a little more came out, yet where was the meat, the information that would allow the police to come to some conclusion?

'Inspector Hill is probing, Mr Montgomery. You do realise this?' Isaac said.

'Insulting the memory of my Matilda, I could not allow that.'

'Let's go back to the beginning. You are not a pleasant man, certainly not charismatic, rude most of the time, dismissive at others. Is that a fair description?'

'I love my family, always have,' Montgomery said.

'Let's clarify what I said originally.'

'Then, yes, I will grant you that. I mean no harm, I commit no crime, pay my taxes, clothe and feed my family. Although they don't always understand.'

'No one would.'

'It was my childhood, harsh and uncaring, a brute for a father, a mother who didn't care.'

'No doubt of interest to a psychoanalyst,' Larry said, 'but it doesn't advance the investigation, does it?'

'I met my wife in my last year at university. We married within three months. Even then I was dismissive of people. But Janice, she understood. We were happy, and then along came Barry, followed by Matilda two years

154

later. It was easy when they were young, always at our coattails, wanting to be with us, listening to what we had to say. Of course, they could be naughty, but it was harmless and childish.'

'What happened?' Isaac asked.

'They grew up. Matilda started to develop adolescent crushes on boys at school, pop singers.'

'The same as my eldest,' Larry said. 'They grow out of it.'

'It was unhealthy, and her schooling suffered, and then she got in with a bad crowd, swearing, answering back to her mother, to me. I had to stop it.'

'Patience and guidance work best.'

'I tried them both, but to Matilda, as well as to Barry, I was steeped in the past.'

'You stopped them finding themselves?'

'Not all the time, and then Matilda came home from school, a flaming row with her mother, abusive towards me.'

'What was said?'

'Matilda was fifteen, almost sixteen. She'd met a young man at school, and…'

'She told you that she had had sex with this young man. Is that what you are trying to say?'

'Yes. After that, I kept her at home as much as I could. Picked her up from school, dropped her off in the morning.'

'How did she respond?'

'I loved her, you know that?'

'We don't doubt that, although what you did doesn't help. She was at an impressionable age, looking to her peers for advice, not to you.'

'I couldn't accept it. I tightened the controls on her, on Barry, but then she left home and went to university.'

'Young men?'

'I don't think so. In truth, Matilda was not an affectionate person, more like me than her mother. But she had wanted to experiment. I could see her getting in with the wrong crowd at university, a repeat of what had happened at school. I went to the house she shared, offered to drive her from home to the university and back every day. I had her interests at heart. I was doing it for her. She was so innocent, a rose amongst thorns.'

'It's obsessive,' Larry said.

'It's parental love. Your children will grow up, want to leave home, start answering back, call you a retarded old fool who should be in a museum.'

'You hit your daughter at the house she shared?'

'Never. I may have grabbed her by her arm, but I could never hit her; she knew that.'

'Then what?'

'Barry was there. The relationship between us was not good. He's more like his mother.'

'Did he intervene?'

'He tried to reason with me, to let Matilda stay at the house. He was taking out one of the housemates, not sure which one. You know about Barry?'

'That he was attractive to women?' Isaac said.

'Young or old, they would always fawn over him. Even when he was young, he had this innate charm. He knew it as well.'

'That's why we've considered that a jealous husband or a former boyfriend could have killed him.'

'It's possible. Matilda loved him more than anyone else in the world, but it was the love of a sister for a brother, and I never touched her. I couldn't, too pure, too innocent.'

'She had a boyfriend a few months ago,' Isaac said. 'We've interviewed him. He said she was emotionally cold. Does that surprise you?'

'She meant no harm, but she could not express herself the way that her mother could, that Barry could.'

'Yet with all this love for Matilda, you never saw her again.'

'I couldn't, don't you understand? She had grown up, and she had boyfriends, lovers. My feelings towards her never changed, but she was tainted goods.'

'You gave her a house.'

'What else could I do? I wanted to protect her, but I couldn't control her anymore. I did the best I could; not good enough, obviously.'

'Let's come back to Barry. What happened after the incident at the shared house?'

'I never saw him again. Not that I didn't want to at first, but then he changed. No longer was he with a woman by choice; now he was selling himself.'

'A male escort?'

'It upset his mother when she found out, and I vowed never to allow his name to be mentioned again.'

'Your wife?'

'She wanted to forgive him, but I forbade it. It would have been too much emotional stress for her to deal with. I did it to protect her.'

'Were you ashamed of your son?'

'Yes.'

'Matilda?'

'Her mother would meet her. I paid all her bills. I hoped that one day she would find a good man, settle down, and then we could have reconciled, but now...'

157

'Thank you, Mr Montgomery,' Isaac said. 'I don't think we have any more questions for now. Sorry, only one. The shared house, do you have its address?'

Montgomery wrote the address on a piece of paper and left the room. The two police officers could see a broken man; a man who had confronted his demons, a man who through his actions had sent his two children on a path from which there was no return.

Chapter 16

There was no doubt in anybody's mind that bringing Stanley Montgomery into Homicide had been a good move. For once they had a new avenue of enquiry that would take them away from the current suspects, and into hitherto unconsidered areas.

Wendy could see the need to meet with Christine Mason again. If, and it seemed clear that it was true, Barry Montgomery, alias Colin Young, alias whoever else, had been selling his services, then had the accounts manager at the Fitzroy Hotel been a client or a paramour? Had the man's feelings for her been genuine, had hers for him? And was the manager, the unpleasant man that Wendy instinctively didn't like and Christine was afraid of, not the villain of the piece, but merely a man who had seen the truth?

'What do you reckon?' Larry asked.

Wendy was still trying to digest all that she was being told, trying to put the pieces together, aiming to identify inconsistencies in Christine Mason's story, her hesitancy, her need to look away at certain times. 'We need to know who paid the bill at the Fitzroy,' she said.

'The credit card, we know it was valid and in the name of Colin Young,' Bridget said.

'If the man was a male escort, then where did he operate from? How do the women make contact with him? And why the Fitzroy?'

'As good a place as any to make contact with his clients,' Larry said.

'Not if Christine Mason was there, it wasn't,' Wendy said. 'We know her to be a jealous woman, and if she had seen anything…'

'Anything what?'

'She would have had her proof. But we know the story about the taxi near to Paddington Station is correct. Why tell us that story if she had known the truth about him before?'

'Unless she was blinded by love,' Isaac said.

The team was in Isaac's office, the investigation was getting hot, the culprit was not far from being discovered, hiding behind a thin disguise. It was the time that DCI Isaac Cook liked the best: the adrenaline rush, the quickening heartbeat, the added passion in the office. Days spent sifting through unknowns, finding solutions, clues, avenues of inquiry, people to interview, and then…

One recalcitrant and disagreeable man who under pressure had revealed a hitherto unknown secret. One so awful that he could not bring himself to say the word, let alone allow his son's name to be spoken again.

'If Christine saw Barry Montgomery with a young and beautiful woman in the taxi, it could have turned her,' Wendy said. 'In the hotel, the man could have been discreet, a sideways glance, a phone number on a piece of paper. And even if Christine had seen him in the hotel talking to other women at the bar, what would she have thought? She was so enamoured of the man that she wouldn't have been able to make the connection. But with Matilda, she didn't know that she was his sister.'

'In the back of a taxi? What would she have seen?' Larry said. 'They're hardly made for a bystander to see inside.'

'Larry's right,' Isaac said. 'If Christine Mason had seen any affection between Montgomery and his sister, it couldn't have been in Paddington.'

'Maybe in Pembridge Mews,' Bridget suggested.

'If that were the case, then she would have known she was his sister,' Wendy said.

'Why? To her, he was Colin Young, not Barry Montgomery. She could have found out Matilda's name, not so difficult to do. And then she could have seen him with Amelia, realised that the man was not only cheating on her with one woman but two.'

'Wendy, focus on Christine Mason. Larry, find out what you can about Barry Montgomery's secret life,' Isaac said. 'I still don't get the reason for the Fitzroy. It's a reputable hotel, not the sort of place to condone such behaviour. What would happen to their reputation if it became known as a place for well-heeled and lonely women to meet up with attractive young men?'

'Its clientele's demographic would change,' Larry said, appreciating the humour.

'Get your mind out of the gutter,' Wendy said. 'We're not all desperate, and don't go standing around in the foyer of a fancy hotel looking for someone to pay you for your time. You'll go hungry if you do.'

'Okay, team, to work,' Isaac said. 'Bridget, work with Larry, check the classifieds. We need a complete history of Barry Montgomery by tomorrow. And why the Fitzroy?'

'What about the shared house where Barry and Stanley Montgomery came to blows?' Larry asked.

'According to Stanley Montgomery, there were no blows, just an argument, some jostling. Is it the most important line of enquiry?'

'It depends on whether the girl Barry was dating can tell us more.'

'Very well. Check it out. But let's be clear, Barry Montgomery was, according to his father, selling himself. So that brings into account jealous women, angry husbands. And unfortunately, more suspects, some in this country, some possibly overseas.'

'It's closer to home than that,' Wendy said.

'How can you be sure?' Isaac said.

'Instinct. It's what Amelia Bentham said about the foxhunting that still continues. Once the hounds have got a sniff of the fox urine that they use, they'll not give in until they've killed something. We've got the smell now, the smell of success.'

To Larry, they were no closer than before.

'Wendy's right,' Isaac said. 'The sixth sense tells me that we're close. Amongst those we have in our sights, one of them is guilty.'

***

Christine Mason did not take kindly to the aspersion that she had known all along what Colin Young was, and that she had been complicit in his prostituting himself to lonely and wealthy women.

'He loved me, I know that now,' she had protested. Too strongly, Wendy thought when she had put the possibility to her. It wasn't as if her approach had been harsh. On the contrary, the two women had met in a park close to the Fitzroy.

Wendy was fully cognisant of the grilling given to Stanley Montgomery, the intimidating surrounds of Challis Street. Not that Isaac and Larry had any intention of holding the man, but fear had been a factor in getting him to open up. Not appropriate for Christine Mason, Wendy had insisted when it had been suggested by Larry.

'I'll do it my way,' Wendy had said.

'Results, no letting the woman slip out from under,' Isaac had said.

'When have I let you down?' Wendy replied. Not that her DCI and DI were wrong. She knew that Christine Mason knew more than she had let on, but what had she seen in the taxi?

And there was another thing that concerned Wendy. She had heard 'beautiful' used twice to describe Barry Montgomery, the first time by Christine, the second by Amelia. Could any man be that beautiful? A description reserved for Adonis, the spouse of Aphrodite, the goddess of beauty and love; for Eros, the god of attraction; for Achilles, the Greek hero of the Trojan war, the son of King Peleus and Thetis, a sea nymph; and for Paris, who had stolen Helen away from Menelaus, the King of Sparta. Not for a man from London, not for someone who was not Greek and not a figure from ancient mythology.

A friendship of sorts had been built up between Sergeant Wendy Gladstone and Christine Mason. She recognised in Christine the effects of age starting to show, the vulnerability that no longer was she a young teen savouring adolescent love, nor a newlywed with a husband who spent all his time with her, and then the children, growing up, forming relationships of their own, grandchildren even, and the stark realisation that life was slowly ebbing away.

Wendy had felt all of these emotions, although they had not affected her to the same degree as the woman she sat with, the woman who dressed younger than she should, applying makeup to cover the imperfections, the possible plastic surgery.

'Christine, I should haul you into Challis Street, give you the third degree.'

'But you haven't. Why?'

'Level with me, please. We know more about your Colin Young than before. There's no doubt that he was sleeping with another woman, younger than you, his age. He was, and we are still trying to prove this, selling himself. Now, that may have been in the past, but we can't be sure. What we do know is that he focussed on vulnerable women, and you are, don't deny it, a classic case. The disinterested husband, the belief that time is passing you by, the need to be convinced that you are still desirable, attractive, able to find another man.'

Christine sat mute, not sure what to say. Tears were starting to form in her eyes. She attempted to speak, a garbled muttering.

'What is it, Christine? The truth this time.'

'I knew what he was doing in the hotel,' she said.

'When? Colin?'

'The first time that he came to the hotel, the way he moved around the bar at night and in the foyer, picking his mark.'

'But why the hotel? There must have been other places, lonely hearts clubs, that sort of thing.'

'I'm not sure he was truly comfortable with what he did. He told me later that he abhorred tricking vulnerable and lonely women out of their money, solely for spending time with him. He was a moral person who knew wrong from right, but a selfish father, an abused childhood, had left him with only one skill.'

'And you believed this nonsense?'

164

'It was true, don't you see it? With me, he was honest and caring, nothing like you portray him. I was the person he relied on, the person who accepted him for what he was, who forgave him.'

'Apart from being delusional, what else is there?' Wendy said. 'Each time we meet, more comes out. Christine, where is this going to end?'

'You will never understand the pure love that existed between us.'

Wendy could see that, yet again, the woman displayed a detached take on reality, as if her senses had deserted her. But that couldn't be true, Wendy thought. The woman was smart, smart enough to separate truth from make-believe. But then a lot of people watched the programmes nightly on the television where a good-looking man has a group of women vying for his attention, professing love, falling out of love, eventually choosing one, a wedding with all the attendant glamour. Even Wendy and Bridget would sit down of a night and watch, having a good laugh, sometimes a tear, but never believing that it was anything more than a scripted programme acted out. Yet Christine Mason seemed to think that life was like that.

'Christine, my patience is wearing thin. I have been advised to bring you into the police station. I resisted because I thought this would work better, yet you're still fobbing me off with sugary rubbish. The truth, please, or I'll declare you a hostile witness.'

'But it is the truth. I must get back to work, the accounts. The manager will be angry if I don't complete my work for the day.'

'To hell with him,' Wendy said, raising her voice.

'He loved me.'

'One more time, the truth. Colin Young is there in your hotel. He's casing the joint, looking for his mark. What time of the day, the first time?'

'Four in the afternoon. I'm standing by the lift, and he comes up to me.'

'He sees you standing there, looking rich and lonely, is that it?'

'I suppose so. We get talking.'

'The smooth talk, how he's been looking for a kindred spirit, and how younger women leave him cold?'

'Something like that.'

'And then, the time in the bar, the sweet words, the "let's go to my room".'

'Tony was away, three weeks that time, but yes.'

'You're an easy lay, you know that?'

'I always was, but he was charming, and I couldn't resist. Don't you understand?'

Wendy could to some degree, but it wasn't the time to talk about her frustrations, it was the time to solve a murder.

'I'm not the person being questioned, you are. You've spent time with him, no mention of money at this time?'

'He told me he was struggling to pay the hotel bill.'

'How much?'

'I gave him five hundred pounds.'

'What has your life consisted of? Didn't you get out as a teenager, didn't you play around with the local boys, doctors and nurses, that sort of thing?' Wendy said. 'You believe the man's story, not for a moment thinking that he's a hustler and that you've just had sex with a male prostitute.'

'I never thought that.'

'He leaves the hotel, returning a few weeks later, and checking in again, correct?'

'Yes. I had no idea where he had been, and he never told me.'

'Not some cock and bull story about him being a secret agent?'

'No, nothing. I was in love, I trusted him.'

'He returns to the hotel. Does he chase after other women?'

'Not at all. We're careful in the hotel, never talking to each other in public.'

'And then, up to his room whenever you got the chance. And?'

'I paid his hotel bill. He'd use his credit card, but I'd give him the money in cash.'

'Embezzlement? You're using the hotel's money by this time. How much?'

'Over twenty thousand pounds.'

'Does anyone know?'

'Yes.'

'Carry on, let's hear the rest.'

A plane flew low overhead, the conversation momentarily halted; a baby cried nearby. An old man sat on the bench beside the two women. Eventually, he walked away, and the conversation resumed.

'I managed to hide the theft. But if there's an audit, then it will be picked up,' Christine said, her face red, her voice clear, her hands steady, as if the unburdening was good for the soul. Wendy knew that her soul may be better, but the woman would face criminal action once the hotel found out.

'You said someone else knew,' Wendy said.

'The manager, that horrible toad of a man, figured it out.'

'He saw you with Colin Young?'

'He saw me coming out of his room. Not that I knew at the time, and he said nothing. After that, he checked the financial records, figured out how I was hiding the theft.'

'Blackmail?'

'Not at the time.'

'When?'

'He came to me one Thursday. Colin had not been in the hotel for some time. He sat across from me in my office, with those leering eyes of his. He took hold of my arm, hurting me as he squeezed. I was frightened, unsure what to say, what to do.'

'The man's a pig, I'll grant you that.'

'He sat there, his grip getting firmer. He leant forward, his breath had the smell of alcohol. "I know all about you and your fancy man", he said. I was frightened, not sure what to say.'

'What happened after he had confronted you?'

'He said nothing for a few minutes, or maybe it was seconds. I can't remember, and then he said, "You've also been fiddling the books, giving the money to him, admit it."'

'You're in trouble. If he follows up on your crime, it's prosecution, a possible custodial sentence.'

'That's not what he wanted.'

'Confession's good for the soul,' Wendy said. 'The full sordid details, please.'

'He could see that I had a talent for embezzlement. He wanted me to take money for him as well.'

'How much?'

'Over ten thousand pounds now.'

'Is that it?'

168

'There's more. You remember when we were sitting in the hotel café, and he came over and spoke to me?'

'The time I told him that you were helping the police with their enquiries?'

'It wasn't the accounts he wanted reconciling.'

'He's blackmailing you for sex?'

'That was part of the agreement, or he'd tell my husband.'

'You agreed?'

'What could I do? I had to have Colin under any conditions. He wouldn't come to the hotel if I couldn't pay for his room, and my husband is an angry man.'

A sad case, Wendy thought. A pathetic woman who had allowed feigned love to put her into intractable positions from which there was no way of extricating herself.

'Firstly, the manager is complicit in the crime,' Wendy said. 'We don't want to jeopardise you if we can avoid it. However, the man is clearly a parasite preying on the weak and stupid, and you qualify on the stupid. There was never any need for any of this to happen.'

'That's the full story,' Christine Mason said.

169

Chapter 17

Bridget had checked out the address of the shared house where Matilda had lived, obtained a copy of the lease agreement from that time.

'Matilda, we heard, all of us,' Amanda Jenkins, the lessee name on the agreement, said when she and Larry met at her house in Tottenham. She was a plain-looking woman with an angular face, blue eyes, a cheery disposition. She was also very pregnant. 'Two weeks,' she said. The house, a two-storey semi-detached, had nothing to recommend it; the garden was neglected, and the house looked as if it could have done with a fresh coat of paint. A dog, no more than something that moved under a matted coat, took one look at Larry and resumed its sleep.

'That's Boris. He doesn't do much these days. Certainly no use as a guard dog, not that we get any trouble around here,' Amanda said. It was a good area, Larry knew that, and there was some advantage in having the worst house in the street. Those on either side were bright and renovated, and worth more than Amanda's.

'John, that's my husband, he intends to fix the place up, but you know how it is.'

Indeed, Larry did. His wife was a stickler for a pristine house, the constant need to update, upgrade, repaint. She would not have appreciated the house where he now sat, although she would have loved the area.

'Tell me about the house you shared,' Larry said. 'About Matilda.'

'Did you meet Barry?'

'Beautiful?' Pre-empting the woman's reply.

'We all thought that. Although Matilda was beautiful too, in a different way.'

'What do you mean? I'll be honest and tell you that I don't expect to gain too much from our conversation. Mainly because we know of their history, their childhood, their personalities, the issues that Matilda had, the effect that Barry had on women.'

'Matilda was a lovely person. Always tidy in the house, never failed to do her chores. We rotated on the vacuuming and washing up the dishes.'

'When it was your turn...?'

'Failed miserably. Matilda used to cover for me, not that the others were any better. We were young, into partying, getting laid. I hope you don't mind my bluntness.'

'Bluntness is fine. Honesty is better. What do you think drove Matilda to commit suicide?'

'Her brother, no one else. None of us could break that impenetrable barrier that she surrounded herself with.'

'We're well aware of their troubled childhood: a hard man for a father, a weak woman for a mother.'

'He was at the house. I remember it well.'

'Your version?'

'An argument, harsh words spoken by the father, Barry coming to the defence of his sister, of us.'

'The man called you whores, and his daughter no better?'

'We made ourselves scarce, although we heard the raised voices. "Whore" came through loud and clear, but Matilda hadn't slept around.'

'Barry had.'

'Yes, with me. Not that I had an issue with that, nor did Matilda. But Matilda never had a man over. We used to tease her about her being the cherry ripe for picking.'

'Her reaction?'

'She would just laugh, and say that in time she would find a good man and settle down. But we didn't believe her.'

'Why?'

'She just didn't seem the sort to fall in love. Emotionally scarred, I'd say now, but back then I would have said she was frigid. Strange how you look at life when you're young.'

'It's not that many years ago.'

'A lifetime for me, and now I'm married, pregnant, and about to give birth.'

'A beautiful man?'

'My husband!' Amanda laughed. 'Short and fat, but he's kind, and he'll not let our child or me down, ever.'

'Barry Montgomery?'

'He wasn't a keeper. He was the good night out, not the stay at home type. Not the person to spend a lifetime with.'

'The other two in the house?'

'One of them, the most promiscuous, found religion. She's doing missionary work somewhere overseas.'

'How do you know this?'

'The internet, Facebook. Everyone's there somewhere.'

'And the other?'

'Hannah, you'll see her on the television every night reading the news. She was the most academic of the four. She may know more than me, but I doubt it.'

'Any reason for any of you to have wanted Barry dead?'

'I never saw him again after the big argument with his father. I was mighty angry at the time, but no, and I don't think we cared either way after a few weeks. And why should we? All we worried about was passing our exams and having a good time. If Matilda wanted to be a wallflower, not that she didn't get plenty of offers, then that was up to her. And believe me, we didn't need the competition. Matilda was the beauty; we weren't. Not unattractive, not stunners either. Still, I'm not complaining. Life's turned out well for me.'

Larry left Amanda and her house, knowing that happiness was to be cherished at all costs. There were times when he imagined a life without his wife and his children, the opportunity to make his own choices without considering others, to get drunk, to smoke more than he should. But he knew he would not change his life for anybody. He, like Amanda Jenkins, was a happy person.

***

'And what do you have in mind? Muscular, gymnastic, overnight, or by the hour? Our men are flexible as to your requirements. If you want them to accompany you to a work's function, office party, they are the soul of discretion.'

Bridget had not immediately let on to the gentlemen for hire companies that she had phoned that day that it was a police matter. Suspicious, she thought, the change in tone when she had finally told them who she was and why she was phoning.

Bridget had looked at and not been offended by the companies' websites, where there were hundreds of men to choose from. The pictures showed some bare-chested, others in dinner jackets, wearing bow ties, the ages varying from the twenties up to the more distinguished in their fifties, greying hair, creases in the face. No mention was made on the websites of the extras, just that the arrangement between the client and whoever they sent was strictly for social purposes. On the phone, before Bridget had identified herself, the extras had been outlined, sometimes in more detail than she required.

'Send us a photo,' the last company said. 'If he's not on the website, then he may have been a past employee.'

'Thank you,' Bridget said. 'We're interested in his movements, not your company.'

'I was a police officer once,' the man said. 'Wales. I made it up to sergeant, so I know our legal position. It's always a grey area, but we're above board.'

'You've got the picture on an email now,' Bridget said.

A pause while the former police officer opened the email. 'Yes, I know him. A few years back, attractive, hit with the ladies. I'll need to check the records, but I don't think he was here for long.'

'I'll send some officers out to your premises. Is that acceptable?'

'The website is our shopfront, not where we're situated. Just a small office in Brixton, up two flights of stairs. Ninety minutes?'

'DCI Isaac Cook and Sergeant Wendy Gladstone will be there.'

174

'Black guy, tall?'

'Don't tell me…'

'We were on a course in the past. He could have made good money back then.'

'He still could,' Bridget said. 'He's an attractive man. It's more than my life's worth if you tell him what I just said.'

'Don't worry. Discretion's my middle name.'

'Apart from that, what other names do you have?'

'Nick Domett, previously of the Cardiff police, currently the proprietor of Gents for Hire.'

'Which do you prefer?'

'My mother was proud of me when I was a police officer, although the money was lousy.'

'It still is,' Bridget said.

'That's why I'm here in this office, raking it in. My mother has never forgiven me, not that I can blame her. We're not breaking any laws, not serious ones, but people still have a perception that what we're doing is somehow wrong.'

'I'm not criticising.'

'A special discount, Bridget,' Domett said, his tone of voice clearly joking.

'You never know,' Bridget said.

'Spoken like a true libertarian. A believer in not passing judgement as long as no one's hurt or offended.'

'I'm not serious. Ninety minutes, two visitors.'

'I'll put the kettle on,' Domett said.

Bridget knew that she and Wendy would have a good laugh about the risqué repartee she had had with the owner of the escort company.

***

There was one thing obvious when Isaac and Wendy met Nick Domett at his office in Brixton: he wasn't one of those whose pictures and physiques figured on the Gents for Hire website.

The man wasn't a beefcake, not even a meat pie, Wendy thought, smiling to herself, having to hide her mouth with her hand.

'Good to see you, Isaac,' Nick Domett said as he got up from his chair. The office stank, as did the man. Stubble on his face, a bandage around one hand, his hair, what was left of it, combed over.

'Nick, good to see you,' Isaac said, not letting on that he had no clue who the man was.

'You've not changed, not one bit. A one for the ladies back then; still are, I suppose.'

'I've got a good woman. No need for others.'

'Shame. I could have found you employment. For me, four times down the aisle, four times in the divorce court. Fun, though.'

Isaac could not remember the man, and instinctively, he did not like Domett, but personal prejudices were not relevant. What the man knew was.

'Colin Young,' Isaac said. 'You recognised him, according to Sergeant Gladstone.'

'Five years back, and he was only on our books for seven months. Not that we ever met, you understand.'

'Why?'

'Not everyone on our books wants to come over to Brixton, not that I can blame them. Some prefer to maintain a distance, adds to the allure, hides the fact that the picture doesn't match the person.'

'That must happen all the time,' Wendy said, remembering the pictures of the girls outside a strip club that had prospered in Paddington ten years previously.

The pictures proudly displayed, Playboy models every one. Inside, Wendy knew, as she had been in a few times to deal with underage girls and women from Europe without visas. All of them, bar the newest and youngest, were haggard, old before their time, turning tricks in a room behind the stage.

'Nick, this is serious,' Isaac said. 'You were a policeman, so you'll understand. Colin Young's been murdered. The man's been playing the field, a younger woman, an older one, old enough to be one of your clients.'

'She might be a regular.'

'I'm talking hypothetically here. She's not on your books, we know that. She seems to be able to find enough men without your assistance.'

'Isaac, I left the police behind. I wasn't cut out for it, more interested in pushing the law at the edges than upholding it. That's an honest answer. I know I'm a reprobate, but it suits me. Each day with the police: the meetings, the reports, the standing to attention. Here, I do what I want, make money, sometimes get hired out.'

'You must be joking,' Wendy said.

'You'd be surprised. Not every female wants a Colin Young or one of the other studs for hire.'

'Smelly, unkempt and dirty, an attribute?'

'It's an acquired taste, the same as I am. Now, what can I tell you about Young?'

'His clients, address, that sort of thing,' Isaac said as he took a seat, wiping his handkerchief over it first.

'I don't run police checks on them.'

'So, they could be lying.'

'Colin Young, no address, other than a post office box.'

'Whereabouts?'

'Bayswater. Not sure that does much for you.'

'It doesn't. How did you pay him?'

'A bank account. You've got the details on that sheet of paper I just gave you.'

'We know the account,' Wendy said. 'It's the same bank where his credit card came from. Nothing to be gained from this.'

'I've checked your website. You set the meetings up online, deal with the payments,' Isaac said.

'It saves any of the men getting smart.'

'Does it stop it?'

'Not totally. Some reckon they're smart and renegotiate another meeting with the client, cutting out the middleman.'

'And if you find out?'

'They'll never work for me again or any other agency.'

'What does that mean? Their pretty looks, their chiselled features gone forever?'

'An unwritten rule amongst the agencies,' Domett said, looking nervously at the clock on the wall.

'Somewhere to go?' Wendy asked. She was still standing, even though her ankles were aching. On the phone, hidden from sight from Bridget, Nick Domett had been charming and humorous. In person, he was a revolting, egotistical specimen of manhood.

'I need to make sure all is in order for tonight. And besides, I've given you a list of who he met, where, and a phone number.'

'The women would have paid with a card,' Isaac said.

'You've got the details. Not all of them are women. As I said, he wasn't here long, and I don't remember our working relationship to be any other than professional. But as I said, I never met the man.'

Chapter 18

Nobody liked being confronted by a police officer with a warrant card, least of all Terry Hislop, the former husband of Gwen, the one-time lover of Christine. Although Wendy, who had been given the task of travelling north up to Liverpool, wasn't sure that the latter accolade was a badge of merit, given what Christine Mason, sensing in Wendy a confidante, had unburdened about her past and present life.

'And the next-door neighbour, when Tony was drunk and out of it,' Christine had said. 'And the man in the library, and then another guest, not beautiful like Colin, but you know.'

Wendy had to confess that she didn't know and that Christine Mason had an unhealthy obsession with sleeping around with stray men, yet her love for the man that Homicide knew as Barry Montgomery remained unabated. 'My one true love, the man I had searched for all my life,' the woman had said.

Terry Hislop may have been a born and bred Liverpudlian, with a scouse accent and his mop-top hair, but he was no Beatle. Unless he was the fat Beatle. There was a fifth Beatle, Wendy remembered, but he had been tossed out in favour of Ringo Starr because he had not wanted to change hairstyle, and he was hopeless on the drums. Yet the man popped up from time to time: documentaries on the Fab Four, the life and times of Britain's most successful musical export. She had missed the mania in the sixties, and there hadn't been much time on the farm, what with collecting the eggs, ensuring that the pigs were fed, mucked out sometimes, and the two-mile walk to school, a two-mile walk back.

The thought of her childhood filled her with nostalgia, and sadness that her parents were no longer alive. Life hadn't been bad for them. Her mother had busied herself around the house, ensuring her man was fed and Wendy was looked after. Neither of her parents had ever travelled, apart from the occasional bus trip into Sheffield, a one-week honeymoon in Scarborough on the North Yorkshire coast, the photos on the sideboard in the farmhouse. And then her mother, still relatively young, a cheery red-faced woman in her early fifties, had keeled over in the kitchen and died. Her father had laboured on at the farm, and then he was gone, and Wendy was perilously edging towards the age when they had died.

'You're here about Christine,' Hislop, a man who clearly enjoyed beer and calorie-rich, oily food, his paunch testament to one, his greasy complexion the other, said.

'I understand that you and she were friendly some years ago.'

The two were sitting in Hislop's office. Down below, the sound of panel beaters at work. To Wendy, the late-model Toyota they were labouring on looked like a write-off.

'Business good?' Wendy asked.

'It's a living. Not as good as it used to be, not so many accidents. I'd do something else, but I've been fixing cars for most of my life.'

'They're better built, not so prone to damage.'

'Nowadays, a lot of plastic, swapping body panels, not a lot of working the metal with the tools. We get the occasional classic in here, and they take our time. But that's not why you're here. You've got a few questions.'

181

'Christine Mason, what can you tell me about her?'

'Beautiful woman in her day, not that I was looking that closely.'

'What do you mean?'

'I was seventeen, hormones going crazy, attempting to grab every stray female I could. I assume you don't want the version that comes with maturity and getting older.'

'You're telling it fine. You're a rampant testosterone-fuelled young man who's trying to get it off with every female.'

'Christine was a looker, probably still is.'

'You've not seen her for some time?'

'Not since I split with her sister.'

'Over twenty years, then.'

'If you say so. I've not been counting, too busy for that.'

'Busy with what?'

'Life. I worked with the tools, and then I bought this business; a couple of wives, a few live-ins.'

'Children?'

'Never been blessed,' Hislop said matter-of-factly.

Wendy wasn't sure whether the words were glib or whether the recollection of what Christine had done still hurt.

'Let's go back to when you were with Christine. What do you know of our interest in her?'

'Only what you told me on the phone, that she had known the man found in the lake.'

'Christine was conducting a clandestine affair with this man.'

'That'd be Christine.'

'What does that mean?'

'I was seventeen, but still, I had a sense of the future. Sure, I wanted to have a few too many drinks, brag to my mates about which woman I'd slept with, which one was begging for it. We all did then. Silly and childish, but when you're young…'

'At least you remember the reality, not that it helped the women, just teenagers struggling to come to terms with growing up, their bodies changing, the confusion that they wanted to be with a man, the knowledge that they'd be called a slag afterwards, the banter of drunken humour.'

'Sorry,' Hislop said. 'I touched a raw nerve.'

'You didn't,' Wendy said. 'I needed to know if you were a decent man; if I could trust you.'

'Can you?'

'Let's proceed. Christine's easy, I know that. Not only back then.'

'I was seventeen, silly and stupid as I said, but I'd known the sisters all my life, even when we were toddlers. It was always Gwen for me, but she's not the same as her sister. She's the ring on the finger type, and I was hot, and there's Christine. That's how it was. It was only a couple of times, and Gwen never knew, married me at nineteen. Happy as could be, I was.'

'You seemed to resent my coming here when I phoned you from London.'

'Just suspicious as to your motives. As I said, it's been a long time since Gwen and Christine.'

'Any chance of a cup of tea?'

Hislop called out through the office door. 'Mavis, a couple of teas if you don't mind. Two sugars and milk for me.'

'The same for me,' Wendy said. Looking at the state of the office, the general decay, the dirt on the floor,

183

it was clear to her that the business wasn't prospering and that money was tight.

Mavis came in, left the teas on Hislop's desk, smiled at Wendy, winked at Hislop. Wendy could see that the man's taste in women was suburban. Mavis was no Christine, not even a Wendy Gladstone, but a woman in her forties, her arms covered in tattoos, even the knuckles of the fingers. She also smelt of mothballs, and her taste in clothing was eclectic. All in all, Wendy had to admit to not being impressed with the man's assistant.

Wendy took a drink from her mug. 'I know about the child,' she said.

'It was only later that we found out that I was at fault. I blamed Gwen, thought that she was not getting pregnant to spite me.'

'But I thought you two were in love, destined for each other.'

'That's what I thought.'

'The marriage soured?'

'No violence, no harsh words, but the love that I felt for her didn't last, the same for her. We divorced, and that was that. I've not seen her for a very long time. How is she?'

'Both women are fine,' Wendy said. She wasn't in Liverpool to reunite old friends, to natter about past loves, lost opportunities. 'When you found out that Christine had miscarried, what did you think?'

'Angry, very angry. Confused, I suppose. When you're young, you see everything as black and white, not shades of grey.'

'And now?'

'I would have liked to be a father, but it doesn't seem so important now.'

184

'Christine through no fault of her own had cheated you out of your one chance. Is that a hatred that could lead to violence?'

'Sergeant, what are you implying? That I travelled to London, and then killed Christine's lover?'

'I need to know your level of anguish. As we feel our mortality, the slowing down, the aches and pains, the waning libido, we all reflect on our past; it's only natural. You have no legacy to pass on to future generations. Does that worry you?'

'Yes, if you must know. But the idea that I would kill someone important to her makes no sense. I'm not a violent man, not vengeful, and my libido's still active. Shooting blanks hasn't helped, but it hasn't harmed me either.'

'An alibi?'

'Whatever you want. I've not been to London in five years, and that was only for a couple of days.'

'Where did you stay?'

'Somewhere central. I can't remember the name.'

'Five stars?'

'It wasn't that good. Somewhere that looked great on the internet with its views of London, but didn't have any, not unless you climbed on the roof.'

'Thank you, Mr Hislop. I'm sorry you've been inconvenienced. You were a person of interest. I had to come and meet with you.'

'If you see either of them, please give them my best wishes.'

'I will. I like Christine, although Gwen is not so easy to read.'

'They've not changed, and yes, Christine's a good person. Did she kill the man?'

'That information is confidential. However, I hope she did not.'

'But she may have?'

'As I said, our enquiries are ongoing. I don't want her to be guilty, but whoever is the murderer, I will do my duty,' Wendy said as she thanked Hislop for his time. She thought she had wasted the day coming north, but the investigation into Terry Hislop was not closed yet.

***

Bridget spent time in the office going through the information that Nick Domett of Gents for Hire had supplied. Wendy's description of the man, charming and entertaining on the phone, disappointing in the flesh, had tempered the women's joking about him and his saucy repartee.

Larry was working with Bridget and following up on the details supplied by Domett. No surprises yet, apart from the fact that the murdered man had swung both ways, and that his clientele had included both men and women. Larry was no fool, and he'd been out on the street and into the underbelly of society. He knew of people's perversions, their needs, their weaknesses.

The first person he met up with, a chartered accountant in the city, a tired-looking man who carried his sixty-six years poorly, did not appreciate having a police inspector in his outer office, his personal assistant curious as to what was going on.

'Mr Cranwell is a great boss. I've been here eight years, and I've never seen the police here before,' the middle-aged woman said. She was an efficient woman, Larry decided. Probably lived on her own, her only company an old cat that looked just like her, minus the accoutrements, of course. But Larry realised that evaluations of people based on appearances could sometimes be wrong. Bridget dressed sensibly in the office and was as efficient as the PA, yet she had had lovers and flings, and he and Isaac always suspected that Bridget's and Wendy's trips to the sun occasionally involved more than the sun, siesta, and a tan, although in Bridget's case it was more a burn than tan.

'Inspector, what can I do for you?' Eustace Cranwell said as he opened his door. His hand outstretched, he grabbed Larry's firmly and shook it vigorously. Defence mechanism, Larry thought. A show for the PA who pretended to be looking at a computer screen, but her eyeballs were angled up. Police training and experience had taught Larry to look for the unseen. No sign of intimacy between the accountant and the woman, but then the man had been using the services of a male prostitute.

Larry walked into the man's office. It was scrupulously clean, a desk in the far corner, close to the window. On one side of the room, a large bookcase, full of mementoes, family photos, and financial books, none of which would have meant much to Larry.

With the door closed, Cranwell's manner changed, no longer the smiling welcome. 'I was disturbed by your phone call, Inspector Hill,' he said as he leaned back on his chair, attempting to look at ease, failing miserably. The man's right hand had a slight tremor: the early sign of illness, or just nerves. Larry decided on close inspection that the redness in Cranwell's face, the sweating, indicated it was nerves. The man had been sprung, and he didn't like it.

'We're investigating the murder of a man you knew as Colin Young.'

'Inspector, surely you must be mistaken. I don't know of any such man.'

'Fine. Here or at Challis Street. It makes no difference to me, but I assume you have a reputation to protect.'

'I'm well respected, a happily married man, three children, all of them making successes of their lives. A scandal would destroy them, me.'

'I'm not the moral police. If you want to indulge in whatever with another consenting male, that's down to your conscience, not mine. We need to solve a crime, and you are only one on our list. Tell me openly and in your own time where and when, and what you knew of the man, and then I'll be on my way. Probably you'll never hear from another police officer or me again. Lie, and it'll be the third degree. Do I make myself clear?'

'Perfectly.'

'In your own time,' Larry said as the man sat quietly, unsure what to say, having to speak words that he did not want to utter.

'I met Colin Young on two occasions. I have a flat near to the office. It's only small, and my wife never visits.'

'Where is your wife?'

'She's in Sevenoaks, not far on the train, but if I've been working late, then I'll stay in London for the night. It's a weakness, but sometimes…'

'I'm not here to pass judgement or to offer an opinion. I need the facts, nothing else.'

'Very well. Sometimes…'

'Please, Mr Cranwell, the sooner you talk, the sooner I'll be out of here.'

'It's just difficult, you must understand.'

'The facts.'

'I remember him well, anyone would.'

'Beautiful?'

'You met him?'

'Never, but that word's been used by others.'

'Men?'

'You're the first. Women mainly.'

'He would come over to the flat. Two hours later he would leave, set your clock by him. There's no more to tell.'

'We had him as heterosexual.'

'He was unemotional during the two hours. To him, it was mechanical.'

'To you?'

'I felt something, but afterwards, I was ashamed. I'm afraid I got drunk with a bottle of whisky after each time.'

'Yet you continued with him.'

'Only two times.'

'What about him? The sort of man to form enemies?'

'The sort of man to fall in love with.'

'Did you?'

'No. But with rejected love comes anger and then hatred then violence.'

'Are you a violent man?'

'I'm just a weak man, nothing more.'

As Larry left, the door behind him being closed quickly, the PA looked up from her laptop. 'Mr Cranwell?' she said. Larry hoped she had not been standing close to the door when the man had unburdened himself.

***

Phillip Strang

'My wife has taken a turn for the worse,' Stanley Montgomery said on the phone to Isaac.

'Serious?' Isaac's reply wasn't what the unpleasant Montgomery wanted to hear.

'If you hadn't interfered, I could have dealt with it, but now she's in the hospital, refusing to eat. They've put her on an intravenous drip, not that it's going to help, not in the long run.'

'If there's anything we can do.' Isaac knew it was the right thing to say, but what did it mean? Neither he nor the Homicide Department could change the fact that the woman's son had been murdered and her daughter had committed suicide.

'I'm holding you personally responsible, and I'll be making a public statement in due course. I'm also investigating legal action against the police in the handling of this matter.'

'That's your prerogative, Mr Montgomery. Tragic as it is, it is still a murder investigation. The truth must be revealed, the murderer brought to justice. You have been inconvenienced, as has your wife. I'm sorry about that, but that's how it is. Take legal advice if you must, talk to the press, but you will achieve little, only more sorrow for yourself and your poor wife.'

'Smooth words, Cook, but what do they mean? My wife is who I care about, not you and your precious police force. My daughter is dead because of you.'

'Because of us?'

'Yes, because of you.'

'How? We never knew of her, not even your son's true identity. If she died, it is because you told her about Barry, which means that you have lied to us. Did you kill your son?'

190

'I did not. We will talk again in the courts. My wife is dying of a broken heart, and I need to be with her.'

'Mr Montgomery, her death is on your account, not mine,' Isaac said in a rare bout of anger.

Afterwards, he sat down and reflected on what had been said, and whether the father was a murderer. But first, he needed to go to the hospital where Mrs Montgomery was. He wasn't sure if it would help; it just seemed the right thing to do.

***

Christine Mason reacted with alarm when Wendy outlined what needed to happen next.

'But you can't. My husband, my career.'

'I'm sorry, but there's no alternative. We need to bring in your manager. He's been blackmailing you, treating you as his personal plaything.'

'I will go to jail,' Christine said. The two women were sitting at the bar in the hotel, the manager hovering, but out of hearing range. They both kept to a fruit juice, although Wendy would have preferred something stiffer. She knew that she had promised to try and keep Christine out of the investigation as much as possible, but embezzlement, blackmail, a young lover, an offensive hotel manager who took his payment in money and sexual services, kept bringing the investigation back to her.

Wendy still hoped that she was innocent, just a hapless person whose weakness for affection and physical contact had brought her centre stage once again.

'I hope not,' Wendy said. 'You've cooperated with the police. That'll go in your favour.'

'My job?'

'The truth must prevail. I can't stop this. Either you work with me on this, or it'll be a black mark.'

'My husband?'

'He needs to be interviewed. We have all the pieces of the jigsaw in front of us. It is now time to complete that puzzle. Others will be hurt, and we know that Colin's mother is close to death.'

'From what? Was she a good woman?'

'Malnutrition, a weak heart, years of being brow-beaten.'

'She has suffered as well. I am sorry for her.'

'Will you cooperate?'

'If I must,' Christine said, her face downcast.

Chapter 19

Larry wasn't prepared for the next person on Domett's list. Cranwell had been polite, even if ashamed of what he had done, but it wouldn't stop him spending time and money with another man in the future. After him, there had been two other men. One was a retired police officer in his seventies, which had not been an easy interview, even though the man had answered the questions, graphically as it turned out.

Larry wasn't naive, but it was a subject he preferred to read about, not hear about, and not in the jargon used by a former police inspector. The man's alibi was watertight and he wasn't ashamed of what had occurred.

The third man, Justin Grinstead, no more than Colin Young's age, was someone who sat behind a computer screen all day, playing video games.

'I'm a nerd,' he said.

'You must need money?' Larry said, looking around him at the discarded packets of crisps, the empty pizza boxes, the general mayhem. Outside the house, it had looked fine, the home of successful people. Inside, decay.

'My parents died young, left me this house.'

'When was the last time you left it?'

'Three weeks. No reason to go out. Order everything online, pay someone to put the rubbish bin out.'

'And clean the house?'

'Sometimes, a lady comes in, but she doesn't come often.'

'Why's that?'

'She doesn't like me, I don't like her. Mutual hate and she thinks I stink. I don't, do I, Inspector?'

'Tell me about Colin Young.'

'Who?'

'Five years ago. A man described as beautiful by more than one person. A person you ordered online.'

'That's a long time ago, a few video games in the past.'

'An addiction?' Larry asked, aware that his son enjoyed video games to the detriment of his studies. There had been a minor disturbance in the Hill household when a computer expert from a local IT shop had come in and put blockers on disturbing sites that were not conducive to the upbringing of a child approaching adolescence. The games had all been deleted as well. But the expert had said, 'He'll find a workaround in a couple of weeks.'

'According to you, it is,' Grinstead said.

An unpleasant, insular individual, Larry realised. 'You've used a company called Gents for Hire?'

'I may have. What's it to you?'

'To me, nothing. I'm from Homicide. A man that you paid for using your credit card has been murdered. And I don't need graphic detail; I've already had that today. Now, do you remember him or do I have to pull the plug on your computer.'

'I've got it backed up.'

Larry walked over to the computer monitor and pressed the off switch.

'You can't do that.'

'I can, and I have. Now, do you remember the man in question?'

'Vaguely. That's it, nothing more.'

'You are obviously intelligent, yet "vaguely" is the best you can come up with?'

'There's thousands online, no need to rent them. Virtual reality, streaming internet; it's wonderful.'

Larry felt sickened by the man and what he was describing.

***

'I remember him well enough,' the owner of the final name on the list supplied by Domett said. The woman lived well, Larry could see that. She was attractive, in her fifties, older than Christine Mason. It was clear that money was not a factor in her life, judging by the antiques and the oil paintings in the penthouse flat.

'I was keen on him,' Nancy Bartlett continued. 'He'd come here sometimes, other times we'd go away for a couple of days in the country.'

'Romantic weekend?' Larry asked. He appreciated the woman's openness.

'With Colin, guaranteed. Tell me why you're here, and then I'll give you the full story. A beer, wine?'

'I'm on duty. I should keep to non-alcoholic.'

'You're not in the army. I'll fetch two beers for us.'

After both had sipped their beers for a few minutes, Larry spoke. 'I'm from Homicide.'

'I know that,' Nancy said. 'It's on the card you gave me. Is he dead?'

'Murdered.'

'The body in the Serpentine? I read about it, thought that there was a possibility that it could be him.'

'But you didn't come forward.'

'I don't see how I could have helped. He was a man who brought out strong emotions in people. Some would feel love; others, hatred and anger.'

'You're a perceptive woman,' Larry said. 'What do you reckon happened?'

'I met him through an agency. We hit it off, had a great time, and for a while I thought that he cared.'

'But he didn't?'

'Outwardly, beautiful and charming, but inside, dark secrets, a coldness.'

'How long did it last?'

'Three months, maybe four. And then the occasional meeting, coming back to here, but I had grown tired of it by then.'

'Why?'

'Marriage and fidelity never suited me, but I'm not without passion. Colin supplied it for a while, and then he was gone.'

'You missed him?'

'Not that much. Business was thriving, I was travelling a lot, and there was always another business deal to handle, another issue to resolve. Since him, the occasional man, but nothing more.'

'You mentioned others who could be moved to hatred and anger.'

'I couldn't have harmed him, but who knows about others.'

'Anyone that you had rejected in favour of the man?'

'There have been some who have attempted to lay claim to me, but I always pushed them to one side. Colin asked for nothing.'

'Money?'

'I gave him some. Gifts though, nothing more. Apart from paying the agency that first time, our relationship was based on mutual respect. I suppose you'd call me a sugar mummy.'

'Let's come back to those who hated him. There must have been some people that you know who would have been shocked by your behaviour.'

'If they were, I don't care. Most weren't though. If you're rich, a different set of rules apply, a different morality.'

Larry had another beer, as did Nancy Bartlett. He was enjoying himself when he shouldn't have been. He drew the line at the third beer and left the flat.

The woman had been open and appeared genuine in her views on love and life, but Colin Young/Barry Montgomery drew out strong emotions in people. Was it possible that the love she had had for the man five years ago had remained intact, the need to avenge his treatment of her a possibility?

***

Isaac wrestled with the complexities of the investigation, not least of all how Matilda Montgomery fitted into the picture. It was clear that she had committed suicide, that had been confirmed, but why? The woman had undoubtedly had issues, possibly severe and psychological, but she had apparently never expressed a morose view of life in general.

Everyone that had been interviewed had agreed that she revealed very little of her life, yet she had stood on a step ladder, thrown a rope over a beam, tied it off, formed a noose and then, either accidentally or intentionally, kicked the step ladder away. The death could not have been pleasant or painless, the woman gasping for breath, searching for support for her feet if she had had a last-minute change of mind. Pills would have been less traumatic, walking out into the River Thames at night, allowing the cold and the water to overcome her, more logical.

And now, another possible suspect for the murder of Barry Montgomery. In the hot seat in the interview room, Archibald 'don't call me Archie' Marshall, the manager of the Fitzroy Hotel.

It was the first time that Isaac had seen him, not the first for Wendy. It would be the two of them sitting across from him. The opportunity to bring in a lawyer of his choice had been offered to Marshall; he had declined, and it had been duly noted.

Wendy could see tension in the man, not sure what was coming. He must have realised something was amiss when Wendy had stopped him outside the hotel as he walked outside to light a cigarette. Her request, she realised on reflection, had not been made with the delicacy that it should have been. She did not like the man, a predator who had preyed on a vulnerable woman, although a woman who was not blameless in herself, a woman who would need to explain her actions in detail and to tell her husband more than she wanted to.

Wendy felt sorrow for Christine Mason, not for Archibald Marshall.

'What's this all about?' Marshall said. He scowled as he spoke, used to the staff at the hotel obeying his commands. It was not going to work at Challis Street.

Isaac said nothing until he had completed the procedure for the interview, informing Marshall of his rights and that 'whatever you say may be used in evidence…'.

Marshall, his arms crossed, nodded when required, shook his head at the appropriate times. Wendy kept her eyes firmly on him.

'Mr Marshall, we are investigating the murder of one of your guests,' Isaac said. Wendy had forewarned Isaac of her dislike of the man, which had required him to remind her that Marshall was innocent until proven guilty. The fact that he was a lecher and that he had been taking liberties with Christine Mason did not alter the need to give the man the respect accorded him by law.

'Colin Young. Yes, I'm aware of who you're referring to,' Marshall replied.

'How did you know about this man?' Wendy asked.

'I came over to Christine, asked her about her responsibilities for the day, and you said clearly that she had seen a fatal accident and that she was a witness.'

'That's what I said, so why Colin Young?'

'I quizzed Christine afterwards.'

'Why?'

'Curiosity, a concern that it may reflect on the hotel.'

'That's not the story that I've been told,' Wendy said. Isaac looked over at her. She understood to hold back for the time being.

'Tell us about Colin Young,' Isaac said.

'What's to tell? I checked the hotel records after Christine had told me the truth. He had stayed at the hotel on a few occasions, always paid his bill, and took nothing from the minibar.'

'Is that it?'

'No. But I don't want to say any more,' Marshall said.

'Why? It's important that full and frank disclosure is made now.'

'I didn't kill the man, never met him. I may have seen him, said hello, wished him well, have a good trip, that sort of thing.'

'You've seen a photo since?'

'Yes. He seemed familiar, that's all.'

'Let's come back to what else you found out,' Wendy said. She was on edge, wanting to push him, to see what else fell out.

'There were anomalies with the accounts,' Marshall said.

'Explain what you mean,' Isaac said.

'I keep an eye on the accounts. I'm not an expert, you understand, but I know enough to find discrepancies.'

'Mr Marshall,' Wendy said, 'you're selling yourself short. You know more about accountancy than you let on.'

'Very well, it's true. A hotel manager must be skilled in many areas, and with time, I picked up expertise in such matters.'

'Have you taken money from the hotel before for your personal use?' Wendy asked. She was treading lightly, not wanting to play her trump card yet.

'No. Why should I?' Marshall squirmed on his seat. 'Has anyone been saying differently? I came here of my own free will, and I'm being subjected to the third degree. I didn't kill Colin Young, you know that.'

'Mr Marshall, we don't know any such thing. You weren't in our focus before, but we have verifiable proof of embezzlement and bribery against you. The connection to murder wouldn't be that difficult,' Wendy said.

'How? Why? I know you're friendly with Christine. Is this some kind of vendetta against me because I'm a tough boss?'

'You know that's not the case.'

'Then what is it?'

'Christine Mason has been taking money from the hotel, giving some of it to Colin Young, some to you. Are you going to deny this?'

'I didn't know when she was giving it to her toy boy.'

'Toy boy, long time since I've heard that term.'

'That's what he was. I saw him prancing around the hotel, chatting up women.'

'Jealous because you didn't have his charm?'

'I manage well enough.'

'And that you do,' Wendy said. 'Not only did you find out about Christine giving him money, you then forced her to give you money as well. And services rendered as an additional benefit.'

'What does that mean?'

'You forced her to have sex with you. Did you fancy her before Colin Young? Did you see her with him, know what was going on?'

'Nothing can be proved.'

'True, nothing can be proved without Christine Mason's corroborating evidence. She's willing to tell all, even though it's her career and probably her marriage.'

'I don't believe you. And yes, we slept together, but it was by mutual consent.'

'You're not a Colin Young,' Wendy said. 'Christine was in love with him and believed it was reciprocated. And then you're putting pressure on her.'

'What you can do, Mr Marshall, is to tell us the truth, the same as Christine Mason. Hopefully, the judge will be lenient,' Isaac said.

'He won't be.'

Which meant to the two police officers that either Marshall had an innate understanding that what he had committed against Christine Mason was wrong or he had a previous criminal conviction. Bridget had checked Marshall out, found that he had been born in London and had worked in several leading hotels, and had advanced from reception into management over the years. There were no apparent black marks against him.

'That's probable. Taking money is one thing, forcing a woman to prostitute herself to protect her family is not something that a jury will warm to.'

'Christine knew the cost. And who said it was forced? It could have been consensual.'

'We'll deal with that in due course. It's not necessarily a criminal matter, even if it's distasteful, but asking her to take money for you, is. Are you willing to admit to it?'

'To what? Yes, I knew what she was doing, and I confided to her that I was willing to let her resolve the situation. There was no pressure from me for her to do anything.'

'It's your word against hers,' Isaac said. He knew Marshall was correct in what he was saying, not that it made him believe his denial. The man had a seedy look, the sort of man that would sit in the front at a strip joint stuffing pound notes into the gyrating woman's underwear, the sort of man that would…

Isaac shuddered at the thought, having spent enough time in such places, even pretending to be an avid spectator on an undercover operation. Larry had enjoyed himself, though, and he had been free and easy with police money. The stripper that night had gone home with taxpayer money, not that it had helped her the next day when she had been arrested for dealing drugs.

'Mr Marshall,' Wendy said, still maintaining her cool, 'what will the hotel say when they find out that you've condoned a crime, been part of it?'

'Nothing,' Marshall said, folding his arms and sitting back on his chair.

'Why?'

'I've already sent a report to head office.'

'Why would you do that?'

'Because I know my job. The money that Christine's taken is not that much; a criminal case against her is bad publicity. The hotel chain's senior management will make a decision as to what to do. And it's not a crime if it's not reported, is it?'

'If the hotel doesn't press charges, then maybe it's not,' Wendy conceded.

'Okay, it's not a crime,' Isaac said. 'If the senior hotel executive corroborates your story, where to from here?'

'There's nowhere. Christine will be removed from her position with a suitable payout, her record of employment unblemished.'

'And you, a criminal, will walk free.'

'Innocent until proven guilty, isn't it? Or do you have a different view?'

'Even though I find you repugnant,' Wendy said, 'there remains the issue that you used this knowledge of her wrongdoing as a lever against her. Doesn't that concern you, don't you have any concept that what you have done is wrong?'

'Ask Christine again,' Marshall said. 'I told her when I first found out about her fiddling the books for her fancy man that I'd protect her. That's what I've done.'

'She gave me a statement,' Wendy said.

'She spoke to you, but she can always rescind the statement. She's not going to jeopardise her freedom, her marriage, her respect in the community, so that you can exact your vengeance on me.'

On the one hand, the man had saved Christine; on the other, he had forced her to sleep with him. Wendy wanted to climb across the table and scratch his eyes out, but she did nothing.

'Will she continue to have sex with you?' Wendy said, her voice unsteady.

'That's up to her. Now, if you'll excuse me, I've a busy day ahead,' Marshall said standing up.'

'Not so fast,' Isaac interrupted the man leaving. 'There is still the murdered man.'

'What's that to do with me?'

'You murdered him.'

Marshall laughed, not sure whether the police officer was serious or not. 'You're clutching at straws,' he said. 'I've protected your sergeant's friend, and now you want to pin a murder on me. Why would I have killed him?'

Wendy wasn't sure of her DCI's strategy, but she'd go along with it.

'You're a smart man, maybe too smart for your own good. You'd seen Christine with the man, and then you found out that she had been taking money. Naivety on her part, but then love does that to people, not that it excuses her actions.'

'Get to the point. I don't have time for this.'

'Making you nervous? You realise where I'm going with this, is that it? Too close to home, too close to the truth? Archibald Marshall, or should I call you Archie, you are just a snivelling little street hustler. We'll be watching you very closely from now on.'

'I have my rights. You can't speak to me like that.'

'I can and I will. Let's start again. You knew that Christine Mason was a vulnerable woman. You'd seen her with Colin Young. Did you have a hidden camera in his room, watching them gyrate on the bed, imagining it was you instead of the murdered man?'

'You, Detective Chief Inspector, have a perverted mind.'

'You became infatuated with her, wanted her for yourself, but how? It consumes you, this jealousy, the realisation that you can't have her, so why should he? You hatch a plan. You're a methodical man. You run the plan through in your head: the positives, the negatives, the flaws.'

'This is errant nonsense.'

'Is it?'

'It took us a long time to find out who he was, but you may have succeeded before us. You knew the man is for hire, or he had been in the past. You had followed Christine Mason that day down to Hyde Park, knew why she was there, who she was waiting for. And then, the next day, you go down to Hyde Park and wait in the same place. The man comes jogging by, you move out quickly, a rock to the head, and he falls into the lake.'

'If I had known about her taking the money, why would I have killed him?'

'A good point,' Isaac said. 'There's one component that's missing.'

'What's that?'

'Even before Colin Young, you had fancied Christine Mason. And then, there she is, madly in love with a young man, a man you could never hope to compete with.'

'I did fancy her, even asked her out once for a meal. Harmless in itself, and she told me about her husband, and what a good man he was and how he'd be so upset.'

'Precisely. She gives you a story. It sounds plausible and you back off. And then, she's in one of the hotel rooms with another man, going hell for leather. How did it feel? The anger, the jealousy, the attempts at a gentle seduction, and a charmer takes her with no trouble. It must have hurt.'

'I did fancy her, what man wouldn't? But I never spied on her, nor did I kill her lover. After that, with him dead, and my knowledge of her embezzlement, I confronted her, told her that I knew and that I would protect her.'

'And she flung herself at you with open arms,' Wendy said.

'It wasn't as sordid as you make it out to be. I had feelings for her.'

'Very well, Mr Marshall, we will accept your statement for now,' Isaac said.

Marshall turned to Wendy. 'Christine is safe as long as you leave it as it is,' he said.

Chapter 20

Wendy wondered how Terry Hislop could have slept with one sister, married the other. But that was in the past, and no doubt he hadn't been as fat or as slovenly back then.

It wasn't important, but what Bridget had found out subsequently was. Terry Hislop had a history of violent and erratic behaviour.

'One year after divorcing from Gwen, the man took to the bottle,' she said.

'What did you find?'

'A drunken brawl at a pub close to Liverpool, three men were taken to hospital, one with a broken bottle pushed into his face, another with a ...'

Wendy interrupted. 'Hislop has a scar on his left cheek,' she said.

'Let me finish,' Bridget continued. 'Another with a broken arm after he had slammed into the bar, and the third was unconscious for two days after his head had been pushed into the floor.'

'Does that mean he's a suspect now?' Wendy said.

'Once in the past is hardly the criterion of a man capable of murder,' Larry said. 'I used to drink in my teens, got belligerent on occasions, yet ended up here at Challis Street.'

'You fixed yourself up,' Wendy said. 'Terry Hislop's not had it so good. He told me that business was fine and he was content, but who can be sure. He's running a panel beater's, and now he's got an ex-biker chick doing the accounts, sleeping with him as well if I was reading the signals correctly.'

'Long way from Christine and her sister,' Isaac said.

'You've met them both. Attractive, educated, well-dressed. His assistant wasn't any of those. He told me that the last time he'd been in London was five years ago. Any way of checking if that's true?'

'Not unless the man admits to it. Bridget said. 'What about the woman in the office? Any chance of her talking?'

'Unlikely. If the tattoos on the knuckles are any indication, she's been on the wrong side of the track on more than one occasion. She was polite to me, but only because she had to be. And Hislop looks like he can't be trusted not to do a quick respray on a stolen car.'

'Larry, any benefit in you and Wendy going up to Liverpool, giving them both the third degree?' Isaac asked.

'Not for me,' Wendy said. 'I've got to meet with Christine Mason again. We need confirmation as to whether Archibald Marshall was telling us the truth or feeding us a line.'

'What he told us will be true,' Isaac said.

'Why do you say that?'

'He knows you'll check with her. He's played it well, destroyed our case against him, protected the woman. She'll not be the same the next time you meet her.'

'Even so, I intend to.'

***

Isaac had made the trip out to the hospital to see how Janice Montgomery, the mother of Matilda and Barry, was faring. It had been a short visit, as Stanley

Montgomery had seen him arrive and had reminded him that it was a family matter, his wife was his responsibility, and that the police fishing for information about anything untoward, or an innuendo, an aside from his wife about an unrevealed truth, was not going to happen. The woman was unconscious, under medication and unlikely to see out the night.

And that was how it was: at one thirty in the morning, when the hospital was at its quietest, Janice Montgomery passed away, the only person at her side, her husband. The man had protected her all her life, or so he believed, but in the end, time and illness and heartbreak had sealed her fate.

Isaac learnt later in the day that Stanley Montgomery had wept uncontrollably at his wife's passing. Isaac felt sorrow for the man, empathy, even though neither liked nor respected the other.

Due to the woman's integral position in the murder investigation, she would be subjected to an autopsy.

Janice Montgomery's death raised ethical questions about how Homicide would continue to investigate a man who had lost two children and a wife in a short space of time, yet could still be a murderer.

Isaac met up with his senior, Chief Superintendent Goddard, a man of wisdom and experience. Goddard's office up on the top floor of the building commanded a view out over the city, whereas Homicide's two levels below looked out on a wall across the road.

'Could he have killed his son?' Goddard asked, from his side of the desk.

'Stanley Montgomery is an anachronism. He has an old-fashioned view on morality, a need to control his family, yet he protected them, and clearly loved his wife and daughter.'

'The son?'

'He had disappointed him.'

'No contact?'

'None that we know of, although our only source on that is Stanley himself. And he's not likely to tell us, not if he's guilty, or even if he's innocent.'

'We can't let a murder enquiry be prolonged out of sentimentality. If you think the man's a strong possibility, then you've got to maintain the pressure, force him to falter. And remember, he's emotionally vulnerable now. It's an easier job for you.'

Isaac left Richard Goddard's office more unsure than when he had gone in. Stanley Montgomery deserved to be left alone to grieve. It was the right thing to do, the humane thing to do, but the man did have a motive, albeit obscure and hard to fathom. But then that was the man, out of step with the modern day, holding onto a belief system that belonged to another century.

Wendy went to meet Christine Mason. The woman was contrite. She sat behind her laptop in her office at the Fitzroy. She averted her gaze, not wanting to look Wendy in the eye.

Archibald Marshall was nowhere to be seen.

'Where is he?' Wendy asked.

'He's at head office,' Christine replied. It was clear that she did not want to speak and was attempting to give Wendy the brush off. It wasn't going to work.

'Saving your skin?'

'I don't know what you mean.'

'Christine, let's get this straight. We know that Marshall has abused his position, committed a crime, even forced you to sleep with him.'

'I misjudged him. He's a good man.'

'Rubbish,' Wendy said. 'Let's be honest with each other. He's going to protect you from criminal prosecution. Now that's fine, and no doubt he thinks he's a regular Boy Scout doing his good deed for the day, but it doesn't stop the fact that he and you are guilty of a crime.'

'You've got it all wrong.'

'Have you considered the fact that he could have killed Colin Young?'

'Why?'

'Marshall's besotted with you.'

'He professes love when we…'

'When he's screwing you, is that it?'

'He wants me to say it to him as well.'

'Have you?'

'Once, but I didn't want to.'

'Christine, hold to your story if you must, but be warned. Archibald Marshall could be a murderer, and you've got the dirt on him. If he thinks his hold over you is weakening, or we're closing in, he could remove the one person who could threaten him. He's not a stupid man. If killing you will help him, he could come up behind you in this office, on the way home, when you're in bed with him. A swift blow to the head, a cord around your neck, and you're gone.'

'He wouldn't do that.'

'Why not?'

'Because he does love me. I've known that for months.'

'How?'

'The way he used to look at me, the attempts to be near me.'

211

'An intensely jealous man, he would have been upset with you and your lover.'

'He never said anything, not once, but I knew.'

'And now he's using blackmail to get what he wants. His love could be an obsession, don't you realise that, and now he's plucked the golden goose, found out that you're mortal, the same as other women.'

'I am safe with him. He will protect me. I can't say any more to you.'

Wendy stood. There was no more to say. Christine Mason was taking the only avenue open to her, but it was a dangerous route she was travelling.

As Wendy pulled the door closed on the way out, she looked back at Christine. 'If he's a murderer, you're in mortal danger. Remember that, and please phone me if you're frightened. The wrath of your husband, a possible prison sentence, are better alternatives than being dead.'

'I can't agree, but I will remember your kindness and understanding,' Christine said.

With the door closed, Christine buried her head in her hands. She knew that Sergeant Wendy Gladstone had been right in what she had said. With Archibald Marshall, her situation was perilous. She would not sleep with him again.

***

Isaac had not expected to hear from Gwen Hislop, but she had phoned him up, asked him to come out to where she lived.

Isaac arrived at the small house in Kingston upon Thames, ten miles to the south west of Challis Street Police Station. It was a tidy house, Isaac had to admit, although lacking in any charm. The garden out front was concrete, and inside the house it was functional, but nothing more. The home of an economical person, Isaac thought.

'Thank you for coming,' Gwen said. She was dressed casually, a tee-shirt that had seen better days, a pair of blue jeans. She wore no shoes, and her hair was uncombed.

'Apologies for the look, but I'm not in court today, working from home.'

'That's fine,' Isaac said as he sat down in a chair that looked old and worn, but was surprisingly comfortable. 'You said it was important.'

'Terry, my former husband, phoned.'

'You still use his surname.'

'I qualified when we were married. It was just easier to continue using it, although I've not heard from him for a long time.'

'Sergeant Gladstone went up to Liverpool to interview him. Did he mention it?'

'He didn't phone for a social chat.'

'Angry?'

'Drunk more than angry, but he wasn't friendly. On the contrary, he resented the suggestion that my sister and I had put him forward as a person of concern.'

'His words?'

'His contained some expletives. I've no intention of repeating them to you.'

'You're a lawyer. You're used to difficult, argumentative, and violent people. Why do you need me here?'

'Off the record, that's why.'

'I'm a police officer, nothing's totally off the record.'

'I can understand that, but I needed to talk to you without others listening in. No recording what we're talking about, okay?'

'Okay.'

'Terry was never violent towards Christine or me, that's a fact.'

'But?'

'After I broke up with him, and before we were divorced, he took out a friend of mine. Spite on his part, stupidity on hers.'

'It didn't go well?'

'She's no longer a friend, obviously. It didn't last long, up until he started bringing Christine and me into the relationship. Telling her that I was a bitch, and that Christine was a better lay, a better person, and he should have chosen her, not me.'

'He told Sergeant Gladstone that it was always you.'

'He had a notion of the virgin wife, I suppose. I was the virgin, Christine was the substitute. Not that I knew when I married him, not about Christine, but you know this already. Anyway, he started to become paranoid, constantly on about the bitch I was with my airs and graces, my education and then becoming qualified, aspirations of becoming a judge, a QC.'

'Was he right?'

'I never shoved it down his throat, and I certainly didn't have airs and graces. Yes, I was ambitious, but for the two of us.'

'He saw himself as the provider?'

'He was fine with me working. It was when I started bringing more money home than him of a week that he felt it. To him, it was a castration, not to me. The

214

money went into our joint account, and he had access to it.'

'An educated man, Terry?'

'Enough to get by in life, not enough to obtain professional qualifications. He wasn't stupid, on the contrary, but he didn't have the interest in completing a degree.'

'Whereas you did.'

'I worked hard, damn hard, another problem with him. He felt neglected; I felt tired.'

'The man's ego has taken a hammering, the marriage falters, and so on. It's not a unique situation.'

'Exactly. We all move on, that's how the world works. I've got my career, he's got my friend.'

'You've still not told me the reason why I'm here,' Isaac said. He enjoyed being in the woman's company, her manner of speaking, her education, both alluring characteristics.

'After this friend of mine has heard him going on about Christine and me for one too many times, she finally snaps, tells him the relationship's off.'

'His reaction?'

'He hits her, and hard.'

'Did she report it to the police?'

'No. She came around to me, asked for my advice, looking for a shoulder to cry on.'

'Were you the shoulder?'

'I was upset with her, but she hadn't done anything wrong, not really. Terry and I were separated, and he was a free agent, so was I.'

'Have you remarried, formed any relationships?'

'Not that it's important, but no. I busied myself with my career, and there has been the occasional fling, nothing serious, and certainly not love. I love my sister,

215

but we're not cast from the same die. She craves love and attention, I don't.'

'Are you worried that Terry has become violent again?'

'I'm concerned. I've no reason to take it any further, and besides, for what? He's abusive on the phone, but that's not a crime.'

'Unnecessary, though.'

'That's not the point. If he can phone me up, give me a piece of his mind, then he can phone Christine, find out where she lives. He could cause trouble.'

'According to Sergeant Gladstone, the man is still bitter about your sister. He's struggling with his business, and he's gone to seed. Old animosities, emotional conflicts could be coming to the forefront again. Could he attack Christine?'

'I don't know. And Christine is a foolish woman around men.'

'We know that. What else do you know about your sister's recent history?'

'I only know what was said at the police station. As I said, she's my sister. We don't always see eye to eye, and I don't approve of her frivolous affairs.'

'Do you know about them all?'

'No, and I don't want to. Such behaviour always leads to trouble.'

'Terry Hislop is still a suspect for the murder of Colin Young, now known to be Barry Montgomery,' Isaac said.

'It seems unlikely though. He would have killed Christine, not her lover.'

'Who knows what the state of his mind is.'

'You're correct. Please don't aggravate Terry, don't let him hurt Christine.'

'And you. He knows your phone number, he must know your address.'

Chapter 21

Janice Montgomery's autopsy revealed nothing unusual, apart from a weak heart and being malnourished, but that had been known. There was nothing to indicate that her husband, Stanley, had been responsible.

Isaac, regardless of Stanley Montgomery's aspersion that the police were to blame for his wife's medical condition before her death, had not heard from the man. Wendy had met with him on one occasion, found him to be quiet with little to say. It had been an uncomfortable conversation, and whereas there were still questions to be asked, she hadn't had the heart to ask them.

In the office at Challis Street, Bridget Halloran continued with the paperwork, ensuring that all reports were in on time, the case for the prosecution was updated.

So far, the murder count stood at one. Nobody wanted Christine Mason added to the total, and Wendy had advised her to be careful. Christine had confided that Archibald Marshall had become extremely upset at her refusal to go with him to one of the vacant rooms upstairs, and as a result he had threatened to withdraw his support for her and to ensure she paid for her crimes.

Wendy's take on Marshall's changed attitude had been to advise the woman to maintain two sets of records, one for the hotel, another for evidence that the man had also been guilty of a crime.

It was not unusual, not with arrogant, manipulative men, scheming women – it was not gender specific – the belief that if they could hoodwink their boss, or in Marshall's case the hotel chain, they could also hoodwink the police.

And with Marshall threatening Christine again, Wendy knew she'd be doubling her efforts to make sure the man did not come out on top.

Homicide Department, the early-morning meeting. The core team were in Detective Chief Inspector Isaac Cook's office. The mood was sombre.

'It's time to wrap up this case,' Isaac said. The team sat attentive, knowing that this was the make-or-break meeting where the facts were laid out before them, when everyone had to stand up and be counted, to justify their actions so far, the plans going forward.

There were enough facts, more than one possible murderer. People would need to be put under pressure, to breaking point if needed.

Isaac sat in his chair, a grimace on his face. 'Larry, what's your status?' he asked.

Larry, standing up with his back against the office door, paused for a moment before speaking. 'It's not that simple,' he said.

Not the answer that Isaac wanted to hear, but it was an open forum. It was for his detective inspector to continue.

'Consider who we have. Stanley Montgomery, the father. And then we have Terry Hislop, a man capable of violence, as well as Archibald Marshall.'

'There's no proof of violence against Marshall,' Wendy said.

'Besotted with Christine Mason? Her messing around with Colin Young? He's still a candidate.'

'Who else?' Isaac asked.

'Christine for the murder of her lover. We know he was playing around with Amelia Bentham, possibly some others.'

'We've not found any more,' Larry said. 'Not since the men and Nancy Bartlett that he was contracted out to by Nick Domett of Gents for Hire.'

'Conclusive that his escorting days were over?'

'No. It's just that we've found no more proof. If he was freelancing, picking up a woman, and as we know now, men, at clubs and hotels in London, then we've not found any evidence. Even though Nancy Bartlett and Christine Mason have admitted to giving him money, it doesn't look as though the man was a total bastard,' Wendy said.

'What do you mean by that?' Isaac asked.

Larry answered the question. 'He could have bled them for a lot more, especially Nancy Bartlett, and Cranwell, the accountant, was seriously embarrassed by his indiscretion. A closet homosexual, Cranwell; he'd not want it bandied around the city, and especially not to his wife.'

'The other men?' Isaac asked.

'I don't think they would have cared. I'd go for either Cranwell or Nancy Bartlett.'

'With Cranwell, it's fear of being outed? With Nancy Bartlett, it's anger at being dumped?' Wendy said.

'That's about it. Mind you, she never gave the impression that she was a vengeful woman nor was she angry when I interviewed her,' Larry said.

'Christine Mason doesn't give the impression that she's a cheating wife, either,' Wendy said.

'Anyone else?' Isaac asked.

'There are more, we just need to prioritise.'

'Amelia Bentham?' Bridget said.

'She made out that the relationship was casual, but she's at the settling down age, not the one-night stand. It could have been serious from her side,' Wendy said.

'And she could have said something to Matilda, the reason that the woman committed suicide.'

'We're clutching at straws,' Isaac said. 'Where are the solid facts? Wendy, you've spent time with Amelia Bentham. What do you think? And none of that "I hope it isn't her".'

'She comes from a stable family background. She's successful, attractive, and she's got a lot going for her.'

'But not ruled out.'

'No. But we have violent men that we need to exclude first.'

'The death of Colin Young didn't require too much strength.'

'Hitting him hard on the head, ensuring that he fell into the water doesn't automatically ensure death, though,' Larry said.

'We've been through this before. The blow was of sufficient force to render the man unconscious, and there was no attempt to rescue him. The water in the Serpentine's not that deep; cold, though.'

'The person who hit him panicked, left the area quickly. It would have been half light, misty, and maybe they were frightened, regretting what they did,' Wendy said.

'You're not a defence lawyer for Christine Mason,' Isaac said. 'You're a police officer. If she hit him and he fell into the water and drowned, it's still murder.'

'I'm not trying to get her off. I'm just stating facts. Stanley Montgomery's not the sort of person to leave the man's death to chance. He would have waited around to be certain that he'd been successful. Terry Hislop would have hit the man hard, but why would he kill him, rather than Christine or Gwen? And why now? After so many years, he comes to London and kills the lover of the woman who had once carried his child? And how would he know about the man?'

'Only if he had been keeping a watch on Christine for some time,' Larry said. 'We've checked his movements on the day of the murder. He's still a low bet for this.'

'He phoned Gwen Hislop, got angry with her, started threatening,' Wendy said.

'Not good enough. He wouldn't have appreciated us dragging him into the local police station, giving him the third degree when we went up there yesterday. He kept his cool with us, but Gwen, she's an easy mark. Unless you've got anything better, he was just venting his spleen, voicing his anger.'

'Stanley Montgomery's a methodical man. He doesn't leave anything to chance. And Terry Hislop's anger is impulsive. Judging by his business, he's not methodical, not much of anything really.'

'Amelia Bentham?'

'An alibi for the day of the murder.'

'Solid?'

'Solid enough,' Wendy said.

'Which brings us back to who?'

'Tony Mason, he's the only person with a possible motive that we've not spoken to.'

'Sorry, Wendy. He's got to be interviewed,' Isaac said.

***

Three women sat down in the front room of Gwen Hislop's house. There had been an attempt at making the place homelier: some flowers in a vase, rearranging the furniture.

Wendy could never ascribe to herself the title of home decorator, yet her house was loved, and she had a family who visited regularly, the grandchildren always bringing a crayon painting for her or a handicraft they had made at school. On her mantelpiece, the framed photos of her two sons when they were young, the buckets and spades on the beach, building sandcastles, her and her husband reclining on deckchairs. And then, over the years, photos of the sons' marriages, the grandchildren soon after birth. But in Gwen Hislop's house, there was not one photo, no sign of anyone else but herself. Wendy thought that it was a sad house, a house that had not known love for many years.

'Sergeant Gladstone, Wendy,' Gwen said. 'Shouldn't we be meeting at the police station?'

'I need to talk to you two. I need you both to know what we must do.'

Gwen had prepared snacks for the three of them, as well as a pot of tea, three cups. Nothing was said while the women ate and drank. The air was heavy in the room, the atmosphere reflecting the fear etched on Christine's face, the importance on Wendy's about what she had to say.

'What is it?' Gwen said, breaking the silence.

'Christine,' Wendy said, looking over at the woman, 'we have interviewed all those with a reason to have wanted to harm Colin Young, or as we know him now, Barry Montgomery.'

'You're evading what you want to say,' Gwen said.

223

'We must bring in Christine's husband. He needs to be interviewed.'

'But you said you'd protect me,' Christine said. Her face showed panic. Archibald Marshall was threatening her, although he wouldn't get far, as Wendy wouldn't allow that, but Tony Mason was another issue.

'I always told you that I could only do my best.'

'It was always going to happen,' Gwen acknowledged.

'But Tony? You promised,' Christine said. She was shaking. 'I don't know what he'll do.'

'Let's be honest here, amongst us three,' Wendy said. 'Colin Young wasn't the first man you had had an affair with, was he?'

'Yes, no…'

'We're trying to help you here.'

'No. He wasn't the first,' Christine admitted. She had already told Wendy on a previous occasion that was the case. Wendy had not wanted to remind her of her earlier admission.

'You were always a slut,' Gwen said. Wendy wasn't sure if she was being critical of her sister, or saying it for effect, light-hearted teasing.

'But Tony?'

'Did your husband ever find out about the other men?' Wendy asked. She knew she was treading lightly, trying to protect a woman who might still be a murderer.

'I never gave him reason to believe there were other men.'

'How?'

'You know how. You don't need me to elaborate, do you?'

'Sergeant Gladstone doesn't,' Gwen said.

'You continued to sleep with your husband, or did you overdo your affections? The candlelit dinner, the soft music, the lingerie, the early night? Any of that when there was another man,' Wendy asked.

'I may have.'

'And your husband said nothing?'

'Never.'

'Let's assume the man's a complete moron, not that I believe he is. Did your husband receive the same special attention when you were with Colin Young?'

'We're not as young as we were.'

'And he still didn't figure it out. Christine, you're a sensual woman, and you're not that old. Your husband's busy with work, he comes home late at night, or he's away for a few weeks, and there you are, cold, passionless.'

'I wasn't cold. I did my duty.'

'Your duty? The man would know you were up to something. He probably knew about the others, but as you said, he's entertaining clients, laying on women for them, taking one or two for himself. You knew when he was, and do you think he didn't sense the change in you?'

'He never said anything.'

'You're there giving him the works. He lies back and thinks of England or something like that. He's got a good thing going, he knows that. He weighs up the options. He can have you eager and willing, as well as other women overseas, whores out of Ukraine, the women that frequent the bars in Dubai and throughout the Middle East. He's got it made, so he makes a decision, but by your own admission, Colin Young comes along. You fall in love, you change towards your husband.'

'I might have, but he never said anything.'

'He's had his fill overseas. You're the icing on the cake, and he's tired, and it's been a long trip. He lets it pass, but he's suspicious.'

'Could he have found out, Christine?' Gwen asked.

'I might have had a phone number on a piece of paper, another phone in my handbag.'

'Your husband has to be told about Colin Young. He needs to convince us that he's not involved in murder,' Wendy said.

'Does he have to know?' Christine said, her voice almost a whisper.

'Either you tell him, or we do.'

'I must, but not on my own. What will happen to my marriage, to me?'

'I don't know. All I know is that we must pursue this investigation. Where is your husband now?'

'At home. He arrived last night.'

'Candlelit dinner, the lingerie, the early night?'

'He was tired.'

'Did you try?'

'No, I couldn't.'

'Why?'

'I'm certain he killed Colin.'

'And when did you come to this conclusion?' Gwen asked. She was not looking at her sister with love.

'Who else would have wanted him dead?' Christine said.

'That's not good enough. Colin Young brought out strong emotions in people. We're going to give them all the third degree, including you before this is finished. I hope for your sake that your conscience is clear and that you are innocent,' Wendy said.

'I will be with my sister,' Gwen said.

'We are going to Christine's home now. Will you be coming?'

'Yes. Christine cannot talk to him alone.'

Chapter 22

Amelia Bentham, freshly returned from a photo shoot overseas, did not mind the visit from Isaac Cook to her house in Pembridge Mews. She was not so keen on him being accompanied by his detective inspector.

Wendy, who had formed a friendship of sorts with the Bentham family, was otherwise occupied with Christine Mason and her sister, and now, Christine's husband.

'Miss Bentham,' Isaac said as the three sat in the main room of the mews house, 'there are still unanswered questions.'

'I've told you all I know,' Amelia replied. Isaac could see that she was an attractive woman, a little on the skinny side for him, but then all top models were. And for someone who had just spent three days in the Caribbean, her skin was still pasty white.

'We know that you've spent time with Sergeant Gladstone and that she's been up to your family home, met your family. Wendy's been thorough, but now we're in the wrap-up stage. It's the time to re-interview all those who might know something more, to re-examine the original statements, to look for the minutiae, the unimportant detail that was not picked up, or which the witness deemed of little relevance or just plain forgot.'

'Nothing to worry about,' Larry said, although he wasn't sure if that was entirely correct.

'You were friendly with Barry and Matilda Montgomery?' Isaac said. He was sitting directly across from Amelia, Larry was off to one side. The decision to interview her in her house rather than at Challis Street Police Station was to keep her calm and relaxed, to gently entice whatever they could from her.

'Matilda was a friend; as much of a friend as she could be.'

'What do you mean by that?'

'We're going over old ground here. Your sergeant knows all this. She must have written a report for you,' Amelia said.

'She has, but humour us. As I said, the minutiae often get missed.'

'There was a barrier with her. Sure, she'd tell you about her family, her life, growing up, but it was only if you asked, and then her replies were short. None of the memories, the anecdotes that a child carries into adulthood.'

'Did you press the point with her?'

'No. Why should I? She was a friend, someone to spend time with, someone I trusted and respected. There's no need for me to know of her past, no need for her to know of mine.'

'According to Sergeant Gladstone, you had a happy childhood, loving parents.'

'I was fortunate. I took Matilda to meet them once when we were in London, a good restaurant in Knightsbridge. They had met her before, but this time it didn't go well.'

'We didn't know about this before,' Larry said.

'It didn't seem important,' Amelia said.

'We'll be the judge of that.'

'Very well. It was a Thursday night, eight in the evening. Matilda and I grabbed a taxi and headed over to the restaurant. She wore a dress, I was wearing jeans and a white blouse. We're a casual family, the Benthams, when

I'm not modelling, or my parents aren't flaunting their title.'

'Wendy said they didn't do that,' Isaac said.

'Never if they could, but sometimes there's a charity function that they need to attend. My parents do what they can to help the less fortunate. Not that it's as much as they'd like, but every little bit helps.'

'Let's come back to the restaurant,' Larry said. 'What happened?'

'We were into the second course, and my mother asks Matilda about her childhood, starts talking about how I had a pony when I was six, and then a horse, and the places I'd been and how much they loved me.'

'And?'

'The more my mother spoke, well-meaning you understand, the more morose Matilda became. It was as if a wall was descending. My mother's a one glass of wine person, but because the atmosphere was so congenial, she was onto her second, and she was talking more than she should have, not reading the signals.'

'How did Matilda respond?'

'That's it, she didn't. She made an excuse about not feeling well, thanked my parents and left the restaurant. It was surreal, her leaving like that. I hadn't warned my parents beforehand that Matilda had a dark side, but with my mother, slightly tipsy, it wouldn't have made any difference.'

'Did you speak to Matilda about it afterwards?'

'I let it pass. I knew her well enough to leave well alone.'

'Barry Montgomery, friend?'

'Wendy's told you, hasn't she?' Amelia said without emotion.

'We know that you were lovers, shared the same bed on occasions.'

'It wasn't a relationship, no declarations of love.'

'Now, this is where we have a problem,' Larry said. 'Everyone that he's been involved with has described him as beautiful, and some have professed love for the man.'

'Your sergeant has told me of some of it. Not that I ever knew. He wasn't in Matilda's house all the time, but when he was, he was the brother; and if I were free, then we'd get together. We didn't talk about much, certainly not about his childhood, and I had no intention of introducing him to my parents.'

'Why not your parents?'

'They'd make a fuss, tell me what a lovely man he was, and how I'd not find better. My mother's keen on grandchildren, someone to maintain the family line.'

'Did you learn anything about his sister and his childhood?'

'Not really. I knew there was a problem, he told me that much, but he didn't elaborate, and I certainly didn't push the point. I suppose I should have some shame telling you this, but I don't. When Barry was here with me, conversation was the last thing on our minds.'

'A good lover?' Isaac asked, slightly envious of the dead man.

'The best,' Amelia said, a grin on her face – aimed at Isaac, not Larry.

'Did Sergeant Gladstone tell you about his time as an escort, his involvement with a married woman?'

'I'm not sure that she told me everything.'

'What she told you, and we'll go over this in a minute, were you shocked?'

'My view, as well of that of my parents, is not to pass judgement on people. If they mind their own business, don't interfere in ours, and don't offend or commit crimes against others, then I don't have an opinion.'

'A broad statement,' Larry said.

'I don't think so,' Amelia said. 'You asked a question, I gave you an answer. Tell me this, did Barry commit any crime?'

'There are some who believe that prostitution, the selling of sexual favours, should be a crime, but no.'

'Then why should I be concerned? If he made some women happy and he was paid in return, then that was his business, not mine.'

'And if he was doing this while sleeping with you?'

'If I had known, then he would have been sleeping in his own bed. As I said, our relationship was casual, and if I needed someone…'

'You have a few you could phone?' Isaac said.

'I wouldn't have, though. I'm not that easy, but Barry not telling me about the others would have been an issue. It's the deception that I would disapprove of, not the act.'

'We know that he was also contracting himself out through an escort agency. Did you know about this?'

'Wendy told me.'

'It wasn't only women,' Larry said.

'While I was sleeping with him?'

'We have no proof of his homosexual activities after he met you.'

'If he was still alive and I knew of this, then I would have been upset with him. But he's dead, and he's not coming back. I have no intention of slandering the dead.'

'The homosexual act offends you?'

'Not in itself. My only concern is my health. I trusted him, and he didn't use a condom. I could have caught something from him.'

'Have you checked yourself out?' Isaac asked.

'The first thing I did after Wendy told me some of the details. I'm fine, nothing to worry about.'

Isaac looked around the room. He could see that she was not a cold woman emotionally: photos of her family, an enlarged picture of a horse on the wall, mementoes from her trips overseas.

'Let us come back to your time with Barry,' Larry said.

'I believe we've exhausted the subject. He was a good man, an even better lover,' she said. 'No emotional entanglements, no discussing the state of the economy, climate warming or whatever. We met, here or once in Matilda's house, and that was it.'

'Barry had a profound effect on everyone he met,' Isaac said, unable to contain the need to confront the woman. 'Why and how have you remained unemotional?'

'Upbringing, emotional restraint,' Amelia replied. The two police officers could see that she was becoming tired of the interview.

'You were a few years younger than Barry. From what we've been told, he was a good catch.'

'Told by whom?'

'Those he was involved with.'

'Gay men and older women, is that it? They're hardly a cross-section of society. I could never allow myself to fall for a man like Barry.'

'Why?'

'I'm not a snob, far from it, but whoever marries me will have a say in the running of the family's business, the ancestral home, access to a lot of money. My emotions are in check until I find the right man.'

'Aristocratic, public school, a friend of royalty?'

'Not at all. My parents would disapprove if I used those as the criteria. I need someone I can understand, an open book.'

'The right school, knows how to use his cutlery?' Isaac was baiting the woman, probing to see if she would make a mistake.

'I wouldn't care if he was government educated, the son of a labourer, even if he grew up on a council estate. Barry, I judged, did not have what I want. And sure, I tried to get through to Matilda, as well as Barry, but both of them were mentally compromised by what I could only judge as a difficult childhood.'

'Have you found anyone suitable yet?'

'Not yet. I'm still young enough, and I'm not a demanding woman looking for an impossible ideal.'

'If you had fallen for him, you would have.'

'I've told you once too often now, I kept my emotions in check. I'm not a foolish or frivolous woman. I'm not looking for an Adonis, just someone who'll look after me and the family name, that's all.'

Isaac deemed that there was no more to be gained. He thanked Amelia Bentham for her time, and he and Larry left the house.

***

Tony Mason sat on a kitchen chair, having refused to make himself more comfortable. The man had been suspicious when it had been Wendy who had entered the house first, her warrant card opened for him to see.

'Sergeant Wendy Gladstone, I'm here with Christine and Gwen,' she said.

'What for?' Mason's reply. 'And why Gwen? She's not been here for years.' He looked over at his wife. 'Friends with your sister again, is that it?'

'I'm in trouble,' Christine said, her face almost stiff, with no movement, no blinking eyes, her nervous tremble a giveaway to Gwen who had her arm around her sister.

'It's serious,' Gwen said. 'I'm here as Christine's sister, also as her lawyer. We've agreed to talk to you here, not at a police station.'

'Are you under arrest?' Mason said to his wife. Wendy observed no sign of affection between the two, just a look of accusation from one to the other.

It was a good house, Wendy could see that. Upmarket, the stockbroker belt for those with high annual incomes, but if, as reported, Tony Mason was selling weapon guidance systems into the Middle East, then his salary had to be high. Higher than the house would suggest, she thought, not that she knew much about weapons' sales, let alone guidance systems.

'No,' Christine replied. 'Nothing like that, but someone's been murdered. I had hoped to keep you out of it, but the police tell me that I can't.'

'Did you kill this person?' Mason said. The tone was accusatory, Wendy noted. She wasn't sure if that was the man's manner or whether there was more to it.

'I've killed no one, but I'm involved. I knew the man,' Christine said. She was also sitting on a chair, her eyes downcast, not making contact with her husband's.

'I don't like other people to be around,' Tony Mason, a less commanding presence than Wendy had imagined, said. She had thought that he would look like a senior politician, distinguished, his voice authoritative and forceful. On the contrary, he was a smallish man, no taller than Christine, with greying hair, a slight paunch, and most noticeably, a squeaky voice.

'It has to be this way, Tony,' Gwen said.

'Then let's get it out in the open,' Mason said. 'It gives us a starting position.'

'This is not a trade deal,' Wendy said. 'This is a serious matter, and you, Mr Mason, by default, are a suspect.'

'*Me*? What have I done? You come in here, tell me there are a few questions and that I'm about to hear bad news, not that I've heard it yet. And now I'm a murderer. Someone had better start talking quick, or I'm out of here.'

'I'm afraid, Mr Mason, I've taken the precaution of making sure there's a police car outside, a couple of uniforms. The only place you can go to from here is Challis Street Police Station. Not that I want to do that, as what you are about to hear is bad enough.'

'Then tell me what it is.'

'I was involved with the man,' Christine said, her eyes still downcast.

Wendy looked at Tony Mason, attempted to see signs of the man's reaction to what to most would be startling news. She could see none.

'An affair? If that's what it is, then say so. I can't stand this beating around the bush. A spade is a spade, not a fork or a shovel. If you've been screwing him, then say so. It'll explain why I've been getting the cold shoulder these last few months. There I am, out there in

236

the desert, attempting to put the food on the table, and what do I get? You, flat on your back. *Thank you very much.'*

It was a reaction, that was plain to see, but whether it was feigned or real, Wendy couldn't tell.

Christine Mason raised her head and looked her husband in the face. 'Yes, it was.'

'Not the first, is it? I had hoped you had got over screwing around, but that was asking for too much, wasn't it?'

Wendy looked over at the woman's sister, hoping to catch her eye, hoping to see if she could gain some inkling from the woman about the exchange between the two people.

'You were away for so long,' Christine said.

'I was working, not screwing around.'

'I need affection.'

'You need something else, and it's not that.'

'Mr Mason, Christine, regardless of the traumatic circumstances of this meeting, we need to address certain issues,' Wendy said.

Tony Mason stood up and walked into the other room. He returned shortly with a glass of whisky. 'You'll forgive me, I'm sure. Today's not turned out well,' he said. He smiled at Wendy, cast a glance at his wife, looked at Gwen, holding his gaze on her for a few seconds. His facial expression gave no sign of emotion, one way or the other.

'Mr Mason, a frank and honest admission,' Wendy said. 'Did you suspect your wife of having an affair?'

'Suspect, yes. But that doesn't mean I killed the man. Or does it? It's happened before. Has Christine told you?'

'We are aware of past relationships.'

'Relationships? That's a fancy word for what she gets up to. Don't expect me to be shocked or upset by what's been revealed. My wife has an unhealthy appetite for men.'

'It's not unhealthy,' Christine said. 'If you hadn't been so career-driven, none of this would have happened.'

Wendy was there as a police officer, not as a marriage guidance counsellor; she needed answers. 'You can discuss your marriage issues afterwards,' she said. 'What I need now is for you, Mr Mason, to tell me what you knew of your wife and Barry Montgomery, Colin Young as she knew him. Did you know?'

'Not about him, but I knew something was happening.'

'Relevant?'

'Not to you, it isn't. I killed no one, never have, never will.'

'Yet you sell weapons to countries that suppress their citizens, wage war on others.'

'Guidance systems, not weapons.'

'The same thing,' Wendy said. 'You must have seen them being used, people being killed.'

'I'm a salesman, government-sanctioned. I do my duty, look after this family. I don't screw around, and I don't kill people. Period! Is that clear?'

'Mr Mason, do you realise that you've raised your voice, that you are angry, that you are capable of killing someone who gets between your wife and you? Do you love your wife?'

'What sort of dumb question is that? I'm meant to love a tart, a woman who screws a younger man because he's more of a stud?'

'No one's mentioned that this man was younger.'

'I assumed he was.'

'Why? According to Christine, her past relationships have been with men more her age. You're holding something back. What's the truth?'

'There is no truth. I don't know any more than I've already told you.'

Wendy took her mobile from her handbag and made a call. 'Inside, now,' she said.

'I'm afraid, Mr Mason, that you will need to be interviewed at Challis Street Police Station, suitably cautioned and with a lawyer present.'

'Are you arresting me for murder?'

'No. But you knew of your wife's affair. You have gone from being a peripheral witness to a major suspect.'

'Gwen, I'll need you with me?' Tony Mason said, looking over at her.

'Yes. And Christine?'

'I still want her, even though she drives me crazy sometimes.'

'Are you coming voluntarily? Wendy said.

'No need for handcuffs. Let me get my coat, and we can go,' Mason said.

Chapter 23

On the way over to Challis Street Police Station, Tony Mason had made a few phone calls from the back seat of the police car, one of the officers telling Wendy afterwards. Not that there was an issue; the man was coming in voluntarily for questioning, he hadn't been charged, and with mobile phones, how could they stop him phoning anyway.

Wendy had to agree with the officers. The man had his rights, innocent until proven guilty, but his reference to a younger man had not been expected.

Mason sat in the interview room; across from him, Isaac and Wendy. To Isaac, he was a man who kept his emotions in check. But then, from what Isaac had read about negotiating commercial deals in the Middle East, it was an extended process involving the initial courtesies, then the outright disagreements, then the consolidation, the renegotiation, the arguments yet again, before patting the other on the back, the words of conciliation and friendship and a lasting relationship. It took a competent man to handle that. To Mason, sitting in Challis Street would be seen as a minor inconvenience.

The reason for Gwen Hislop to be representing him was unclear. If the man had connections, then he would have been phoning for a QC, not asking for his wife's sister, competent as a lawyer, but not with a murder investigation.

'Mr Mason,' Isaac said after the formalities had been dealt with, 'Sergeant Gladstone was not satisfied with your responses to some of the questions that were asked at your house.'

'Chief Inspector, my wife tells me that she's having an affair. How do you expect me to answer? I was upset, not thinking straight,' Mason replied.

Isaac was aware that he would need to be on his guard with Mason. He liked to control the questioning in the interview room and to ensure that the person opposite him wasn't able to take control. But Tony Mason was a skilled negotiator, a man who could hold his own against the very best. And even now, was Mason telling the truth, or was it all a show? Was the man seething about his wife? Or was it a feigned response? And what about the reference to a younger man? A stab in the dark, a lucky guess?

'Could you please explain your reaction to your wife's confession?'

'Stunned. Not that it was unexpected. It was just that it was so sudden, and then Gwen's there, a woman who I've not seen for years. Not only that,' Mason said, 'a police sergeant is waving her badge under my nose, asking if she can come in. What do you expect me to say or do? How would you feel if your house was invaded, and then your wife tells you she's been screwing around with a murdered man?'

Isaac had to concede the man had a point, not that it meant that what he had told Wendy at the house, and what he intended to say in the current interview, was the truth.

'I'll grant you that it was difficult for you. But now, we must focus on what you know about the murdered man.' Isaac said.

'Nothing. I assumed he was younger. Christine's got wandering eyes. A few drinks in her, and well, you never know.'

'Your wife has told us about the murdered man and three other men. Did you know about the others?'

'One of them. I suspected another, but I never said anything.'

'The normal reaction would have been to confront the man, ask your wife to her face.'

'Normal, what's normal, Chief Inspector? How would you have handled it?'

'I'm not the person being questioned. You are.'

'Both times I let it pass, gave it a few weeks. Once she had got it out of her system, she changed back to what she had been before. And besides, the children were young, and I didn't want to disturb their lives.'

'Mr Mason, have you had an affair?'

'What sort of dumb question is that?'

'It's not dumb, only necessary. You're overseas, negotiating substantial export deals for your company. The temptation must be there.'

'Business is conducted differently over there, but you must know that.'

'I'm aware of what happens. You've still not answered the question.'

'I have. What more do you want from me?'

The door to the interview room opened, a ginger-haired, freckled-faced constable came in. 'Apologies, but you're needed outside, DCI,' he said. Isaac acknowledged the man. He paused the interview, knowing that interruption could only mean one thing: someone senior needed to talk to him.

Outside in the corridor, Detective Chief Superintendent Goddard. 'You've got Tony Mason in there?' he said.

'We have reason to believe that he is concealing evidence,' Isaac said.

'Is he the murderer?'

'He's not the only suspect. We've got no proof, but his testimony has given us reason for concern.'

'I've had Commissioner Davies on the phone.'

'And?'

'He's the head of the London Metropolitan Police, as you well know. "And" is not an appropriate response.'

'Government interference?'

'Are you likely to charge Mason with murder?'

'Are we being told to back off?'

'No. Davies is worried. Your Mr Mason is currently negotiating a deal to sell more than one hundred million pounds of technology to Saudi Arabia. If he secures that, then there are other companies lining up behind him to sell even more. The man's important, and he's sat in the interview room getting the third degree from you.'

Isaac didn't like it, but it wasn't the first time that he had come across 'in the national interest' in a murder investigation.

'What do you want us to do?'

'Unless you can prove it…'

'Not yet. But he knows something, I know it.'

'A hunch is no good with Mason. If you've got proof, I'll back you up.'

'Commissioner Davies?'

'He has people to report to; we all do.'

'A murderer could walk free. Until he's concluded the deal in the Middle East, is that it?'

'The politicians will tell you there are hundreds, possibly thousands of British jobs at stake. They'll not say they've got their fingers in the trough, and it's their seat in Parliament that's at risk.'

'And a murderer walking free is the cost?'

'Not while I'm the chief superintendent, it won't be.'

***

Wendy had not been pleased when Isaac had returned to the interview room and ended the interview, citing additional evidence, and saying that Mason was free to go.

She had watched the three people leave the station. Tony Mason had got into the back seat of a Jaguar. Christine and Gwen had taken a taxi. To Wendy, the investigation into Mason was not over, but as her DCI had explained, 'We're being told to back off, and only to question Tony Mason when we have proof.'

'What then?'

'We need to inform Chief Superintendent Goddard first, is that it? Ask for permission to charge a murderer?'

'We still do our job.'

Isaac could understand his sergeant's frustration, but there was still more to do. Mason was a person of interest, although he had been out of the country when Colin Young/Barry Montgomery had died. Not conclusive in itself as the man had influential friends, people who would return a favour for him, or place him in their debt.

Isaac could see that they were heading into the realm of conspiracy theory, and if it was someone unknown who had committed the murder, then it was a safe bet that the person would have been professional. Hitting the man on the head in Hyde Park, his subsequent drowning, still had the feel of amateurism. He dismissed his previous thought and walked over to Larry Hill's desk.

'Someone up high forcing their hand again, is that it?' Larry said. He was leaning back, his hands behind his neck.

'Thinking again? Isaac said sarcastically, although he knew his inspector was not a man to be idle for long.

'Just going over the investigation in my mind. We're focussing on the more likely characters, the men, and all three of them have negatives against them. Mason trades in weapons of death, Terry Hislop had a spell as a drunken brawler, and Archibald Marshall comes across as a despicable individual.

'What's your point?'

'It seems illogical, leaving the man's death to chance. What if he had managed to get himself ashore and onto the bank?'

'We've spoken about this before. The man didn't, and it's still murder.'

'But it could have been an accident, the man falling in, the other person not remaining there; or if they had, not knowing what to do. Not everyone can swim, and early in the morning, a light mist, the water cold, maybe whoever it was panicked.'

'We're making excuses. We need whoever it is, then we can decide on the charge. The judge and jury can decide on the penalty.'

'Terry Hislop's a strong man, but Gordon Windsor said that the blow could have been inflicted by a weaker person. Mason's not in the country, and Archibald Marshall is a lecher, embezzler, but we've no evidence of violence against him.'

'Are you saying we refocus on the women?'

'Them or a gay lover.'

'Apart from the man selling himself in the past, we've got no reason to doubt that he was anything other than heterosexual.'

'He can't have been. What he did with those men would have been abhorrent if he was totally straight. He was bisexual at the very least. There may still be someone out there that we don't know of.'

'Any suggestions as to how we find out?'

'Your policing friend, Nick Domett.'

'I don't even remember the man,' Isaac said, conceding that Larry had a point.

'Haul him in, give him the third degree if you think it will help.'

'We could sweat Christine Mason, Wendy's sure that she's holding something back, or we could subject Amelia Bentham to a more intensive interview.'

'Pursue the angle of another lover,' Isaac said. 'If we have something else against the women, then bring them in. No holding back this time.'

'Not unless they're Tony Mason with his political friends.'

'I doubt if they're friends.'

***

Nick Domett sat glum-faced in the interview room at Challis Street Police Station. Isaac studied the man through a two-way mirror, still trying to figure out if he remembered him, whether there was anything from back then that could be used to advantage in the interview. Finally, Isaac conceded that the man was a mystery to him from back then, a mystery now.

Domett ran a male escort business out of a seedy office, an impressive website as its front to the world. And there, clearly laid out, the fact the men were supplied for social activities, not sexual. It was a joke in that no one believed what they read, and that anyone who paid plenty for the men to be with them wanted them for affection, for sex. And in Colin Young/Barry Montgomery's case, it had been both men and women who had used his services.

Yet none of the women that currently knew him personally believed that he was gay or that he was bisexual. Christine Mason had been indignant at the suggestion; Amelia Bentham had adopted a more laissez-faire approach, restating that her sleeping with the man was purely physical, with no emotional content, and if he swung both ways, it didn't concern her, unless her health had been endangered.

Amelia Bentham concerned the team, even Wendy. Attractive, successful, a capable and confident woman, they would all agree, yet the unemotional reaction about the murdered man didn't hold up. She had a cat in her house, a neighbour feeding it while she was away, which she showed affection to. And she was close to her parents. Wendy hadn't said it, not to anyone in the station, but she had gone through a promiscuous period, and even if the men had not always been the most attractive, she had to admit that she had felt a degree of affection for them.

But in the case of the dead man, Amelia held to her story of no emotional content. She had not even shed a tear over Matilda Montgomery. Upset and shocked at the time of finding the woman's body hanging from a beam in her house, she had soon recovered.

But Amelia wasn't the person in the hot seat. It was Nick Domett, and he was edgy, barely able to sit still. Across from him were Isaac and Larry.

What's this all about?' Domett said.

'We're drawing blanks on this case,' Isaac said.

'I told you all I know. What else do you want from me?' The procurer of men for hire had a manner that irritated, a voice that was rasping, an open-necked shirt that looked as though it would benefit from a washing machine and an iron.

'That's the problem,' Larry said. 'Have you? Have you told us everything that you know about the man? You were able to give us the records from five years back about the man and who he had been rented out to. Too easy for us to trust you.'

'I keep meticulous records,' Domett said. 'What do you want from me? I run a legitimate business, pay my taxes the same as everyone else.'

'This is not personal,' Isaac said. 'You were a policeman, you know the drill.'

'A man who I never met is murdered, and just because I employed him, contracted him out, took a percentage of what the man earned, I'm somehow involved.'

'An interesting point you've raised there. Are you involved?'

'This is in the realm of fantasy. I've got my rights, and unless the law has changed since I was a police officer, then I'm here voluntarily, and I can leave at any time.'

'And we can follow up on what you said to our Bridget Halloran, check if you've detailed the sexual

248

services to others that you offered to her. You must have disgruntled clients who were expecting a night of high romance and sexual ecstasy, only to be provided with a boring man who could barely maintain an erection.'

'Satisfaction guaranteed, that's the company's motto.'

'Don't force us to check. Tell us what we need to know, and we'll not get the vice squad to go through your records and your clientele.'

'I've nothing to hide.'

'Even if that's true, it'll destroy your business. Word gets around quickly, and confidentiality is all important.'

'You're right, of course. Some of my clients wouldn't want the facts known.'

'Then let's go back to the dead man. You gave us names, one of which was a woman. Were there more? Who were they?'

'Seeing that I was one of the police force's finest…' Domett said. He had a look of resignation.

'The London Metropolitan Police would not regard you as that if you've been holding back,' Isaac said.

Domett ignored the slight on his character. 'I never met Colin Young back when he worked for me, and that's the truth. Quite frankly, the man was difficult to work with.'

'Why?' Larry asked.

'He was good, and he knew it. He wanted more money than I could pay. The woman was the most demanding. She wanted him more than once, but when I told her the increased price, she backed off, called me a few words I'd rather not use.'

'Angry?'

'She'd got it bad. Sometimes the women, the men occasionally that use Gents for Hire, regard it as more than a commercial agreement, start to feel love. Most of the men that I use are emotionally drained, traumas in their lives. You'd not believe how many of the men that spend time with the women are gay, and they're not into a normal heterosexual man-woman relationship.'

'Nancy Bartlett, that's the woman's name,' Larry said. 'I've met with her, and she's not short of money. Why would she have had trouble paying you what you wanted?'

'I've no idea. Those with the real money don't always throw it around, the reason they became rich in the first place, I suppose. Not that I'd know. I can make a good income, ten times what I did as a police officer, but I like to live well: good food, good drink, a better than average car.'

Not on personal hygiene, Isaac thought but kept it to himself.

'Women?' Larry asked.

'Ambivalent,' Domett said. 'I'm not gay, but I prefer to be on my own most of the time. If the need takes me, not that it does that often, I've got a phone number.'

Let's come back to Nancy Bartlett,' Isaac said.

'She met with the man on more than one occasion,' Larry said.

'It happens. The agreement is that if there's an ongoing arrangement agreed on between the client and the escort, then the escort makes sure that I receive a commission.'

'How many of the escorts honour that?'

'What do you reckon?'

'Zero.'

'Correct. I didn't know that the woman and my man had made a separate deal, and if they had, then what was I going to do?'

'Accost the woman and the escort.'

'Sure, I'll make a phone call, and if the phone is answered I'll let them know that contractually they're legally obliged to pay me.'

'Waste of time,' Isaac said. 'Is that all you can tell us about Colin Young?'

'Seeing I'm here.'

'Then talk,' Larry said. 'We've got a cold cell downstairs if you keep procrastinating.'

'Six to seven months ago, I can't remember the exact date, so don't ask, I receive a phone call.'

'Colin Young?'

'Who else do you think I'm referring to? The man's pleasant, he asks if we can meet.'

'And you agreed?'

'I had no reason not to. We met not far from here, a small restaurant. I can show it to you if it's of interest, not that it will help you.'

'We'll be the judge of that,' Larry said.

'It was the first time I'd met him. I'd seen his photo before, and I'd spoken to him on the phone in the past, and that's the truth. He's a good-looking man, I'll give him that.'

'Beautiful is the word we've heard mentioned.'

'Maybe he was. He didn't do much for me, but if you say he was, then we'll go with that description.'

'Why the meeting?' Isaac asked.

'Bizarre. I'm not sure how else to describe it.'

'Explain what you mean.'

'He doesn't ask for anything directly. We order a meal, he's paying. I had fish, he had meat, and we shared a bottle of wine. I'm more of a whisky man, but he's got the money, and I'm there with him. I'll grant that there's something about him. Normally, I would have eaten the meal, drunk the wine, made some small talk and left. But he's got a likeable personality, the type of person you don't mind spending time with. The same as you, Isaac, from what I can remember of you back in the past.'

'I'm not the subject of interest,' Isaac reminded him. 'And you've been withholding vital evidence.'

'The man's agreeable, he wants to chat, asks me about business, and how he's considering returning. We discussed the financial remuneration, and whether he wants it straight or gay.'

'His response?'

'Straight. He was adamant on that point.'

'He came back to work for you?'

'Not then.'

'Why have you held back on this?'

'I have a special clientele,' Domett said. 'You'll not find them in my records. They'll pay more for confidentiality.'

'Do you know who they are?'

'Strictly cash, brown envelope.'

'Brown envelope? Larry asked.

'An envelope, sometimes a parcel, arrives at my office. Inside, the money. Credit cards are never used and these people phone on a landline, so I can't see their mobile number. There's no way to trace them.'

'We could try,' Isaac said.

'You could, not that you'll get far.'

'The dead man is back on the books, you're organising clients for him, paying him what he wants?'

'Not until four weeks ago, but there are complications.'

'What sort?'

'My special clientele, they're men.'

'And you indicated that Colin Young was not interested.'

'He made that clear when we met before. But now, he wants money, and they will pay whatever I ask. He's got no option.'

'Did he say why he wanted the money?'

'He said he wanted to buy a house, not that I believed him.'

'Why?'

'Too clichéd, I hear it too often from my escorts. But he was different.'

'Explain what you mean.'

'I couldn't figure him out. He was an attractive man who could easily find himself a woman his age, and he was educated. No problems for him to make good money in London; not selling himself, obviously.'

'He was involved with an older woman, taking money from her. We're not sure if he was emotionally involved.'

'It's unlikely,' Domett said. He had a smug look about him as if he was telling two serving police officers what they should have already deduced.

'How many times?'

'If you're referring to how many times he was rented out to the specials, then twice.'

'Any feedback from Colin Young about them?'

'Nothing from Young. He took the money, that's all. I imagine he was repulsed by what he had done, although he was willing to continue. The first of the specials hired him again, the second never came back.'

'We need their names,' Larry said.

'I've told you already. Cash delivered to my office, an address with a time and date inside. That's all there is.'

'You have the details?'

'Not on my computer.'

'But you do have them?' Isaac asked.

'In a notebook, but you're heading into places you might regret.' Domett reached into the inside pocket of his jacket and withdrew a tattered leather-covered notebook. He handed it over to Isaac.

'We'll follow up, and you're still guilty of withholding vital evidence.'

'My life's worth more than what you can penalise me with. I know the sort of people we're dealing with here. They will not allow you to get too close, to blow their cover.'

'We've met their type before. We know what we're up against. Nick Domett, you'd better hope that what you've given us is the complete truth."

'It is. If you want me, you have my phone number. I'll be keeping out of sight for a few days.'

'An address where you'll be.'

'Don't worry. I'll answer the phone, and besides, you've got my email. Once you start ruffling feathers, it's going to become unpredictable. If you find yourself out of the police force or dead in the gutter, don't come complaining to me.'

'Or dead in Hyde Park,' Larry quipped.

'As you say,' Domett replied. He stood up and left the police station.

'Here's where it gets dangerous,' Larry said.

'It's also where we solve the case. We may have found the motive,' Isaac said. He knew he'd have to talk to Detective Chief Superintendent Goddard about the latest development.

Chapter 24

Christine Mason held to her story that Archibald Marshall, her manager and now confidante, was no longer pressuring her for money and sexual favours. Wendy Gladstone had spoken to the woman on two occasions since the meeting at the Masons' home, where Christine had finally told her husband the truth about her involvement with a younger man.

The first time the two women had spoken after Christine's revelation, it had been a five-minute conversation over the phone. That time, Christine had updated Wendy that she was staying with her sister for the time being as her husband was still angry, and she knew that if she went back to her house, he would be asking penetrating questions, questions she did not want to answer.

The second time the women met, it was not far from the hotel where Christine worked. It was a good day, clear and bright, warm even. The two women walked around the small park, a casual conversation, no prodding from Wendy.

'It's Gwen,' Christine said. 'She's starting to drive me crazy.'

'Past issues raising their ugly head?' Wendy said. She wasn't surprised as she knew what had happened in the past, the illicit love affair of Christine and Terry Hislop when he had been courting Gwen, and she had been playing hard to get, and Christine hadn't.

'It's always there, but we were never that close as children. Different personalities, and my being there with her in that small house; well, we're starting to argue. Over the dirty dishes in the sink last night, can you believe it?'

Wendy could. After Bridget had moved in with her, they had had the occasional flare up, always about the silly things: the cat scratching the furniture, the washing not out on the line.

'I can. What are you going to do about it?'

'Go home. Tony's off overseas again, and we've been speaking. He wants to try counselling, not that I'm so keen.'

'You believe it won't help?'

'I loved Colin, I can't help that. If Tony wants me back, I'll go, but I'm not going to be a changed person. It's strange when you think about it now, but I suited Terry more than Gwen, and Tony and Gwen would have been a good match.'

'Life takes twists and turns, but we make compromises,' Wendy said. 'Are you still holding to that story about Marshall?'

'It's not a story, it's the truth,' Christine said, but not so firmly as she had on previous occasions. Wendy noticed the change.

'Sleeping with Marshall, the truth?'

A pause before Christine responded. 'No.'

'Christine, you're an adult, not a teenager behind the bike shed at school. This is the real world, you've children who have grown up, a husband who must care about you, and you still jeopardise your life.'

'You sound like Gwen. She's a good one to lecture.'

'What does that mean?'

'She's not been the vestal virgin all her life.'

'Tony?'

'Neither of them knows that I'm aware of it, and it was a long time ago. I didn't tell them then, I don't intend to now.'

'Why?'

'Ironic, isn't it? I'm an open book, yet others who profess piety are no better.'

'That's the way it is, not that it matters. What does is who killed your lover. We're still considering Marshall.'

'And me?'

'Aren't you concerned when Marshall's pawing you that he could be a killer?'

'I'm more concerned about ensuring he's finished as quickly as possible.'

'Not a pleasant experience?'

'He's not the most attractive of men.'

'Christine, you know where I am,' Wendy said. 'When you're ready, call me. There's no need to allow the man to treat you like a piece of meat.'

'There is, and you know it.'

Wendy walked away, shaking her head in despair.

***

'You know what this means?' Richard Goddard said. He and Isaac were in the chief superintendent's office on the top floor of Challis Street. In Isaac's hand, the leather-covered notebook that Domett had handed over.

'Whoever's in here could be important, influential,' Isaac said as he held the notebook up.

'Some of the pages are missing,' Goddard said as he flicked through them.

'Domett was prepared. He knew that if we pushed too hard, attempted to make the connection between the murder and him, he had a bargaining tool, proof positive that it wasn't him.'

'Is it?'

'Proof positive? No, we don't think so, although Domett's street smart, he's not the type to murder anyone. He's ripped the pages out to protect other special clientele.'

'Do you want to go there?' Goddard said, referring to whoever had been in the book.

'We want the murderer, not those who indulge in nefarious activities.'

'Domett? Anything against him?'

'The vice squad might be interested, but it's unlikely. Two names in the notebook are of interest.'

'Names?'

'Domett's used a code, but we're sure that he doesn't know who they are, not unless he attempted to find out.'

'And you don't believe that he did.'

'He's a lazy man, makes enough money to live on without working too hard. Unambitious, the reason he never succeeded as a police officer.'

'Yet he makes more money than me,' Goddard said.

'One of life's injustices. Not really relevant, is it?'

'Not really. What does the notebook tell you?'

'A date, a time, and a location.'

'Nothing more?'

'Two phone numbers. We've checked them out, nothing there. Larry Hill's checking the first location now. I'll be assisting him as soon as we've concluded here.'

'Then why are you here?'

'Just giving you a forewarning. The two men could have influence. You could receive a phone call to tell us to back off.'

'If I do, I'll let you know.'

'And then?'

'Keep investigating. We want this murderer. If it's one of the two men, then give me the name, and I'll follow through. And take care, we don't know who or what we're up against.'

'We do,' Isaac said. 'It's not the first time we've come up against one law for the powerful, another for everyone else.'

'You're right. Keep me posted,' Goddard said.

***

Isaac knew that the investigation was not over yet, but back at his flat, Jenny was packing the suitcases. It had only been two days before that he had come home more optimistic of a breakthrough than he had been for some time. His parents' wedding anniversary was in seven days, and it had looked promising that the two of them would make it to the celebrations in Kingston, the Jamaican capital. His parents had purchased a three-bedroom house, complete with swimming pool, in Barbican on Millsborough Avenue, upmarket from where they had both been born in Trench Town.

Trench Town had been dangerous when they had lived there over forty years before, and it still was. It may have been where Bob Marley and reggae had come from, but it was still the centre of violence, not a place to drive through at night, and not in the day if it could be avoided.

It wasn't as if Barbican was entirely crime free, and Isaac's parents had upgraded the security on their property twice already in the year since they had returned to Jamaica. The first time was after they had returned from the Mahogany Bar at Devon House, the former mansion of a Jamaican who had made his money in Venezuela. That time the burglars had made a run for it. The second time, three men, more determined and carrying guns. Isaac's father, seeing them as he entered the driveway, had slammed the car into reverse and driven fast to the police station, two minutes away. Being the parents of a detective chief inspector in England carried weight. A police car arrived at the property within five minutes. There were four policemen, and all were armed. The robbers were arrogantly loading the entire contents of the house into a van. A shootout, two of the robbers died at the scene, the third attempted to make a run for it, two policemen in hot pursuit. He died with two bullets to the chest, one to the head.

Isaac had pleaded with his parents to return to England, but they were adamant. Jamaica was their spiritual home, the place where their extended family could visit, not that Isaac had yet. Always too busy the reason, but he had been born in England, and to him, England was home, not somewhere where the police shot first, asked questions later.

Jenny, regardless of Isaac's trepidation, had every intention of enjoying herself, the chance to soak up the sun, to visit Boston Bay and to eat Jerk Chicken at Shaggy's, and then to go up the winding road to Firefly, the home of Noel Coward, the place where he had died, his grave in the grounds overlooking the sea down below. And to visit Ocho Rios and climb the Dunn River Falls, where James Bond had encountered Honey Rider coming out of the sea. And if time permitted, a weekend at

Negril, the haunt of hippies in the sixties, the wealthy in the seventies, and to jump off the cliffs.

But the visit wouldn't be yet; he knew that, as did the team. Isaac reflected on previous cases when there had been more than one suspect. Then, as now, it was a case of intensifying the process, pushing that bit harder, working extended hours.

Larry and Wendy focussed on the two special clients that Nick Domett's notebook revealed. The dates and the locations could be correlated, although the phone numbers proved to be of no value. The first date, a Thursday, the time, seven in the evening, the location, an address in the country. The two police officers made the trip out to the place, a thatched cottage of picture postcard beauty. A car was in the gravel driveway to one side of the cottage and smoke was coming out of the chimney.

'Strange,' Larry said. 'It's not that cold. Why would someone have a fire?'

Wendy had seen the car, noticed the confetti on the rear window. The people inside were honeymooners, and they were about to be disturbed on the one night that two people in love should have to themselves.

It was Wendy who rapped on the cottage door, using a brass knocker in the shape of a lion's head with a ring in its mouth. After what seemed a long time, the door opened. The face of a young man in his thirties peered round it. Through the gap in the door, Wendy could see the reflection in a mirror on the wall at the other end of the room – the man was naked.

'Sorry to disturb you,' Wendy said. 'We're from Homicide, Sergeant Gladstone and Inspector Hill.'

'It's not a good time,' the reply.

'Unfortunately, we must insist.'

The door closed, to reopen after three minutes. This time the man was clothed, as was his wife. They were an attractive couple. By this time, Larry had been wised up by Wendy as to the situation. He smiled at the newly-weds: a sign of friendliness, remembering his own honeymoon.

'We've a few questions,' Larry said.

'About us?'

'No. About this house. What can you tell us about it?'

'Nothing. We rented it through Airbnb, nothing more. It had good reviews, mostly from people looking for a romantic weekend, so we booked it online.'

'How long ago?'

'Four to five weeks. What's this about?' the young woman said. Her husband had identified himself as James Corcoran, adding that they were both lawyers, the same firm, and that they had indeed been married that day in a church ten miles down the road.

'This place was rented out to a person of interest.'

'How long ago?'

'Four weeks. We have a date and time and this location.'

'We can't help you. We booked online, and then we received a receipt and instructions. The key to the cottage was in a box at the rear, a tumbler lock on it. That's all we know of the place.'

Larry phoned Bridget to ask her to conduct a search on Airbnb and to find out who the owner was. The only factor in their favour was that the rental accommodation company required payment with a credit card.

Wendy phoned for a couple of uniforms from the local police station to conduct a door knock in the area, although she didn't hold out much hope for it. Standard procedure, that was all, and the cottage had probably only been rented for the one day and night. And if Barry Montgomery/Colin Young – having two names was confusing – had been in the cottage, it would have been night-time when he had arrived, and still dark when he had left. Whoever he had met might have come in the day, but even so, if the man was influential, or well-known, then he would have been smart enough not to have been seen.

The second location was a hotel near Windsor, not far from the castle. The cheerful person at the reception, a woman in her forties, had scanned the records, checked who had been in and out that day, even checked the possibility that the room may have been rented for more than the allotted time.

'We do get those who rent the rooms for more than a good night's sleep,' the receptionist said.

'Prostitution?' Larry said. Not that he thought that was what the woman had meant, but her comment had been ambiguous.

'Young lovers, adulterers, not that we'd know.'

'This would have been two men, one young, the other we are assuming is older.' Wendy produced a photo of the murdered man and pushed it across the counter. 'Any recollection? Think carefully before you answer.'

'That's Colin, Colin Young,' the woman said.

Wendy let out a sigh, and mumbled under her breath, *not again*.

Yet the woman was not like Christine Mason. She was on the heavy side, with bright red lipstick and too much perfume.

'What can you tell us about him?' Wendy asked, taking one step back to take a more detailed look at the woman. Christine Mason had exuded wealth, the receptionist did not. She was dressed smartly, but the look was dowdy. Colin Young's conquests, even if he was willing to take women young or old, money or no money, were always attractive. Christine Mason certainly was, so was Amelia Bentham, and according to Larry, so was Nancy Bartlett.

But the receptionist, her name badge showing that her name was Ingrid Conlon, was not of the calibre of the dead man's conquests.

'He stayed here a few times.'

'Why?'

'I don't know. He was very agreeable, a lovely man.'

'Beautiful?'

'Oh, yes. He had a way with words, made you positively go weak at the knees.'

'We'll need the dates,' Larry said.

'I'll get them for you later. You mentioned prostitution,' Ingrid Conlon said.

'Colin Young is dead,' Wendy said. 'Are you surprised by that?'

A look of shock on the woman's face. 'I'm not sure what to say. He was a guest, but he was the sort of person you felt you knew.'

'What does that mean?'

'Nothing in itself. I only ever spoke to him here. He was on one side of the counter, I was on the other.'

'The man has a history of seduction. Were you one?'

'No, I was not,' the indignant reply.

'We'll accept that for now,' Larry said.

'You'll accept it, *full stop*. I can be enamoured of the man, enjoy talking to him, share a joke, some harmless humour, but I'll have you know that I'm a happily married woman.'

The two police officers had heard the pious defence before from murderers, fraudsters, violent criminals. It wasn't a defence in itself, but Wendy thought that it was probably true.

The three of them moved away from the reception, another woman taking Ingrid's place.

Wendy ordered a tea; the other two, coffee. They were sitting on comfortable chairs in the hotel foyer. There was no hovering manager.

'Mrs Conlon,' Larry said. 'Colin Young, whose real name was Barry Montgomery, was a man who used his charms to seduce vulnerable and lonely women.'

'Then he must have made plenty. I'm not a prude, and I'm not shocked by what you're saying. All I ever noticed was that he made people cheerful in his presence. Old Mrs Winterly always sought him out when he was here.'

'Old Mrs Winterly?' Wendy asked.

'She's not that old, only seventy-five, but she always calls herself that.'

'Tell us about her?'

'She obviously has a lot of money. It was about nine months ago that she first checked in. For some reason she's never left, each week renewing her booking, paying up front.'

'Are you saying she lives here?'

'She told us she enjoyed it in the hotel, good friends, room service, the bed made every day. "Why leave?", her words, not mine.'

'An active woman?'

'Every day she goes out for a walk. She feeds the pigeons in the park, bread from the hotel, not that we

265

mind. There's a sign that says they shouldn't be fed, but Old Mrs Winterly, she doesn't pay heed to rules and regulations. She used to be a businesswoman, very successful, according to her. Not that I nor anyone else was prying, but she did like to talk, and she did like Colin.'

'A relationship?'

'I wouldn't know, and that's the truth, but she's got a mischievous eye, and if you're saying that Colin was selling himself, then who knows?'

'We'll need to talk to her,' Larry said. 'Any other women he was friendly with?'

'Only Old Mrs Winterly.'

'On one occasion, Colin Young came to this hotel to meet with someone else.'

'I wouldn't know if he had.'

'This time, it was to meet a man. We assume him to be older, probably prominent or influential.'

'Yet again, I don't know how I can help you. We see the occasional celebrity in here, but I can't remember Colin meeting anyone. And besides, if the man in question had booked a room, then they needn't have met in the foyer.'

'We'll need a copy of the guests for the date or dates we specify.'

'I'm sure we can arrange that.'

'Where is Mrs Winterly now?'

'She'll be back soon. I'll let her know you're waiting for her.'

Ingrid Conlon left and went back to the reception counter.

'What do you reckon?' Wendy asked Larry.

'I need a beer,' his reply. 'We thought we were on the home run, and now another development, another rich woman.'

266

'Ingrid Conlon?'

'Innocent, unless there is evidence to the contrary.'

'That's what I thought, but this Mrs Winterly is an unknown.'

Chapter 25

Isaac, after the visit with his chief superintendent, had intended meeting up with Larry Hill, taking the opportunity to get out of the office and to do some real policing. That plan was waylaid; a phone call, another development.

The first person that Isaac saw as he entered Pathology was Siobhan O'Riley, cheerful as always.

Isaac and Graham Picket, the pathologist, had a complicated relationship, and each and every encounter of the two was strictly professional, none of the usual banter.

'You'll find a change today,' Siobhan said.

'It'll be a first,' Isaac's reply. He always enjoyed talking to Picket's assistant, never to the man himself.

Picket sat at his desk. For once it was clear of the usual papers, the laptop and monitor pushed to one side. The office was no bigger, no better than Isaac's in Challis Street, although he had the benefit of a plant in one corner, his qualifications framed and up on the wall. Picket had nothing except for a calendar on one wall and a copy of a memo he had circulated to the Pathology Department reminding the staff about documenting, ensuring due diligence, and not to circumvent the process, not to make any assumptions in an autopsy, and to check and double check. And now Isaac could see that the man had an expression that he had not seen before. It was almost friendly, but still no smile.

'Chief Inspector,' Picket said, clearing his throat. A sign of nerves, Isaac thought. 'We've re-evaluated our findings into the death of Matilda Montgomery.'

'You said it was suicide,' Isaac responded.

'We hold to that. We conducted a toxicology test at the time and came back with nothing.'

'Are you saying that the woman was taking drugs?'

'Detection is not always that easy. Blood will show it for up to a day, saliva, up to ten, and then there's urine and hair follicles.

'What are you saying, precisely?'

'Toxicology takes time, not how they want to portray it on a television crime show with their instant results, almost warp speed.'

'Picket, get to the point. If there's additional information about the woman's death, then spit it out,' Isaac said. It felt good to be belligerent with the man.

'Very well. It had been over a month since she had used cocaine, maybe up to three. She wouldn't have been under the effects when she killed herself.'

'Her brother, Barry?'

'We've not concluded our tests. A lot of people do, and most would argue that it's no more harmful than alcohol.'

'We're not here to discuss the rights and wrongs of the drug. What more can you tell me?'

'That's about it. If she had taken it recently, then she could have killed herself as it was wearing off, depression, mood swings, tension, anxiety.'

'But that's not the case, is it?'

'No.'

'I'm not sure if it has any bearing on our investigation.'

'We found no signs of long-term cocaine usage, no damage to the nasal lining or the septum, cerebral atrophy, no sign of injection.'

Isaac did not mention that as a student before he had joined the police force, he had snorted cocaine once, and apart from the initial rush, the feelings of euphoria, it had done little for him, but then, he had never understood why people smoked dead leaves wrapped in paper.

After that one time with cocaine, he had never tried it again, and he had never smoked. Wendy, his sergeant, had been a heavy smoker in her time, and he had had to speak to her about it on a couple of occasions, but now she smoked less than before, and the air in the Homicide Department was pleasant and fresh.

'It's still illegal. The question is where she obtained it.'

'And if it's relevant to your enquiry,' Picket added.

'We need to know if her brother was using cocaine.'

'Assume he is. A final confirmation will be available in a couple of days.'

'Their mother, Janice Montgomery?'

'The original report stands.'

***

With the new information from Pathology and Forensics, another element had come into the investigation. Although taking the drug was illegal, it wasn't Homicide's primary focus. But whoever had been dealing in the drug could well be a person of interest. Yet another twist and turn in a case that had had more than its fair share.

Larry and Wendy were sitting in the foyer of the hotel in Windsor when Old Mrs Winterly walked through the front door; a nod from Ingrid Conlon, the receptionist, to indicate who she was.

As Ingrid had said, 'Old' was how Mrs Winterly referred to herself, and the two police officers assumed she would be showing her age, attempting to push it back by the liberal application of makeup and wearing designer clothes.

That was not what they saw.

For one thing, the woman did not look seventy-five and would have passed for someone ten to fifteen years younger. Her complexion was clear, her figure still firm, her step sprightly.

It was Wendy who introduced herself and asked her to come and sit with her and Larry and to answer a few questions. The woman acceded to the request, not showing any concern that it was a police matter. In one hand, she held a designer bag, and it was expensive; Wendy knew such things, though never having the money to buy one for herself. In the other, a Harrods' bag, green, with the store's logo emblazoned in gold.

The store was so strongly identified with the English capital that the bag had in itself become a souvenir, and it was possible to buy one without buying anything else. But that wasn't the case with Mrs Winterly; hers was full of purchases from the shop.

'What's this all about?' Mrs Winterly asked; Larry and Wendy were unable to see her as 'Old' anymore.

'Colin Young,' Wendy said.

'An old woman's folly,' came the reply, without hesitation.

'Are you admitting to having a relationship with the man?' Larry asked.

271

'*Why not?*'

'Please, Mrs Winterly, we're not here to comment.'

'It doesn't matter to me either way. I'm just making the best of my life, the same as everyone else. I could afford him, and he made me happy. There's nothing wrong in that.'

Wendy had to agree, although she could see that Larry, more straight-laced than he'd care to admit, was not so sure. To Wendy, his view smacked of hypocrisy. A man in his seventies could proudly display a twenty-something on his arm and in his bed, but when the position was reversed, out came the prejudices.

'Unfortunately, we must tell you that Colin Young is dead,' Wendy said.

'I'm sorry to hear that. He was good fun, and he kept me entertained.'

'No more than that?'

'What do you want me to say? How did he die?'

'He was murdered in Hyde Park.'

'I saw something about that, but I didn't take much notice.'

'Weren't you surprised that he hadn't been here to see you?'

'No, why should I be? He was a free agent, the same as I am. If he wanted to spend time with me, then great. But if he was occupied elsewhere, then that was fine as well.'

'Do you mean with other women?'

'Other women, other men, it wasn't my concern.'

'You have a healthy attitude,' Wendy said. 'But it doesn't explain your ambivalence towards him.'

'I think it does. What do you know about me?'

'We've only recently become aware of you. We understand that you are seventy-five years of age and that you moved into the hotel about nine months ago.'

'And that I had a young lover.'

'That's about it,' Wendy said.

'If you want me to talk, I need a glass of wine. And call me Dorothy.' She raised her hand in the direction of the bar at the far end of the foyer. 'He knows what I want. How about you two? Or are you on duty, not allowed to drink?'

'I'll have a beer,' Larry said.

'A glass of wine,' Wendy added.

With all three holding a drink, Dorothy Winterly commenced the story of her life. The conversation was being recorded, with her permission.

'I married at twenty-five, a good man, as ambitious as me. We were married for nearly fifty years until he died eighteen months ago.'

'I'm sorry to hear that,' Wendy said.

'No need to be. We had a good life together, and he was suffering at the end. We were close, loving, faithful, and we raised two sons and a daughter. My daughter is married and living in America, my sons are still in England. All of them are well-balanced and successful in their own right, and before you ask, yes, they are older than Colin was.'

'Did they express concern about you living here and about Colin Young.'

'It wasn't any of their business, and even if I told them, they would have wished me well. As I was saying, over time and with a lot of hard work, we started to improve our situation. We could see that betterment required self-discipline and sacrifice. For years, it was us and the children and the business. My husband never

273

enjoyed the benefit at the end of the rainbow, the chance to put his feet up, to do what successful people are meant to do. Once a year, two weeks holiday with the children. When they first came along, a week at Brighton or Cornwall, a tent for all of us, and then later the holidays became better and more exotic.

'My husband became ill, and we discussed our life together, the children and what was to become of me. If was he who said for me to break the chain and to enjoy myself. Our two sons look after the business, and money is not an issue for me. There's a perfectly good house for me in the country with plenty of room, and it's beautiful, but I like it here.'

'Your children? Do you meet with them?'

'All the time, but they never come here.'

'Would they be concerned by a young lover?'

'Why should they? They knew their father's view on how I should live my life after he'd gone. And I don't intend to be the grieving widow.'

'But you must be sad,' Larry said.

'I was relieved when he died. He was in a lot of pain; there was no quality of life for him.'

'Dorothy, we will check your story,' Wendy said.

'Check if you want to, but you'll find it to be true. One day I may tire of being here in this hotel and day tripping up to London. Then I might go back to my home, or take a cruise around the world, but I'm not ready for either yet. Colin made me happy whenever I saw him, and if he was making someone else happy, then good for him, good for them.'

'He was also acting as an escort,' Larry said.

'Yet again, it's not my concern.'

'Did you give him money?'

'For services rendered?'

'Yes.'

'I gave him presents. Sometimes it was money, sometimes clothes or whatever else he wanted. He never asked, and I had no issue with looking after him. After all, he looked after me. Did anyone else tell you that he was beautiful?'

'On more than one occasion,' Wendy said. 'And a good lover?'

'You're not expecting me to be coy now, after all I've told you?'

'No.'

'Then he was.'

'Do you know of anyone who might have wanted him dead?'

'Check if you must, even talk to my children, but no, there is no one.'

'And you, after we leave here?'

'I will feel sorrow for Colin. What about his family?'

'That is another sad story,' Wendy said.

'Then tell me no more. Sadness is not something I want to deal with,' Dorothy Winterly said.

***

It was Wendy who made the phone call to Amelia Bentham; the updated information from the pathologist needed to be followed up. Not that the team in Homicide felt that it was critical in itself, not sure if the fact that both Barry and Matilda Montgomery had low-level traces of cocaine affected the murder enquiry.

Amelia came into Challis Street at 10.20 a.m. It was raining outside. 'We were going to do an outside shoot down by the river, the latest summer range. No chance today.'

Isaac joined the two women in the interview room. An air of cordiality existed.

'Amelia, we've been informed that Matilda and her brother had used cocaine in the past,' Isaac said.

'Matilda, she tried to rebel occasionally, to go against her inherently conservative nature.'

'You do not deny the cocaine?'

'It was at a party. The three of us were there, and everyone was getting high on alcohol and whatever else.'

'Drugs?'

'Social, nothing heavy. No heroin, nothing like that.'

'Cocaine?'

'Chief Inspector, you're a man of the world. You know it exists.'

'That's why we're meeting here for a chat.'

'No bright lights, no truncheons, thumbscrews?'

Wendy could see Amelia flirting with Isaac, not that she could blame her, but it was an unusual reaction to witness in a police station.

Isaac ignored the woman's attempts at light-hearted repartee, realising that it could be an attempt to conceal nervousness. 'We know that cocaine is freely available, and most parties, especially with the upwardly mobile, the affluent, would have someone snorting it. Are you one of those people?'

'Never in my house, and that's the truth.'

'Why?' Wendy asked.

'My parents. You've met them, found them to be easy-going on most matters, but drugs are anathema to them. It's the one thing they draw the line at.'

'Good people, but why the abhorrence of drugs?'

'If you must know, when they were younger, they went off the rails for a while, transcendental meditation, hallucinogenic drugs, the obligatory trip to India.'

'But that was in the sixties and the seventies,' Isaac said.

'Late developers, my father would say. But the truth is that it still existed for a couple of decades after. Now my parents will barely take an aspirin.'

'But you will?'

'An aspirin, of course. And cocaine, but very occasionally. It doesn't do much for me, and it didn't do much for Matilda. That one time she snorted it, she was talking silly for about thirty minutes, and then she was sat in a corner crying her eyes out.'

'It would take more than the one time for it to have remained in her system.'

'I only saw her snort it once, and that's the truth. Maybe she did with Barry, but I wouldn't know. As I've told you on more than one occasion, Matilda was a friend, but we weren't in each other's pockets, and Barry used to come over to my place of a night-time. And he wasn't snorting cocaine with me.'

'We met another woman yesterday, an older woman, who was involved with him,' Wendy said.

'Sleeping with him?'

'The same as you, casual sex. Amelia, was it casual with you? Or did you harbour feelings of love for him? An attractive man, and you're at the clucky age, the age of wanting children.'

'I'm too busy to contemplate the possibility,' Amelia said.

'Falling in love, wanting children, are not conscious actions formed by modern values and society,'

Wendy said. 'They are base instincts, primordial, unalterable, uncontrollable.'

'Very well. I did want more from him, but he wasn't giving that to me. When he was with me, I was happy; when he wasn't, I busied myself with work and other thoughts.'

'But the love was there, the need for children. Am I correct?'

'It could have been love if he had let me through the barrier that surrounded him. But he never did. I'm a pragmatist, not a foolish lovestruck teenager. He wasn't going to change, not then, and probably not in the future.'

'Why not?'

'Because Matilda was shaped from the same mould. I never knew either of them, not truly, not the way my father and mother know each other.'

'Love is a strong emotion,' Isaac said. 'So is hatred, the need for revenge, for retribution.'

'I rejected love as a wasted emotion,' Amelia said.

'Sometimes people have a distorted view of life, and they feel the need to lash out at those who have affected their balance, thrown it into confusion.'

'This is ludicrous. I came here at your request, and now you're virtually accusing me of murder. I couldn't have done that, not to him.'

'Because you hadn't rejected love, but because you had embraced it, even though he would not reciprocate.'

'Okay, you win. Yes, I loved him. Is that what you wanted to hear?' Amelia said. 'And now he's dead, and I don't know who killed him, nor do you.'

'Thank you for being honest. Now, what else don't we know?'

'Matilda knew how I felt about her brother.'

'Did she tell him?'

'She may have, but I don't think so. She was possessive of her brother. From what I understood, their childhood must have formed an unbreakable bond, the reason that both of them were incapable of unconditional love.'

'The cocaine, other drugs?'

'That's all I know, and that's the truth. I wish that Barry was still alive, not that it would have helped me. He wouldn't have been mine, apart for the occasional one-night stand.'

Wendy felt sad for the woman who had a good moral compass from her parents, but not the love of a man her age that she craved.

Amelia Bentham left Challis Street and hailed a taxi. She gave Wendy a hug as she was getting into the vehicle. 'I miss him, but life goes on,' she said.

'It takes time, that's the hard part,' Wendy said, remembering the feeling of emptiness when her husband had passed away.

Chapter 26

Christine Mason left the hotel where she had worked for the last four years, three months, and eight days: the period clearly stated on the severance notice she had received when she had been called into Archibald Marshall's office and summarily dismissed.

Marshall had been professional, she might have agreed, if she had not been shocked by the suddenness of the dismissal. Alongside him in the office was a senior manager from head office, as well as the hotel group's chief accountant.

'There'll be no reference,' Marshall had said. 'Embezzlement is a serious crime.'

The pot calling the kettle black, she should have said, but did not. And as the time since her removal from the hotel extended, Christine reflected on it. There were questions with no answers. Why did it need a chief accountant? Why did it need someone from head office? The woman had said she was the head of Human Resources, but Christine had never heard of her before.

She was guilty of rank stupidity, she knew that, in giving money to Colin whom she had loved, and then to Marshall whom she detested and had slept with because he protected her. And then telling her husband of her infidelity, remembering her sister and her husband entwined. Remembering Terry, Gwen's former husband, and her bearing his unborn child in her teens. All that she had suffered, yet Archibald Marshall had come out of the sordid and shabby business at the hotel as though he smelt of roses.

Christine Mason was determined to find out the truth, and, as her shock abated to be replaced by bewilderment and then anger, she made a phone call. 'The park bench where we met before,' she said.

From her handbag she withdrew the severance notice detailing the financial settlement, the confidentiality agreement. It did not mention the specifics, only the generalisations about not discussing internal hotel procedures and finances, and not to reveal anything that could be of benefit to a competitor. Not that she intended to work for another hotel, anyway. It was a small world, and she knew that her departure from the hotel would be gossip for the next week, the rumour mill working overtime trying to figure out what had gone on, and why.

There'd be some who would say it was due to incompetence, although it hadn't been. Others would say it was a witch hunt, another sign of male domination of a weak and defenceless woman. Few, if any, would realise that she was the sacrificial goat to protect the hotel's reputation and that of its manager. But why Marshall? He was equally guilty, and she had the proof.

Isaac dropped Wendy off at the park entrance. It wasn't that far from Challis Street, and parking in inner London was a nightmare, even for a police car. And Wendy was sure that she did not intend to rush away from her meeting with Christine Mason. Bridget was still trying to find out who the specials were on Domett's list, Amelia Bentham had brought a degree of uncertainty to her situation, and Terry Hislop had met up with his former wife in London.

There was a belief that an imminent breakthrough was about to happen, but the team had felt that before, only for them to fall flat on their face.

281

Wendy found Christine Mason sitting on the bench, as agreed. From a distance, she looked a lonely and lost soul.

'What is it, Christine?' Wendy said as she sat down beside her.

The enveloping hug from the woman was not expected. 'I've been dismissed,' she said. Her voice was tremulous.

'This was always expected. Was there any mention of the money you took?'

'It was intimidating. There were three of them; one of me.'

Outside the park, a small café. Wendy walked over, ordered two coffees, and came back, handing one to Christine, taking one for herself.

Wendy did not object to being a shoulder to cry on, but she could not feel a lot of sympathy for a person whose woes were self-inflicted due to her lack of moral restraint. Yet she still liked the woman, the sort of person who was easy to talk to, not like Gwen, her sister, who was now meeting with her ex, Terry Hislop, a man who had shown the capability to act violently.

'You mentioned three,' Wendy said as she sipped her coffee. It was lukewarm, with too little milk and not enough sugar. Any other time, she would have complained.

'Archibald Marshall, an accountant, and a woman, the head of Human Resources.'

'Did you know the other two?'

'Not personally, although I've no reason to doubt they are who they said.'

'Let's assume they are. We can check later. Now, what was the gist of the meeting?'

'Archibald Marshall told me that I had been dismissed and that I would be leaving the building immediately.'

'Immediately?'

'It always upsets people, but I did have access to the hotel's money and privileged information: passwords, bank account details, that sort of thing.'

'You were taking their money, giving it to your fancy man, and then to Marshall. Any mention made of that?'

'Not in detail and they must have known about Archibald. It's only logical.'

'He wasn't a stupid man. He could have altered the records.'

'I would have seen if he had, and so would head office. Those two with him knew that he was guilty.'

'And he's free of all blame, is that it?'

'But why? Why would they do that?' Christine asked. Wendy thought it had to be a rhetorical question.

'They've not finished with him yet. He'll get a sweetheart deal, and the whole sorry saga will be swept under the table. The hotel maintains its reputation, worth more than what you stole.'

'It's so unfair.'

'Christine, what happens to him is not your concern, just accept it as one of life's lessons learnt.'

'He followed Colin once.'

'*Who*? Marshall?'

'The last time that Colin was in the hotel. Not that Colin ever knew, but I saw Archibald walk out of the hotel not long after Colin and follow him down the road.'

'Are you sure he was following? He could have just been heading in the same direction.'

'I'm certain of it. At the end of the road, Colin had hurried across the road, and Archibald had run after him, almost getting hit by a car. I followed from a distance. I could see that Colin was unaware of what was going on.'

'And?'

'Colin went into a building on Westbourne Terrace.'

The address intrigued Wendy. 'The number?'

'It was 125. Does it mean anything?'

'What did you do?'

'I stayed there for a few minutes on the street. Archibald was still watching, and I was worried that he'd see me.'

'How long was this before Colin was murdered?'

'Four to five weeks. I can't remember the exact date, but he was staying at the hotel, so you must be able to find out.'

'Christine, what I suggest you do is to go home, take a long hot bath, drink a glass of wine, and forget today. That's my recommendation, but you're on self-destruct, and you may well ignore my advice. So far, you're free and innocent of all charges. Don't jeopardise this.'

'I won't. I'll do what you said.'

Wendy wasn't convinced that she would.

***

Isaac was conscious of Jenny's packing back at the flat they shared, her growing excitement about her first trip to the Caribbean. He thought that she may have the notion of a wedding proposal on a starlit beach, the waves gently lapping on the seashore, a harp playing in the background. He had to admit that was on his mind to, although not the harp. Maybe a guitar in Jamaica, a Rasta selling drugs down one end of the beach, the noise of cars beeping their horns in the distance.

Jenny's notion of the Caribbean, he realised, was tempered by the movies and the travel brochures, not the reality. He knew that behind the gloss there was crime and poverty and misery. In the resorts, she would see very little of them, but they were going to stay with his parents. She had grown up in a small town in Sussex, a county on the coast to the south of London. Her childhood had consisted of country life, a school for the girls of gentlefolk, a safe and happy environment where the family house was separated from the world outside by a privet hedge, not the electric fence that surrounded his parents' house.

'Nancy Bartlett lied to you?' Isaac said to Larry, Wendy was standing beside him. This three of them were at Challis Street. It was Wendy who had come back with the latest revelation from Christine Mason.

'It's her address, 125, Westbourne Terrace, but why?' What did she hope to gain? If she was still paying him for services rendered, then why didn't she tell us? I'll go with Wendy, check her out.'

'We could bring her into the station.'

'If needed, we will.'

'Has anyone checked on the father?'

'Not recently. According to Amelia Bentham, he's been around at Matilda's house since she died,' Wendy said. 'Apparently he wants to sell the place.'

'A discounted price if anyone finds out the truth of what happened in there.'

'We've never satisfactorily answered the question as to why the woman committed suicide,' Larry said.

'She died because of the trauma in her life, the death of her brother.'

'But she was dead when we found out about the house, which means she either killed him, or she had been told.'

'Or she had read the newspaper, seen a photo and a description on the internet.'

'Let's assume that she had realised who it was. What's the normal reaction?'

'To contact the police, to break down in hysterics.'

'Not to commit suicide, is that what we're saying?'

'It is. Yet there's an inconsistency. Matilda Montgomery was measured in her suicide. It was all too neat. Only a calm person could have done that, and why hanging? Melodramatic, don't you think?'

'It was a statement. Not to us, but to someone else.'

'Her father?'

'She wanted him to feel the pain that he had caused them over the years. Remember, he loved his daughter and his wife, even his son. And he felt that whatever he had inflicted on them was the act of a loving father, not that either of the children believed it. And with her death, Matilda was finally saying to him, "you were wrong, it was you who destroyed our lives, made my mother miserable, drove my brother away, made me an emotional vacuum". And what if she believed it was her father who had murdered his own son, her brother?'

'She would have been frightened of coming to the police, frightened to confront her father. All his life he had been the dominant figure, good or bad. It would be inconceivable for her to ask him for the truth, impossible for her to tell us what she believed.'

'The woman must have been half-crazy.'

'If she was half, then what is her father?'

***

Nancy Bartlett was initially pleased to open the door of her penthouse flat to Larry; not so keen on him entering with Wendy.

'This is Sergeant Gladstone,' Larry said. On the dining room table, three bottles of wine, a plate of snacks. Some candles lit the main room, the windows closed, an incense stick burning somewhere, its smell permeating the room.

'It's not convenient,' Nancy Bartlett said as the two police officers stood in her flat. She was dressed in a pair of designer jeans and a white blouse. Her hair, as usual, was coiffured, her makeup flawless, her lips, as were her fingernails, a bright shade of red.

Larry thought she looked good; Wendy did not. She had seen enough painted tarts in her time, and the flat was set up for seduction, or one was already occurring.

'Are you alone?' Wendy asked.

'No,' the woman replied. Wendy smiled at what they had interrupted, envied the woman in some ways, disapproved in another.

'Important information regarding you and Colin Young has come to light. We need to know the answer, and we need to know now,' Larry said.

A blustering reply from Nancy Bartlett, an attempt to close a bedroom door. Wendy walked over in that general direction, attempting to look unconcerned. The woman wasn't suspected of murder, and her alibi had been checked by Bridget and found to be tight. The police had no right to search the flat, but Wendy was a woman; she could sense that something was amiss.

Wendy returned to where Larry and Nancy Bartlett were. 'Good view you've got here,' she said as she casually looked out of the window, the previously closed curtains now fully open.

'Yes, it is,' the woman's meek reply. 'What's this all about?'

'You lied to us,' Wendy said.

'When have I lied? Inspector Hill was here a few days ago, and I told him all that I knew.'

'Not the fact that you've been screwing one of our suspects.'

'And what's that supposed to mean?'

Wendy walked back over to the bedroom door and pushed it wide open. 'You'd better join us,' she said.

A sheepish Archibald Marshall came out of the room and over to where Larry and Nancy Bartlett were sitting. 'I've done nothing wrong,' he said.

'What's this here with you two?' Wendy said.

'What does it look like?' Nancy Bartlett said. 'Charades?' A nervous attempt at humour to defuse what was a compromising situation.

'How long have you two been involved?' Larry asked.

'A few weeks,' Marshall replied.

'Another lie?' Wendy said.

For one moment, she hoped he was guilty of murder as that would ensure Christine Mason's innocence.

But now there was Nancy Bartlett, a woman whom Larry had regarded as a bit player in the saga.

'When I was here last time, you told me that you hadn't seen Colin Young for some years,' Larry said.

'That was true.'

'He knocked on your door four weeks ago. We have the date. Do you deny this?'

'I kept in contact with Colin. Occasionally we'd meet. Sometimes for a meal or a drink in the pub, and sometimes we'd come back here. It wasn't a commercial arrangement, although sometimes I gave him something.'

'So why the lying?'

'I didn't want to become involved in your investigation. I was frightened you'd want to blame me.'

'And now you're with Archibald Marshall. Are you aware of his involvement?'

'Archibald is a friend, nothing more. I know that Colin used to stay at his hotel, and he was sleeping with one of the staff.'

'Were you upset?'

'With Colin sleeping around? Not at all.'

'Archibald Marshall is no Colin Young,' Wendy said, looking over at the pathetic lump of humanity.

'He followed Colin here one day, so he knew my address. He knocked on the door two days after Colin had been identified as the dead body in Hyde Park.'

'Yet you acted as though you didn't know when I told you,' Larry reminded her.

'What did you expect of me? I know how the law works, guilty by association.'

'That's what's happened to me, isn't it?' Marshall said. He had pulled over a dining chair and was sitting sideways on it.

'Is it?' Wendy asked. 'I met with Christine not long after you dismissed her.'

'And you believed her version?'

'Not totally.'

'She told you what a bastard I was, and how I had mistreated her, and then had her sacked.'

'Something like that,' Wendy admitted.

'She's right. I did have her sacked, but I worked behind the scenes to ensure that she'd leave the hotel with no crime against her name, and a substantial payout. Did she tell you how much she received?'

'Not the details.'

'That's Christine, isn't it? I'll tell you that she received the usual payments, plus a full year's salary. And all she had to do was to sign a confidentiality agreement that she wouldn't reveal the truth of what she had taken, what she had done. The woman was consorting with a murdered man, a man who sold himself, having sex with him in the hotel. She did well out of it.'

'And you?'

'I've got three months before I receive a similar deal.'

'Why not now?'

'Two people in management leaving at the same time raises suspicion. One only causes gossip.'

'Will they honour their side of the bargain?'

'They will. I've got it in writing.'

'You forced Christine to sleep with you?'

'Force? A strong word, if you don't mind me saying,' Marshall said. It was clear that he was feeling increasingly comfortable with the situation.

Though he didn't like him, Larry could see that the man might be telling the truth. Christine Mason was hardly the best character witness; yet the perception that she was the most truthful was based on the fact that she was attractive, Marshall was not.

'Are you saying it was mutual?' Wendy asked.

'Not totally, not that I forced her either. Christine is not the saint that you want to portray her as. She was embezzling money before I found out, and she easily took on board my suggestion. I may be disreputable, according to her, but I'm not the villain of the piece here.'

'Mr Marshall, you are, and you know it. But you're right, Christine is no saint. But how about Nancy Bartlett?' Wendy said. 'What's your story?'

'There is no story. I have money, enough to see me out. Check me out if you want, but you'll not find any dirt against me.'

'But you met with Colin Young not long before he died. You must be regarded as suspect.'

'I liked him, but that was all.'

Larry and Wendy left the two not-so-young lovers in their love nest and left the flat. Another unexpected element to the murder investigation.

Chapter 27

It was Gwen Hislop who phoned Isaac, not on account of her sister, but because of the visit to her house by Terry Hislop. Her sister had mentioned it once before to Wendy, but then there had been no significance attached to it. But now, Christine Mason's sister, as well as being her lawyer, was saying that there was more to it.

Isaac, alone in the office and glad of the opportunity to get out, visited the woman at her house.

'Terry has been here,' Gwen said. Old news to Isaac, but he decided not to mention that Homicide knew of Terry Hislop being in London.

'You've asked me here,' Isaac said. There was no cup of tea, no chat about the weather and life in general, nothing that transformed Gwen Hislop from hard and severe to soft and agreeable. She was, he decided, the sort of woman who would have no trouble finding a man to keep her company, but from what the department had found out and from what her sister had said, she had been on her own since her marriage to Terry. And that was a long time ago, more than twenty years.

'He's been twice. The first time he was disagreeable, yet I let him into the house. He wanted to reflect on good times in the past.'

'And you?'

'I indulged him with his fantasies.'

'Are you saying that there were no good times?'

'Not that I can remember, and certainly not after my dear sister,' sarcastically said, Isaac noted, 'told me that she had been screwing him behind my back.'

'I thought you were friends again.' Isaac had to admit that she had a colourful manner in the way she spoke, and she was articulate, her choice of words entertaining.

'Not friends, sisters.'

'Does Christine know all of this?'

'We're not talking at this time. She left here and went back to her house, and good riddance to her. It's a good job I don't have a dog, or she would have taken it as well.'

'The parting was acrimonious?'

'You could say that. No doubt you and your officers think she's a lovely person, liberal with her favours, but basically, harmless and agreeable?'

'To some extent. But we're not naive. She committed a criminal act, but we're not charging her, no proof. And, as you say, "liberal with her favours".'

'Forget about her for the moment,' Gwen said. 'A coffee.'

Wendy would have said it was the Isaac charm, softening the hardest heart. 'That'd be fine,' he said.

'The second time,' Gwen Hislop said after she had returned with two cups, 'Terry had been drinking. I didn't want to let him in, but he stuck his shoe in the door as I tried to close it.'

'Did he harm you?'

'No.'

'In the past?'

'Statute of limitations on that far back. Let's focus on his last visit.'

'He's in your house, he's drunk, he's angry.'

'Not drunk, just a little unsteady on his feet. It used to be a joke in our courting days, how I could down

293

four pints of beer and still walk a straight line and he'd be struggling to stand up.'

'He's not committed a criminal act by visiting you, then?'

'He frightened me, but no. I'd say he'd drunk two to three pints, enough to think we were still married, and I was there for him.'

'Amorous advances?'

'He thought they were, I didn't. I don't need a lecher pawing me, not now.'

'You live alone,' Isaac said.

'I've just become used to my own company. I'm not a man hater, not anything really. Terry was enough for me, and the years passed by. For the first five, I was definitely anti-men, and then I had my career and my own cosy environment.'

'Terry?' Isaac reminded her why he was in the house.

'He starts going on about the past, and how I had cheated him out of a child, conveniently forgetting that he had been checked out and found to be the fault.'

'Not something a virile man would want to accept. He wouldn't have been down the pub of a Saturday night bragging to his friends about it.'

'Easier to blame me. He's here and he's fluctuating between anger and amorous advances. The first is getting my back up, the second is about to get him a rolling pin to the head.'

'Rolling pin?'

'You know what I mean. Anyway, he's going on about Christine and me, slandering her, maligning me.'

'Is that it?'

'He's got verbal diarrhoea by now, and he starts talking nonsense. I can't remember him being keen on

children anyway. He wasn't the paternal type, not that I
ever saw.'

'An affront to his manhood, not having children.'

'Peer pressure from his friends whose partners
were pushing them out at a rapid rate. And there I am,
barren, the Virgin Queen.'

'Why the Virgin Queen?'

'It was his friends, their women, they all thought I
was looking down on them, ramming my education down
their throats. Terry was a common man. He had left
school with a couple of O Levels and an ambition to
drive fast cars and to fix them up. He's good at one, not
the other.'

'Lousy driver?'

'No coordination. He could never manage to
heel-and-toe; you know where you combine braking and
changing down a gear, matching the engine's revolutions.
He always thought it was the car, and if he had something
better, then he'd be able to do it.'

'But he couldn't, not in the better car?'

'Terry? We had a ten-year-old Ford, a bomb it
was. The one time I tried heel-and-toe, I aced it after the
second attempt. He drank more than he should that
night, said that I was lucky, and that tomorrow he'd show
me how it was done, how a professional racing driver
would have achieved the feat, not a woman with the luck
of the Irish.'

'You're not Irish?'

'And he wasn't sober either. The next day, he's out
with his friends, and he's there hurtling around the
country lanes not far from where we lived. He ended up
heel-and-toeing the three of them into the hospital after
he blipped the throttle when he should have been
braking. Ended up in a field, the car rolling twice. Terry

got out of it with a broken arm, two broken ribs, and a bruised ego.'

'What about the other two?'

'One was unharmed, a few bruises, that's all. The other man, an uncouth individual who peppered every three words with an expletive, is still in a wheelchair. So much for Terry's attempt at winning the Formula One World Championship.'

'So Terry's here in the house with you; he's angry or fancying his chances,' Isaac said.

'He starts to blame me for his life, and "that bitch Christine", his words, not mine, for denying him fatherhood. As I said, I believe it was not that important all those years ago, and I doubt if it is now. But that's Terry, a mouth that works overtime. He starts making statements, such as how he had sorted out Christine's fancy man, how he was going to have his revenge, how he knew about her and what she had got up to over the years. He even found a couple of men that I had supposedly had affairs with, even the individual in the wheelchair. As I said, he's talking nonsense, and he's irritating me.'

'How long did he stay in the house?'

'Twenty-eight minutes. A lawyer's attention to detail and I documented all that happened and what he said. At the time, I thought nothing to it. I was used to him, and I've met more than my fair share of deluded fools, drunks, and ne'er-do-wells, the same as you have.'

'Yet you called me,' Isaac said.

'He said that he had been in London and he had seen the dead man jogging alongside the Serpentine, and that…'

'Is that it?'

'He clammed up, said no more. After that, he got up from the chair and walked out of the house. He never said goodbye. He closed the front door gently, not banging it as he was apt to do after we had had an argument.'

'Are you suggesting that he could have killed Colin Young?'

'I'm not suggesting anything. It was him probably sounding off, a touch of bravado, an attempt to frighten me, to get his revenge.'

'If he killed the man, then he could come for you and Christine,' Isaac said.

'I can't see it, but it's a possibility, especially if he's had a few drinks. I'm not certain if he's mentally stable, either. According to you and your team, his business is shaky, the woman he's with is on the rough side. Embittered men commit terrible crimes.'

'Have you told your sister what you've just told me?'

'Not yet.'

'We'll get the police up in Liverpool to check on his movements, and it may be a good idea if you move out of your house. For a few days, that is.'

'I have enough money. I'll pay for twenty-four-hour security for the house and for me. It's not the first time that I've been threatened, occupational hazard if you've been a prosecuting lawyer.'

'Or a police officer,' Isaac said. 'Your sister?'

'She can come and stay here if she wants.'

'If she doesn't?'

'I'll ensure that her house is watched. She's my sister, and she drives me crazy, but blood is thicker than water.'

Isaac hoped that the reference to blood was metaphorical and that Homicide would not see any more in the current murder enquiry.

***

The consensus in Homicide was that the special clients of Colin Young/Barry Montgomery were not going to be found easily. The first location where the dead man had met with one of the 'specials', a cottage in the countryside, picturesque and available through Airbnb, had had a succession of different people occupying it, mostly couples looking for a romantic weekend, a wedding night, or just a break from the hustle and bustle of the city.

Bridget had found the owners, a professional couple who lived in Brighton, a city about seventy miles south of London. A favourite holiday destination on the coast in the past, but now, with discount airlines and trips to Europe and further afield affordable and in the reach of most people, some of its lustre had been lost. The Prince Regent built the Royal Pavilion there in the late eighteenth century, finally completing it in 1823. The prince, later to become George IV, maintained the building, designed in the Indo-Saracenic style, as a discreet location for his liaisons with his long-time companion, Maria Fitzherbert, later marrying her in secret.

Wendy and Larry drove past it to their meeting with the Goldworths, the owners of the thatched cottage, a building whose style had appealed to Wendy: homely, inviting, loved.

'We can't help you,' Brent Goldworth said. He and his wife were sitting in the alcove of the bay window in their third-floor flat on Brighton's promenade, overlooking the sea.

'My husband's correct. We go up there every couple of weeks to check everything's in order, though we don't clean the place. We pay an agency to do that and to ensure it's ready for whoever's coming. If it's newly-weds, we ensure that there's a bottle of champagne in the fridge, flower petals on the bed, but that's all. Credit card payment or PayPal, and there's a key around the back, hidden, a password to open where it is.'

'The agency?'

'A couple in the area. They've made a good business looking after rentals for absent landlords. Not that we're really absent, but we prefer to keep hands-off. If we're up there, Brent's fussing over what needs to be fixed up, a scratch on the wall, the television's getting old. As for me, I'm checking under the bed, in the cupboards, worrying as to who's been there, what they've been up to. We lived in it for a long time, until Brent was transferred down here, a company promotion. We should have sold the cottage, but it holds fond memories, and we'd prefer to leave it shut up, but that serves no purpose. Life's expensive enough as it is, and every little helps.'

Larry assumed that the Goldworths did not bother to tell Her Majesty's Revenue & Customs about their additional income. The short-term letting of property had become a lucrative black-market activity, and cities across the world were trying to crack down, ostensibly to maintain standards, although he knew, as did everyone else, that it was all to do with money. The hotels couldn't compete, their occupancy rates were down, and they weren't paying as much in taxes as they had before.

'We gave Bridget Halloran all that she requested,' Brent Goldworth said.

'Unfortunately, it didn't help. As you said, a credit card.'

'A name on it?'

'The murdered man had paid for it; no doubt whoever he met paid him back.'

'It's disturbing to think that someone who died had been in our cottage,' Emilia Goldworth said.

'And for the purposes of prostitution,' Wendy added.

'That's worse. We've considered selling the cottage after what has happened. Do you have any problem with that?'

'That's up to you. It's some time since the man was there with his lover. The crime scene investigators won't find anything, and we've not asked them to look. Besides, we're not sure what we're looking for. The place will be full of fingerprints, needle in a haystack to find Colin Young's, let alone who he was with.'

'You could try the agency we use.'

Larry and Wendy visited the agency on the way back to London.

'We don't make a habit of welcoming the visitors. Sometimes we'll go around if there's a problem, but that's rare, and we can't recollect a couple of men there. Are you sure about them? The Goldworths are a bit sensitive about that sort of thing,' a friendly red-faced man said. For someone who made a living looking after other peoples' properties, he didn't look particularly fit.

'Two men, that's it,' Wendy said.

'We can't help you, sorry.'

There was no need to visit the hotel in Windsor again. Mrs Winterly had provided the information that Colin Young had been there for her, and the date when he had been in the hotel with the 'special' coincided with a week when she had gone to see a friend in Cornwall.

Chapter 28

It was Larry who found Terry Hislop at a pub in
Paddington. It wasn't one of the trendy pubs that serve
gourmet food, boutique beer, or even a cup of coffee. It
was a serious drinking man's pub, the place that the
affluent kept well clear of.

'Made a fool of yourself,' Larry said as he sidled
up alongside the man sitting on a bar stool, leaning on the
bar, steadying himself to focus.

Hislop looked Larry's way, unable to make the
connection.

'Inspector Larry Hill, Homicide.'

'I've killed no one,' Hislop said, still struggling to
focus. It was as Gwen Hislop had told Isaac: Terry Hislop
wasn't a drinker, even if he wanted to be.

'We met in Liverpool. I came up with Sergeant
Wendy Gladstone.'

'I remember her well enough. She came to my
office.'

'That's it. You were polite then, and then the two
of us met you in the local police station. Coming back to
you now?'

'Gwen threw me out of her house.'

'Why not? You've been divorced from her for a
long time.'

'Maybe, maybe not.'

Larry looked over at the barman. 'No more drinks
for him,' pointing at Hislop.

'Who are you to tell me who to serve or not? His
money's as good as anyone else, and he's not drunk.'

Larry withdrew his warrant card from his inside jacket pocket and flashed it in the direction of the barman. 'As I said, no more drinks.'

'It's hard enough to make a living without you telling me what to do.'

'Don't give me any more of your lip. Once I've finished having a chat with this man, then he's yours to fleece.'

'As you say.'

Larry ignored the barman, not even asking if he was the licensee of the pub, although he probably was. It was an unattractive building with a dated interior, white tiles halfway up the walls, tiles on the floor as well. The pubs that were doing good business had diversified, gone upmarket.

'Now here's the deal, Hislop,' Larry said. 'We can have a nice little chat here, or you can be hauled down to Challis Street Police Station. What's it to be?'

'Can't a man have a quiet drink?'

'Not if they go around to their ex-wife's house and threaten her and her sister.'

'I didn't threaten. Maybe I had had a few drinks and said a few words I shouldn't have, but that's all. Gwen and me, we go back a long way. She was keen on me in the early days. She's still keen, I could tell.'

'Do you seriously believe that, or is it the beer talking?'

'I know my women.'

'Gwen Hislop is an educated woman, so is her sister. When you were all younger, and you carried less weight, then they may have seen something in you, but now? I don't think so. I'm told you're going around with a slapper up in Liverpool.'

'How dare you talk about Cynthia like that. I'll grant you that she doesn't look the best, but she doesn't complain about my drinking, and she doesn't accuse me of murder.'

Larry knew that character assassination and belittling the man's current girlfriend were wrong, but he needed a reaction, and once Hislop was sober, he would start to think before he spoke.

None of the Homicide team believed that he was the murderer, but he had made statements that indicated that he knew the story. Even that wasn't conclusive, as anyone with access to the internet, or a newspaper, could have learnt as much as he had; but most people nowadays neither had the time nor the interest to follow what was an increasingly stale crime.

'We've not accused you of murder, *yet*. Either you tell me why you were at Gwen's and why you cast certain aspersions, or I'll haul you in. Now, what's it to be?'

Larry looked over at the barman. 'Two pints of your best.'

'About time too. We're not a social club.'

Larry couldn't blame the man for his attitude. He would be barely covering costs, and possibly even making a loss each week; once, the pub's licence would have been worth a lot of money, now it was probably worth a lot less than when the man had paid for it. He was cursed financially whatever decisions he made.

Hislop downed half the contents of his glass before Larry had had a chance to take his first sip. If this is the pub's best, Larry thought, then he was glad he hadn't ordered the worst.

'You visited Gwen on two occasions.'

'Twice, that's it. She was really friendly the first time,' Hislop replied.

304

'Don't give me any nonsense about how your boyish charm won her over, and that she was yours. Hislop, you're a pathetic man who keeps getting himself into trouble. How about this business of yours? Strictly legal, no dodgy resprays, filing off the engine numbers?'

'What are you talking about? You know that doesn't happen anymore, too many rules and regulations. Nowadays, I change body parts, that's all. I was a craftsman when I first started out, made a good living. Gwen knows that.'

'And Cynthia?'

'My business, as with my women, has gone downhill. Gwen and her sister are classy women, and once both of them were putty in my hands. Christine's putting it about from what I've heard, and maybe I should give her a call, no harm in that.'

'If you don't want to spend a night in the cells, then I suggest you keep well clear.'

'A threat?'

'A fact. You visited Gwen the first time, nothing happened. I'll accept that.'

'Nothing happened the second time, either. If Gwen's told you differently, then she's lying.'

'I'm not saying she has. What's your story?'

Hislop had an issue with alcohol, a love-hate relationship, as did Larry. And Hislop had intellectual limitations. It was not as though the man was stupid, the same as for Larry: an inspector who wanted to be more, but he had come to realise that even if he devoted the time necessary, he just couldn't summon the intellectual stamina required to push his career on.

'Okay, I went around to her house. I wasn't planning to, but I'd had a few, and you know how it is?'

'Not really, but carry on. Why are you in London? A special trip to meet up with the sisters?'

'I'll admit to that. With you and your sergeant reopening old wounds, asking questions, it got me to thinking. Gwen's still on her own, and I am, more or less.'

'Cynthia?'

'It's casual. No doubt she'd like to take it to the next level, move in with me, but she won't.'

'Why not?'

'Where do you think I live?'

'Over the business.'

'It's not a home, is it? I had a place, but I couldn't keep up the payments. It wasn't much better, but at least it had a bathroom. All I've got now is a hose downstairs and a toilet in the back of the workshop. Hardly the sort of place for two people.'

'Would she mind?'

'Probably not. She's got a place, a one-bedroom flat courtesy of the council, but they'd get funny if I moved in there.'

'Would they find out?'

'Who knows? There are always nosey neighbours.'

'And you keep using it as an excuse.'

'I've still got some money, and I thought Gwen might have been responsive. After all, we did have something, and we're both getting on a bit. If she had had me back, then I would have played it fair and square.'

'You'd have still been after Christine.'

'Not this time.'

'I can't believe you. That's not the point, though, is it? You're with Gwen in her house; she's not enamoured of your drunken attempts at seduction. She's telling you to leave, you're getting angry.'

'She's an educated woman, spends too much time defending someone or other. I'm trying to reason with her, but she's not biting. She starts using words I can barely understand, making out that I'm stupid.'

'Did she? Or are you making this up to justify what you said about Christine and the dead man?'

'What did I say?'

'Your final words were, and I'm quoting from what Gwen said, and DCI Cook recorded, "He said that he had been in London and he had seen the dead man jogging alongside the Serpentine, and that…".'

'What then?'

'You left the house.'

'I deny it.'

'Deny all you want. I'll take Gwen's account of what was said over yours any day.'

'I'll admit that I knew Christine was working in that hotel, and that Gwen was a hotshot lawyer.'

'How?'

'I've got a laptop and the internet. You can find anyone if you look hard enough. Gwen was easy enough to find, and there were court transcripts, a photo of her, and Christine's into Facebook, photos of her with the children, her husband, a dog.'

Larry felt that the man's answer was plausible. He had reconnected with some friends from school using Facebook, met with a couple of them: one had become an actor, the other, a schoolteacher. After an hour of talking to each of them, it was evident that time had moved on and the child was not the man, and he had little in common with either of them.

But Terry Hislop still believed in the possibility of a connection with his former wife.

'I'll buy into how you knew about Gwen and Christine. It still doesn't explain why you said you saw the dead man jogging.'

'It does. The internet, updates on the news. You interviewed two joggers, they told you they had seen someone, and then after he had been identified, his name, his story.'

'Not on the front page of the newspapers.'

'What does that matter? I set an alert for any information relating to the murder, no matter how obscure. You can find anything on the internet, you know that?'

Larry had to concede that Bridget could. It was possible that, given time, Terry Hislop could as well.

'What are your plans?'

'I'm going back to Liverpool.'

'Cynthia?'

'Any port in a storm.'

'Then I suggest you go. If you go near Gwen or Christine, they'll be trouble for you. Do you understand?'

'Christine could have still killed him, you know that?'

'Amateur detective, are you?'

'Statistically, the murderer is often the nearest and dearest, a family member. Isn't that correct?'

'The internet?'

'That's what I read.'

'You may be right, but Christine Mason is not high on our list of potential suspects. However, you are. Hislop, I suggest you leave London tonight. In fact, I'll put you on the train myself.'

'Up to you.'

Larry finished his drink and took hold of Hislop's arm. 'Where are you staying?'

'Next door, a budget hotel. It's not much to look at, but it's clean.'

'With a shower?'

'And a bath. Luxury after what I've had to put up with for the last few months.'

Sixty-five minutes later, Terry Hislop boarded his train. Larry hoped it was the last that he saw of him. He had not killed Colin Young/Barry Montgomery, that much was known, as his movements could be accounted for in Liverpool at the time and date when the man had met his fate in that cold lake early in the morning.

***

Nobody in Homicide had intended going back to Pembridge Mews so soon. Its significance in the investigation was that it was where Matilda Montgomery had lived and committed suicide and where Amelia Bentham, who lived in another mews house, had bedded Matilda's brother.

And now, as the team drove up to Matilda's house, a sign outside, placed there by an estate agent, announced that it was for sale.

Typically, just one or two from Homicide would have attended the scene, but the old man with the walking stick and the limp had been adamant.

'Come quick,' he had said to Wendy when he had phoned. 'Bring your DCI.'

The man ended the phone call soon after. Another time Wendy would have regarded the request as that of an old man looking for attention, feeling the loneliness of age, but this was different.

'I don't know,' she said to the others in the office. 'It seems serious to me. We'd better go.'

Larry had phoned for a patrol car to be at the scene, to wait out on the main road and not in the cul-de-sac.

'It's inside,' the old man said as the three of them, Isaac, Larry and Wendy, got out of their car.

'What's inside?' Larry asked. He had figured from his previous encounters with the man that he was the person in the street – every street seemed to have one – that kept an eye on the comings and goings, who was sleeping with who, who had just bought some new furniture, who had argued with their spouse. Not the sort of person you always wanted living near to you, but handy in a murder investigation.

'Matilda's father. I saw him enter three days ago and I never saw him leave.'

'That doesn't mean he's inside.'

'There are no lights on, not even at night, and there's a smell.'

Wendy pressed her nose close to the front door. 'He's right,' she said.

'We don't need a warrant for this,' Isaac said. 'Ask the uniforms in the patrol car if they have an enforcer.'

'No need for a battering ram,' Wendy said. 'If Amelia's at home, she'll probably have a spare key.'

Two minutes later the door to Matilda Montgomery's house was opened, the key having been supplied by Amelia Bentham. Isaac entered on his own, ensuring that he had shoe protectors on his feet, nitrile gloves on his hands. The old man had wanted to go in too, but Larry had told him firmly that if anything was untoward then the fewer people inside, the better.

The old man didn't understand. To him, he had alerted the police and that somehow gave him privileged status. A small crowd was starting to form outside the building; Amelia standing to one side with Wendy.

'What do you reckon?' Wendy asked the young woman. 'Stanley Montgomery, have you seen him recently?'

'Once, but that was when they put it up for sale. He acknowledged my presence, but he didn't want to talk, never asked if I had a spare key. Unusual, I thought at the time, and why he didn't change the lock, I don't know.'

'Has the place been painted, carpet changed, that sort of thing?'

'Not that I know of. What if someone buys it, moves in, and then finds out that Matilda committed suicide in there?'

'I'd say they had a lousy solicitor. The estate agent will only address questions asked, and he'll definitely not be proffering that fact. It'll only lower the price, render if virtually unsaleable.'

'That's what I thought. Why would he want to sell it so soon after? It makes no sense.'

'Nor did the treatment of his wife and his children, and they're all dead.'

Isaac walked along the small hallway, opening a door to one side and entering an open-plan area. Nothing appeared out of order apart from a distinctive smell. He quickly found that it was because the fridge door was open, some cheese inside a delicate mouldy blue. Also, a milk carton was open, its contents gone off.

Isaac felt that there was no more to see and that the small house was in otherwise good order. He checked in the pantry at the rear, nothing to see. He then climbed the stairs to the two bedrooms upstairs. There was no sign of anyone in the first. The second room, the room where Matilda Montgomery had killed herself, was in front of him. Gingerly, Isaac opened the door, not so much from a sense of trepidation, more from a belief that he was interfering in the domain of the dead.

Inside, what he had hoped not to see loomed in front of him. He retreated from the room, retracing his steps, and rejoined Larry and Wendy outside.

Wendy could see from his face that something was wrong.

'Call Gordon Windsor, tell him to bring his team here,' Isaac said as he walked away. 'And get the uniforms to establish a crime scene.'

'Stanley Montgomery?' Larry asked.

'Swinging from the same beam as his daughter. No need to rush in and check his pulse. He's been there for a couple of days from what I can see.'

The old man adopted a look of 'I told you so'. Amelia Bentham shed a tear.

'So much tragedy for one family,' Wendy said.

'Is there a suicide letter?' Larry called to Isaac.

'There's one. Wait for Gordon Windsor to give us the all-clear and then we'll get to read it.'

'We could read it now,' Wendy said. 'It could be important.'

'It could be, but wait. The man's dead, and it's suicide. A couple of hours is not going to make any difference either way.'

Chapter 29

A full team of crime scene investigators were in the house in Pembridge Mews, as were Isaac and Larry. A smell continued to permeate it, no longer coming from the opened fridge but from upstairs where the body of Stanley Montgomery hung.

'The letter?' Isaac asked Windsor, the senior crime scene investigator.

'It's bagged.'

'We need to read it.'

'As long as you sign for it. There's no doubt that he killed himself, messy though.'

'That's what suicide is.'

'You've confirmed it's the father. She had made a decent knot, even though she would have been strangled, not broken her neck. But he would have suffered for longer. The knot wasn't tight, and if he had tried, he could have probably used his weight to break the beam, or failing that to have stretched the rope sufficiently for him to touch the floor.'

'He would still have died.'

'Probably. What was his state of mind?' Windsor asked.

'His son had been murdered, his daughter hanged from the same beam, his wife dead in hospital from a broken heart and malnutrition,' Larry said.

'Not much to live for then. There's a half-empty bottle of whisky under the bed, also a bottle of sedatives.'

'The daughter committed suicide without any of those.'

'It makes no difference,' Windsor said.'

'Agreed. Now the letter,' Isaac said.

'Is it his writing?' Windsor asked as he handed the letter over.

'I can't be sure. What had you hoped to gain from bagging it?'

'Confirmation that the man had written it. Obvious, I'll grant you that, considering that it was in the room with him, and no one else has been in. It may help you if we know whether it was written in here, or if he brought it with him. Whether he had contemplated suicide or whether it was spur of the moment.'

'He had to buy the rope,' Isaac said.

'Is his car nearby?' Windsor asked.

'Not that we know of.'

Isaac took hold of the letter and left the house with Larry. They both removed their protective clothing on leaving.

The old man, who had a smug look, was standing in the middle of the mews. Larry moved over closer to him.

'Rum do,' the man said. The excitement appeared to have perked him up, and he was not leaning so heavily on his walking stick.

'There must have been some noise,' Larry said.

'Amelia had one of her parties a couple of nights ago. If he had done it then, nobody would have heard.'

'Yet you suspected something?'

'I keep a watch on what goes on here, not like some.'

'What does that mean?'

'Amelia cares, not that she's here all the time. But some of the others, they're here during the week, and then at the weekend they're off somewhere or other.'

'People live busy lives,' Larry said. He knew the old man was a busybody, but he was a decent person, and according to what Amelia had told Wendy, he was well-liked by his neighbours, never complaining if there was a party, as long as he got an invite, the chance for one or two drinks.

'You're right, but I'm here all the time. If people look after their places, then that's fine. We had a rogue down the other end of the mews, a couple of years back now, who was dealing in drugs. The police picked him up soon enough.'

'Did you report him?'

'He caused no trouble, and the only times I saw him, he was extremely polite. You never know who people are really, do you?'

'Not really,' Larry agreed. 'You've still not explained why you phoned us to come to Pembridge Mews urgently.'

'I was right, wasn't I?'

'Lucky guess, or is there more to it?'

'What do you know about me, Inspector Hill?'

'What you told me and what we've checked on since.'

'SAS, Special Air Service when I was younger, behind enemy lines. I wasn't always an old man. You'll not find any reference to my full military record on any website, no matter how hard you try. And it's confidential, so don't go putting it into any report.'

'I need to report what I see and hear, you know that.'

'I prefer to live my life in cold reflection of what I saw and did, not to become involved in a police investigation.'

'But you have.'

'I've acted as a responsible citizen, that's all. Pembridge Mews is important to me, so are the people who live here. I missed picking up on Matilda, but I wasn't looking for clues then. I'm trained to observe and to remember, more of a subconscious reaction nowadays. I saw her father going into the house, I never saw him come out.'

'Did he have a rope when he went in?'

'He was carrying a bag with him. There could have been a rope in there.'

'Why did you believe we'd find him dead?'

'I'm trained to observe, I told you that, to ascertain a person's frame of mind. Whether they're cheerful or sad, and if their body language contradicts how they appear. A subtle art, and no doubt I could teach you a thing or two about it.'

'Once this is over, maybe you could,' Larry said. He had to feel admiration for the man who was maintaining his wish to live out his remaining years in tranquillity, not interfering, just observing, helping where he could. Larry realised that the man had trusted him with privileged information. He would respect his wishes, although in confidence he would need to tell his DCI.

'I can give you a few pointers. The father goes into the house, he's carrying a heavy bag. I can see his face. It's not the face of a contented man. I can see the lines etched into his forehead, the drawn expression, the obvious signs that he's not been eating properly for some time, and that he's been drinking.'

'You can tell all that?'

'If you're behind enemy lines, you need to be able to judge quickly. Is the man standing in front of you ready to shoot or is he just a local peasant trying to feed his family, not interested in getting involved in petty squabbles and violence?'

'Afghanistan?'

'Other countries, not there. My time with the military was over before that became a war zone. Don't ask too many questions. Not everyone understands or agrees with what we had to do.'

'Do you agree, on reflection?'

'I was a soldier, following orders. And besides, we're talking about Stanley Montgomery.'

'Sorry for diverging. It sounds interesting.'

'It was bloody and dirty and sometimes boring. We did things that no man should ever be forced to do, experienced things that I don't need to talk about.'

'The limp?'

'A bullet in the leg, but mainly it's old age.'

'My apologies for resurrecting the past.'

'Sometimes it's good to talk. Coming back to Montgomery. He enters the house, closing the door behind him. He moves through to the kitchen at the rear, and opens the fridge.'

'You could see this?'

'Through a gap in the curtains. I'm suspicious, not because I'm interested in what he's up to, but as I said, I've seen the man's face.'

'Then what?'

'A group of Amelia's friends appear, and they beckon me over.'

'A couple of drinks and you no longer took any interest in Montgomery?'

'That's it. I couldn't have known what his ultimate intent was. Maybe he didn't either.'

'But he had a rope.'

'Having and doing are two different things. And I'm not the Samaritans. If the man's intention had been clearer, then I'd have probably knocked on the door and had a chat to him, but it wasn't. I liked Matilda, even her brother, so I can understand the father being upset. Most people deal with it in time, but he didn't.

'And then you phone us?'

'The house had been quiet, the lights off. He could have been drowning his sorrows for all I know, but then the smell from the kitchen. And yes, I did stick my nose to the front door, the same as your sergeant. That was the signal that something was amiss.'

'That's when you phoned us?'

'In my army days, it was a clear indicator that if the food was rotten, then no one was at home or they were dead, but I knew he was inside.'

'You were certain of your facts when you phoned us?'

'As certain as I could be. Of course, he could have left, and I had missed it, but why the open fridge, the rotting food, the smell of burnt meat?'

Larry left the man and joined Isaac and Wendy who were sitting in Isaac's car. He couldn't help but think that he had been talking to Sherlock Holmes and James Bond, both wrapped up into one man who walked with a limp.

***

Isaac removed the letter from the evidence bag. On the front of the envelope, 'To whom it may concern'. He then withdrew the letter and unfolded it. The writing was firm and legible, the signature on the third page that of Stanley Montgomery.

'What does it say?' Wendy asked.

'There's a lot here,' Isaac said as he scanned it.

'Give us the précised version,' Larry said. He didn't need to know all the details, only if the letter was a confession.

> *I, Stanley Edward Montgomery, of sound mind and in control of all of my faculties, confess to the murder of my son, Barry Montgomery. I am also responsible for the suicide of my daughter, Matilda, the death of my wife, Janice.*

None of the three in Isaac's vehicle concurred with the man's view of himself as sane.

'There's a page relating to the distribution of assets,' Isaac said. 'A brother in Scotland, a sister in Wales. No mention of his wife's family, no bequests to charity.'

'Is that it?' Larry said.

'There's more.

> *I am sorry for what happened to Barry, and I wish that it could have been different. But he had chosen a different path in life. The need to rebel was strong in him, and whereas I had given him and his sister strong discipline and good values, he rejected them. I knew of his descent into depravity, his prostituting himself for money, something I abhor. It could not be allowed to continue, to sully the good name of Montgomery, to upset his mother, a fragile person but kindly and loving.*

'It's a confession,' Wendy said.

'It's a suicide letter, an unburdening of the man's soul,' Isaac said. 'Wait till I've finished reading before commenting.'

Matilda, a young woman of good values, committed suicide because of my intractability, my unwillingness to embrace her brother, a person she loved dearly, as did her mother. My anger towards him had abated to some extent, and I had hoped that in time he would understand the devotion I had given to the family, the desire to protect them from the evils of the world, the wanton greed, the promiscuity. I now realise that I had failed and that Janice, my wife, and the mother of Barry and Matilda, was unwilling to continue. She died in great sorrow, and yet, even though I had wished to join her, I could not. My body is too strong, my resolve would not allow it. There was only one solution to my dilemma, and if you are now reading this letter, then I have been successful.

'That's it,' Isaac said, 'apart from his signature at the bottom.'

'Date?' Larry asked.

'Two days ago.'

'Is that it?' Wendy said. 'Stanley Montgomery was the murderer?'

'He's confessed but given no proof,' Larry said.

'That's the crux of it,' Isaac said. 'We could accept the man's letter at face value, and wrap up the investigation, but where's the proof? What he's admitted to is that he was responsible for his son's murder. Does that mean that he hit his son on the head in Hyde Park and left him to drown in the Serpentine, or is he confessing that he failed to guide his son as a child, and then the man had left the family home and sunk into depravity and despair, which had ultimately resulted in his murder.

'I'd say the latter,' Larry said.

'Are we agreed that this investigation is not concluded?' Isaac asked.

'We have to. If we don't, then a murderer could still be free.'

Isaac knew that Jenny was out buying presents to take to Jamaica, and time was marching against them making the flight, but murder was murder; he couldn't allow the easy option to take precedence over his professional responsibilities.

Chapter 30

Isaac was gratified that his team were not willing to accept the suicide letter as a murderer's confession. Other police officers would not have been as thorough; some would have wrapped up the case, hoping that no one else was murdered. However, that wasn't how he worked, although Richard Goddard, his chief superintendent, wasn't pleased that the murder inquiry wasn't over yet.

'Are you certain on this?' Goddard asked. He was in Isaac's office.

'He could have killed his son, that's true.'

'You're not convinced?'

'Not yet. We've not been able to connect him to the murder scene, although his alibi was weak. And then, he's claiming that he was responsible for his daughter's death, but why?'

'His mind was disturbed.'

'We can agree on that, and no doubt the trauma he had put his family through over the years rendered them all unstable, to some extent. Barry Montgomery seems to have been the sanest of the lot in that he got away from his father.'

'But selling himself doesn't seem such a great idea.'

'Not in itself, although from what we've been told, he was a man in control of himself. Janice Montgomery, the mother, wasn't, but then she had a weak personality, easily led.'

'Or Stanley Montgomery had beaten her into submission,' Goddard said.

'We've no proof of violence against the man.'

'Constant brow-beating, interminable criticism of whatever she did.'

'There's no crime against him for his wife's death, but I'll go along with your assessment. It still doesn't explain Matilda Montgomery's suicide though.'

'It depends on your perspective.'

Isaac had great respect for his chief superintendent, a man of experience and clear thought.

'If, as you say, Matilda Montgomery committed suicide, with no other person in the house, then what was going through her mind?' Goddard continued.

'We don't know. There was no letter from her, unusual in a suicide.'

'Why didn't she write a letter? Have you considered that?'

'Statistically, she would have been expected to.'

'Statistics aside, she took time arranging her death. She may have been under great strain but she was careful to be tidy, and according to Windsor's report, she had tied the knot in the rope with care and precision.'

'Cold and passionless, some would say.'

'Why? I'd say that she was a highly emotional woman who had decided on a course of action, and nothing could dissuade her. You've said before that her life was ordered, and that there were no broken romances, no issues at work, and that she had sufficient money in her bank account.'

'Where's this going?' Isaac asked.

'You've interpreted a suicide letter as a possible confession.'

'But we've not accepted it at face value. We still need to prove it one way or the other.'

'Credit to you and your team for that, but it's raised a concern. Your focus is now on Stanley Montgomery at the expense of your other suspects.'

'To some degree.'

'Not some, a lot. And if I was the senior investigating officer in this case, that's the approach that I'd be taking. The others who could have done it have alibis, weak motives, or neither the strength nor the malice to commit murder.'

'There wasn't a lot of strength required, but you're right about the malice. A discarded woman, a hotel manager who has proven himself to be a despicable character, a husband who now knows of his wife's involvement with the murdered man, an ex-husband of the sister who felt that Christine Mason had cheated him of fatherhood. None of them shows the necessary intent to kill.'

'But Stanley Montgomery does.'

'An intense man, a man with deep and hidden thoughts, a dark heart.'

'Yet you say that he loved his family with intense emotion.'

'His family, he may have, but he had little affection for others, those that had disappointed him.'

'Barry Montgomery?'

'Exactly. Stanley felt anger towards him, there was the probability of violence.'

'Coming back to Matilda. The woman was smart, and from what we know, she had emotional problems.'

'Everyone has issues, but yes, according to Amelia Bentham, the only person who could claim to know her, Matilda could throw up a wall if anyone got too close.'

'Matilda, from what she's read about the body in Hyde Park, is certain that it's her brother. Possible?'

'That's what we believe. In fact, we had placed a photo in the newspapers and on the television.'

'But no one came forward. Why was that?'

'The body didn't look like the Barry Montgomery that Matilda would have known. He had dyed his hair, had it cut short.'

'A sister would know, and what about Amelia Bentham? Even Christine Mason and the other women he was messing around with?'

'Amelia Bentham was out of the country, and Barry and Matilda Montgomery's parents don't have a television, not even a radio. Stanley didn't want the wickedness, the licentiousness of the world to enter his domain.'

'Matilda's figured out that her brother's been murdered,' Goddard said. 'She doesn't know about the other people, probably doesn't know that he's been prostituting himself. To her, he's the one constant in her life, the one person who understands, the one person she truly loves. The woman is still struggling with her upbringing, still racked with emotional issues, and there's her brother, the rock in her life, the one person she can talk to, and now he's dead.'

'Are you suggesting that she killed herself because of that?'

'Why not? Her brother's dead, and she shuts down emotionally. She doesn't know what to do, how to react, but then she starts thinking. Remember she doesn't know about the other people in her brother's life, apart from Amelia.'

'Matilda knew that Amelia was in love with her brother.'

'So she's not blaming her. There's only one possibility, her father.'

'That's what he had written.'

'Stanley Montgomery's letter was succinct and to the point. Matilda's was non-existent. Other people write pages of semi-coherent nonsense, about life and love and the problems with the world, but with her, nothing.'

'If she had written anything, it would have been to say that she blamed her father and that he was the murderer.'

'But she couldn't,' Goddard said. 'Her father was another constant in her life, even if he had not been a constant for good, and he was a man who demanded loyalty, and Matilda had to consider her mother. If she had written that letter, it would have accused her father, and she couldn't. Detached from reality, her suicide would have been a robotic act. She wouldn't have felt pain or suffering, just her life slipping away.'

'It doesn't make Stanley Montgomery a murderer,' Isaac said.

'I'd agree with that hypothesis. I suggest you find out who it is before too long.'

***

Nick Domett, part-time male escort – if you were desperate, Wendy thought – sat across from her and Larry. His escorting activities were not of interest, his position as the principal of Gents for Hire was.

'We were fellow officers once,' Domett said. 'Give me a break. I've broken no law, and I've helped you where I can.'

'The specials?' Larry said. 'We can't find out who they are. The case has gone cold, and you're the missing link in the chain.'

'I told you before, more than once. An envelope, sometimes a parcel, money inside, and where to go. That's all I know.'

'An ex-police officer is inherently nosey; you know that as well as we do.'

'So what if I was nosey? If someone wants to keep their identity confidential, who am I to worry? Good money, much better than the usual, and if their demands were perverted, what concern was it of mine?'

'Perverted? How do you know this? Did Colin Young tell you this?'

'Not him. He was always careful in what he said, but some of the others, they like to talk from time to time. Almost a badge of honour to some of them, what happened.'

'Define perverted,' Wendy said. The three were in Domett's office, and for once, it was clean.

'Whips, bondage, submission, that sort of thing.'

'Is that it?'

'Polite company. Do you want me to tell you more? You've both been around, you both know how far people can sink.'

'We do,' Larry said. He, for one, did not want Domett to recount tales of beatings, and bodily fluids, and carnal savagery. He had come across a place once before at his previous station, in the cellar of a Victorian terrace house, implements on the walls and hanging from the ceiling.

'There was none of that with Colin Young, not in a cottage or a hotel room,' Wendy said.

'He wasn't into that, not too much of it anyway. Tying up the client and humiliating him, he would have done that. It's some of the other men I employ who are more willing.'

327

'The same specials as Colin Young?'

'Not that I'm aware of. If you're trying to find out who they are through me, then you're wasting your time. I just don't know, and that's the truth.'

'And if you did, you wouldn't tell us.'

'I gave you all that I had. If you can't find out who these men were, then either you're not good police officers or they've covered their tracks well.'

Larry did not appreciate the slur on his and Wendy's abilities, not from a man who by his own admission had failed as a police officer, concealed the fact by pretending that a company that hired out men for sex was more profitable. And judging by the look of the office and the man, that may not have been true.

Domett, Larry and Wendy agreed after they had left him to his phone calls and organising that night's activities, wasn't going to give them much more.

'He's smart enough to take his special clientele's money, smart enough not to ask too many questions,' Larry said.

Wendy had to agree and nodded her head, unable to speak as she took the first bite of a McDonald's burger. Larry knew that his wife would have a few words if she knew that he was joining his sergeant, but it did not stop him ordering one for himself.

***

It wasn't usual; in fact, Isaac couldn't remember it happening before, but he was in a conference room at Challis Street and across from him were Gordon Windsor and Graham Picket.

'I don't appreciate your chief superintendent pulling rank,' Picket said. 'I've got an autopsy on this morning, a ninety-year-old man. You'd think they'd let him rest in peace, but his family are known tearaways, and he had plenty of money. No point opening me up when I'm gone, I can barely pay the bills as it is.'

Isaac had never seen the man so verbose. In his office or if he was bent over a cadaver in Pathology, he said very little, only answering questions when asked.

'What's the aim of this meeting?' Gordon Windsor asked. An agreeable and competent man, he was also a friend of Isaac's.

'We need to decide if Stanley Montgomery murdered his son, and if not, then who did.'

'Agreed, but where do Picket and I come into this? We conducted our investigations, filed our reports.'

'We're not convinced that Montgomery killed his son.'

'Specifics,' Picket said. 'The man's confessed, so I'm told, yet you want me and Windsor to give you a hitherto hidden fact to either validate the man's claim or to disprove it.'

'In a nutshell, yes.'

'Stanley Montgomery was a robust man of sixty-three. He could have killed his son. Is that what you want?'

'Can we prove it wasn't him?'

'How?' Windsor asked. 'We submitted our reports. The rock hit the man at an oblique angle. It also leads us to believe that the person was right-handed, and that force was applied.'

'Enough to kill?'

'If it had hit at the right place; if the dead man hadn't pulled away.'

'Too many variables, that's what you're saying?'

'Isaac, we're not sure where you're going with this. The father could have killed the son, so could any number of other people.'

'Amelia Bentham?'

'If this is going nowhere, I need to leave,' Windsor said.

'I'll be right behind you,' Picket added.

There's one possibility,' Isaac said. 'Matilda Montgomery.'

'Wild speculation on your part, or is there any reason to bring her in as a possible suspect?'

'She's the one person we've not considered. Was she strong enough?'

'She wasn't a bodybuilder, nothing like that, but it was clear when I examined her that she was fit, as was her brother.'

'She wasn't a jogger, we know that.'

'Swimming, walking, visits to the gym, that sort of thing.'

'My apologies for bringing you both here today,' Isaac said. 'You've both helped a great deal.'

'We said nothing new,' Gordon Windsor said.

'Neither of you did, but it helped to clarify the investigation for me.'

'Matilda Montgomery?'

'It's a possibility. A tragedy if it was.'

Chapter 31

Amelia Bentham wasn't much help, Wendy had to admit as the two of them sat in a café not far from Pembridge Mews. It was eleven in the morning, and Amelia was anxious to get away by midday for a photo shoot. The woman's behaviour was out of character, Wendy thought, as in the past she had always been cooperative, willing to chat, wanting to assist as best she could, but now she was holding back.

'It's been a hard week,' Amelia, as attractive as ever, said.

'Amelia, she was your friend, and now my chief inspector's got this bee in his bonnet that Matilda could have killed her brother.' Wendy knew that Isaac wasn't fixated on the woman's guilt, had purely raised the possibility, but she wasn't going to let Amelia know that. She wanted more from the woman, and she was sure there was more: the evasive answers, avoiding eye contact, both indicators that something was amiss.

'I must go,' Amelia insisted, rising from her chair, Wendy taking hold of her shoulder, pushing her back down again.

'I'm sorry, but you're going to tell me what you've been trying to avoid since we came in here.'

'There's nothing, honestly.'

Not good enough for Wendy. She had come to like the well-balanced woman from an aristocratic family who did not use that fact for her benefit, no more than her parents. She was willing to work hard, and to make her way in the world, successfully as it turned out.

Wendy had bought a magazine from her local newsagent two days previously, and there was Amelia on the front cover, standing on a sandy beach in a bikini. Definitely not the wear for today, as outside the café there was a steady drizzle and a cold bite in the air.

'I'm not willing to let Matilda be labelled a murderer, are you?' Wendy said, hoping to get through to the woman about the seriousness of the situation.

'I've no more to say. I must go. I thought with her father's death that would be the end of it.'

'You thought wrong. He's admitted that he was responsible for killing his son, also that he was guilty of his daughter's suicide, his wife's death. We know that two of the three are not correct, not the actual act. We've no proof that he was in Hyde Park either. But you, Amelia, have admitted to being in love with Barry, yet you've never said what Matilda thought of it.'

'I've told you. She knew about my love for him, his neutrality towards me. Just someone to sleep with when he wasn't whoring.'

'You knew about that, didn't you? Admit it now, or I'll know you're lying.'

'I suspected that he was. There was a woman outside Matilda's house once, someone I hadn't seen before.'

'New evidence? Why have you kept this secret?'

'It was the day before he died. I didn't think much of it at the time. She stayed for a few minutes and then left. It's only with you asking questions, and then confirming that Barry was putting it about, that I've started to think more about it.'

'Yet you still never came to me with this, knowing that I wouldn't judge you and I would have followed through on it.'

'I was frightened to tell you anything.'

'Describe the woman.'

'Blonde, mid to late forties, attractive, starting to put on weight. I didn't look at her for too long, but I could see that she would have been a stunner in her day.'

'Tall?'

'Tall enough to have been a model. That's what they want these days, tall, skinny, androgynous if they can.'

'The person I have in mind wouldn't qualify on the androgynous. You'd better make a phone call, tell the photographer that you'll be late. Is this the woman?' Wendy scrolled through the photos on her smartphone and showed the selected image to Amelia.

'Her hair was longer, but yes, that's her.'

'That's what I thought. I'm sorry, you'll have to reschedule or cancel. This is serious.'

Amelia made a call. 'We've rescheduled for tomorrow,' she said to Wendy after she had finished the call. 'It's a nuisance, and the makeup artist and photographer will want extra money now.'

'Your money?'

'No, but that's not the point. It's my reputation that suffers. The models who get the work are the ones who turn up on time, healthy and able to pose.'

'Some don't?'

'Some of them don't eat, or they've got a love affair with recreational drugs.'

'The same as you?'

'A casual acquaintance, that's all.'

'We can either talk here or at your place.'

'Here's fine. The memories back there are starting to get to me. I've considered moving, but the price of the place will be down on account of what's happened across the road.'

'The truth, not the shortened version that you've been feeding me,' Wendy said.

'It doesn't look good for me, I'm afraid.'

'Why?'

'Matilda knew about Barry and me. She accepted it when it was casual. But then it started to become more serious.'

'Barry as well?'

'He was more reticent, but with time, or maybe I was just hopelessly in love and deluded, I'm not sure which. I felt that he was coming out of his shell and that the two of us could have made a go of it.'

'There's still this bond between Barry and Matilda.'

'It was sibling love, nothing physical. And back then, I never knew of the life the two of them had had as children. Even if I had known, I wouldn't have known how to react. I'd grown up in the country, the child of wealthy parents, a horse for my birthday, a stately home to live in.'

'I had a horse,' Wendy said. 'It pulled a cart sometimes, not that it was much good for that. Sometimes I'd ride it, bareback.'

'Our lives, so different, yet we can be friends.'

'It depends on what you tell me.'

'Still friends, regardless. You know, Wendy, that you are a thoroughly decent person. No wonder my parents liked you, and once this is over, you and your friend Bridget must come up and stay with us, sample my father's wines, and I'll take you horse riding.'

'We're getting away from what we were talking about.'

'It was the day before Barry died. We had spent the night together, not that Matilda knew. For some reason, she had come home late the previous day, and Barry had come to my place first. He said that he was in love with me.'

'Had he said it before?'

'In the throes of passion, but men tend to do that sort of thing.'

'This time it wasn't lust?'

'Not much of it anyway. We're sitting downstairs having a glass of wine, and he leans over and says the words. I'm not sure what to say and do.'

'Why?'

'Matilda. I knew enough of her to know her reaction. She had to be told before I could reciprocate. I didn't want to allow what I felt for him to become an overriding obsession, knowing what could happen if we made a mistake. I've got my parents as a reference, and I wanted what they had for each other. Matilda could have been a complication that I couldn't deal with.'

'Love is blind, conquers all obstacles,' Wendy said.

'Poetical, but that's not reality, is it?'

Wendy thought it was.

'Why haven't you told us this before?'

'I blocked it out. I had to, don't you understand?'

Wendy could understand that a person might want to; there was only so much bad news that any one person could take.

'I take it that you confronted Matilda with what Barry had professed to you.'

'I didn't know about the other women. If I had, I wouldn't have fallen in love with him.'

'Where did you think his money came from?'

335

'Matilda had money, and he told me that he did some modelling, not that I had ever seen his work anywhere, and that he helped out a friend with his business. Quite frankly, I wasn't overthinking about it. He always dressed well, he didn't have a car, and he stayed with Matilda most of the time, and I'm sure he never gave her any money.'

'She could have given him some.'

'I never asked. It wasn't my business to pry, and the two of them were my friends.'

'One was more than that.'

'A good friend, yes.'

'Matilda?'

'She came over, and we sat around the kitchen table. I asked her if she would object if Barry moved in with me.'

'Her reaction?'

'At first, she was supportive. She said she understood, and that she was pleased for us.'

'Did you believe her?'

'I was initially pleased with her reaction, but then she started to throw up negatives. How were we going to survive financially? How could we maintain a relationship with me away modelling? Barry without a career? Her mood was becoming morose. We both could see that she had only wished us well out of courtesy, the same as you do when a work colleague tells you she's pregnant or getting married.'

'It ended badly?'

'Matilda started to become animated. And remember, this is a woman who rarely showed emotion.'

'She became violent?'

'She accused me of being a bitch for seducing her brother, and Barry for being such a fool. Her anger was directed against me, not against him.'

'We believed you weren't in the country.'

'I didn't openly deceive you or your fellow officers. I just preferred to forget, and then, Barry disappears, and I find out he's dead, and Matilda's hanged herself. It was just too much to comprehend.'

'Let's come back to when you told Matilda about you and Barry,' Wendy said. She waved over to the waitress, two fingers, not in an offensive salute, but as an indicator for two coffees to be brought to the table. She also pointed to cheesecake in a glass-fronted cabinet, two fingers again.

'Matilda started accusing Barry of deserting her. He stayed calm, brooding under the surface. I don't believe he could ever say a word against her, not to me, never to her. I could see that the bond was unbreakable between the two and that it would have been a marriage of three. I accused Barry of not being a man, irrational on reflection, but he wasn't under the thumb of an oppressive parent, he was under Matilda's thumb.'

'Is that it?'

'Not totally. Barry left in a huff, not saying a word to me. I swore at him. Matilda stayed with me, and within ten minutes, she's talking about this and that, not looking smug, nothing that you would sense as unusual. The Chinese might call it inscrutable, but to me, she was still seething. She left soon after to go to her cottage, and I hailed a taxi for the airport. That was the last time I saw either of them alive.'

'What's missing?'

'Nothing,' Amelia said as she drank her coffee, prodded her cheesecake. Wendy imagined that she would be a secret food purger if she felt that her weight was increasing.

'You've thrown the investigation wide open by telling me all this. You'd better tell me the rest.'

'I was livid, and I told Barry that he had destroyed my life, and if I ever saw him again, I'd kill him.'

'Angry people say stupid things. Were you that angry? Did you kill him?'

'I was overseas when he died. I wanted Barry, more than anything else in the world.'

'Matilda?'

'Who knows what was going through her mind. Did anyone ever know? The next time I saw her was when I found her hanging from that beam. It still gives me nightmares.'

'Could Matilda have killed Barry?'

'I don't know. Honestly, I don't.'

'Could she swim?'

'Not a stroke.'

***

Christine Mason had been hauled into Challis Street. Amelia had confirmed that she had been in Pembridge Mews, which meant that she, like others, had been economical with the truth.

It was four in the afternoon, and the woman was fretting, having been confined to the police station for two hours and thirty-five minutes already.

Isaac sat beside Wendy; Christine Mason beside Gwen Hislop. The four were in the interview room. Four bottles of water were on the table that separated the police officers from the sisters.

Isaac went through the formalities, informing Christine of her rights, the procedure to be followed, the usual. He could say it all verbatim, and Gwen Hislop knew it equally well.

Christine Mason sat calmly, although she was picking at her fingernails, and her lipstick had been applied with a nervous hand sometime before. Gwen Hislop, whom Isaac admired, for her professionalism and the fact that she was representing her sister, someone who, by her own admission, she did not like very much.

'Mrs Mason, you were seen outside Barry Montgomery's sister's house. You know him as Colin Young.'

'I hope we're not going over old ground here, Chief Inspector,' Gwen Hislop said. 'My client's had a difficult few days, and if this is another attempt to draw more information from her, then I will regard this as more than the diligent carrying out of your police duties.'

Isaac did not respond, aware that the woman was trying to throw him off track.

'Christine, are you denying that you were in Pembridge Mews one day before Colin Young's death?'

'I went to find him in Hyde Park, you know that.'

'We know this well enough, but we never knew about Pembridge Mews. Why?'

'Why what?' Gwen Hislop asked. 'You're beating around the bush on this. My client has given a full account of her actions, explained where and when she was, who she was sleeping with.'

'We can prove that Christine was in Pembridge Mews on the same day that she was in Hyde Park,' Isaac said. 'We can understand her knowing about the man's jogging habit, and where he liked to run and the time. That's one issue we'll accept, although one day before he

339

died is suspicious. However, we didn't know about Pembridge Mews, and if your client knew that address, then she knew his real name, that of his sister as well. All in all, damning evidence.'

'Okay, I knew,' Christine blurted out. Her sister looked at her with a scowl.

Gwen Hislop realised that she was tasked with defending the indefensible. 'Five-minute break,' she said.

Isaac and Wendy left the room, meeting Larry outside. The three each took a coffee from the machine in the hallway. It tasted awful, but for once it didn't matter. Christine Mason was in the hot seat, and the evidence against her was mounting.

The five minutes stretched to ten; two coffees from a café across the road were delivered to the two women in the interview room.

None of the officers sat down, and Chief Superintendent Goddard had joined them, bringing a coffee with him. 'I'm not drinking that,' he said, looking over at the machine. 'A confession?'

'Not yet. It's still circumstantial. Just because she's been at two of the key sites, doesn't give us a cast-iron case. It's her word against ours, and her lawyer's no fool. No doubt she's berating her for admitting that she was in Pembridge Mews,' Isaac said.

'The witness, solid?'

'Amelia Bentham has been careful not to say too much. If a defence lawyer for Christine Mason got to know that she's been holding back vital information, then she'd be soon discredited.'

'Best of luck,' Goddard said as he walked away.

'He's going easy on us, none of the normal rallying of the troops speech,' Larry said.

'He knows it's a matter of hours before we wrap up this case.'

'But we're not proving this, only pressuring others to come clean.'

'Amelia, could she have killed the man?' Isaac asked Wendy.

'She was overseas at the time,' Wendy replied.

'Proven?'

'It has been now.'

'Then it's not her. Is this it, the end of the investigation?' Isaac asked. 'Christine Mason admits her guilt if we pressure her?'

'I'm not convinced,' Wendy said. 'Christine Mason's a pawn, not one of the major pieces, certainly not a bishop or a rook, definitely not a queen. Things happen to her due to her submissive nature. I don't believe she could maintain the rage long enough to harm anyone.'

A uniform summoned Isaac and Wendy back to the interview room. It was clear that the two sisters were not comfortable with each other, the chairs they had been sitting on marginally further apart from their previous positions.

Isaac recommenced the interview.

'My client has a statement,' Gwen Hislop said. Christine Mason shifted uneasily on her seat; she did not look over at her sister.

'I admit that I was in Hyde Park,' Christine Mason commenced, 'and that my purpose was to confront Colin Young, who I believed was fond of me. Naivety may be what others will say, but to me the love that we shared was real. And even though I had not seen him for some time, I accepted that was the nature of his business. When I saw him in that taxi with a woman, I was alarmed. Not necessarily because he was with her, although I could see that they were happy and laughing, and she was attractive, not showing her age as I am.'

It was clear to Isaac that Christine had drafted the statement, her sister only checking it for incriminating words or descriptions of actions that could damn the woman. It was a clever document, though, in that it showed Christine to be a woman with neuroses, unable to separate fact from fiction. If she did claim to be the murderer, or she was charged with murder, then evaluation of her statement, her known behaviour, would all be valuable in deeming her as having diminished responsibility.

Isaac's estimation of Gwen Hislop took another leap up. Wendy, not as astute as Isaac, saw it differently. She was worried for Christine Mason, certain that she was about to confess.

'I never saw him in the park, and where I had waited was coincidental,' Christine continued. 'I needed to know if his love for me was real or whether it was feigned. I was beside myself with worry, not that the relationship was floundering, but because I had assisted him with money. I had seen the taxi, taken its number.'

'Photographic memory, we remember,' Wendy said.

'I've not finished my statement,' Christine said.

'Apologies, continue.'

'I recognised the taxi as it sometimes picked up people at the hotel, let them off. I phoned the taxi company, they let me have the driver's phone number. I knew his name. He told me about the fare and where he had picked them up, where he had dropped them off.

'I went to the address in Pembridge Mews, not sure what to do or what to say. If he had been there, it would have been suspicious. If he was inside with the woman, then maybe they were together. I was confused, so I left. That's the end of the statement.'

'I don't think there's any more to say, do you?' Gwen Hislop said. She had a look of satisfaction, as if she was going to call a halt to the proceedings and take her and her sister out of the police station.

'We can probably accept that Christine found the taxi and the driver,' Wendy said. 'However, there's one flaw.'

'Clutching at straws, trying to pin this murder on my client, will not work. We all recognise her weak personality, her lack of confidence in herself.'

Isaac could see that the sister made up for Christine's failings in bucketfuls.

'Barry and Matilda Montgomery took a taxi at the end of Pembridge Mews,' Wendy continued. 'It's a cul-de-sac. There's no way that your client would have found out the address from the taxi driver. He would not have waited at the address.' She knew that she was placing the woman in the line of fire again, her previous statement shot down in flames.

'Is this true?' Gwen looked over at her sister, forgetting momentarily she was there as the lawyer, not as her sister.

'No, yes…'

'What is it, Christine?' Isaac said. The woman was on the ropes, the confession was about to come; he was sure of it.

Christine buried her face in her hands. 'I knew the address. The taxi driver only confirmed where he had picked up the two of them.'

'The truth this time.'

'I knew that Colin wasn't his real name, or maybe the other one wasn't.'

'You knew that he also went by the name of Barry Montgomery?'

'He left his wallet by the side of the bed once. I looked inside it. He was asleep, he never knew.'

'You knew of his subterfuge?'

'Not really. I never knew what he was doing when he wasn't with me. I assumed it was something to do with the government, but I never asked.'

'It could have been criminal.'

'Not Colin, never. He was too smart for that, too beautiful.'

Gwen said nothing, just sat back with her arms folded. Her sister was doing a good job without her help.

'Did you check on who owned the address in Pembridge Mews?'

'I didn't stay long. I could see a woman in the window of the house behind me, an old man coming out of a door.'

'You're convinced that he's been unfaithful with this other woman. Is that why you murdered him?'

'No. I've lied to you, I know that. But I never murdered him, I never could. I loved him so much.'

'Mrs Mason, you'll be remanded on suspicion of involvement in the death of Barry Montgomery, also known as Colin Young.'

'DCI Cook, you can't do that to my sister, my client,' Gwen Hislop said. 'Consider her fragile mental state.'

'A doctor will be assigned to her. He can make that judgement, prescribe the necessary medicines if needed.'

'She has not admitted her guilt. You don't have enough evidence.'

'I'm afraid we do. And you as an experienced lawyer know that. Appealing to my good nature will not help. The continuing lies, the attempts at subterfuge, the denial of your client being in Hyde Park and then Pembridge Mews is damning. We also have the embezzlement of the hotel's funds. Your client may be as she says, as you say, naive, but it does not excuse her from the crime.'

Outside the interview room, Wendy spoke to Isaac. 'You were harsh in there.'

'I did my duty. Do you have a problem with that?' Isaac replied tersely.

'I just wish it could have been handled differently.'

'It couldn't, and you know it.'

'I know, but the evidence is still circumstantial.'

'It always will be. We can't rely on Forensics and Pathology to help us here. It's either a full confession or sufficient evidence. And with Christine Mason, there's plenty.'

'I still don't believe she did it, a gut feeling.'

'Then get your gut to tell your feet to get walking. Find the killer, and the woman walks free.'

'I will.'

'I hope you're successful. We've encountered a few rogues, that Archibald Marshall for one, Tony Mason for another, and I wouldn't give much creditability to Nick Domett. Make them sweat, and whoever else.'

Isaac walked away, not pleased that he had spoken to his sergeant abruptly, aware that his gut also told him that the case was not over yet.

Chapter 32

'The truth, Domett,' Larry said. The two of them, along with Isaac, were sitting in Domett's office. It was six in the evening, and the man had been on the phone when the two police officers walked in.

'I've got a business to run. You can't just barge in here,' Domett said. He was dressed casually, an open-necked shirt, a pair of jeans. He was sweating, not unexpected as the room was hot, and the fan in the corner didn't work. Not much worked in that office, Isaac conceded, not even Domett.

Isaac cast a critical eye over the man, vaguely remembered a fellow trainee from the past with body odour and bad breath.

Another man came into the office. He was dressed formally, and he wore a bow tie.

'Jerome, there's an address out in Hampstead, a company dinner. You're accompanying the person,' Domett said.

Jerome, the two police officers saw, was a black man, almost as tall as Isaac, his close-cropped hair greying. He was a good-looking man, one of the men on the Gents for Hire website.

'Male or female?' Jerome asked.

'The name on the credit card is Lesley, or it could be Leslie. Take your pick.'

'Fair enough. The normal rate?'

'The normal. It's dinner, that's all.'

Jerome looked over at Isaac. 'Are you new here?'

'Detective Chief Inspector Cook, Challis Street Homicide.'

Larry could tell that Jerome had not seen him as another escort. He was slightly insulted by the man's assessment. Domett had said that he was occasionally hired out, and compared to him, Larry was sure he was a more impressive figure. But Isaac and Jerome stood out. If they had not been there in the office, Isaac and Larry would not have picked Jerome as a man who sold himself.

'Not trouble, I hope,' Jerome said.

'I thought your people never came to the office,' Larry said to Domett.

'Jerome lives locally. We sometimes meet up for a beer after work; a friend, not that I have many,' Domett's reply.

'What about you, Jerome? What's your story?'

'Is this a bust? It's only dinner, that's all.'

'We weren't born yesterday, and besides, that's not why we're here. Did you know Colin Young?'

'If he worked for Nick, then no.'

'As I said, nobody comes here, only Jerome.' Domett leaned over from his chair. 'Now, if you don't mind, I'm busy. Unless you've got a warrant, then I've got the right to ask you to leave.'

'If there's nothing else, I'll go,' Jerome said.

'We checked you out,' Isaac said to Domett after Jerome had left the office, closing the door behind him.

'And what did you find? How I resigned from the police force? There's no blemish against my name.'

Domett continued to email and message, not looking away from his computer and phone, his back to Isaac and Larry.

'We made a few enquiries at your last police station,' Larry said. 'It seems you had a bit of a reputation.'

'I was tough, so what? I got results, arrested more than my fair share.'

'That's the official line. Detective Chief Inspector Harry Galsworthy, remember him?'

'Tough bastard, wasn't shy of slapping the occasional villain.'

'He reckoned you were taking backhanders from the pimps, looking the other way, getting freebies from the girls.'

'He's lying.'

'Maybe he is, maybe he isn't, but we'd take his word over yours,' Isaac said.

'Look here, Isaac,' Domett said, swivelling his chair around and resting his elbows on his knees. 'It was a tough station, tough neighbourhood. We didn't have any of your gentlemen villains, the same as you do in Challis Street, up around Kensington and Bayswater. Our villains were hard men who gave as good as they got.'

'We've got enough of those, but that's not what we're talking about, is it?'

'It is to me. It's easy to cast an aspersion, to claim that a police officer was on the take, another was handy with his fists, another was screwing the local whores, turning a blind eye to the people traffickers, the drug pushers.'

'We know the drill, but Galsworthy said there was proof.'

'If there was, then why wasn't I charged?'

'According to him, you had a good record, although he didn't rate you as a police officer. But you had arrested more than a few in your time, occasionally doctoring your notebook to get a conviction.'

'Supposition, hearsay, just nonsense. I played it fair, others didn't. I was framed, forced to take the blame for others in the station, even your precious DCI Galsworthy.'

'We verified it with another source.'

'Name? Who is this malignant piece of filth?'

'That person remains nameless. What we do know is that on account of your arrest record, the fact that the station would be subjected to an audit, one rotten apple spoiling the barrel, a decision was made for you to resign voluntarily.'

'I was still framed.'

'We're not forming a judgement here, but we want the truth from you. Is that too much to ask for?'

'I still can't help you with the "specials" that Colin Young serviced.'

'We've moved on from them at this time,' Isaac said. 'We've remanded a woman for Colin Young's murder, but my sergeant doesn't believe it's her, and Inspector Hill's not so sure, either.'

'Then why remand her? Insufficient proof means no conviction.'

'We don't hold with falsifying the evidence, something that your record indicates you're capable of. We want the murderer, not someone we can stitch up for the crime.'

'Then why are you here? I'm not a murderer, and yes, they asked me to leave. The sacrificial lamb for the good name of the police station and the chief superintendent. A hearing into my supposed misdemeanours would have sullied his copybook.'

'Did you know that Colin Young's real name was Barry Montgomery?'

'Why? Should I?'

'Domett, if you don't stop answering a question with a question, we'll haul you and your pathetic arse down to Challis Street. Now, one more time. Did you know that he was also known as Barry Montgomery?'

'A lot of them have other names, nothing special in that.'

'Answer the question.'

'Once, when he answered his phone. He must have forgotten who he was talking to, which phone he was using. It was just the one time, and I didn't think much to it.'

'Did you know that he was visiting Nancy Bartlett, one of your clients, and taking money from her direct?'

'I found out. I phoned her up a few weeks back, trying to drum up business, and don't ask the exact date. I'm not police anymore, so I don't detail everything.'

'You would have. What did she tell you?'

'That she was fine, and she had herself a beautiful man.'

'Which meant she had Colin Young.'

'It did. Who else was referred to as beautiful? You saw Brent, one of our most popular. A good-looking man, the same as you, and neither of you would be called beautiful. Handsome, masculine, manly, but never beautiful.'

'What did you do?'

'I knew how much money she had, how much money she had paid for Colin when she came through me. I remonstrated with her, told her that contractually she was obliged to pay my commission. I'm running a business here, not a charity.'

'Her response?'

'Polite, calm, no money.'

'And you?'

'Angry. What else would I have been?'

'Angry enough to have slapped her, to slap Colin, to hit him over the head in Hyde Park and to watch him drown?'

'Cook, I may not be your idea of the perfect police officer, but I'm not a fool. Money is one thing, murder is another. At some stage the murderer makes a mistake, a missed clue, someone says something, and then it all comes together.'

'Not like screwing the local tarts, taking a backhander when you were in the force. You got away with those. Domett, you're in the firing line. Don't be surprised if we're not back with an arrest warrant.'

'What for? Telling you the facts of life?'

'Another question, when you should have given an answer. Be very careful from here on as to what you do, who you see, what you say.'

***

'I've got a hotel to run,' Archibald Marshall said from the sanctity of his side of the desk. 'You've arrested Christine. Damn stupid thing for her to do, killing the man.'

It was seven in the evening, and Wendy and Larry were with the man. Neither would admit to liking him, but he had a point if indeed Christine had killed her lover.

'She's been remanded. Sergeant Gladstone's not sure of her guilt. She's still got her money on you,' Larry said.

'For what? I got her out of this hotel with no criminal convictions against her name. I must get some credit for that.'

'Not from me, you don't,' Wendy said. She was not comfortable sitting in the same room as the manager, knowing full well his history, the leverage that he had exerted over Christine Mason, the sexual favours he had received as part of the deal, the money he had taken.

'How long before you leave the hotel?' Larry asked.

'Fourteen days, maybe fifteen.'

'Another job?' Wendy snarled.

'Overseas. A resort, part of the hotel group's foreign acquisitions. I'm taking control, dealing with the local bureaucracy.'

'Greasing the palms of every crooked official, is that it?'

'Not officially,' Marshall said. Wendy didn't like the way the man spoke; a self-assuredness that he had got away with embezzlement, the harassment of a fellow employee who now languished in the cells at Challis Street.

'Whereabouts?' Larry asked.

'Barbados.'

'A promotion?'

'It's a tough job, and I'm good at what I do.'

'You may be that, but I still don't hold with Christine being labelled a murderer. You had reason to want him dead.'

'What for? Just because Christine was soiling the bed linen upstairs with him doesn't mean that I'd want to murder him. The hotel's senior management has seen fit to reassign me out of the country. They're having a tough time down there with their expansion plans, the builders, the government.'

'Christine is thrown out, not so much as a reference, and you bask in the glory.'

'Not glory. I'd rather stay here, but they've offered the deal, they call the tune.'

'And you, one of the children, follow the Pied Piper, not caring that a woman who we are certain you felt some fondness for is sentenced to ten years, probably more, for second-degree murder.'

'Manslaughter, I would have thought.'

'You know about these sorts of things? Did you check on the internet what you would get if we arrested you?'

'Ludicrous, and need I say, slanderous.'

'It's a police investigation, slander doesn't apply. You're still a criminal, even if your management wants to sweep it under the table.'

'As you say. Now if you don't mind, I'm busy.'

It had been a wasted visit, Larry and Wendy knew that. And Wendy was acutely aware that one more piece of damning evidence against Christine Mason would put the final nail in the coffin, and her conviction would be assured.

Back in the office, Gwen Hislop sat with her sister. She had a legal practice that required her time, but her sister had taken precedence. An air of calm existed between the two, due to Christine being mildly sedated, and Gwen feeling guilty for distancing herself from her for years over Terry, her former husband.

Isaac sat in his office wrestling with paperwork, attempting to figure out what to tell Jenny if the trip back

to the ancestral homeland was off. He couldn't hold
Christine Mason indefinitely; he didn't want to formally
charge her and have her sent to a woman's prison. There
was a niggling feeling inside him, the same as there was
with Wendy, that somehow they were missing something,
an already known fact that was crucial to the
investigation.

The sixth sense, some police officers called it; the
innate knowledge garnered after years of policing that
made the difference to knowing someone was guilty or
not. Christine Mason, her own worst enemy, had not
helped the investigation, and by her own admission she
was passionate and jealous.

Tony Mason, who had been out of the country
when Christine had been remanded, entered Challis Street
and headed up to Homicide. Two uniforms blocked his
way into the department, only to have Isaac wave them
aside.

'Mr Mason, we can talk in a room down the hall,'
Isaac said. He could see that the man was not happy,
although that was understandable given the
circumstances.

'My wife,' the man blustered. 'You've arrested her
for what? I know she can be stupid sometimes, but
murder? You've got to be joking.'

Finally, the man sat down in the room that Isaac
had led them to. Mason was red in the face, not having
waited for the lift up to Homicide, having instead bolted
up the stairs. He had a suitcase with him, and it should
have been scanned downstairs, but hadn't been.

'Your case,' Isaac said as a uniform stood at the
door to the room. 'Any weapons in there?'

'I sell guidance systems, not guns.'

'You never know who could come through the door. A police station is as good as anywhere else for the terrorists.'

Isaac gestured to the uniform standing nearby to check, Mason handing him the key. 'I packed it myself if that's what you're about to ask.'

'Any of your company's products inside?' Isaac asked.

'No, there aren't, just my clothes and brochures. We ship the product and samples through couriers, the proper documentation in place, export licences, whatever else the government throws at us. We make plenty of money for this country, yet they still get in our way.'

'Your products kill a lot of people, as well.'

'What are you? A policeman with a soul?'

'Mr Mason, your wife has consistently lied to us. We can place her in Hyde Park on the day before the murder; we can place her outside the house of the man's sister, the same place that she and her father committed suicide.'

'A double act?'

'A foul thought, Mr Mason. We've had our suspicions about you for some time. It appears that you've spent too long around violence and death, no doubt seen your products in action, probably seen people dead as a result.'

'Do you know how many people look after their families in this country as a result of the UK selling weapons overseas?'

'A lot, I've no doubt. But we're talking about your wife, not indulging in the justification of what you do. We also know that your wife knew of the man's true identity and that she was embezzling hotel funds, sleeping with the hotel manager. He was bribing her for that.'

'Okay, damning, but she's my wife. A forced confession?'

'Not here. Justice in this country is innocent until proven guilty. And why so much concern about your wife? You've not shown it before, and you've not been holding back on supplying women to win a contract.'

'It's a tough business. We produce a quality product, but that doesn't guarantee sales. You must know that. You're a smart man.'

'Coming back to your wife. You'll be free to see her, and her sister's with her.'

'What do I need to do to get her out of here?'

'Provide us with a murderer. Failing that, she stays where she is.'

'I need a drink,' Mason said.

The uniform left the room, having concluded his checks of the case.

Larry messaged Isaac soon after. *Interview room, conduct it by the book, advise Mason of his rights.*

***

'Smart lad is Constable Bradley,' Larry said after the preliminaries had been dealt with by Isaac. Tony Mason, on advice from Isaac, had brought Gwen Hislop along as his legal adviser. A touching reunion between Mason and his wife just before the interview.

Isaac had been updated by Larry in the twenty minutes since the text message from Larry and before the four people convened in the interview room. Larry sat with his arms crossed, a look of satisfaction on his face. Tony Mason looked bewildered, unsure what to say. A sinking feeling, Isaac thought, as his lawyer had been briefed as to what was to happen, that new evidence had been found.

Isaac looked over at Tony Mason. 'We are willing to release your wife, Christine. We do not believe that she is guilty of murder. There are other crimes that she has committed, but it is not our intention to pursue those.'

'I've been told by Gwen that much. What else do you have? What are you basing her innocence on?'

'Your suitcase.'

'You checked it, found nothing.'

'No weapons, that's for sure. You were right about the brochures, not that we understood much of what they were promoting.'

Bradley, a tall, fresh-faced young man of twenty-five, entered the interview room. He carried the suitcase with him, duly tagged as evidence. He placed it on another table to one side of the room.

'What's the point of all this?' Mason said.

'Fastidious man, are you?' Larry said. Isaac felt that he was enjoying the moment too much, not that he could blame him.

'I like everything in its place,' Mason said. Gwen Hislop sat apprehensively to his side.

'Is this your suitcase, Mr Mason?' Isaac asked. A nylon strap had been put around it after the initial examination.

'You know it is. Chief Inspector, where is this heading? You've had one of your officers go through it.'

'Get to the point,' Gwen Hislop said. 'I want Christine out of the cells.'

'And Tony in?'

'That's not what I said.'

Mason looked over at Constable Bradley but said nothing. Isaac could see that the man was sweating, although the temperature in the interview room was moderate.

'Mr Mason,' Isaac said, 'as Inspector Hill asked before, are you a fastidious man, a man who likes to keep a record of who he's meeting, whose palm he's greasing, the deals he's making, and so on?'

'I am, but what's that got to do with my sitting here?'

'You've told us that there's incriminating evidence,' Gwen Hislop said.

'Constable, open the case,' Larry said.

Bradley followed instructions and withdrew a small notebook, the type that could be bought in any newsagents.

'Is this yours?' Isaac asked as it was placed on the table between the two police officers and the interviewee and his lawyer.

'What use is this to you?' Mason said. Isaac noticed he was becoming more agitated.

'Please answer the question.'

'It's mine. I still prefer to write key details down, notes of meetings that I've had, people I've met. Nothing wrong in that.'

'As you say, nothing wrong. But that's not what we're talking about, is it?'

'Get to the point,' Gwen Hislop said.

'Don't worry. Your sister's sitting upstairs with Sergeant Gladstone, no doubt enjoying a cup of tea.'

'Mr Mason,' Larry said, looking straight into the eyes of the man opposite, 'we held your wife due to circumstantial evidence. She had been the closest to Colin Young/Barry Montgomery, and she had consistently lied to us. She told us that she had not been in Hyde Park, and then that was found to be false. She told us that she did not know where the murdered man lived, but she did, even knew his true name, though she never found out that the woman she had seen him with was his sister. She has lied and cheated through this entire investigation, while you, Mr Mason, have played the indignant husband, upset about your wife's affairs, dismissive of our charges against her. Did you think of her and what she was going through?'

'We're lost over on this side of the table,' Gwen Hislop said. 'Is this a character assassination? You've released my sister so you can focus on her husband?'

Isaac picked up the notebook and turned to the back page. 'Is this your handwriting?' he asked, showing it to Mason.

'It's my notebook.'

'That wasn't the question.'

'Very well, it's my writing.'

'There's a map here with a date in the top corner.'

'It was a demonstration in one of the countries that I visit.'

'Which one?'

'That's confidential.'

'We've checked it against a map of London. It's Hyde Park, isn't it?'

'I can't remember any weapons being fired there, can you?'

'Mr Mason, before we continue, let me ask you a question, although I can't be sure of an honest answer.'

'This is a farce,' Gwen Hislop said. 'If this is the extent of your proof, then I would suggest that you end this interview and allow my clients to go back to their home.'

Isaac ignored the lawyer, maintaining his focus on Mason. 'Do you love your wife? Or was the touching scene in the cells put on for the uniform to duly report to us?'

'Admittedly Christine could get up to mischief occasionally, but she's been a good wife, a good mother.'

'The difference was that this time she would have left you for another. A dalliance, such as she has had from time to time, is one thing, but Christine was in love with a younger man. You couldn't compete, you knew that. You had contacts who could keep a watch on her, advise you of her indiscretions. You're living the good life overseas, and you don't want it jeopardised, but now, there's something about to derail it.'

'If you have evidence, present it,' Gwen Hislop said.

'Very well. It is a map of Hyde Park in the notebook, a cross marked where the Peter Pan statue is, an outline of the Serpentine, the lake that vaguely forms the shape of a snake.'

'That's not what I drew,' Tony Mason said.

'It is. And the writing is in code, or should I say Arabic. Do you speak the language?'

'A few words, that's all. I always have a translator with me.'

'But you can write it?'

'Some, but what's the point here? If my wife is free, I should take her home.'

'I would agree,' Isaac said, 'but there's more, isn't there, Mr Mason?'

'Not that I know of.'

'Constable Bradley has an Egyptian wife. He's been studying her language for a few years, not getting too far by his own admission. He has translated what he can in the notebook, the damning parts anyway.'

'Industrial espionage is rife.'

'I don't think so. If you are travelling to Arabic countries, then where's the advantage in using their language? It was your clumsy attempt to hide the fact that you've been well aware of what your wife's been up to.'

'I'm subject to security checks at the highest level. I needed to know if Christine was going to impact on that, or if I could be subjected to blackmail and coercion.'

'You've known about your wife and the dead man for some time. It's all in the notebook. It will be translated by someone qualified for it to be acceptable in a court of law.'

'It's not all in Arabic.'

'The date and the time at the top of the map are.'

'It was the date that Christine was there looking for the man.'

'You admit to that now?'

'I was not there. I was overseas.'

'And if you were visiting countries which England has sanctions against, yet still does business with, especially weapons, would it be possible to falsify a passport entry? Or did you travel to wherever, then catch a plane back to France, and then another passport, another name, and you re-entered England, committed murder and left?'

'The date and time?' Gwen Hislop said.

'It's in Arabic, but Constable Bradley understood what was written,' Larry said. 'It's the date and time of the murder. You, Mr Mason, killed the man because you knew that the relationship was becoming serious, more than you could deal with. It was either concern about the life you were living or concern that your possession, namely your wife, was getting away. The notebook, the small writing, the Arabic, indicates a fastidious person, a person who wants everything compartmentalised and in its box. And one of those boxes was about to be emptied, and you had to act.'

'This is conjecture,' Gwen Hislop said, yet it was not said with the fervour of someone defending her client against the evidence. Isaac could see that she believed the man's guilt, and it had been her sister that he had been willing to throw to the wolves.

'It's murder,' Isaac said. 'Mr Mason, you will be formally charged with murder.'

'I had to, you must realise,' Mason said feebly. He was a broken man, yet neither Isaac nor Larry could feel any sympathy for him. He was a man who would have let his wife be punished for what he had done to keep her.

Outside the interview room, Isaac phoned Jenny. 'Give me one day, and then we're off to the airport.'

One day wasn't enough to complete all of the paperwork, Isaac knew that, and he would have stayed if he could, but this time, he'd break the habit of a lifetime. He would leave it to others to complete. He would leave it to his team in Homicide. He knew they would not let him down.

The End

ALSO BY THE AUTHOR

Death by a Dead Man's Hand – A DI Tremayne Thriller

A flawed heist of forty gold bars from a security van late at night. One of the perpetrators is killed by his brother as they argue over what they have stolen.

Eighteen years later, the murderer, released after serving his sentence for his brother's murder, waits in a church for a man purporting to be the brother he killed. And then he too is killed.

The threads stretch back a long way, and now more people are dying in the search for the missing gold bars.

Detective Inspector Tremayne, his health causing him concern, and Sergeant Clare Yarwood, still seeking romance, are pushed to the limit solving the murder, attempting to prevent any more.

Death at Coombe Farm – A DI Tremayne Thriller

A warring family. A disputed inheritance. A recipe for death.

If it hadn't been for the circumstances, Detective Inspector Keith Tremayne would have said the view was outstanding. Up high, overlooking the farmhouse in the valley below, the panoramic vista of Salisbury Plain stretching out beyond. The only problem was that near where he stood with his sergeant, Clare Yarwood, there was a body, and it wasn't a pleasant sight.

Death and the Lucky Man – A DI Tremayne Thriller

Sixty-eight million pounds and dead. Hardly the outcome expected for the luckiest man in England the day his lottery ticket was drawn out of the barrel. But then, Alan Winters' rags-to-riches story had never been conventional, and there were those who had benefited, but others who hadn't.

Death and the Assassin's Blade – A DI Tremayne Thriller

It was meant to be high drama, not murder, but someone's switched the daggers. The man's death took place in plain view of two serving police officers.

He was not meant to die; the daggers were only theatrical props, plastic and harmless. A summer's night, a production of Julius Caesar amongst the ruins of an Anglo-Saxon fort. Detective Inspector Tremayne is there with his sergeant, Clare Yarwood. In the assassination scene, Caesar collapses to the ground. Brutus defends his actions; Mark Antony rebukes him.

They're a disparate group, the amateur actors. One's an estate agent, another an accountant. And then there is the teenage school student, the gay man, the funeral director. And what about the women? They could be involved.

They've each got a secret, but which of those on the stage wanted Gordon Mason, the actor who had portrayed Caesar, dead?

Death Unholy – A DI Tremayne Thriller

All that remained were the man's two legs and a chair full of greasy and fetid ash. Little did DI Keith Tremayne know that it was the beginning of a journey into the murky world of paganism and its ancient rituals. And it was going to get very dangerous.

'Do you believe in spontaneous human combustion?' Detective Inspector Keith Tremayne asked.

'Not me. I've read about it. Who hasn't?' Sergeant Clare Yarwood answered.

'I haven't,' Tremayne replied, which did not surprise his young sergeant. In the months they had been working together, she had come to realise that he was a man who had little interest in the world. When he had a cigarette in his mouth, a beer in his hand, and a murder to solve he was about the happiest she ever saw him, but even then he could hardly be regarded as one of life's most sociable people. And as for reading? The most he managed was an occasional police report, an early morning newspaper, turning first to the back pages for the racing results.

Murder has no Guilt – A DCI Cook Thriller

No one knows who was the target or why, but there are eight dead. The men seem the most likely, or could have it been one of the two women, the attractive Gillian Dickenson, or even the celebrity-obsessed Sal Maynard?

There's a gang war brewing, and if there are deaths, it doesn't matter to them as long as it's not them. But to Detective Chief Inspector Isaac Cook, it's his area of London, and it does.

It's dirty and unpredictable, and initially, it had been the West Indian gangs. But then a more vicious Romanian gangster had usurped them. And now he's being marginalised by the Russians. And the leader of the most vicious Russian mafia organisation is in London, and he's got money and influence, the ear of those in power.

Murder of a Silent Man – A DCI Cook Thriller

No one gave much credence to the man when he was alive. In fact, most people never knew who he was, although those who had lived in the area for many years recognised the tired-looking and shabbily-dressed man as he shuffled along, regular as clockwork on a Thursday afternoon at seven in the evening to the local off-licence. It was always the same: a bottle of whisky, premium brand, and a packet of cigarettes. He paid his money over the counter, took hold of his plastic bag containing his purchases, and then walked back down the road with the same rhythmic shuffle. He said not one word to anyone on the street or in the shop.

✓ Murder in Room 346 – A DCI Cook Thriller

'Coitus interruptus, that's what it is,' Detective Chief Inspector Isaac Cook said. On the bed, in a downmarket hotel in Bayswater, lay the naked bodies of a man and a woman.

'Bullet in the head's not the way to go,' Larry Hill, Isaac Cook's detective inspector, said. He had not expected such a flippant comment from his senior, not when they were standing near to two people who had, apparently in the final throes of passion, succumbed to what appeared to be a professional assassination.

'You know this will be all over the media within the hour,' Isaac said.

'James Holden, moral crusader, a proponent of the sanctity of the marital bed, man and wife. It's bound to be.'

Murder in Notting Hill – A DCI Cook Thriller

One murderer, two bodies, two locations, and the murders have been committed within an hour of each other.

They're separated by a couple of miles, and neither woman has anything in common with the other. One is young and wealthy, the daughter of a famous man; the other is poor, hardworking and unknown.

Isaac Cook and his team at Challis Street Police Station are baffled about why they've been killed. There must be a connection, but what is it?

Murder is the Only Option – A DCI Cook Thriller

A man, thought to be long dead, returns to exact revenge against those who had blighted his life. His only concern is to protect his wife and daughter. He will stop at nothing to achieve his aim.

'Big Greg, I never expected to see you around here at this time of night.'

'I've told you enough times.'

'I've no idea what you're talking about,' Robertson replied. He looked up at the man, only to see a metal pole coming down at him. Robertson fell down, cracking his head against a concrete kerb.

Two vagrants, no more than twenty feet away, did not stir and did not even look in the direction of the noise. If they had, they would have seen a dead body, another man walking away.

✔ **Murder in Little Venice – A DCI Cook Thriller**
✔ " " HYDE PARK

A dismembered corpse floats in the canal in Little Venice, an upmarket tourist haven in London. Its identity is unknown, but what is its significance?

DCI Isaac Cook is baffled about why it's there. Is it gang-related, or is it something more?

Whatever the reason, it's clearly a warning, and Isaac and his team are sure it's not the last body that they'll have to deal with.

Murder is Only a Number – A DCI Cook Thriller

Before she left she carved a number in blood on his chest. But why the number 2, if this was her first murder?

The woman prowls the streets of London. Her targets are men who have wronged her. Or have they? And why is she keeping count?

DCI Cook and his team finally know who she is, but not before she's murdered four men. The whole team are looking for her, but the woman keeps disappearing in plain sight. The pressure's on to stop her, but she's always one step ahead.

And this time, DCS Goddard can't protect his protégé, Isaac Cook, from the wrath of the new commissioner at the Met.

Murder House – A DCI Cook Thriller

A corpse in the fireplace of an old house. It's been there for thirty years, but who is it?

It's murder, but who is the victim and what connection does the body have to the previous owners of the house. What is the motive? And why is the body in a fireplace? It was bound to be discovered eventually but was that what the murderer wanted? The main suspects are all old and dying, or already dead.

Isaac Cook and his team have their work cut out trying to put the pieces together. Those who know are not talking because of an old-fashioned belief that a family's dirty laundry should not be aired in public, and never to a policeman – even if that means the murderer is never brought to justice!

Murder is a Tricky Business – A DCI Cook Thriller

A television actress is missing, and DCI Isaac Cook, the Senior Investigation Officer of the Murder Investigation Team at Challis Street Police Station in London, is searching for her.

Why has he been taken away from more important crimes to search for the woman? It's not the first time she's gone missing, so why does everyone assume she's been murdered?

There's a secret, that much is certain, but who knows it? The missing woman? The executive producer? His eavesdropping assistant? Or the actor who portrayed her fictional brother in the TV soap opera?

Murder Without Reason – A DCI Cook Thriller

DCI Cook faces his greatest challenge. The Islamic State is waging war in England, and they are winning.

Not only does Isaac Cook have to contend with finding the perpetrators, but he is also being forced to commit actions contrary to his mandate as a police officer.

And then there is Anne Argento, the prime minister's deputy. The prime minister has shown himself to be a pacifist and is not up to the task. She needs to take his job if the country is to fight back against the Islamists.

Vane and Martin have provided the solution. Will DCI
Cook and Anne Argento be willing to follow it through?
Are they able to act for the good of England, knowing
that a criminal and murderous action is about to take
place? Do they have an option?

The Haberman Virus

A remote and isolated village in the Hindu Kush
mountain range in North Eastern Afghanistan is wiped
out by a virus unlike any seen before.

A mysterious visitor clad in a space suit checks his
handiwork, a female American doctor succumbs to the
disease, and the woman sent to trap the person
responsible falls in love with him – the man who would
cause the deaths of millions.

Hostage of Islam

Three are to die at the Mission in Nigeria: the pastor and
his wife in a blazing chapel; another gunned down while
trying to defend them from the Islamist fighters.

Kate McDonald, an American, grieving over her
boyfriend's death and Helen Campbell, whose life had
been troubled by drugs and prostitution, are taken by the
attackers.

Kate is sold to a slave trader who intends to sell her
virginity to an Arab Prince. Helen, to ensure their
survival, gives herself to the murderer of her friends.

Malika's Revenge

Malika, a drug-addicted prostitute, waits in a smugglers' village for the next Afghan tribesman or Tajik gangster to pay her price, a few scraps of heroin.

Yusup Baroyev, a drug lord, enjoys a lifestyle many would envy. An Afghan warlord sees the resurgence of the Taliban. A Russian white-collar criminal portrays himself as a good and honest citizen in Moscow.

All of them are linked to an audacious plan to increase the quantity of heroin shipped out of Afghanistan and into Russia and ultimately the West.

Some will succeed, some will die, some will be rescued from their plight and others will rue the day they became involved.

ABOUT THE AUTHOR

Phillip Strang was born in England in the late forties. He was an avid reader of science fiction in his teenage years: Isaac Asimov, Frank Herbert, the masters of the genre. Still an avid reader, the author now mainly reads thrillers.

In his early twenties, the author, with a degree in electronics engineering and a desire to see the world, left England for Sydney, Australia. Now, forty years later, he still resides in Australia, although many intervening years were spent in a myriad of countries, some calm and safe, others no more than war zones.

Made in the USA
Coppell, TX
28 December 2020

47243579R00218